This is a work of fiction. Names, characters, places, and incidents either are the product of the author's imagination or are used fictiously. Any resemblance to actual persons, living or dead, events, or locales is entirely coincidental.

Copyright © 2024 by Jennifer Jurcakova

All rights reserved. No part of this book may be reproduced or used in any manner without written permission of the copyright owner except for the use of quotations in a book review. For more information, address: jennyjurcakovalib@gmail.com

First paperback edition June 2024

Book and cover design by Jessica Cvilo

ISBN 979-8-9907315-0-9 (paperback)

Instagram: jurcakjenslibrary

THE VILE ELF

JENNIFER
JURCAKOVA

To my mom,
Who I know would be proud.

CHAPTER ZERO

I LAY IN A PUDDLE OF MY BLOOD.

My eyes shot open, the darkness forcing them to adjust to the dim glow of moonlight. I can feel the blood surrounding my body, staining my skin. The warm comfort of my bed pulled me deeper into the depths of security. Only this sense of security felt false; this sense of security felt more like captivity. It was the same bed in which I had fallen asleep - but it wasn't. My room was empty, uncomfortable, and cold - as if somebody had raided its contents. The walls were bare; nothing was on the floor or covering the windows. There wasn't anything in my closet.

My entire body instantly became glued to the bed. Not even closing my eyes was an option anymore. One minute went by… then another. Finally, after what felt like an eternity, my body melted back into its original, natural, comfortable state.

I could move again. I curled my fingers into the sheets, feeling the blood-stained cotton wrapping around my fists. I lifted my head slightly, looking left and right. I heard a voice telling me, "Don't move, Blanche. Just fall asleep." My feet moved independently, disobeying me, and lifted me from my supine position. The only thing that was still visible in the room of my dream-like reality was my wooden door.

My hands were shaking, and my legs were weak. My ocean eyes were weary, and my dark brown hair was pushed behind me, flowing down my back. I could tell that I was in my normal nightwear - a black nightgown. I planted my feet on the ground, and my feet felt cold and wet. I looked down nervously and saw vermillion under my feet.

I noticed my entire floor covered in blood. It was dark red – so dark, you couldn't see the hardwood underneath it. I approached the door, ignoring the blood seeping between my toes. I turned the doorknob and pushed the door open. The hall was empty – just like my room. The blood on the floor flowed through the upper level and dripped down the stairs.

I walked forward, making my way over to the railing, and looked down the staircase. I watched every last drop of blood hit the ground. I didn't know what to do next – or where to go. I should have stayed in my bed. I shouldn't even be exploring this reality – it isn't safe. I frowned, looking around. My dad – where is he?

"Dad, are you there?" I called out, my voice echoing through the house. Is he even in this dream void? I headed downstairs. Every time I stepped down the staircase, another ounce of horror coursed through my veins, frightening me – tormenting me. I took the final step down the stairs and looked up. Everything was the same – empty, uncomfortable, bloody. He's nowhere to be seen – my father isn't here with me. "Dad?" I called out again.

The silence was deafening, and I felt my knees grow weak. I feared they would buckle, and my entire body would plunge into the blood. I walked into the living room and looked around. My eyes widened when I saw crimson written on the wall, ever so neatly. It almost looked innocent:

The man who is most important to you shall die on the day that you need him the most.

Out of nowhere, I could hear the faint voices of two men and three women whisper behind me… in front of me… inside my head. The most distinct voice, though, belonged to a man. It was as clear as day: *"Be afraid of me."* My teeth chattered as I listened on. The man's voice grew darker and lower, and I could hear it right next to my ear. *"I crave you. I need you."* That last statement could've been genuine if the voice wasn't so…disturbing…

I wanted to scream. I hoped the voice would leave me alone. I took off running towards the front door, only to have it disappear when I reached for the doorknob. "No, please!" I shouted, my fists pounding against the phantom of where the door once stood.

"Let me out! I want to go! Please!" I was begging, pleading… for my life.

"You can't escape me," the voice cooly taunted behind me. *"You can never escape me."*

"Please, I want to get out!" I thrashed against the wall, hoping my entire body might be able to break it down. The dream world thought otherwise. The wall didn't even dent, not even a minor scratch of paint. "No… I want to leave. Please, I want to go home!" My eyes welled up with tears, and I hugged myself, my figure sliding down the phantom door. "Please… take me back," I begged, "Please."

I wanted to cry and be free, but it didn't seem possible in this dream world. I was surrounded by panic and anxiety. Looking up, I saw someone towering over me. He was tall and muscular. His arms and legs are strong enough to strangle me. He had ebony hair, and his eyes felt cold as ice. His visage was expressionless as he kneeled in front of me. This man - who is he?

"Please…" I begged.

He put a finger under my chin and lifted my face to his. I could tell he was vile by how he grinned at my fear and taunted me with his obsidian eyes. "Where do you think you're going?"

Without hesitation, he lunged at me, wrapping his arms around my neck and pushing me toward the ground. I let out an ear-piercing scream that echoed through the entire house. I knew no one could hear me. He lifted my arms, so my hands were pinned towards the floor, his hand forcing my wrists to shake, pain shooting through them.

The last thing I saw were his eyes, slowly starting to glow a bright red, and his sneer revealing razor-sharp fangs. The moment his fangs pierced through the tender skin on my neck, I was knocked out cold, and the walls around me slowly faded into a black abyss.

LONDON
1943

CHAPTER ONE

Sweat falls down the side of my face like a cascading waterfall. My legs and hands tremble, but my body doesn't move from its position on the bed. I can feel my numb hands and am unable to move. However, only a second later, I felt my body relax, and I sit up. My whole body feels on fire, and I'm desperate to be doused. My hands and legs are twitching, and my limbs are weak. Sleep paralysis is what the midwife told me I had.

I threw the hot blanket off of me and looked at myself in the mirror. I look sick. My eyes are droopy, my cheeks and nose are red, and my black nightgown sticks to my body. These nightmares are getting worse. They are disturbing and sick, and ever since the war started, they have been plaguing my mind like a virus.

I hear distant voices ring just outside my closed door. One of the voices was my father, while the other sounded too familiar, the chief of Ansalona, Berlin. He's here for the third time this week, which means something is wrong.

I throw my feet off my bed, touching the cold, bare floor. My feet wobble, and I grip the headboard to steady myself. I sit up and walk towards my closet. I've got many shirts and pants, dresses, and skirts to wear, all sewn by the neighborhood elves.

I throw on the first thing I see, a dark green dress that my neighbor, Anastasia, had got me for my birthday last year. She had got it from outside the forest, where the mortals lived. I had never seen that part, and my father always told me to avoid it. He said it was dangerous for people like me.

I walk over to my dresser, pull open a drawer, and look at my holster. I slide it under my dress, clipping it around my thigh, and then grab the dagger beside my nightstand - the blade my mother used to use.

Then I walk into the hallway, closing my door behind me quietly. It's empty, just as I expected. My father and Berlin are talking downstairs - I can hear the isolated tone of Berlin's voice from the kitchen. I peer over the edge and look down the stairs. Just a moment ago, I could have sworn I was there, the blood written on the wall, while voices whispered in my ear.

"Christ, Berlin, are you insane?!" My father's frantic voice yells. I walk down the staircase despite my limp legs shaking. As soon as I reach the bottom floor, I peek into the combined kitchen and living room.

Since I was born, Berlin has been best friends with my father. They have been friends since they were children, which makes them closer than the relationship I have with my father.

"Do you have a better solution, then? We don't have many options left, Brenner." Irritated, rubbing his chin with his fingers, he says. "I can't keep draining myself like this. The others will start to notice soon."

There's a silence between them for a minute, my father threading carefully with his words. Then my father said: "We'll need to find a hiding place. Magic isn't helping us anymore." He sits next to Berlin and then tells him something silently - something I can't hear.

Berlin says something back and then stands. "I'll see what I can do. Good luck," he says and then pats him on the back. I hide behind the big banister by the stairs and watch him leave the house.

"You can come out now." My father says, and I shut my eyes, my hands curling around the railing. Not until then do I come out of my hiding spot and see the defeated look on my father's face. He's upset - with me? With Berlin? I didn't know.

"I didn't hear much," I explain.

"It's alright," he retorts and then turns around, looking around in the kitchen. "Are you hungry? I can make you something to eat." He looks over his shoulder at me, but I shake my head. I feel the taste of blood in my mouth, and I swallow the gag that almost erupts from my mouth.

"No. I was going to visit Anastasia." I walked closer to him but kept my distance. My father was tense, and I wanted to know why. "I know she's just gotten back from her trip."

"She arrived this morning." My father exclaims. "I saw her. She looked happy to be back." He fully turned to me until I could see his old gray hair, the stubble of hair on his chin, and big blue eyes staring at mine. "Before you go, I want to talk to you. In the office," he finished.

Before I could ask what was wrong, he walked away, heading into his office. My mouth parts slightly. I stare at the empty kitchen.

I'm never allowed in his office. It's why he keeps it locked – there are three locks, and it never is unlocked. The only time I've ever gone in was when I was little, and my father left it unlocked by accident. I'd never seen him so mad at me that day – he yelled at me never to go back in there. He has many books in there, some of which he forced me to read daily. Especially when my powers didn't show, he had made me study every element and urge for my abilities to show – it never worked.

To this day, I still cannot use my powers because I don't have any. Not ones that appeared physically, at least.

I haven't dared to go back into that office since.

As I walked to his office, I saw the open door, and my nerves skyrocketed. I knock on the door first and then peek into the small office.

It's a standard desk, but behind it are shelves and massive documents that I couldn't believe my father owned. He's sitting at his desk when he sees me. He smiles. "Come on in." He ushers me to the seat on the opposite side of the desk. Christ, what had I done to deserve this?

Unable to help myself, I ask: "Am I in trouble?"

He looks at me and chuckles. "No, but I would like it if you sat down so I could talk to you." I close the door behind me as I stroll forward, taking a seat. I feel the cushion under me. I love my dad, but facing him now, I'm terrified of what he has to say.

He grabs something from a drawer. It's a round brown paper rolled into a map. He hands it to me. "Go on. I want you to look at it."

I unfold the map and look at it. From what it looks like, it looks like a layout of the entire forest. Our forest is extensive, and this map captures every area – where the werewolves live and where all the elven towns are. The only thing I don't see is the vampire kingdom and its small village around it. Mainly because it was not located anywhere near this forest.

I spot my little town and see the dark green specks in it. "What are these-" My heart leaps when the dots suddenly move as if they are taking small steps. "What the-"

"The dots represent all the elves, werewolves, and vampires living in the forest. I'm sure you see more elves than anything." I look at them all moving. All of them amaze me. Even in my small town, the dots move gracefully.

I want to ask him about it, but his voice rings through the room before I do. "A few weeks earlier, Berlin sent some elves to get food and supplies for the town, but they never returned. They were attacked by a group of vampires that were on their way." I look away from the map and up at my father. "That's when Berlin knew the war was spreading, not only here but also to other parts. Eventually, I imagine the vampires will find us. Berlin set up a force field, but his magic faded, and it didn't take long until King Castor located us."

"What does that mean?" I ask.

"It means our town is in danger. We can use magic however we want, but Castor knows where we are now, and if he knows, he can do anything he wants with this town." He then pulls out something else. "And it wasn't until two days ago that I found this letter on our doorstep. A snake was delivering it."

He handed it to me. "Go ahead. Read it."

I unfold it and read.

Hello uncle. I've meant to write to you for a while now, but it's been rough with times like these. We may not have seen each other in a few years, but I hope you remember me. I'm your niece, Devyn Everard. Recently, I've been living alone in the same cabin that you often visited.

I come from a family of witches, you see. I've been wondering about your and Blanche's safety. I know that most elves are more immune to the whole dying part, but I still worry. At that, I heard that Castor plans to find the Warlord's dagger and intends to use it on the elves. He wants power more than he already has, and I fear for your safety. Please write back.

Oh, and if you can gladly tell Blanche to read my letters and write back, that would also be excellent.

Sincerely,
    Devyn Everard

Devyn
I haven't seen my niece since I was ten years old. It's been… eight years. Yes, I remember going to her cabin when I was younger, but we had stopped precisely when my mother left us. My father was distraught, so sick that he couldn't move from his bed for months. He was crushed, and so was I. We hadn't bothered to go back since.

Her letters. What letters?

The Warlord's dagger is known to kill Elves, taking away all their powers and killing them. For years, it's remained hidden. That was until Rufus Percival, the former king, found it. He hid it in his castle, ensuring it was never touched by the wrong hands, except a sociopath killed Rufus during the night. His family mourned exceedingly his son, Castor, who was now the king, and he was bloodthirsty for revenge.

He didn't bother trying to find the murderer. No, he decided to make everyone pay. He started a war.

"Castor can't use it on all of us. There's too many of us," I say.

"Except the number of us is decreasing. Our villages are being burned down. People are dying, and we might not be able to die from a simple knife, but fire can hurt us badly. Elves are dying from weariness and grief, and I don't want that to be you, Blanche."

"We have to do something," I argue. "We can't just let them win. They've burnt down enough villages. Why must they go after ours?"

"Because Castor hates us all." My father retorted.

"We didn't even do anything!" I argue, my chair flinging back as I stand up and fist the map. "It's brainless to go after all of us for something one person did."

A pause. "I cannot do anything about it." My father says.

I opened my mouth to argue, but a hard knock banged on our front door. I don't take my eyes off my father, and when the knocks don't relent, my father stands up and ushers me to get it. I bite my tongue, resisting the urge to curse at him before I swing around and go and get it. He follows close behind.

When I opened the door, Anastasia stood, a basket of blueberries there. Her brown skin glows in the sunlight, reflecting the brown freckles that circle her face. She has her brown hair in a ponytail. "Morning, Blanche. Brenner."

"Hi," I say.

My father nods at her.

"I hope I'm not interrupting anything." She gives me a sly smile. "I was hoping we could catch up." It's at the tip of my tongue to say no and go back to the conversation with my father, but I don't even get to open my mouth.

He yells out. "Go on, Blanche. We'll finish our conversation later."

He walks away, leaving me at the doorway. Ana smiles gleefully, and I close the door behind me. It's when I look down and see that I still have the map in my hands.

We turn to go. I tuck it into my back pocket for now.

CHAPTER TWO

"D id you have another nightmare?" Anastasia asks me. I open my mouth to deny, but her worried expression keeps my mouth closed. "Have you been getting them a lot recently?"

"I've had one every night this month," I admit, my breath stutters. I sat down on her sofa. "The dreams…they just keep getting worse…graphic."

Anastasia places the basket of blueberries on the wooden kitchen counter before sitting down next to me. She's taller than me, even sitting up. I cannot fathom how she is only two years older than me. "It might be the war - the knowledge of it could be setting your mind in various directions. You should see a midwife."

"I've seen enough midwives in the last couple of months," I argue and lean my body on the arm of the sofa. "They all say the same thing anyway."

They were all wrong. I've had the same statement said to me over and over again since I was a child. I was naive then and believed it, and so did my father, but I'm not daft.

"*It is typical coping*," They said, "Losing a mother so suddenly is challenging for a twelve-year-old. Give her time."

"Do you remember your dream?" Anastasia asked, plopping a blueberry into her mouth.

"No," I lied. I watch her cock her head, but I look away from her. "I just remember being afraid." I take a look at her and see her watching me. Anastasia always knew what to say, but now, she said nothing. Was it because she didn't know what to say? Or did she truly think I was crazy now?

"What about you?" I asked, and she raised an eyebrow. "How was your trip?"

Anastasia gets up, grabs the basket of blueberries and gives me a sad smile. "The forest seems so foreign to me." She looks down at the basket of blueberries, her eyebrows scrunched together. "It's so…quiet." She looks back at me. "It's unnerving."

Anastasia was gone for a month, traveling through the big forest. The emerald forest is one of the biggest forests in London. Humans stay out of most forests because our existence enough is to terrify them. Though they don't specifically know of elves in general. They hated the witches the most, mostly because they believed witchcraft was demonic and its main purpose was to summon the devil.

Of course that was not true.

"It's not our fault." I finally responded back and watched her mouth curve into a mischievous smirk. She takes a blueberry, but instead of eating it, she throws it straight at my cheek, leaving a sticky blue stain on my cheek. I open my mouth, trying to act offended, as I jog to the bowl and grab a blueberry and throw it at her.

I miss her face, tragically.

Anastasia and I were close. She was my only friend.

I hear Anastasia giggle before she stands back up. "Alright. Want to help me make some blueberry pie?" She asks.

I stand up and open my mouth to retort, but my voice stops, and my throat tightens as I hear a blood-churning scream from outside. My heart flips, and we both whirl towards the window, right above the sofa we just sat on.

I feel Anastasia freeze, and she looks out the window. Her eyes are huge as she scans what's happening. I back away from the window until I stand right next to Anastasia. "What's going on?" I whisper.

Just then, the air is ruptured with the sound of breaking glass, and something whirls my way. I grab Anastasia's arm and push us to the side until I collapse onto her. My hair flies over my face onto Anastasia, who gasps. I roll off of her and look at the object that was thrown at us.

A torch. It's blazing.

I curse, jumping up to my feet and looking at the shattered window. My heart accelerates, seeing the shards lying on the sofa, the floor…everywhere. Then, another scream, and Anastasia was fast on her feet; she looked out the window. Her eyes roamed frantically around outside, and then they widened with terror. "We have to get out of here, now," she says, a little too calmly.

"What's happening?" I demand.

"The village…" I see her eyes water. "They're burning it down. They're burning everything down."

I rush over to her, pushing beside her to see out the broken window. However, before I could take a good look, Anastasia ran, yanking me with her, towards her bedroom. She grabs a small satchel from her closet and starts shoving loads of clothes. "It's enchanted," she explained, rushing to fit everything inside. "Grab everything you can. We need to leave!"

Leave? My heart stutters, and I exhale, feeling my heart rapidly beat against my chest. "M-my father.," I realize, backing away from Anastasia. "He's out there. I need to find him."

Anastasia stands. "No, Blanche. You can't go out there."

I rush to turn around, but she grabs my hand, yanking me towards her. "Let me go!" I shove her away and make a run towards the front door. The door flies open, and I rush down the steps and see the chaos that stirs.

At the bottom of the steps, my body freezes.

There is so much fire - everywhere.

My eyes skim over the town I used to know, the houses that once stood. They erupted with fire. Elves ran with their children towards the woods, desperate to get out, while others lay unconscious…beheaded on the floor. Others had their hearts ripped out of their bodies. A scream comes from behind me, and I whirl around and watch as Anastasia's house swarms with hungry flames.

"Anastasia!" I yell, just as the porch lights on fire.

Among the fires, I see Anastasia appear, rushing down the steps. "Come, please! We can leave now!" She grabs my hand, but I push her away.

"I need to find my father. I'm not leaving without him!" I argue and watch as her eyes grow big. I turn towards my house. Despite the whole village being on fire, our house seems…fine. The roof is slightly lit on fire, and black smoke exits the chimney.

My heart is exploding. I run up my steps, about to open my door, when a crackling sound comes, and the space around me isn't visible anymore. Something lifts me off my feet, and I feel the magnitude of my body start to float. Some kind of force pushes me back. My vision goes blurry, and my feet buckle when the force throws me back violently down the steps.

My head bounces on the ground harshly, and the blistering pain sizzles at the back of my scalp. The air has been sucked out of me, my lungs breathless, begging..begging. Blood rushes down my nose and my head, and I open my eyes, lifting my head to see my house.

My house has been blown up.

Tears form at the edge of my eyes as I stare at my home. I don't care much about the house, but I do care about my father. Was he in there? Is he dead?

I look around. The elves were being ripped apart to shreds. Elves cannot die easily, as most creatures think we are immortal. However, there were creative ways to kill an elf, and I watched as those ways came to life.

We can burn into ashes. We can lose so much blood to the point where we can never wake up. We can die from grief. Elves can die in so many ways, and the vampires have figured this out. They burned down every village in this forest and burned down so many in others.

I watch as my neighbors turn into piles of ashes. I watch as my town turns into hellfire. The vampires are dressed in all black, dark black masks covering their faces. My hands bawl into fists. All I can think about is murdering every single one. Even with no power in me, I wish all of them a horrible death.

My hands shook as I stood up. Ana was behind me; I could feel her coming closer. "Blanche-" She tried to say. I turned around, and at the same time, Anastasia's house blew up in flames, causing both of us to fly toward the other side of the neighborhood.

I landed on the grass, just inches away from the other house. I coughed, breathing in the stomach-churning smoke. My vision grew dizzy as I looked at the grass and looked at the others being murdered. My eyes swerved around. "Ana?!" I shouted and looked around for her.

My eyes landed on the dwelling on fire and spotted her body.

I gasped when I saw her slumped body, consumed in the fire. I shout something, a tear escaping my eye. I gather the strength to force myself onto my knees and run towards the fire. Covering my mouth with my hand, I take her leg with one hand and pull her towards the grass.

The fire has burned off most of her skin, and her hair is slightly lit on fire. I grab my dagger and, with no hesitation, slice off her hair that burns at the tips. She might kill me later, but I'm saving her life.

Her stomach rolls up and down, and her shallow breaths are starting to slowly get slower. "Blanche, it hurts - it hurts really bad." She sobs, her body limp and pale as I take a look at her.

"Ana, please, can you stand?" I demand, trying to lift her up myself, but that causes her even more pain, and she puts a hand on my chest, her eyebrows scrunching together, eyes closed. I drop her instantly, and she lands on the floor, her hand shooting up to her chest, right above her heart.

She's got burn marks so deep the muscle has been burned off completely. I need to swallow down to stop from spewing.

"P-please, just leave me be," she stutters.

"Ana, we have to go. Please, let me help you stand," I argue.

"No," she retorts, eyebrows fluttering. "I can't move. Just leave me right here."

"Ana-" When I look at her now, I see her eyes roll back so that I see the whites of her eyes, the red veins appearing like lightning strikes. Then her eyes close, and I stay still for a moment. Suddenly, I can't hear the voices around me. I can't hear or smell the fire. Everything just...disappears.

A sob erupts from my throat as I look at my dear friend. Anastasia is the only friend that I have ever had. I cover my mouth with my hand as the tears flow down my face like a cascade of waterfalls. My throat starts to scream, but I can't even breathe as I look at my lifeless friend.

Then reality hits me back. Blinking away my tears, I realize I'm in the middle of a burning village. I noticed the satchel around her arm. I wipe away my tears and pray that she will forgive me in the afterlife. I take the satchel that she carries and put it over my own shoulder.

I take one last look around and see as the vampires slowly

come to a finish. Berlin still stands, and I see him off in the distance, fighting a few vampires with the help of some guards, but my father is not one of them. I look at my childhood. No, he was not dead.

I refused to think he was, but I could not look for him anymore. I would surely end up dead, just like Anastasia.

I took off in the opposite direction, heading straight out of my village. I looked back one more time and prayed that my father would make it out alive and safe. Then I would find him.

CHAPTER THREE

I found myself crawling into the nearest cave that I could come across. My legs shake from the cold. It was in the middle of September, and it was already freezing. London got cold around this time, and it was colder out in the forest than in the cities. I drop the pouch on the ground as I start up a fire.

Anastasia had brought a lighter; from what it looked like, it was from the city, which meant she had traveled there on her trip. All I needed was some dry grass and a few wooden sticks. I gathered some rocks around the small fire pit. I lit the grass first and watched the fire spread to the wood.

I sat down against the stone wall, reaching my hands out. It was dark, and the fire was the only light that illuminated my surroundings. It had nearly been a whole day since my village burnt down and my best friend died. I sniffle and blink away the tears that threaten to escape.

Now, I sat in this cave alone.

My stomach hollered, and I clenched my stomach with one of my hands. Unfortunately, Anastasia hadn't packed food, so I would have to hunt instead. I had spent most of the day trying to find a village, but my luck was unfortunate.

I groan just as my stomach growls again. I stand up and walk out of the cave. I look around. It's a chilly night, and I have nothing but Anastasia's clothes to cover up. I grab the pouch and grab a knitted sweater Anastasia packed. I throw it over my head before I hang the satchel over my shoulder and walk out of the cave.

I needed food and water. If I had to eat a fox tonight, fine, but

I needed it now.

I reach for my dagger, but something crinkles in my back pocket, and I reach back, only to feel the brown paper parcel that my father had made me keep.

That's right. I still had the map.

I unfold it and look at where I am on the map. I'm the dark green spot near the south cave, just next to a cold stream. My eyes are heavy, and even though I only want to crawl back into the cave and sleep next to the fire, I continue away from it.

I would need food eventually. The worst things come out at night, anyway.

Not many vampires usually roamed the Emerald Forest, not in London, but I imagined many would be here, especially after burning my village down. My hands curled into fists as I walked alongside the stream. The water was brown, full of tree chunks that had fallen off the trees.

I walked along the rocks until I was on the other side, farther away from my fire. I recheck the map and see if a vampire is nearby. I spot one red dot only a few miles from where I am. Unless he's headed in my direction, I'm not in trouble.

I shuffle forward, feeling the weight of my shoes poke at my feet. I grab my dagger from my holster and tuck the map inside the satchel. The trees encircle me inside the darkness.

I set out to find animals, at least something to eat tonight, before I starve to death.

I could have been out there for ages, or maybe it was minutes, but I spot a fox near a tree, sniffing the grass on the ground. It lifts his head slightly and then back to the ground again. Its fur is red and white.

It's beautiful, and I hate to waste the creature's life, but I need food. I try to hurry closer from where I'm at with as little noise. It snaps its head up when I move, and I freeze next to another tree. It looks around, but it doesn't spot me.

I'm almost ready to lunge at it and stick my dagger in its stomach when the fox starts to wine, and its stomach goes up and down rapidly. It plops to the ground with an agonizing cry. I frown. That is not how a fox should act.

I get up from my position and walk over to it. It doesn't scramble away. Instead, the fox looks away from me, down at the ground.

Its eyes are half closed, and its body is unmoving. I kneel towards it and see its stomach rapidly up and down again. I place my hand on its coat and immediately pull back when I feel something move.

I look at the fox. I understand now. She's giving birth.

"It's alright," I encourage, though the fox looks to have given up. I reach for it, but at the same time, something cracks from above. I whip my head up, and I can see part of a branch starts to fall toward me. I gasp, jumping away from the falling unit. I don't see it happen, but when I look back, the branch is laid on top of the fox, crushing it beneath it.

I look around for my dagger, only to see it's gone.

"Looking for this?"

I whip my head. A vampire stands only a few feet away from me, dressed in black jeans and a red t-shirt, but his cloak covers most of his outfit. It wears the same black mask that I saw them wear earlier. In his right hand, he holds my mother's dagger.

Shit.

I look back at the fox and the branch that crushes it. I feel horrible. I want to help it, but if I turn my back now to him, I'll be the one that's dead.

"Now, what shall we do with you?" The male vampire starts to say. He brings the dagger towards his mouth, tapping the pointy blade against his lips. He takes leisurely steps toward me. I use my hands to crawl backward until my back hits the nearest tree.

He continues forward, though, and he gets so close that I can practically smell his breath. His hand wraps around my throat and lifts me with ease. My back scratches against the tree, and he has no mercy as he presses me harder into it.

His grasp is hard. I can feel the block in my throat, restricting my breathing. His dark hair grazes my forward, and I suck in a breath as he leans toward my throat. I groan, trying to push away from him - please, don't.

"What's a pretty thing like you doing out here?"

I don't say anything, trying to get out of his grip. "Don't you know it's unsafe to wander around at night?" He says, his breath on my neck. My hands hit his chest desperately, trying to push him away. He grabs them with his other hand, stopping my movements. "Now, little lady, you ought to stop moving."

My rage burns. I see red and lift my head, hitting him in the groin. He yelps, letting me go instantly, as he falls to the floor. The dagger scatters on the ground, and I rush toward it. When I grab the blade, I faced the vampire, who had already recovered from the injury.

He looks angrier now. He tries to lunge at me, but I grab his hand and twist it away. He groans just as I throw him towards his ground. However, I don't expect him to recover so quickly, and he's up again. This time, he's got me pinned to the ground.

He tries to suffocate me to death, even as he yanks the dagger out of my hand and puts it against my throat. My mouth opens on reflex, even as my throat constricts and begs for air. "You're quite the troublemaker, darling," he comments and leans down. "We ought to punish you, shouldn't we?"

I grunted under him and saw my vision get so blurry. I felt the blade right under my throat. I needed a way for him to loosen it so that I could try to kill him. Like a maniac, I smiled up at him. "So easily?"

He raised an eyebrow and smiled down at me. "Yes, so very easily."

He tightens his hold on my throat harder, and my eyes roll to the side of my head before my hand shoots out toward his face, punching him in the nose. It was so unexpected, and I didn't expect it to happen, but I grabbed the dagger as fast as possible.

"You fucking–"

My instincts were quick. I raised the dagger, and then I stabbed him. No, but I wasn't just stabbing him in the stomach. No, I had stabbed him in his eye. I felt the splatter of blood spray on my face, and the rest of his blood oozed onto my clothing.

I learned how to fight from a young age. My father made sure to teach me in case of situations like these. He taught me how to wield and not be afraid to kill when defending myself. Shortly after my mother left, he ensured I was skilled enough for it. He didn't want anyone to hurt me, so instead of crying, I could remove my sadness and replace it with anger.

After all, I wasn't prey to vampires.

I lay still on the ground for a minute or two, trying to figure out what I had just done. I looked over at the vampire – his chest heaving up and down. He was still alive, barely, but he would be able to function in just a few minutes as soon as he recovered.

Plus, he would be outraged after learning he lost an eye. I look at his limp body. Do I regret it?

No.

I made sure the dagger was in my holster, grabbed the map, and shoved it inside the bag, and as fast as lightning, I sprinted across the forest floor. Like an earthquake, I felt oddly tense and terrified. He would wake up soon - would he smell my scent? I assumed he had at least an idea of my scent - I just hoped it wasn't too much. Terrified to look back, I didn't realize I was heading in a different direction than where I was supposed to go.

There was blood on my hands, my skin, my clothes, and my mouth. I could feel the metallic blood on my tongue - but it wasn't my blood; it was his blood.

I rustled through the trees until it led to one opening, and I came in contact with the risen crescent of the moon. There was a small grassland and a pond in front of me, but what most sparked my curiosity was the small cottage on the small hill in front of me. Someone made it entirely out of wood.

The gaps in the cottage were replaced with fine windows. Even my home wasn't as beautiful as the one before me. The light brown door only brought out the house's strangeness. What was it doing here? Indeed, one couldn't have lived in it. Vampires would have spotted it.

I walked towards it, climbing up the small hill before I reached the cottage. Oh, how lovely it was. It was a capturing sight, and the best part was that I didn't hear anything. Something about the silence and peacefulness made me feel welcomed. I climbed the steps, and then I looked through the windows. It was much smaller from the inside, but it was still beautiful. The dark green counters were unflattering, but I didn't mind. A refrigerator was inside - if it had food, I could take some. My stomach growled at the thought of it. I looked around for anyone. I didn't see anyone. I was turning the knob. It was unlocked...I smiled.

I should have stopped then, but I was compelled to go in. As soon as I entered and the door behind me closed, I was met with darkness. There were no lights, only my creative navigation skills. I stuck my hands out and felt the things around me. First, I felt the furniture, which appeared to be old yet tidy. I was then sitting on it, feeling the cushion.

It seems it hasn't been tended to in a long time. The dust lingered on it, and I wiped my finger across it. Whoever lived here once had died. I could smell the death and the eeriness in this cottage.

It seems that the cottage had been left alone a long time ago.

So just as I was to lay down, I heard something shuffle...no, someone. I turned my head towards the sound, my heart moaning loudly. Had the vampire already gone out and traced my scent? How is that possible?

It was only a few minutes ago that I had run away. Recovery for vampires was quick, but this quick? No, this was no vampire. I could feel the goosebumps appear on my arms and legs. My hand drifted towards my dagger, where I looked around. Another shift, and I jumped when I saw the shadowy figure appear in the darkness for a split moment.

"Who's there?" I demand, grabbing my dagger and keeping it at my side. "Show yourself."

I was pressed so close against the couch that I thought I had melted into it.

Where are you?

I braced myself for the impact, but when I felt nothing, my eyebrows furrowed, and I slowly let my dagger dangle at my side. I was not deranged. I had just seen the figure. "Hello?" I tried once again.

I frowned, my shoulders slumping as I put the dagger back into my holster. Truly, I was crazy. It was the fear or the anxiety. Perhaps this was one of my nightmares, trying to terrify me like they always wanted to do. Was this what my nightmares wanted? To make me insane? To drive me into being a monster?

Except then, it became clear that I wasn't alone. Something shifted, louder...harder than before.

Then I felt something on my throat. One mighty hand choked me slightly as it pinned me against the wall, and I was trapped in the figures barrier. Their legs stood between mine, crouched, touching the wall I was tackled on. I felt heat form in the pit of my stomach and rise vibrations, especially the sensitive skin between my thighs. This creature was different.

I felt my lips quiver and the stranger's breath near my lips.I bit back the groan, especially from the burning sensation in my neck and back. They slammed me on the wall harshly, knocking the pictures behind me to the ground. The image was now lying on the floor, shards of glass splattered everywhere.

I could barely make out the picture, but it was a silhouette of two people with short hair. They both looked like boys, but I could have assumed wrong. I gulped, and I exhaled, closing my eyes slightly. Whoever was pinning me against the wall had a lot of strength because I couldn't move. I couldn't breathe. I can only see their figure in the darkness.

"Well...aren't you a bloody ray of sunshine."

My whole body became stiff as a board, to the point where I felt paralyzed. I could hear only my shaky breaths in the awkward silence. The stranger was right before me, his face just inches away, but I could not see his features clearly. It sounded like he had just woken up, and I might be to blame.

I almost gasped when he said, "Well, I certainly didn't expect this." I kept my mouth shut and made no noise or movement. My head was spinning.

But why was he here?

"Cat, got your tongue, little elf?" He says, with a slight edge of amusement dripping off his voice. I wanted to kick him in the face but stayed silent instead.

"You're a quiet one, aren't you?" He muttered, and his other hand skimmed the length of my sweater. "And short." My hands bent into fists, and I scowled. He might not be able to see it in the darkness, but the thought of kicking him in the balls made me joyful.

"Shut up," I whispered.

He drew back, and I could feel him smirking. "Ah, so the elf speaks..." He slowly let me drop to the ground, my shoes crushing the leftover glass shards. "I thought you might have gone mute, or was it just my daring looks?" I scoffed at his arrogant nature, and he let out a chuckle. "Ah, so you're denying it?"

"I can't deny anything," I found my voice, my fists curling. "I can't even see you."

"Do you wish to see me?" He asked in a calm voice as if he

was signaling something to me. I didn't know the answer to that. Why would I want to see him? Why..why was he even here? Was he another elf? Or perhaps he might be a werewolf.

"What are you doing here?" I whispered, keeping my voice low and firm.

He grumbled. "Why do I need a reason to sleep in my house?"

I let out a quivered breath. I felt like such an fool. Of course, this was his house. I stared at his black silhouetted face, feeling the seriousness of the situation. This was his home. I broke into his house. I look at the front door - I need to leave. I try to break free from his excruciating close barrier, pushing my entire body to his, but my efforts go to waste because his hand flies out towards my shoulder, shoving me to the wall. I was even closer than I was before. "Now, the real question is, what are you doing here?"

I stared at him for a moment. "Don't be quiet on me now. You barge into my home, wake me up, and expect to leave? How rude."

"Let me go," I threatened, my hands flying out towards his chest and trying to shove him away. I realized then that my hands meet skin, and my fingertips feel the muscle he carries

"Or what?" He teased, catching one of my hands with his. "Are you going to scream?"

I looked at his face and felt the way his breath cascaded on my face. "I might," I retorted, but with a simple tug of his hand, I lowered him to my height. "Or maybe I'll just kill you."

I was bluffing. I wouldn't intentionally kill someone, and honestly, I never planned on it. Perhaps if a vampire attacked me and in dire circumstances, I would need to protect myself by killing, but this man had not hurt me quite yet. I'm only waiting for him to make the wrong mistake.

He goes quiet for a few seconds. I wonder if my words had lingered on him. Another fatal mistake I make before he bends down, and his hand that had pinned me against the wall is now on my hip, slowly making its way up to the medial fold of my breasts, trailing up my clothes. My breath hitched, and I shuddered. My head hit the wall behind me, eyes widened. I close my eyes. I had never interacted with a boy like this before.

I never let a man touch me. I had never even kissed someone, let alone be alone with a man in the same room for five minutes. I usually was locked away in my house, studying or training.

I let him touch me; his finger ended right at the center of my neck. Then he returned and leaned in, saying: "Liar," he says, and it all becomes clear to me. He was doing this to test me. He was playing with me. I lifted my knee, missing the target that I was trying to take.

The sudden abrupt change caused his posture to fall back, taking me with him. His hands enclosed my hips, and we fell to the ground. The slice of glass would have hit me, but the man in front of me took my fall, and he slammed into the ground, the shards of glass cutting into his skin. I find my face buried deep in his chest, and my lip curls, looking at him.

His face was a bit clearer in this angle, especially from the silver moonlight in the room hitting his face perfectly, revealing all his features. His bronze eyes were scintillated in the moonlight, and his hair was a shade of dirty blonde. His jawline was sharp, nothing as I had ever imagined a man wearing. He was shirtless with black sweatpants. I swallowed, embarrassment settling in.

He got up, the little bits of glass falling out of his back. I gasped, throwing myself off of him and rolling into the shadows. He frowns, looking at me. "Are you okay?" I asked quietly, my voice lower than before.

He smirked. "Where are you? I know you saw me... It's only fair I see who my intruder is now," My eyes widened, going deeper into the shadows so that that man wouldn't be able to find me. "Don't be hard, little elf. You don't want me to come to look for you," I tried to run...I tried.

Before I knew it, his hand circled my waist, and he roughly pulled me into his chest. It knocked all the air out of me, and I gasped. Hadn't the glass struck his skin? Wasn't he in pain? "Hey, let me go!" This time, I was yelling. He let me go, his eyes wide.

"How rude. Glass is stuck inside my back, and you would rather hide than help me," He taunted.

I elbowed him in the stomach and heard him groan, staggering back. "Don't touch me," I scowled. He tried to go forward, but I stepped back. "I'm serious. Don't touch me."

"Will you hurt me again?" He asked, cocking his head.

"I've barely hurt you," I responded. When he went silent, I looked down nervously. "Come here," I tell him to follow me, pointing to where the moonlight meets the window. He casually sits there, looking straight at me. I look closely at his face and his ears and see round ears, just like mine. "Turn around."

"So bossy," He commented before turning around. I drew closer, my eyes growing. The glass was piercing his skin, the blood soaking down his back.

"This might hurt," I warned him before I pulled out the glass one at a time. He didn't wince, cringe, or even make a sound. He went to turn around, but I stopped him. "What are you?"

He chuckled. "Why does it matter? What matters now is that I see my trespasser," And he turned around, his eyes landing on me. My face was exposed to him by only the moonlight, and I looked away, trying to escape his eyes, but he reached out, grabbed my chin, and forcefully made me look down. "Look at me, little elf. I want to see everything."

When he let go of my chin, I asked: "Answer my question. What are you?"

"What do you think I am?" he asked. I groan. Can this man reply with a straight answer?

"Your back is fine now, so you heal quickly," I say. "You show signs that you're an elf, your height, but your stance- you act as if you own the bloody place. A werewolf has so much power like yours, so how should I know? As for elf qualities, your ears are round"

"Observant, you are," he admitted.

I prevented the smile from coming to my face. "So, what are you?"

He spoke low and in a whisper. "My ears don't show unless I sense something, just like yours, I see. You hide your ears, right?" My eyes widened. I hid my ears under my hair, but how did he know... I'm not too sure. "I'm an elf just like you." It was hard to believe at first, but I stood there, mesmerized by him.

"What's your name?" I asked, raising an eyebrow. "I can't imagine it's something simple."

He chuckled at that. "My name is Beckett Brooker. And what title do you hold?" He was smirking at me, roaming my body with his eyes. It was the same way the other vampire had looked at me. However, this was different. His eyes didn't feel like they were burning me. Instead, it felt like a desire or some compliment. I crossed my hands.

"Why should I give you my name?" I asked.

"Probably because you are in my home that you trespassed,"

He looked out the window, biting down on his lower lip. "And I'm sure that if I kick you out, you won't last ten minutes without a vampire tracking you down," My eyes jerked away from him. He was right, but I would never admit that. "So...name?"

I sighed. "It's Blanche Everard."

"Everard, may I ask why you have blood on your face and clothes?" I looked down and registered that the blood was still evident on my body. I tried to run back into the shadows, but he caught my hand, dragging me back. I looked up at him, dampening my lips. "Please tell me you killed someone."

I shook my head. I snatched my hand back, snarling. "I didn't kill anyone, and refrain from touching me again before I take a knife and stab you in the eye." I almost chuckled. I had done that to the vampire earlier.

"I would love to see you try," he sneered. "A little elf like you could barely reach my height," I glared at him. I went to grab my dagger, but my mouth dried when I felt nothing in my holster. I felt around for it, but nothing.

I looked around the room, seeing the dagger nowhere on the floor. "Where is-"

"This dagger is much too shiny for someone like you." I look at the elf and see him with the dagger between his hands. He's examining it, even with the blood on it. "Did you think you could hide this from me?"

I shuffle forward. "Give that back, now."

"Or what?" He asked, cocking his head to the side. His mouth formed into a mischievous sneer. "Are you going to stab me?"

My hands fold together angrily, and he chuckles, twirling the dagger before he lowers it to me. He lifts it up again as I reach for it, and I stop and stare at the elf. "Are you serious?"

"Don't be so bland," he remarks. "Go ahead and grab it."

He lowers it again, but I don't dare grab it. I won't play his silly games, not anytime soon. "Fuck off. You can keep the dagger."

He clicks his tongue in dismay. "Giving up so soon?"

"I'm not going to play your game just so you're satisfied," I tell him, and as I walk past him, I elbow him square in the side, causing him to groan, and his arm wavers, which gives me a chance to snatch my dagger back.

As soon as he realizes I have it, he glares at me. "My violent little elf."

"Stop calling me a little elf. It's offensive and annoying coming from you," I retorted, storing the dagger in the holster. He was extremely tall, much taller than any guy I knew.

"You admit you're short?" He asked. I scowled, walking towards the entrance, and then my hand found the light, and the small dangling light above me was brought to life. I hadn't seen that earlier. I could see where everything was more clearly. I turned to him slowly, admiring how he looked. I looked him up and down, and my cheeks slowly grew red.

I see his abs. They are sculpted on his chest, running down his abdomen. His body is lean, and I see the dark veins extending from his hands. He has muscles that run up his arms, and each time he moves his hands, the muscles flex and grow larger by size. I haven't seen such a muscular man in a very long time. He was very attractive.

Then I see the scars. White scars are barely visible on the surface, but it doesn't pass my eyes.

He sneered. "I have a few questions," He walks closer, taking my arm and pulling me towards the couch, shoving me on top of it. He sat on the opposite couch, crossing his hands.

"I'm not answering any of your questions," I say.

"You will if you don't want to get eaten by vampires," he snaps. I glare at him. "Now, answer my question."

I dig my fingers into my knees and find my voice. "The door was unlocked. I didn't think anybody lived here."

He drew back, eyes raised. He almost looks confused, but then he looks at my white blouse stained with vermillion blood. "And the blood? What happened?"

I shrugged. "A vampire."

"Did you kill it?" He demanded.

"No," I say, my hands tightening into fists. I do not appreciate how demanding he is, nor do I like this interrogation. "I stabbed him in the eye."

He chuckled a little before standing up. "That's all then. You can leave now."

I stand up, glaring at him. "And how do you have an open place in the middle of the forest? A vampire can come in here any time it wants and kill you. What will you do then?" I demand.

"That's the thing, Everard," he says and then looks back at me. "We have a force field specifically to keep things out…," he says and shrugs. "I'm not quite sure how you even were able to see this house. Let alone get in it."

I shake my head. "Well, then, it was weak. I could see it from down the hill."

"No, it wasn't," Beckett argued. "My brother and I had been keeping us invisible for years, and our power together is dangerously strong, and now that you've broken it, others will be able to see us."

"Broken it?!" I say, almost offended. "I didn't break anything. I walked up the hill and came here."

He looks down at me. "Enough talk. Get out."

"Let me stay," I hated how desperate I sounded. Beckett seems pleased by that, smirking.

"And what will I get in return?" He asks, venom coating his voice. Before I can give him anything, he extends his hand and eyes my bag. I look at him, scowling before throwing it at him.

He zips it open and reaches in. He throws all the clothes on the floor, digging for something he can find. That's when he pulls out the map, and my eyes immediately widen. "No, you can't take that," I say, going to reach for it, but he pulls it high above so that I can't get it and looks at it. I can almost see the way his face lights up looking at it. "I'm serious, don't-"

"It doesn't matter what you say now, Everard," he says calmly. "I don't care if you stay or leave, but I'll be keeping this."

"Give it to me!" I shout, jumping for it. He lifts it higher, catching my arm and pushing me back. "What the hell is your problem? It's my map!"

"Not anymore," he comments and then rolls it up. "I don't know where you got this map, but it'll help me in the long run."

"My father gave that to me. It doesn't belong to you," I argue.

He smiled at that and shrugged. "Change out of your clothes, little elf. You smell foul."

"Don't call me that."

He ignored me and looked down at my clothes, which were stained vermillion. "Towels are in the kitchens. Clean the blood up. Put the dirty clothes in the sink," he instructs. "Now, I'm going to bed. Please don't wake me up again."

I scowled. I was fuming, Beckett's voice ringing in my head

like an annoying brass section. He starts to open the door to his bedroom when suddenly, he looks back, giving me another daring sneer. "Goodnight, little elf."

Before he closed the door, I took my shoe off, hurling it towards the door. It hits the door before it can hit him. I wanted to go after him and punch him, but I went to the kitchen, still fuming, stripped myself of the blood-soaked clothes, and threw it into the sink. I then grabbed a towel from the inside of a cabinet and wiped off the remaining blood on my skin. His lingering touch remained, as if making me. I would never let him touch me like that again.

I picked up all the clothes from the floor, put them back in the bag, and then put on the night dress that Ana had packed. It smelled of her, and my entire body almost fell from the dizziness.

After getting ready, I went towards the light switch, ready to turn it off, but I looked out the window.

I knew this was the safest place I could spend the night. Even if I was spending it in the same house as Beckett Brooker. I turned the light switch off and went back to the couch.

The couch wasn't like my comfy bed at home, but it was better than sleeping in a cave and getting my throat torn out. I went to the couch. I shivered. Beckett could have at least given me a bloody blanket.

That was the first night in the month that my sleep paralysis didn't come for me in the dark.

CHAPTER FIVE

I was the first one to wake up in the morning.

I was shivering, the flesh on my hands and legs covered in tiny goosebumps. The sun had risen and shined through one of the windows. I didn't know what time it was. I only knew the date: September 30th, 1943.

I've been able to count the days and memorize the months, so they were imprinted in my mind. Being in the forest is more challenging since there is no technology to help us. Humans in the cities can access payphones, trains, buses, and cars, but here, there is nothing but us. We can only take care of ourselves.

I could feel the cold material of my dagger strapped to my thigh. It didn't matter if I was safe. I needed to be ready at all times.

My stomach screams. I still hadn't eaten, and I was craving anything.

I got up from the firm coach and proceeded to walk into the kitchen. I'm not sure if Brooker would mind, but I didn't care about his opinion at the moment. I opened the door to the refrigerator. There wasn't a lot, only a few vegetables and berries that he must have picked outside. Blueberries were in a bowl, and my heart sank as I remembered Anastasia.

Blueberries were her favorite fruit.

"Who the hell are you?" A confused yet offended voice pierced through the air. I whirled around to see.... Beckett? No, the man in front of me was not Beckett, but he was so familiar it made me speechless. His hair was the same color, and his eyes were light blue. He had the tiniest facial hair that Beckett didn't have under his nose.

"Who are you?" I demand.

"I asked you first." He stepped forward, and I watched his face contort into something threatening. "Answer the question. Who are you?"

My back is against the refrigerator, my hand slowly grazing toward the dagger I had strapped along my leg. "My name is Everard," I say only my last name, so I don't reveal too much. "Who are you?"

The man's eyebrows shoot up, and he chuckles, looking up at the air before he looks back at me. "Don't tell me...Did Beckett bring you here?"

"Uh-" I don't know how to explain to him that I broke into this house and how Beckett let me stay despite the trouble I've caused already. I don't even know who this man is, but by the looks of it, he lives here too.

I open my mouth to explain, but at the same time, Beckett emerges into the kitchen, hands running through his hair. He looks back and forth between the other male and me and raises an eyebrow. His attention is on me when he says: "Good morning," he greets.

"Who is this?" The other male asks Beckett. "Is she..." He looks at me and then back at Beckett.

How embarrassing. I should have left last night.

"This is Everard," he introduces me to him. Then he looks at me. "Everard, this is my twin brother, Edwin." he strolls forward, and his hand flies towards the refrigerator. He takes a look at me. "Step aside, little elf." At the mention of the nickname, my face contorts into a glare, and I push myself off the fridge and towards Edwin.

I extended my hand forward. "I'm sorry we met so suddenly. My name is Blanche."

He looked down at my hand and almost recoiled for a second before he gathered himself and then grabbed my hand with his. He didn't say a word as he observed me. He seemed to look me up and down, and I wasn't sure what he was thinking. "Did Beckett bring you here?" He asked after a few moments.

"Well..."

"You wouldn't believe it, older brother," Beckett says. We both turn to him, and he closes the fridge at the same, having the bowl of blueberries. He leans against the refrigerator. His face contorted into a sneer. "Our elf here broke in last night. She even broke the force field," He plops the blueberry in his mouth and shrugs. "Somehow, she did."

Edwin looks terrified, face contorting into anger, but it's not towards me. He looks at Beckett. "What? It's been down all night?!" Edwin demands and then peers out the kitchen window. "You should have woken me up when the barrier was broken." He looks back at me. "How did you break it?"

"Good question," Beckett says, looking at me. "How did you break it?"

I scoff, shrugging my shoulders. "I just walked through…"

"You just walked through," Beckett recited and then chuckled. I wanted to hurt him for acting this way. Was it hard to admit their powerful force field wasn't as good as they thought it was?

"That's impossible," Edwin replied. "That force field has been up for years. This house is invisible to the public; we've been here for years without any trouble. So now that you've broken it…"

"I didn't break it!" I argued. "I just saw the house and walked up to it."

"But you shouldn't have," Edwin retorted. "That's the whole point."

"We'll set it back up," Beckett said, putting the blueberries on the green counter. "Once the company leaves, we'll set up a better one." He looks at me. "One that even my little elf can't see."

"Why do you refer to me as yours?" I demanded and crossed my hands. "Nobody is responsible for me other than myself."

How dare he call me names? How dare he mock me? Yes, I've broken into his house, but it was supposed to be invisible in the first place. So why does he persist? I belong to no one but myself.

Beckett smirked and looked at his brother, whose eyes were glued onto me. "What kind of power do you wield?" He asked.

I watched as Beckett looked back at me, interested in my answer. The tightness in my throat happened, and my anxiety pooled inside me like harsh waves. "I… don't have any."

"Bullshit," Beckett snapped.

"I'm serious," I stated. "I don't have any."

"Every elf has a power," Edwin explained. "You might not have found it yet."

"A little too old now, huh?" Beckett comes, his mouth curving into a smirk. "It's alright, little elf. I'm sure you will find them soon."

I glare up at him. "Would you stop calling me that?!"

"No."

I can't stand to be in the same room anymore - it's suffocating and irritating, and all of it is because of him. He's incredibly frustrating, and I can't read him the way I can with others. "Maybe I should just go," I said.

Beckett doesn't say anything for a moment, and even Edwin contemplates it for a moment, but he inches towards the window instead, peering out of it. "Very well then," Beckett replies. "Gather your stuff."

"My map," I state, and he raises an eyebrow as if he doesn't know what I'm talking about. "I need my map back. I can't navigate without it."

"That's not my concern," Beckett retorted. "You stayed the night because you agreed to give me the map."

"I didn't agree to anything," I argued. "You took it without my permission. I demand you give it back to me."

He stood up, marching towards me until his whole body towered over me. I tried to look confident, but goddamn, he was taller. "Oh, what will you do to get it back? You surely didn't think you could spend the night without a price. It was a risk having you here after all."

"Beckett." Edwin inches towards the window, his voice alarming, but Beckett pays no mind to him as he argues with me.

"I have important matters to tend to."

"You live in a forest," I snap. "What could you possibly have to do?" I push at him with my strength. I sent him flying back a few steps. "You don't even need that map!" I start to push him harder, but he grabs my hands mid-air. "I need that map. Give it back, now!"

He smirks. "And what makes you think I take demands from you?"

I go to kick him, but just then, Edwin's voice rings yet again. "Beckett!" He looks over at his brother and then says: "Vampires! Outside!" Beckett's face falls, his hands dropping mine instantly. He rushes towards his brother and peers out of the window— I stand, frozen, a flare of emotions erupting inside my body.

Beckett comments: "The barrier." Suddenly, he pins the small table underneath the door handle. "It won't do much, but it'll hold for a few seconds." He then spun around, licking at his suddenly dry lips.

"How many are there?" I asked.

"A lot," Edwin answered and turned around. "We might have to use the cellar to get out." The two brothers looked between each other and then right back at me.

"Or we could just throw her out," Beckett suggests and shrugs.

I scowl, grabbing my backpack from the ground. "You're horrible." I jump when I hear something bang against the door. "What is this cellar you guys are talking about?"

Edwin stepped forward. "Ever heard of the death Cascades?" I shake my head. "Well, you'll find out today."

CHAPTER SIX

The vampires crash against the door, pounding wildly. I wince as the door slowly starts jamming open.

"Get downstairs now!" Edwin shouts. Beckett races down, and Edwin grabs my dress, hurling me down with them.

There is a flight of stairs heading down into the house's foundation. Into the lower part, which I had not yet explored.

Drip. Drip. Drip.

The pipes squeak against the wall, and the water drips onto the floor. One droplet landed on my forehead, trailing down my nose and into my mouth, where I tasted the salty flavor explode on my tongue.

Edwin and Beckett stop in front of a metal door. Something pounds and then rattles the floor above us. I gasp, looking behind me. "They broke through the door. Hurry!" Edwin panics. Beckett presses the keys, and it opens before we both go inside.

Just as he closes it, I see a few vampires appear in the hallway.

They lunge at the door as we shut it, locking us inside the small room. I look around, complete darkness around me. "Where are we?" I ask in confusion, shooting my hands out to gather my surroundings.

I feel something grab my hand instead, and I recoil, gasping. "Relax," I hear Beckett's stern voice command. He grabs my hand roughly, yanking me towards something. Then I see something light up, just a tiny space away from us. I realize it's Edwin's hand shooting up, and he does it effortlessly.

He brings his hand to the ceiling, and I watch the lightbulb flicker on for numerous seconds before lighting up and then into a chandelier, where all the candles light up. I scoff, quite amused. "I wish I could do that."

"Maybe you will," Edwin suggested.

"Stop chatting and help me find this bloody entrance," Beckett instructed and headed towards one of the bookshelves. I looked around, looking for something to find when I heard the metal door pound. When I looked over, I saw the vampires had created a dent in the door.

They're breaking down the door.

"We have to hurry!" I shouted. I run towards the desk, look through the pictures, and look for clues, but I don't discover anything. Only a picture of which I think is Beckett and Edwin's parents.

I reach to grab the picture, but then, my hand freezes and is pushed back by Beckett, who hovers over me, a glare embowed. "Don't touch anything and help us find this entrance."

I snatch my hand back, glaring at him. I stomp towards the bookshelves, and he joins me. "And what would this entrance look like?" I ask.

"It's not visible to the eye, Everard. It's specifically hidden so that someone who knows it can make a quick escape."

The batters on the door grow louder, and there are multiple dents on the door now. Anxiety pools in me, and I search for it. "Found it!" Edwin shouts, and we turn around. A bookshelf before him has opened, and a small black hole appears. "We'll have to crawl into it."

Edwin then disappears as he crawls into the dark hole. We race to it, and just then, the door breaks down, and there isn't only one vampire - not two - but over ten, squishing their way through.

"Go!" Beckett demands. He pulls out a knife and shields his body before mine. "I'll hold them off." I hesitate momentarily, wondering if I should fight with the man before me, but I decide otherwise when he sends me a glare.

I get on my knees and start crawling. Beckett won't be able to beat ten vampires at once, at least not with just a dagger. I squeeze my feet into the hole. "Beckett, come on!" Edwin yells from beside me.

I can't see Beckett from where I'm standing. All I can see are the feet of a few vampires. "Blanche, get that rock from the corner. Once Beckett crawls through, we'll need to close off the hole so that the other vampires can't get in." Edwin kneels, shouting through the open hole. "Beckett, let's go!"

I hurry and grab the rock, rolling it till it's right next to the hole. "Beckett!" Edwin groans, peeking through the hole. "Get in here!" Then Beckett appears, eyebrows bent in pain. When his legs are inside, I shut the doorway with the rock, and the darkness overcomes us.

"You're a bloody idiot," Edwin curses. "You didn't have to kill them all."

Beckett said into the darkness: "Yeah, well, they sure as hell deserved it." Edwin's hands light up again and shoot at the ceiling. This time, it's a line of candles that light up the tunnel. I see a long, narrow stone hallway leading down into the abyss.

I breathe out. "So where is this place that you speak of, then?"

"Down the tunnel. It might take us a few hours, but if we walk for the entire day, we'll be able to reach the end of it."

The entire day? Just how long is this tunnel? Where is this place? I glance at Beckett and see a gash on his cheek and a bite mark on his neck. A part of me wants to feel sorry, but then I push it away, looking at Edwin. "Then we should start walking, right?" I say and start walking forward.

Edwin and Beckett follow close behind.

A clap of thunder erupts, and I wince at the sound. The blasting noise echoes as I desperately try to tune it out. I've gathered that we're underground somewhere. Though they are dripping and old, I can still hear the pipes, indicating that this tunnel was built many years ago.

I look back at the two boys, seeing them make small conversation, quiet enough that I cannot hear anything. When I focused on Beckett's neck, I noticed that the bite had vanished, replaced with freshly made skin.

Despite being unable to manipulate the earth as the others do, elves' healing abilities were quite powerful. However, his healing was extremely fast. As I step forward, something brushes against my foot, and I jump, frightened by the creature. I look down at the hairy beast and see its rotten eyes looking up at me.

Its wicked stare digs into my soul. The hairs on its body go up, but then it makes a slight whining noise, rushing past me and towards the boys, gliding past them. "It's just a rat, Everard," Beckett claimed, watching me resentfully.

"Perhaps we should sit down for a few minutes. Some of us are quite on edge," Edwin suggested.

"We don't need to stop because of me."

"Yes, well, I would like to sit down." He sits down, leaning his body against the stone walls. Beckett is next to sit, still frowning at our situation. I'm the next, throwing my backpack on the floor, crossing my legs in front of me, and letting my body relax against the wall.

"How far until we reach this "Death Cascades" you two speak of?" I asked.

"Far," Beckett answers, keeping a blank face as he answers. Suddenly, he seems distant, angry, or sour towards me.

The silence is overwhelming - it's too loud. For once, I don't know what to think either. Once I end up at this place, what will I do then? I'll be left stranded, all because I couldn't stay in my damn cave because I was hungry.

I pull my feet up into my chest. I catch sight of Beckett watching me, frowning at me. Does he hate me that much? I haven't done much to him. "Stop doing that," he suddenly flares.

"Doing what?"

"Looking at me. You do it too much," he says, making my cheeks red with uneasiness. I had done it a lot, but I never thought he noticed.

"I'll look at you when I want to," I retort, returning his glower. I had only met him ten hours ago, and he annoyed me more than anyone I knew.

A beat. "Watch your mouth, Everard."

"Or what?" I tested him. "Are you going to shut me up?"

A keen blade drags on the floor, and I look at the dagger he drags on the floor, delivering a promise - a threat. "Sure, I can shut you up," he says and sneers. "But I would much rather cut that tongue of yours out." He looks at my mouth, completely memorized.

I groaned when I saw another rat run across the stone floor.

Just then, Beckett's hand shot out, and as the rat jumped, it stopped and fell to the ground, crying and squeaking, as its body juddered its rapid movements, its head twisting to its side, going all the way around its head, before it's neck snapping, and then… nothing. Its body falls limp on the floor, and it's dead.

I look down at the rat and see its lifeless body. Then, a black shadow swept its body into ashes. I know it's a sort of threat from Beckett, showing how much he can kill me in seconds. Yet the thrill of the kill sent shivers down my back, excitement radiating in me while it cowered against it. I didn't know what the feeling was.

"You didn't have to do that," I say, lifting my legs higher until my thigh is revealed to him. His eyes are fixed on my thigh, and when I glance down, I notice the dagger I had hidden away in my holster. I lowered the dress to hide the blade, but it was too late. He had seen it.

"Your dagger." I cover my thigh with my dress. "Can you fight, or do you have that just for show?"

Thoroughly vexed, I watch as his expression fades into amusement. "You're an asshole."

"No, I'm just asking a question," he snaps back and leans his back against the stone wall. "Is that why you didn't try to fight the vampires? Because you can't fight?"

"I can fight," I say, wanting to prove that I can. I needed to know how to fight, especially being the epitome of disappointment.

"Prove it. Fight me," Beckett says.

I scoff. "Don't be daft."

"I'm not daft, but I would enjoy the thought of you on your ass."

I clench my teeth together, and my hand flies straight toward my dagger, but before I can make any movement toward him, Edwin interrupts.

"Enough," Edwin thunders and then rolls his eyes. "You guys are acting childish." He then stands up, glaring at us both. "I think we should start moving again. I don't know the time of the day, but if we want to get there before nighttime, we don't want to waste any more time."

Without uttering another word, he walks forward. Beckett and I get up, but I grab my backpack before he can leave me alone and hurry to walk alongside him. "Why are you being like this?" I ask. "If this is about last night–"

"Everard," he interrupts. "This has nothing to do with last night. This is about you breaking into my house and dragging my brother and me out of it."

Was it all my fault? "Honestly, I'm not sure why you're complaining. You live in a cottage in the middle of the forest with a weak force field. It's no wonder I was able to see your house. I would suggest working on your magic. I don't deserve all this blame."

"You deserve enough of it," Beckett answers.

"I dislike you," I say.

There is silence, and then I look up at him and see him looking at me carefully. "I'm glad the feelings are mutual then."

The next few hours go on with a bore. Edwin stays ahead most of the time, guiding the way. Beckett and I stay close to each other, but the tension between us is not forgotten. Though we don't say a word to each other, it feels like some force is wrapping around my throat, suffocating me.

"We're almost there!" Edwin shouts, and I see the dim glow of light from afar. Relief fills me as I feel my feet grow tired. My eyes squint as the light appears brighter. I never realized just how bright the sky was at sunset. As the view became more apparent, I saw the magnificent place Edwin had been discussing: a waterfall, the smell of salty rain falling into the pond as it pounded against the surface.

Edwin was the first to see daylight, followed by Beckett and me. The waterfall was strange. Throughout this entire war in the forest, it had managed to stay clean, with not a single leaf floating across its surface. Rocks surround it, high enough that you can climb and see the water.

"How is it so...clean?" I asked, not expecting anyone to answer me.

Beckett did answer, however. "It's called Death Cascades for many reasons. It has many powers. It may look beautiful and majestic from the outside, but that's where its beauty ends." The information falls off his lips with such calmness. "It's got death in its name. Anyone who steps foot into the water or touches it at all will burn, and I am not referring to a fire-related kind of burn. I'm talking from the inside. Hallucinations. Nightmares. Things that will rattle you for a long time to come. It will make you mad."

"How does it kill you?" I asked.

"Well, surely if you turn mad, you don't have the right mind," he adds, "If I went mad enough, I would end up slitting my own throat." My face drops the minute he says it, and I stop walking.

"So, it...makes you..."

"Yes," He says before I can finish it. He strolls forward, and I follow behind. He follows his brother to the rocks while I stay back. What should I do now? Is this where we part ways and never see each other again? I wouldn't be too upset about never seeing Beckett again, but Edwin…had at least treated me nicely.

I walk up to them, seeing them exchange glances between them and me. "I should be going. It will be nighttime soon, and I need to find shelter."

"It was a pleasure meeting you, Blanche." Edwin patted me on the shoulder. I don't expect Beckett to say goodbye, and when he stares at me blankly, I am proven right again. I just hoped he wasn't looking for a goodbye, either.

"You as well, Edwin," I say. I'm about to turn around when suddenly something whizzes past my ear, almost hitting me. Then a grunt, and I turn around to see Edwin as he clutches a silver arrow into his stomach—red blood seeps from his wound, staining his white shirt.

"Shit-" Beckett curses, attempting to reach for his dagger, but then another arrow comes, and it hits Beckett straight in his shoulder.

They both slumped on the ground, the impact making them collapse. I exhale loudly and look around for the source of violence. Anxiety pools in my stomach, and instinct tells me to grab the dagger in my holster. I reach for it-

"Don't move," I hear a voice, and then from the trees appears a woman. Her hair is black, in a low ponytail. Goosebumps cover her brown skin as the breeze hits her. She wears some black leather boots, with a dull-colored dress that ends right at the end of her knees. I would have thought she was someone who didn't fight, but her face says otherwise.

She glares at me with a burning passion inside her. She's young…very young. In her hands, she points a bow and arrow straight at my head. "Don't move, or I'll kill you."

"Please," I say. I throw my hands up. "I don't mean any harm."

She doesn't say anything, only cocks her head to get a better angle to look at me.

Then her hands let go, and the arrow flies towards my head.

CHAPTER SEVEN

My hand shoots out in front of me. The arrow stops right in front of my face. The point is only inches from my nose, but I've caught the shaft with just one hand. My reflexes surprise me, but I throw it toward the side, only to see the wide-eyed women staring at me.

Just then, Edwin sits up, groaning as he pulls the arrow out of his stomach. He looks at the shooter, sneering. I approach her, only to see her raise her bow and arrow again at me. She doesn't seem as confident now. She seems nervous. "Don't come any closer," she demands, taking a step back.

Beckett stands up now, his shoulder wholly healed. The bloody arrow lies in the grass. "Well, that was rude," Beckett comments, and his smile is covered in malice when he stands beside me. "Edwin." He ushers him. Edwin smiles at his brother and then lifts his hand. Then, with a wave of his hand, her body lifts into the air.

"What the-" She says before the air suddenly chokes her. Her eyes widen, and she uses her hands to reach for her throat. Then she flips upside down. Unfortunately, her dresses fall. Fortunately, she wears shorts underneath.

The strangulation stops, and she's now floating in mid-air, right before us. "Let me down, now!" She demands, trying to wiggle her way down, although it proves her no help. We all stare at her until she stops, defeat written on her features. "What do you want?"

I almost laughed. Was she not trying to kill us a few moments ago?

I grab the dagger from my holster and move forward until I'm beside her. "What do *you* want?" I ask, then ensure the blade is right underneath her chin. Her throat bobs up and down. I trail the dagger around her neck, indicating how sharp it is.

Her hands form into fists. "I'm just protecting my territory," she admits, her back straightening when my dagger drags. For a hostile woman, she sure does have a warm voice. "You are at my waterfall. It is my duty to kill anyone who nears it."

"Your waterfall?" I ask, smiling against her neck. "Oh, does it have your name written on it?" She snarls, and she trashes against me. The knife slowly cuts the tip of her skin, and she inhales. The blood coats just a bit of her neck before it trickles down her throat. "I would not try that if I were you."

Suddenly, Edwin's power lets up, and she goes crashing toward the ground. She groans for only a second before she's on full alert again. She tries to run towards her bow and arrow, but Beckett marches forward and yanks her hand to bring her back before she can.

"Explain what you want," Beckett orders. The woman doesn't even glance his way as she tries to move away from his arms. He could hold her for a while, but eventually, her strength would overpower his.

"Do you not hear me?!" Beckett's angry voice breaks down. The woman stops, giving up on her attempts, and then glares at the elf.

"You are on my territory," she states.

"From what I know, the waterfall is free for all," Beckett says. "What makes you think it is yours?"

"I've been living here for the past few months. I have every right to protect my home." She has stopped struggling entirely.

"That is impossible." Edwin scowls. "No one can touch this water."

"I live in the cave, right behind the waterfall," she says. We all turn. From here, it is not visible. The cave is beyond sight, and its opening is deep inside the waterfall, too far to see. Suddenly, she uses her free hand to punch Beckett in the stomach. He groans, dropping her hand before she tries to run for her bow and arrow again.

However, Beckett recovers faster, and he grabs onto the girl next and, with his strength, uses it to lift her until her feet dangle in the air. "Let me go, you bloody elf!" She choked as his hold slowly grew tighter. She shakes, her feet kicking in the air and hands clawing at her throat. "Let me-"

With abrupt movements, Beckett stood on a rock just above the waterfall. His hair blew back, his fury brightening, and I could see his eyes flare as he held her up above the water. He holds her effortlessly. The woman gasped. "You are a fool. There are three of us and one of you. You would not be able to beat us," he stated.

The woman choked but smirked at his words. "Well, I almost did, didn't I?" She attempted to say, mostly coming out as a whisper. I stood only a few feet away, and no matter what I did, I couldn't move. The spot paralyzed my feet. If he lets her fall, the woman is as good as dead.

Maybe she deserved it.

He glared at her before his fingers seemed to slowly slip.

My eyes widened. Indeed, if she had dropped, she wouldn't break immediately, but her fate would await. My feet moved on their own before I stepped up.

"Don't you dare drop her!" I yelled. He stopped, his eyes remaining on her before slowly glancing at me. He looked at me with utter intensity.

"What did you say?" Beckett demanded. As far as we were concerned, this woman was not a vampire nor our enemy. It would be more appropriate to use her instead.

"You heard me, Brooker. Don't you dare kill her, or I'll kill you myself." He cocks his head, and I can see his lips curve, but then he stops himself. The woman screeched and tried to rattle out of his grip. "She has a cave, don't you see? I don't know about you, but I need a place to stay. We can use her."

Edwin walks to my side. "She is right. This woman is a murderous creature, but surely, her home is better than sleeping outside," Beckett sighed, looked at the struggling woman in his hands, and threw her beside him. She coughed up her saliva. She breathed heavily, and for a moment, I thought she would cry.

"You will let us stay the night tonight," Beckett said.

"Absolutely not," the woman protested.

"If not, I will throw you into the waterfall. Would you like that instead?" He cooed, his lips curving into a sinister smirk. The woman looked up at him, and there was nothing but red fury behind her eyes.

Edwin walked towards her. "Let me help you up."

"Do not touch me," She snapped, standing on her own two feet by herself. After brushing off the dust and dirt from her clothing, she looked directly at us. "Very well then. I will let you stay the night, but at dawn, all of you leave."

She grabs her bow and arrow and latches it onto her back.

All of us seem a little rattled.

Despite the anger radiating off the woman, she seems calm. She lets her brown hair fall loose, allowing her curls to flow around her. The woman leads us behind the waterfall, jumping over a few keen rocks. "Don't fall," she comments, hiding a sneer.

She jumps over the rocks, and once at the edge, she jumps onto the stone platform, the waterfall barely an inch from it. "Well, go on," Edwin says, shoving me. "Ladies first."

I scowl behind him, knowing that if I make a mistake, I'll fall into the water below me. I grab onto the edge of the rock and root myself up until I'm balancing on it. I swallow, straightening myself so I don't fall over. One look at the water sends my anxiety spiraling.

I jump, landing on the rock next to it. "Hurry up!" I hear the woman shout. I glare at her before jumping to the next rock, and as I do so, my arm seems to slip, and my legs dangle over the stone as I clutch onto it. The water pounds underneath me, and I breathe heavily.

I push myself up until I'm standing up again. I cursed, looking behind me. Beckett is behind me, helping his brother to the one he's standing on. I look at the woman, and she stretches her hand, welcoming me. I take her hand but stop and look up at her. I see her frown. I pull my hand away. "I cannot trust you," I say.

Her hair blows back, the strands flying across her face, and she leans back, raising her eyebrows. "Fall to your death, then," she says, and steps back further. I waste no time jumping, landing on the rugged platform. I look at her, raising my eyebrow. I dare her to insult me again.

She doesn't say a word as the boys are near. "Please tell me you aren't associated with them," she says, and I fix my clothes.

"I just met them," I state, crossing my hands over my chest. I see Edwin shout something at Beckett, his expression turning hard as he slowly catches up with him. Beckett's eyebrows furrowed with dismay, his usually blank face contorting into a frustrated one.

"I'm not a witch, but you can tell those two are trouble." She tells me.

I predicted that the moment I met Beckett. The danger was

written all over their faces. I furrowed my eyebrows. But how dangerous were they?

"What is your name?" I ask the woman. She stares ahead and then glances at me. The shimmer of her eyes shows trust, but I can see the restraint. I'm only an elf, and I'm not to be trusted by anyone. It didn't matter if I was innocent or harmful. Nobody trusted no one.

She huffed. "Arabella Vandas." She extended her hand, and I didn't hesitate to reach out and take her hand. Once our hands clasped together, she pulled me closer until our foreheads touched, and her breath lingered on my face a second too long. "If you tell anyone that I live or betray me in any other way, I will rip you to shreds."

I smile, interlacing my hands with hers. "How lovely."

"And yours?" She asked. I looked at her, confusion washing over me. "What is your name, elf?" She lets go of my hand. Arabella was young; she might be my age or a bit younger. She's even shorter than me. Her jawline was sharp, but her delicate features showed the young woman's youth.

"Blanche Everard," I say.

Just then, the boys jump to the platform, first Beckett, landing gracefully, and then Edwin. "Follow me," Arabella instructed, walking down the forum until we reached the rock, a sliver of it cut off. She slipped through it quickly. I stopped and looked back at the boys.

I then turn my body to the side as I slip into the crack. I trip, feeling myself stumble, and grab onto the nearest thing I can, which happens to be Arabella. She recoiled, rolling her shoulder away from me.

She walked before me, and then bright lights illuminated the cave. Her steps stopped, and then I saw the home that belonged to Arabella Vandas. Despite being an old cave and the thundering noise from the waterfall, it's a lovely little cave. The entrance is rounded, and inside stands a tiny little kitchen.

The kitchen is made of wood, and the table beside it has four chairs. "This is all for yourself?" I ask, a little bewildered. It must have taken months to build, and the war had been going on for a year—a slight crack on the table and a bit of blood stained on the side.

Arabella lies on the couch, her legs lying across the wool cushions and her head on a small pillow. My eyes roam the space, hearing the noisiness of the waterfall. This could be considered a lovely home.

A small entrance leads to a small bedroom, which I believe to be Arabella's. "How long have you been here for?" I ask. Edwin grunts from the side, and I see he's slipped through and is now examining his surroundings.

"Only a few months," Arabella says. When she sees Edwin, she shoots up, and resentment resides on her face as she takes the elf in. Her fists curl into balls, and that's when Beckett comes in, grunting at the tiny little crack.

"This is where.." Edwin trails off, looking at everything. "Where will we sleep?"

"You guys can make yourself comfortable on the couch or floor," she states.

"That seems impolite," Beckett comments, raising an eyebrow at Arabella. "We are your guests, after all."

"You threatened to kill me!" She shouted and then reached to grab her bow and arrow. I grab her wrist before she tries to kill us again.

"Yes, well, you did try to kill us," Beckett comments, walking forward and inspecting everything. My breath hitches as I see his dirty blonde curls fall over his forehead, his jawline cut sharp from where I stand. He is mesmerizingly beautiful, I will admit. His aura, though, is nothing but hazardous.

He seems to know how to walk, even when he has nowhere to go. I want to step away from him, but he lures me in every time I see him.

"I'm done talking to all of you," Arabella snaps. "I need to take a shower," She says, striding to her bedroom and slamming it closed behind her.

Edwin rolled his eyes, looking at his brother. "What a lovely lady she is."

CHAPTER EIGHT

The first thing I felt was the stone ground. Goosebumps appeared on my hands and legs right after. When I opened my eyes, it was dark. I felt my breath get stuck in my throat. It smelled ghastly, and I could barely understand where I was. I was just on the couch, lying down with a thin blanket over me, but now I wasn't.

On the right of me, I saw a bed. It was not a standard bed - it was small, dusty, and grimy. Chains were hanging from the stone wall over the bed, and when I looked closer, I saw fresh blood dripping down them. Then, right next to it was a small toilet.

This wasn't the cave I fell asleep in. It felt like I was in prison.

I pushed myself up from the ground and felt my arms' soreness. I advanced to the bars and gripped them, both hands touching the rusty material while my head fitted between two bars. I pulled at them, but they would not budge.

"Hello?" I shouted out, rattling the bars as I trashed against them. Locked away into the night, I screamed for several minutes. "Let me out!" I shouted.

There was yet to be a response from anyone. However, I still felt as if someone's eyes were fixed on me.

Drip. Drip. Drip. Drip.

The leaky water dripped down the ceiling and then landed on my head. I grabbed at my head as my headache drummed harshly. The skeletons of my brain pounded to get out - to get out of this bloody cell. I held my head, closing my eyes at the agony. I realized then this wasn't real.

I wasn't screaming or rattling in the cage. I wasn't actually in a cell. I was sleeping and, again, forced to play a role in my dream reality.

"Wake up. Wake up. Wake up," I pleaded to myself. I cried when something banged across from me, and I jumped.

The cell suddenly opened as the floor's stone screamed at it to stop. Something moved, and my heart skipped a beat. I thought it was a shadow, but I could see the body lying, not a single limb moving on her fragile body. Her hair was the same shade as mine, and I could see the ears...elf ears. They had spots of blood, and from the side, I could see the two fang marks notable on her neck.

Had she been alive, I would not have been hesitant to run to her, but her stomach did not move, and her hair was covering her face.. I took careful steps, my hands rubbing my temples. I watched the body lay there and approached her with slow steps. My nose scrunched at the smell, and I lowered myself as I kneeled towards her.

Then, the realization came over me as I heard the one thing that terrified me. A heartbeat. This woman was not dead – she was still alive. Reaching my hand over her arm, I flipped her so that she was flat on her back, and I could see her face. Her hair covered her features, her pale hands unmoving. "Hello? Can you hear me?" I whispered to her, scared that someone would hear me.

Silence.

I used my hand to remove the pile of hair on her face and took a good look. I backed away immediately, my eyes widening and my entire body shaking. I felt the cold bars hit my back and wanted to shout. I felt the tears prickle my eyes and put my hands over my mouth, silencing the scream that tore out of me.

Although it did not occur in person, it seemed so natural – as if she was in front of me, but she was not. She had disappeared. It was no longer possible for her to be a part of my life. Is there a reason why she appeared in my dream?

"You look just like her."

"You're just like her."

"You are pathetic."

"Not real...not real...not real," I repeated, covering my eyes. "Wake up, please."

The whispers slowly started to turn into shouts.

"You can't escape me!"

"I am apart of you!"
"You are a fool!"
I shook my head, blocking them out. My eyes were covered, and my knees cuddled into my chest. I was scared to look. I didn't want to see her dead body again - she wasn't here - she never was.

Then the voices stopped—the silence gifting my ears instead of the horrid whispers that plucked at my ears.

Slowly, my head lifted, horror dawning over me as I faced the body lying just a few feet away from me. Her nose was so close to mine, and a cry left my lips. My mother stared at me with blank white eyes. Something rattled inside me as I felt something shake, and I cried, wanting to puke.

Then I screamed, and I fell back into the pitiful darkness.

Someone was shaking me. My eyes flew open at the contact of hands on my skin, and I abruptly sat up, eyes full of empty tears. My hands and legs shook, and my lungs couldn't keep up with my rapidly beating heart.

Hands. Hands were on me.

His hands. Why are his hands on me?

Beckett was kneeling just beside the sofa I was lying on. I looked over at where Edwin was. He was fast asleep, facing the opposite direction I had met. They had allowed me to have the sofa. I looked at his hand, which was lightly touching my arm. "Stop touching me," I snapped.

He didn't immediately let go. He waited until my breaths were normal, and then he stopped. "What was that?" He suddenly asked. I looked down at my feet, trying to think of something. It seemed more natural. I knew I could permanently block it out whenever I was dreaming, but it felt different this time.

I felt her arms - how cold they had been. She was dead but also alive, which is equally as terrifying. The only thing I could tell myself was that it was not real.

My mind was playing tricks on me.

"I'm not sure what you mean," I answer Beckett.

He draws back, raising an eyebrow. "You were screaming, Everard."

I whirl my head toward him. "Screaming?"

I dreamed of awful terrors, but I had never screamed. I had been stuck to my bed several times, sweating but unable to move because of the fear. "I was screaming?"

"Yes and talking in your sleep. You're lucky Edwin is a heavy sleeper," Beckett answered and stood up. My head moved up, and I saw how he stared down at me. "I'm not so pretty when I don't get eight hours of sleep, so do mind the noise you make. Otherwise, I'll have to throw you into the waterfall."

My nose scrunches up, and I cock my head. "Leave me alone," I turned away from him, grabbing my legs so they huddled against my chest. He stands there momentarily, and I wish he would go away and pretend none of this happened. I want to cry, but...I can't. I cannot form tears to do so.

I exhale, and that's when Beckett finally walks away from me. Relief washes over me, but it doesn't last long as he grabs his pillow and the thin blanket and walks over to me. He throws them on the ground, right beside the couch.

I glare down at him. "What are you doing?"

"Going to sleep," he casually says, then sits down, patting his pillow, and then lies down. I put my hands over my face, rubbing the temples of my head.

"Why does it have to be next to me?" I demand.

"I can suffocate you if you start to scream again." Amused, he responds. Scoffing at his comment, I lie down on my pillow. There is a brief shuffle right beside, followed by silence.

Why is he so rude?

I close my eyes to sleep, but when I do, the flash of white eyes reappears in my vision, and my eyes slam open, my heart growing faster. My fingers fidget with one another under the blanket. I lean over slightly over the bed and see Beckett lying down, his eyes closed, attempting to fall asleep.

"Do you ever get nightmares?" I questioned.

His eyes opened then, connecting with mine. His eyebrows were hunched closer as if he were thinking, but then he said: "No."

I get up on one of my elbows, looking down at him. "Not even once?"

He shook his head. "No, I haven't," He then turns to his side. "Go to sleep, Everard."

His words repeated in my ears. I didn't have many responses to my childhood other than my nightmares, which made me stand out like a sore thumb. I was the only one who had nightmares like this.

There may be something wrong with me.

I lay my head on the pillow to distract myself from my mother, forcing my eyes to close and think about anything but her. A few hours later, I fell asleep.

My eyes adjust to the dim lighting of the cave. The first thing I notice is that I'm on my stomach, the side of my head on my pillow. My hand hangs over the coach. I groan, lifting my head from my pillow. Next, I noticed that Edwin was no longer on the floor. His blanket is thrown aside, away from his pillow.

"It's about time you woke up," I hear Arabella's cynical voice. I look over at the small kitchen through weary eyes. She's sitting in one of the chairs. She's reading a book. I sit up, pulling the sheets over my body. On the other hand, she drinks something in a wooden cup, bringing it towards her mouth. I watch as her throat bobs up and down.

I look around right next me. Both of the twins are gone.

"Where are they?"

"Out." She puts her book down and then gets up, pushing her chair in. "They've gone hunting for food, is what they said." She walked towards me. The hothead looks me up and down. I wasn't too sure of her feelings toward me yet. She seemed to be kind but then grew angry the next. Her trust meant nothing to me if I had no proof of it. Yet, I knew I hadn't been the most trustworthy either. Arabella had almost been killed, and I had used it to my advantage.

My stomach grumbles. "I'm starving. Do you have anything to eat at all?"

"Do you like squirrels?" She asks, raising an eyebrow. I scrunch my eyebrow, repelling in disgust. She chuckles. "I guess not."

"Do you even know how to cook?" I ask.

She stands up, sitting next to me, crossing her legs. "I'm afraid that I was never taught how to cook. I was going to by the time I reached sixteen, but the plans were delayed." In the background, the waterfall hammers. A cave should not be so warm, yet I'm so hot I think I might explode. I drop the sheets.

I'm still wearing the same clothes as yesterday. I cock my head towards the girl. "Sixteen is young. How old are you now?"

"I'll be eighteen soon. "She admitted. "I still have many years to go before I reach a certain age and stop growing. The perks of being a werewolf, I suppose." Her hand rests beside her on the sofa, beside my own hands. Looking into her eyes, I notice she is staring at my clothes.

"Is there something wrong?" I asked.

"Your clothes are so dirty. Have you ever thought to wash them once in a while?" She cocked her head.

"I'm limited in clothes, unfortunately," I responded, kicking my legs off the coach. I think she'll leave it alone for a moment, but then she stands up and hovers above me.

"Well, that won't do," she argued. "You can borrow some of mine." I shake my head, but she extends her hand, not taking no for an answer. Why was she being so persistent?

I took her hand, and she led me to the door next to the kitchen. She shuts it behind us, and I glance around her small room. She's got a small bed in the corner with a wooden nightstand. Arabella opens another door leading into a small space on the opposite side. "You'll need something warm!" She shouts. "Sit on the bed."

I go over to her bed, my hands roaming around the sheets, feeling how warm the blankets are. It was opposite to what my blanket was. I had been shivering all night, and Arabella had been lying in what seemed like heaven. I never had such luxury at home.

The question was, how did she get all of this?

Arabella walks out of the closet as I get comfortable in her bed. "I couldn't find much. Usually, when the weather gets cold, I get food and wood for the winter and stay in the cave, so I never go out. This is the only thing I could find." She plops down a long black bodysuit with long sleeves. "Try it on."

I plant my feet on the ground and reach for the clothing. I wait

momentarily until I realize that Arabella is looking at me. "Um…
may I have a moment?" I asked.

"Oh, right," Arabella says and turns around, ducking her head low.

Then I slip on the bodysuit. It's not too tight. It fits just right.
"You can look now," I say.

Arabella turns around, and her eyes roam up and down my
figure. Her eyes stopped at my waist, and she walked forward, her
eyes traveling to mine. "May I?" She asks and extends her hands
toward my waist. When I nod, she steps closer until her head is
next to my neck, and her hands move around my waist. I realize
she's adjusting the material to make it fit me better.

I feel her hands on the bodysuit, then they leave. All I could
feel was the coldness that I felt that her hands had left.

Suddenly, a voice yelled: "We're back!"

A groan escapes Arabella's throat, and she steps back. "Let's
go." She walks away towards the kitchen, and I follow behind her.
I see Edwin carrying in a dead bird next while Beckett gathers
some wood.

"You were gone for three hours, and all you could catch was one
dead bird?" Arabella demands and walks closer, crossing her hands.

"It was the only thing we could find right now," Edwin snapped
and shoved past her towards the kitchen. He places the dead bird
on the kitchen counter, where he takes out his knife and works
on cutting it up. My eyes roam over to Beckett, who places the
firewood just by the cave wall and claps the residue off his hands.

Then his eyes snapped to me. Instinctively, I look away from
the elf.

"Everard," he calls my name now and walks forward. He stops
at the table and sits in a chair. "Sit with me," he says, his hand
ushering me to sit. He seemed amused, but when did he not? He
got a kick out of being irritating.

"I'd rather not," I responded.

"Oh, but you'll want to hear this." He reached for something
in his pocket and pulled out the map he had stolen from me only
a day earlier.

"That's my map," I argue.

His voice grew stern as he said: "Come here. We have much to
discuss." I shoot him a glower that has him smirking from where
he sits. Arabella had left my side to grab some food, and I gathered

myself, strolling over to the table and sitting directly across from him. "Good girl."

He looked at me more intensely, just like when we first met. His stare was like venom, and it made me want to run but touch him at the same time. It was a power that could bring you to your knees. I crossed my hands, hoping not to look affected. "What is this about?"

He rolled the map out and then slid it over to me. There, on the map, he had drawn a circle. From what it looked like, a small house was inside of it. My eyes widened, and I went to grab it, but he pulled it away, his smile contorting into a malicious smirk. "What is this?" He then pulled it up so I could see it face-to-face.

The map pointed at one specific area. It had not been there before, but the red lines circled one area. Just beyond the crystal lake stood a plot of land. My hands tightened into fists at the familiar area. "I was looking at this map and realized elf magic was hidden. I only had to convince my shadows to reverse the effects, but this was circled, and it is your map," Beckett explained.

I frowned at the magic. My father was the last one to touch this before I had. He had circled it for the sole reason. He must have known that Ansalona would burn down sooner or later. This entire time, he had prepared for it, but he was never able to tell me face to face as time was running out.

"Don't worry about it," I snap. "It's nothing anyways."

"It has elf magic on it," he replies. "It has to mean something."

"And if it doesn't?"

"Then you will have no problem telling me about it anyway," he says. I knew he would not let up. As annoying as this elf was, he was also very stubborn. I should have learned from the start that he was nothing but devious. As if horns sprouted on his head, he sneered his devilish charm and leaned forward. "Do not go silent on me, Everard. Tell me what this place is."

"It is none of your business," I snap. Just then, Arabella sits next to me, crossing her legs, putting a plate of food under me, and then herself. I mumble a thank you, but she does not respond.

"What are we talking about?" Edwin asked as he plopped down next to Beckett.

"Everard won't tell me why there is elf magic on this map," Beckett said throwing the map on the table. Arabella glared at the elf, stuffing a piece of charred meat in her mouth.

"I don't need to tell you anything," I snapped. I didn't dare look away from him or give him the satisfaction of knowing he had control. With me, he didn't have any. However, instead of getting angry, his eyes lightened up. He reached over, grabbing the plate of food before tipping it all over my clothes. I gasp, standing up as the food stains my clothes. The meat smells jerky and takes up the odor of the cave. I look at him and see the small pleasure in his smile.

"Beckett! Do you know how long that took to make?!" Edwin screeches, eyes wide. I should beat both of them for being so insensitive. "I'm not cleaning that up."

"How mature," I comment, stalking away toward the kitchen. I can feel his eyes on me before I take the brown rag hanging on the oven and then wipe the stains off my new bodysuit. I look back and stomp over to the table. I attempt to grab the map, but his hand comes around my wrist.

He slowly sits up, and as he towers over me, I can feel his anger travel through his veins, searching for mine. "You are getting on my last nerve. You will tell me about this map now, or I will throw you, and this map into the death cascades before you can even utter another word."

"The threat is getting old, Brooker. Come up with another," I retorted.

The suffocating feeling of his hand around me tightens my entire body. His hair - his body - his whole being, completely smothering me. God bless that Beckett did not get his way. For if he didn't, someone would end up dead. He almost did it with Arabella - so why wouldn't he do it to me as well? Everything about me wants to defy him and see what he might do, but his stare spirals me back. He was vicious.

"Let me go!" I shouted, trying to twist away.

"Are you still trying to stop me?" He asked, and then his hand wrapped around my throat tightening as he hauled me against the cave walls. I tried to wrestle out of his grip, but his grip was like an anchor sinking deeper into the ocean.

With a final attempt to escape him, I use my leg to kick him hard - right where I know it will hurt most. The kick rattled him, and his hand came loose around my neck, his eyes squinting in pain. He falls to the ground. Edwin covers his mouth at that exact moment, almost as if he could feel the pain that Beckett was perceiving. His other hand covers his body, and he turns away, closing his eyes.

Arabella glanced at Beckett, and her body shook with laughter. She finished the final meat on her plate and then stood up, wiping her mouth clean with a white handkerchief he had gotten from her pocket. "Well, that was entertaining."

Edwin overcame the pain that had resonated off of his brother and stood up. "I think it's time we leave now."

"We go…" Beckett tried to say and then looked at me. "… Where she goes."

I roll my eyes. "Must you really do that?"

He only glared up at me, and if a stare had been a dagger, I'm sure it would have pierced my face. "Then I shall go with you," Arabella suddenly said, and her firm face told us everything - she would not be stopped this time. She then gazed at me. "I have nothing to do nowadays. Perhaps you three can entertain me."

I knew exactly where I would be going, and even though I was not too fond of the thought of all of them with Devyn, I knew if I had to stay safe, I needed to have people with me. I would not survive out there by myself. "Well then, pack everything you need. We will be out there for a while."

"And where exactly are we going?" Edwin asks, his eyes glancing between his brother and I. Beckett looks up at the three of us in front of him, and no matter how hard I try to feel bad for him, I cannot find it in my heart to do so.

"My cousin's."

CHAPTER NINE

Devyn Everard was the only witch that I knew. Besides being a close cousin of mine, she had meant more to me than anyone I ever knew. She was more intelligent than anyone I knew. Her knowledge of books and education was greatly appreciated, especially by her parents.

The last time I saw her was when I was only ten years old, and she was twelve. I have no recollection of our memories besides the one time I had spent the night at her cabin. We had both decided to sleep outside and watch the stars.

"Did you know the stars and moon talk to each other?" She had once said it, and I couldn't help but watch the sunshine above my head. The sun resembles the beautiful freedom that was bestowed upon us. The moon and stars always represented the peace and liberty that invited us in, but now, circumstances are different.

"Keep up, Everard. I hate slow walkers," Arabella said, bumping her shoulders into mine. I was still not aware of what her intentions were. Whether they were not to be left alone or if she wanted something for her own gain.

We had been traveling for hours on foot.

Arabella had her bow and arrow tied to the back of her backpack. She had pulled her black hair into a ponytail while on our travels. She was merely a year younger than me, but she still held the authority of an adult. I looked at her angry expression - she was always mad at everyone.

As if she could sense my eyes, she glances back at me and cocks an eyebrow. "Hurry up," she demands and then starts walking faster. She has stayed as far away from the brothers as possible, too uncertain about their loyalties.

Edwin keeps to himself, and his only comments are only to his brother. He didn't bother to wash his hair this morning, having argued with Arabella on whether or not the shower she used was sanitary enough. Arabella had nearly killed him on the spot.

As for Beckett, he won't talk to me.

I caught up with Arabella, clutching onto my backpack. Nightfall would be coming, and we would need to find shelter soon. I didn't know how close we were to Crystal Lake, only that we were close enough to smell the musky water from where I was walking.

"Where exactly are we going?" Arabella asked.

"Her name is Devyn. She's a witch that can help us," I told her. Devyn was a witch - a powerful one, and knowing her, I knew she would be able to help us. When I arrived, I planned to figure out what had happened to my father - whether he was dead or alive. Then, I needed to figure out how to get to my father before actual harm was bestowed upon him.

The avalanche of emotions comes over me suddenly, and I shiver. I stop walking, my eyes enlarging as all my senses slam through me with exhilaration and fear. The grass seems too sharp, poking at my ankles. As if drowning in my sorrow, I look around, feeling the anxiety finally peak.

"Blanche?" Arabella stops to examine me. "What is wrong?"

The boys have noticed my nonmoving figure and have come to my side. Edwin reaches over, puts his hand on my shoulder, and steadies me from limping. Beckett kneels so his face is the same length as mine, and I see the same anxiety. "What is the matter?"

I look, and my ears are suddenly too sensitive as the sounds around me are squealing too loudly. The crickets are howling with displeasure, and the fire that burns in hell erupts into the sky. "I don't know," I finally say, looking around. "I don't-"

"Calm yourself," Beckett instructed. I looked at him and took in his displeasure. "Tell me what the problem is."

"Everything, there is -" I stop again, but this time, I hear a ringing in my head, and I grip my head for stability. Like the blistering sun is raining down on me, my head splits into fragments of my mind. "Hell, it hurts," I moan. Hands come around my wrists, and I see Beckett's face, forcing me to look up at him.

"Beckett, my head, it hurts."

"Is it your senses?" He asks.

"My head, it-"

Crack.

I freeze, and suddenly, my headache is gone. It's replaced with a tiny little voice telling me to *"Run, Blanche."* I frowned as all of us looked behind us. The bushes seem to be moving. *"Blanche, run!"* The cracks get louder, and the voice gets louder each time I don't listen to it.

Then silence.

The voice in my head fades, but when I look around, I stop and see the movement of it in the tree. Then I see all of them freeze like they are experiencing it, too.

"Everyone, don't move," I whisper, and they oblige, slowly turning their heads not to cause any suspicion. What moves in front of us is neither an animal nor a human. Its body is carved in all bones as if it were a skeleton that had lifted itself from its grave. Its faded figure moves around in a tree, unaware of our presence near it.

Its ghastly figure only feeds on anything that is near it. It craves the bodies of the ones living, able to take control of their body. It is a ghost that has been trapped in this world, and the only thing they depend on is their bodies - our natural bodies to keep them alive.

"Dybbuk," Arabella mumbles and then slowly takes a step back, but in doing so, she steps on a twig behind her, causing it to snap. We all freeze, and suddenly, the Dybbuk rotates its head while its body stays precisely the same. Its deformed figure twitches just as its eyes turn white with lust.

The Dybbuk then launches onto the ground as it takes the form of a little girl, blood leaking from her blue eyes. Without any warning, she starts to run at us.

"Run!" Arabella screeches.

Edwin lets out a high-pitched screech before we all dart away. Arabella and I take off side by side, grabbing our weapons while the brothers run in the opposite direction. "A dybbuk won't die from a weapon!" I yell at her while I hear the cackling sound of a little girl behind us. I look behind and see it's gotten on all floors, running at us like a wolf.

I've read many things about Dybbuk's. One of the essential things about Dybbuk was its natural form. It was a skeleton, a ghost-like entity still living in the world, feeding off the living. One of their tricks was being able to transform into any of the human bodies or any living thing they could provide. If a dybbuk were to kill us, it could take the shape and form of our bodies.

We dart over the trees, jumping over the logs as we shift to the right. Arabella grabs her bow and arrow and then aims it back toward her. With thundering steps, the Dybbuk is advancing on us with no mercy in its eyes. We cannot let it get close. "Arabella, that will not work!" I shout as the Dybbuk gets closer. "We need to use magic on it!"

Except, I have no magic.

She grabs my hand, pulling me towards a tree. She uses her other hand to shoot back a line of fire before it burns the Dybbuk's chest. It screeches for a minute before recovering and returning to our trail. A little girl is not chasing us anymore. Instead, it's in its natural form. The Dybbuk launched towards us at the last minute, and Arabella and I ducked behind a series of trees, and then we ran back to where we had started. "We need Beckett and Edwin!" I shout.

"Use your magic!" Arabella demands—my head pounds, hating how useless I've become in this situation. The sunny sky had been replaced with a gloomy cloud, and then my entire body vibrated as I realized – the ground. The ground is moving!

"We need to get on the tree!" I command. We both ran towards a great oak tree. She climbs up the tree and then lends me a hand, pulling me up before the Dybbuk can grab me. "Holy –" I hear Arabella mutter and look to the ground.

My mouth dries at the scene as the ground continues to move and wholly split open as if thunder has struck the earth with a death omen. Crows squeak through the sky, and I watch as the Dybbuk summons more. Thousands of skeletons crawl up from the bottom of the earth. The bones crack in unusual ways, and I have never seen such things before.

"Blanche, surely you can get rid of them, right?" Arabella's panicked voice comes through, grabbing my shoulders, shaking me so hard that I almost fall off the tree. "I can only burn Blanche. Please tell me you have a solution to this."

"I- "I try to answer, but I know she will be disappointed by my answer. "I don't know…"

She frowns. "What do you mean?"

The Dybbuks moaned and started running straight at us. Some of them take the form of young women and men, while others take the bodies of soldiers and commanders. The other ones stayed precisely how they were.

You could not kill them with knives or arrows, but that did not mean they couldn't be harmed. I tried to remember when I read those books in the study. How do you get rid of them? How do you-

"We must exercise them," I blurt out. "A ritual. I know how to do it." I remembered the inky pages of my father's books in the study.

A dybbuk, a rare species of Mythology, is a malicious possessing spirit believed to be the dislocated soul of a dead person. It supposedly leaves the host's body once it has accomplished its goal of killing the subject at hand. It is believed that the Dybbuk is scared of holy water and can be eliminated if exercised by a dramatic and terrifying ritual to force the reluctant spirit it is controlling. While some dybbuk's use this to hunt, others use their power to grant others the power to see them one last time, however not without a price to pay.

The sky blows harshly on my skin, and the Dybbuk's are getting angrier. They start climbing up the tree, clawing at the wood as if it is mere plastic. "Blanche!" Arabella says as she starts to climb her way up farther, but I stay. I have no magic - I won't be able to do the ritual.

I need someone else to do it with me.

As one claws on my leg, it immediately lets go as all the Dybbuks fall. I gaze down at them, terrified, as their high-pitched screams burn my ears. I look at the other side of the grassland to see the two brothers standing next to each other. Edwin is staring at the Dybbuks, a sinister smile on his face.

Beckett stands next to him, his hair blowing back as he raises his hand, and the Dybbuks fall to the ground, wailing in their torment. Shadows sprout out of his body in a rush before they settle into the Dybbuk's bodies. The shadows are torturing their minds.. As if he wasn't already dangerous enough, the shadows around him erupted into the sky as it slithered on the ground, clawing at the Dybbuk's faces.

Their cries are loud, and I look at Beckett's eyes. "I need to get to him," I mutter to myself. I look up at Arabella and see the terror she is fighting. "You stay here!" I then jump in terror while she calls out for me. I need to make a move now. Beckett can only torture their being for some time before it loosens; when he does, the Dybbuks will be angrier than before.

I sprint, avoiding the piles of phantoms on the floor. On the other hand, Edwin runs in the opposite direction, where Arabella is. When I reach the tyrant, I grab his arm to get his attention. He floats as his sepia eyes look down at me. His magic stops.

"You can't kill a dybbuk with magic and weapons. It's already dead!" The spirits rise from the ground. Edwin hops into the tree to protect himself from their wrath. "We have to exercise it!" I shout, and his eyes glow red with anger. "I know how to do the ritual. I need your magic for it."

He grabs my hand, pushing us to the side as a tree launches at us. He hides us behind a tree. His curls fall loosely on his forehead, and he looks at the grassland, looking as the restless spirits make their way towards the tree where Edwin and Arabella reside. He keeps us hidden away so that no Dybbuk can see us, but it doesn't help because the Dybbuks are starting to enclose on the tree. Edwin climbs it up farther to escape.

A flare of sunshine shoots from his hand as to blind them, but the Dybbuk merely blocks it as its menacing smile starts to crawl up the tree. One of them is slowly cutting the tree off its root, and if we did not act fast, the tree would fall, and Arabella and Edwin would be doomed.

Arabella grabs Edwin's arms, shouting something at him while she hauls him upwards, then slams a hand towards the Dybbuk's body, causing it to roar and roll off the tree. She pulls him up until they're on the highest branch.

"I can do it," I say, but with no magic in my system, I couldn't do it. "But Beckett, I need your magic- "

"Channel it. If I don't distract them, my brother will die," he says and then looks back at me. "Get rid of them." He then runs as his shadows sprout through the ground, and the shadows pull at the Dybbuk's bodies. He manages to get them off the tree, but they are strong, and Beckett pushes harder as his shadows drag the spirits away from the wolf and his brother.

With panicked hands, I ran out into the field—the ritual. I have never done anything that included exercising, and though I knew the words, I knew that this might go terribly wrong, but I needed it to work. If it didn't, we would all be dead.

Exercising is dark witchcraft, after all, and for some, it would be considered unholy, but for this, I would need all of the under-worlds help to drag them to hell. I run towards the trees, snapping off the twigs. I run back into my spot and stack the sticks on the top, crossing each other in a star.

I look at the three. Beckett's powers are fading, but with the help of Edwin, he shoots light from his hand. Arabella has no magic left as she fights off all she can. No matter what, the three were struggling to stay alive. I turned back, focusing on the initial ritual.

My head pounds as it did mere moments before the battle. The cries of the fight are no longer heard as the ringing in my head reverberates. The walls of my mind seem to crumble, and I have to hold my head straight to keep on going. My hands shake as I grab the dagger from my holster, holding it to my arm.

I don't know how deep I cut my hand, though; I know my vision gets blurry because of the amount of pain. I wince as I bring my hand above the pentagram and let the blood slide down my hand, my fingers coated in vermillion. One drop drips, then another until the tiny droplets are on the sticks.

The blood slides down the sticks until they drop into the grass. I watch the blood, and I…laugh. The pain makes me delirious, and I'm unsure if I like it. I then kneel on the ground and bring my hands together, so the blood coats them. The incantation is simple, though I never had a good memory of my childhood. It's a Latin phrasing, one of the most critical chants to know, and my mind still can't remember it.

Edwin's screaming and Arabella's grunting fill the background of the void, and I find it - I feel the Latin phrasing come over my senses as my mouth starts to move at the remembrance of it. The adrenaline drives me wild, and I close my eyes as I bring my hands up into the air, chanting so loud that the wind sings with me. My hair blows back as I manage to stand up.

I do not look. I only feel the depressing souls of the Dybbuk's scream as I feel their bodies being dragged down to the bottom of the earth – where they belong. I feel their sorrow and pain pass through me, and I almost cry when I see the trauma they have endured.

I grab only their sorrow and slowly, with the guilt of it, drag them further until I feel absolutely nothing anymore. Everything stops – no breaths, no crying, no screaming. Only the sharp breaths of me, and I don't want to open my eyes, in fear that it might not have worked. This was not usual practice for an elf. It was not normal at all.

Hands come around my shoulders and whisper. "Are you alright?" Arabella's soothing voice makes me open my eyes. The brothers are standing just a few feet away, and the Dybbuk's are gone. Edwin has a bloody gash on his forehead, which heals very quickly.

"You did magic, you wonderful elf!" Edwin cheers before hauling me up and pulling me in a hug tightly. When he releases me, he kisses my cheek so fast; I almost don't realize that it happens. I did not know how to do such magic, and this might have been the only kind of magic I could perform, but I was exhilarated but exhausted at the same time. It seems the ritual took all the energy out of me. When I stand up without Edwin's support, I immediately fall, and Arabella wraps her hands around me before anyone else can.

"She needs rest," Beckett says and walks towards me. The last thing I remember is his hand reaching towards my cheek before my eyes close.

CHAPTER TEN

My eyes fluttered to the warmth that they greeted me. I had no recollection of my nightmares. I only felt the soft blanket underneath me and the pillow beneath my head.

My head pounded from the previous events, all coming in a blur. I looked down at my hands to see no cuts from earlier. My cuts were deep, so typically, it would take a few hours to heal. How long had I been sleeping?

I pushed off my elbows, looking at where I slept. The shelter of fabric created the walls and ceiling of the building. I lay on a sleeping bag, and on the other side of the tent, the other sleeping bag was occupied by Arabella. She planted her legs on the sleeping bag as they bent to her lap. A book lay there as she read the ink.

She turned to me as if sensing my attention, and our eyes met. She raised an eyebrow, shutting the book. It thumped in the silence, and she crossed her legs as she gazed at me with emerald eyes. "Oh good, you're awake." She let the book fall to the floor as she got up, strolling towards me. "I did not think you would wake up so soon."

"Where are we?" I asked, feeling just how much energy was drained from me. I had no idea this was how magic felt like - like falling down a rabbit hole that had no end. You just kept sinking…sinking…sinking.

"Well, after you passed out on us, we had to find shelter," Arabella said, moving towards the little nightstand in the corner. "We had found this tent; inside were dead humans, drained of their blood. We moved them and settled down here."

I groaned, sitting up straighter. "So where are the brothers?"

She scoffed. "As if I know. They disappeared into the woods somewhere. I tried to warn them that vampires might be out currently, but they didn't seem to care."

"Hello, ladies," Edwin cooed as he stepped into the tent. Behind him, Beckett trailed inside as he zipped up the tent. Both of them looked at me then, and Edwin broke out into a smile. "I thought you had died for a minute, sunshine." He walked forward, sitting beside me, nearly crushing my legs. "So, tell me, how is it like doing magic?"

I scoff. "That was hardly magic. Pure luck, I would say." And it had been because if it weren't for the adrenaline and the Latin phrasing, I would not be able to perform it. It was simply luck that I had remembered - luck that I had not died.

"Yes, it might have been, but you got rid of those nasty creatures, did you not?" He asked, a sly smirk spreading across his face. Beckett and Edwin were similar in a few aspects. The only thing different about them was their eyes. Beckett's were dark brown, while Edwin's were light blue. In every way, he radiated danger, but his jokes were endless; it was hard not to trust this man. He was the light at the end of the tunnel that you can run into and know you'll be safe.

Beckett was utterly different. I could feel the indifference from him. A man who held no sympathy or emotion, while the other felt so much. He was the darkness in the tunnel that kept going deeper until you had lost yourself completely.

I met Beckett's eyes and saw how he watched my mouth as if he was interested in what I wanted to say. He scowled before he looked away. Or perhaps, I didn't know Beckett as well as I thought.

"I sure did," I said before swinging my legs off the sleeping bag. "What time is it?"

"The sun is about to set. We'll need to rest here for tonight. The tent is guarded with a force field so that if anyone gets too close, they'll be blinded by sunlight," Arabella stated and looked at Edwin. "Due to Edwin."

He sneered at her. "Yes, thanks to me."

I looked for the other two sleeping bags, only to find that they weren't there.

"Where will you two be sleeping?" I asked.

Edwin smiles. "Why on the floor, since Arabella has kingly refused to share the sleeping bag with me." Arabella only glares at him before looking away and grabbing her book again. I look up at Beckett and see his eyes narrow on my figure. His intimidating stare catches my breath, and I feel like the wind blows me away.

He's so damn irritating. I decide not to cower under his stare like I usually would. I see the slight edges of his mouth extend to a simper.

"Well, I am quite tired. Unlike our sleeping elf, I haven't slept." He walks towards the edge of the tent. In exchange for a sleeping bag, he had packed a pillow and a blanket, placed it on the ground, and then patted the other side next to him. "Well, come on, Beckett."

Beckett lets out a small breath before walking over and pulling the covers over Edwin and him. As the sun finally set down for the night, I heard the howls of the neighboring wolves. Arabella had not responded to either of them as she finally settled in her sleeping bag. Dressed in her smelly clothes, she fell asleep.

I was very awake. The nap from earlier had made all my tiredness vanish, and I felt my energy course through me slowly. In the pitch-dark tent, I lay down, legs stretched out, and I let my arms curl up inside my chest. Thoughts of my father consumed my mind. My house had exploded, so did that mean he had exploded?

Or had he escaped beforehand?

Maybe if I had looked for him more, I wouldn't be in my current position. I had grown to like Edwin more and hoped Arabella could be trusted. However, it was the other elf that made me grow nervous. I didn't understand what made me think this way, but the way he acted – the way he moved and talked, there was something else beneath his tough exterior. His loyalty was somewhere else.

He was hiding something – I was sure of it.

I groaned soundlessly. I threw the blanket off me before walking outside the tent. I needed some air. I felt like I was suffocating.

I knelt on the ground, playing with the strands of grass. "It's not safe to be in the dark alone," I hear his voice say. I didn't need to turn around to see who it was. His voice was so familiar to me now. He was an echo in the hollow of my mind, implanting himself as a weed. It's so bothersome – so beautiful.

"Don't bother me," I say as I tear the grass from the ground, twirling them around my digits and then flicking them away. His presence remains behind me, and I close my eyes in irritation. His footsteps got louder, and then he appeared beside me. I look up and see his tall figure regarding me.

I did not understand how he did it. He held such commanding respect, but he was nothing but rude. It had been better when he talked to me - at least then, I knew what he was thinking.

Why aren't you asleep?" He asked, taking a seat right next to me, and I almost smiled but refrained from doing so. The weakness of my happiness would be my undoing. "After what you did earlier, I think you would be the most tired."

"I am far from tired," I say.

"I can see," he said. I turn my head, and our eyes meet. The midnight sky has covered his brown eyes, and the only thing I can see behind his eyes is the pitch darkness. "Where did you learn that kind of magic? It's not normal practice."

"My father," I blurted out before I could stop myself. "My father made me study many things at a young age, and I learned how to do rituals."

My father would wake me up at eight o'clock, he would drag me out of bed and place me in his living room. He would make me read some books- I didn't even understand them as they weren't in the correct language. Some days, I learned and trained so much that I didn't have time to eat. That's all I did. Eventually, I realized that being smart was the only way to defeat opponents. Some days would be more challenging than others.

So, for the days we did not train, I would have my head stuffed in a book and then be quizzed over what I learned. That was my childhood.

Beckett glanced at my hand, loaded with wet grass. He was a stunning creature. His features were made from a fiend - so devilishly beautiful that it was hypnotizing. The curls on his hair fell, and for a moment, I believed I was just a sad woman, and he was just a man comforting me.

He reached his hand closer to mine but stopped over it as if contemplating whether to touch me. He only grabbed the piece of grass still in my palm and threw it away. "Yes, your father must have been a smart man. If he had not taught you that, I am unsure if we could have made it out alive without your knowledge."

I frowned. "Of course." I not only felt the disappointment seep into me, but I also felt the raw emotion of sadness make its way into my system.

"Power like yours is scarce. I can't imagine what you could do to an army of vampires, little elf." I look over at him. He's sneering.

"I won't use this power again," I say, and he frowns, looking at me like I'm delusional. "I have other power in me that I still have yet to see, and I can't cause such death again."

"Death is war." He argued. "No matter how much you try to avoid it, it will always lead to that." As if seeing me was unbearable, he looked away, shaking his head. "You would be so selfish as not to kill a dying man after he begs you to?"

I scoff. "I'm not being selfish. " I reach over, my fingers grazing his chin. That has him freezing, but I force him to look at me. "I have never killed before, but I've seen it and the damage it causes." Then I lean forward so he knows I'm serious. "Would you kill your brother if he begged you too?" I raise my eyebrows and wait for his answer. However, it never comes. His silence is eerie, and I'm unsure what he thinks. I draw back, confused.

"You don't understand. I have plans, ones that I need to do, and if I have to kill someone to get to them, so be it. It's their lives for a hundred others." He was rambling, the plans at the tips of his tongue to tell me, but they die, and he draws back, realizing he's said too much.

I knew my senses were right. His loyalties are somewhere else.

"Do you ever plan to tell me your plans?" I ask, cocking my head. "I'm stuck with you after all."

He sighs, getting up from his seated position and patting off the grass from his knees. "Goodnight." Without another word, he walks back from the tent, and I'm left feeling defeated again.

I shouldn't trust him after all.

CHAPTER ELEVEN

I could not sleep for the rest of the night. After the empty hours, Arabella was the first to wake up from her slumber. She lifted her body, stretching out her sore back. Her hair was a mop on her head, and she only fell back to the bed, turning around to look at me. Her eyes scanned to see the brothers sleeping. "What time is it?"

I shrugged, only knowing that it was early in the morning. "We must leave soon to get to my cousin's house by nightfall."

Arabella's tiny body lounges on the sleeping bag. The sun had started to shine slightly through the fabric. The brothers twisted in their sleep. Beckett rested on his side, facing away from everyone.

Edwin snored slightly in his sleep, and I managed not to kick him in the face during the entire night. Arabella groaned into her pillow, her words becoming muffled.

We had no clothes. When battling the dybbuk's, we had not bothered to look for our bags. They had vanished with the ritual I had casted. Arabella was the only one who still managed to find her bag in the midst of the battle.

"It's time to wake the boys up," I say.

"Hold on," she said. getting up, before walking out of the tent in a hurry. She returned with a cup of water in her hands only seconds later. Her smirk grew wider as she let it all drop on Edwin's head. It hit him like a tsunami, and he sat upwards, coughing as he choked up the water he had accidentally swallowed.

He looked up at the wolf, and he growled. "You bloody women." That's all it took for Beckett to turn to his side and slowly open his eyes to the commotion.

"Time to wake up," she said, and walked towards her sleeping bag, grabbing the book she seemed interested in. "We must leave and go to the Crystal lake. We'll figure out what to do from there." She gathered all of her stuff, put it all in her backpack, and then hooked the quiver to her back, letting the bow and arrows rest there in case of emergencies.

"And you had to splash water on my face to tell me that?" muttered Edwin.

Edwin had looked like he wanted to strangle the girl on the spot. Beckett sat up from the bed, arching his back to stretch. The recollection of last night was still fresh in my mind, and I still heard the coo of his voice as it tormented me mentally.

He looked just as handsome as he did last night. Only his hair was spiraling out of place, falling in different directions. He looked at me for a moment then used his hands to raise himself from the ground. "Christ, you stink," he said to his brother.

"As if you're one to talk," Edwin shot back, irritated. His hair was wet from the water, and no matter what instinct told him to claw out the wolf's eyes, he refrained, wiping his face clean with just a wave of his hand.

Beckett stepped over Edwin's body, running his hands through his messy hair and then stepping outside. The sun illuminates, sending the rays and warmth in, and I follow behind him, peeping out of the fabric. The night had felt too long, and without sleep, the sun seemed too bright for my eyes.

Arabella squeezed between my body, letting herself out of the tent before covering her eyes. "Hell, I didn't know the sun was this bright," she exclaimed.

"Are you going to stay there all day?" Edwin's voice questioned, and I looked back at him. The collar of his shirt was drenched in the water, and I only watched as his expression fell flat.

I raised an eyebrow, challenging him. "You seem a little irritated."

"Don't push it," he warned before pushing me out of the tent. "Well, let's get a move on then. I'm not sure about the rest of you, but I do not want to sleep in that tent again."

The Crystal Lake was brought into this forest by no other than elves. That's what my history book said. It's full of delicious ocean-blue water that tastes like salt. It was said to heal any elf that had been injured. I never believed it myself until I had gotten an injury myself. My father panicked and poured water on my legs. It was healed within minutes, when normally an elf would heal within a few hours.

A beautiful bridge was on top of it, allowing you to cross whenever. Not many visitors went to the crystal lake, but my father and I would cross when we would travel to Devyn's hut. It was back when my mother was still with us.

Except now, this crystal lake was not so beautiful. It's replaced with murky brown wastewater. The bridge has collapsed from the ongoing fire in the forest. It's the creatures inside that were the most terrifying. Usually, they would have been harmless, but now, they like to defend themselves from troubles, as the trauma of the war has scared them into fighting back.

The wind blows harshly, the sun blazing down at us. The sweat on my hair drips down my forehead, down my cheek. I wipe it away, walking towards the lake. I take a breath as I look down at the wastewater. The leeches are the worst - there are hundreds of them - thousands.

"How do we get across?" Edwin asked, looking at me.

"Can't you just use magic to get across?" Arabella queried, leaning back against the root of the tree. Her breaths are uneven from the ongoing travel that has seemed to take a toll on her.

"The crystal lake is full of magic. By the looks of it, it's endured a lot, meaning it'll only reflect the magic back," Beckett spoke up, walking forward. With just the swipe of his finger, he let his finger feel the water. He rubbed the water between his fingers when he brought it back up. "Unfortunately, we are not water elves."

Arabella looks at me this time. "How about you? Can't you do that ritual thing?"

I raise my eyebrows. "And risk my energy for the rest of the day?" I cross my hands. "I think I'll pass."

"Well, there has to be a way around it," Edwin argued, huffing in irritation. After the wake-up started with the water plunging into his face, he was not in a decent mood. He was cranky as an old man who had not slept all night. Lucky him. I did not sleep at all last night.

I wondered if the others could see it.

My eyes fell over the silent wolf. She looked at the lake, and her eyes seemed to light up. "I can try jumping over it," she volunteered. "If I turn into a wolf, I might have enough power to jump over the lake, but you would all need to go on my back." She fidgeted with the sleeves of her shirt nervously. "I just.. don't know if I'll be able to make it over."

"How good are you at jumping?" Edwin demanded.

"Good enough," Arabella replied, looking at the rest of us. "There's always that option."

I looked over at Beckett just as he looked back at me. Then he turned his head to the wolf. "It's a better solution than nothing," he says.

Arabella looked at all three of us, her eyes shining green with nervousness. She closed her eyes, and we all watched in amazement as the hair on her arms grew longer and darker. Her eyes shine brightly, and Beckett leans in to see the wolf's transformation. She falls to the ground as her arms - her paws now, grow vicious claws. Her dress is no longer visible as it rips off her body. Her white coat takes over her body. Her legs are lean and big, snapping so harshly I winced. As she takes the shift of her wolf, she stares at us with appreciation, and her head moves to the side.

"That is impressive," Edwin compliments, extending his hand to pet the wolf's back, but her growl is evident and warns him to back off. He draws back, smirking at the wolf. "Someone doesn't like back rubs."

The wolf grunts and then turns towards the lake. She lowers her body to the ground and then lays her head. That is our cue to get on. Beckett is at my side at once. "Ladies first," he says. His presence goes straight through me until I'm melting, and I step forward, grabbing onto the fur and pulling myself up to her back. The wolf yaps in vexation and patiently waits for the others. I hurry up until I'm at her collar and put my hands around her big neck.

The next one is Beckett, and he takes no consideration to her displeasure as he scoots himself right up against me, except he takes pride in the space he gives me. My heart thumps against the wolf's chest when feeling the terror on my face. He grabs onto my waist, pulls me back to him, and then adjusts me so I don't fall while she jumps. "If you hold onto her neck like that, you'll end up choking her."

"Weird, I thought you would like that," I remark.

I face forward, but my comment isn't glossed over, and his voice settles close to my ear. His breath skims the lower part of my ear, and I freeze at the closeness of his body. "Maybe I do," he says and then falls back away just as quickly.

Arabella growls as Edwin is the last to make his way up. He grabs onto her fur harshly, and she almost sends him flying toward the tree. She kicks her legs on the ground in a warning. He rolls his eyes, reaching the top and securing himself on the fur.

"Are we ready?" Beckett asks us. When we all don't say anything, he instructs Arabella to go. I did not know how high were-wolves could jump, but I knew it was high enough.

The wolf starts running, and I close my eyes when she launches into the air. When I feel the heaviness of my body sink into her body, I open my eyes. The minute I looked down, I see the Crystal Lake. We were jumping higher than the trees.

The grasslands were surrounded, and just beyond the trees, I could see several villages and then a tiny exit out of the forest, which I only could wonder if that was where mortals lived. The air up here was not as it was down at the ground - it was thicker and heavier to breathe. The oxygen that I breathed felt like vinegar sliding down my throat.

Behind me, Beckett stayed silent, and I glanced behind me to see him staring at the trees. Edwin howled in cheer at the sight before him, amused by the entire thing. Then my weight felt heavier, like I was falling down the mountains, the earth's core slicing me from the inside.

Then, all of it vanishes when I feel Arabella hit the ground with a grunt. It takes me a second to get a steady mind, and then I look back. We made it across the lake. She launches us off her body, letting us all plunge into the soil. Edwin groans, and Beckett even winces as they start getting up. I sit on my butt and watch as Arabella transforms into her usual self.

"Hell, you guys are heavy," she states, fixing her messy hair. Arabella's face grows red when she realizes she's completely naked before us, so she turns away. "Well, don't just stand there and stare at me. Give me a bloody shirt!" Arabella demands.

Edwin blushes before he unbuttons his shirt and then walks up to her. He hands it over her shoulder and lets her button it herself.

"We must keep moving," Beckett said, hoisting himself up, and I stood up, cleaning the dirt off my pants. "So, little elf, where do we go from here?" I looked at the pattern of the trees. I remember it was right.

Walking around the right path had been longer than I initially remembered. It circled the trees and then rounded the left way to avoid danger. I had never been down the left path and did not intend to do it soon. The oak trees had grown darker, and the air around us looked as if it were night. The wind had picked up, and with each step back, my hair blew back and forced my body backward.

Beckett was by my side. His hair blew back from his face, and his expression grew frustrated by the whirlwind. He cursed.

Behind us, Arabella walked by herself, and Edwin was a few feet behind her. The shirt he had lent her earlier was a small help. She had no pants to protect her from the cold, and Edwin seemed just as frozen. We all desperately needed clothes.

Lightning spiked, and I winced at the sound. We had made our way around the trees and now slowly turned. If we hurry, we could be there in a few minutes, but the wind is causing our downfall.

"Are you tired?" Beckett suddenly asked.

My head snapped toward him. "No."

"Liar."

I didn't say anything, hoping he would stop talking to me, but when he remained close to me, his gaze glued to mine, I realized he was waiting for a reply. Then he sighed. "How close are we?"

"Excited, are we?" I asked, smirking at him before kicking my feet against the ground to make him fall back. He glowered at my behavior and then brought his foot over mine, stomping on it hard enough for me to wince. "Ow! You-"

"Upset, are we?" He asked, and then my eyes widened at my words thrown back at me. "Your behavior is completely unnecessary."

"Stop talking," I interrupted, whipping my hair back until it blew in his face. "I don't have time to argue with you. We will arrive there in a few minutes." It was my fault to take his silence as his understanding; he only pulled me back, which had me tripping on my feet. "Brooker, I swear -"

He lets go suddenly, and that has me falling on my butt. I fall with an "oof" and then glare at the elf. "You have horrible manners."

"As if you are one to talk! You have been tormenting me ever since I met you!" I shout and shoot up to my feet. His body is mere inches away from me, and I push at him hard. Unfortunately, his body is like a brick, and it only moves slightly by my push.

"Well, my apologies if I don't like people breaking into my home and dragging us out." He shoots back and then turns around to walk away.

I walk after him, not done with him just yet. "Don't walk away from me when I'm talking to you!" The irritation radiates off his back, and he doesn't acknowledge my presence. "There is more to it, isn't it?"

He stops, turns around, his face masked with rage, but I can see the dent of confusion, the dent of his ego slowly coming apart. "What are you talking about?"

"Oh, you know exactly what I'm talking about-"

"Shut it, both of you!" Arabella shouted, and we both turned to look at her. She looked around as if cautious of our surroundings, and Beckett strode to her side. "Do you hear that?"

My senses are awake, and I hear the cries of a wailing woman…not too far away. I had been so busy arguing with Beckett, that I hadn't realized the lurking danger approaching us. I put my hand on my dagger.

I heard the voice whimper, and that is when the woman's footsteps move closer, and I grasped the dagger harder. "From the right," I utter, and we all turn to see the mysterious woman appear by the trees.

She gasped, and then blood seeped out of her mouth.

CHAPTER TWELVE

he woman with pale skin stood in front of us. Her throat slit at the center of her neck as if the perfectly carved cut had been sculpted. She was an older woman, perhaps the age of twenty to thirty. It was no mistake that the world had let her come upon us. She was no danger to us but looked at us with relief.

Her mouth was covered in crimson, blood seeping out of her chapped lips. The woman's hair had been shaved off completely, leaving her bloody scalp bare and fragile. The skin of her arms had been cut off, and the muscle on her skin was beating loudly, trying to talk - trying to get help. It had no skin to live off of. This woman should not have been alive. If this is what torture looked like, I would rather die than go through that.

The only thing that spoke pure to her were her eyes, the deepest shade of hazel. She approached us slowly, and Arabella raised her bow and arrow, perhaps to shoot, and she stopped. She could not move her mouth - I could see that now. Her teeth had been removed.

I took a step forward slowly and watched as she winced. "You are hurt," I tell her, reaching out to her, letting her know I would not endanger her. I took small steps to get to her, and when I did, I reached out; the horror on her face showed the trauma she had experienced.

"Sit down," I told her. She collapsed against the ground, the sadness streaming down her red eyes, her cheeks stained with tears. I looked at her frail body and saw her fingernails had been removed from her cuticles, and I tried hard not to look away in disgust. "It's alright. We can help you."

She shook her head. Arabella and the brothers circled her. I frowned at the woman's behavior. "We can use magic to make you better. It will be alright," I assure her, but she shakes her head aggressively, closing her eyes. She sobs, lifting her skeleton fingers to her face.

"Blanche," Arabella mutters and then bends down to me. "Look at her. She has been tortured, and she cannot talk. Surely, you know what she is trying to tell you." I look at the wolf momentarily, and the realization washes over me when I look back at the woman. Whatever she was – vampire, elf, or wolf – she did not deserve this. She did not want to live knowing she would be this human skeleton, an example of what happens when you risk your life.

She wanted to die.

The crows squeaked loudly, a death omen sent from the skies.

Arabella got to the ground, taking the dagger out of my holster. She looked at the woman. Arabella removed her fingers from her face and placed them on the ground.

Arabella was no coward. Her black hair, as dark as the obsidian core, blew away from her face. Her eyes held a past that no one could see. Her entire childhood was gone.

Arabella lifted the dagger, her hands shaking. She gulped, her throat bobbing up and down. "May your soul rest in peace," she declared before she swung the knife down on her tortured body, letting the blood coat her fingers; she had made sure to stab her right in the chest, right at the center of the heart, where her slow-breathing heart finally stopped.

Silence.

We knew this woman for only a few minutes, and it felt like I had known her for too long. The reality of it had my heart hammering. The wolf pulled her hands towards her chest and crossed them like the woman's hand earlier. She then let her hands drop and grabbed a rag from one of her bags, wiping her fingers clean.

Edwin sat on the other side of me and only looked at the woman with wonder, but it held no sympathy – no sadness or anger. My eyes traveled up to the tyrant who stood behind us. He leaned forward to examine the dead woman. He, too, had the same expression he usually wore, except his eyebrows lifted with curiosity.

"We should go," Arabella's tiny voice welcomed the silence. "Where do we go from here, Blanche?"

I pointed to the left. "Through those trees and around the stream. There will be a cabin at the end of it," I say. I pushed myself up with my hands, helping Arabella to her feet. The dead woman rotted next to us, and the rest of the skin she had left would slowly turn into bone, just like the rest of her body. Was it such a bad thing to put her out of her misery?

One glance at Arabella's face told me everything. We did the right thing.

The rain had no mercy as it poured down on us. My hair is soaked, my clothes are sticking to my body, and I can't see anything in front of me anymore. My hands were slick from the moisture, and we continued down the stream. The droplets dropped into the lake, creating ripples around it. The sunshine had been replaced with stormy clouds as lightning struck above us.

As we took the last steps, we passed the rest of the trees, and then it opened to an empty grassland. Where Devyn's house should have been was nothing anymore. My eyebrows scrunched, and the people behind me stopped at my abrupt position.

I turned around to the other three. They watched me. "Where is it?" Beckett asked.

I pinched my fingers together and looked up at them. I had known many had moved during the war, but Devyn had never told us she was moving. This means…I had led us here for nothing.

"I…uh.." I look back at the grassland and then back at the group. "I thought it was here."

Arabella groaned now. "You've got to be joking."

I shrugged my shoulders, my mouth opening to explain, but Beckett beat me to it. "Hold on," He walked to me, but instead of stopping, he kept walking forward until he suddenly stopped. I walked towards him until I saw what he was seeing. It wasn't something you could see. It was a feeling.

A twinkle of witchcraft was in the air. It was intense and overwhelming, and I grabbed Beckett's shirt to keep myself steady. At that, he turned towards me, and I immediately let go. I turned around. "Can anyone break a barrier?" I asked, my mind still fogged with magic. It was powerful magic, and even though it had not been directly used on me, my senses reached out to it, pulling at the strands of it, hoping to get a feel of it, and it was dark.

"I'm sure I can," Edwin said, playing with the collar of his wet shirt. He had gotten his shirt back from Arabella, while she put on some new clothes she still had packed. The rain picked up and started hailing down at us with vicious attacks. I reached out and felt the barrier around my mind.

Edwin pulled his sleeves up, stained with the blood from the dybbuk's and the witnesses from the rain, and then put his hands close to each other, only they did not touch as I had anticipated. Instead, his fingers were over each other, and his eyes closed.

"Step back," Beckett warned. The boy lifted his hand, and the gravel beneath us shook with terror. Arabella gasped when the air around us suddenly swirled as if Edwin was collecting it in his palms.

Beckett leaned his back against the tree, stuffing his hands in his pants pocket. The slightest smile appeared on his face.

Unlike his brother's dark powers, his sorcery was centered on mainly the earth. Genes that he must have gotten from his parents. He had manipulated the air around, letting the air collect the oxygen from the air around us and twirl it around into a vast monsoon. The wind was harsh, and it headed for us, but Edwin directed it towards the grassland, and then it crashed, the barrier slamming against the wind's tough circulation.

The force field then revealed itself. The purple light radiated off of it, and inside, the shape of a cabin appeared, though it was blurry. "I need more power!" The whistling sound of the wind grew so loud that I covered my ears. Arabella was starting to blow back as her back hit a nearby tree.

I rooted my back on the oak tree. The hems of my shirt flew backward, and I bent down, grabbing onto the edges so it did not reveal too much. Edwin's hair was much longer than Beckett's, and the hair soared backward. With as much force as he could, he used the light from his powers to clash them all together in the hurricane - desperate to break this barrier.

The particles clashed, and the clouds above looked down approvingly as they moved away. With a thrust, he slammed the force into the barrier - no luck. He did it again - no luck. He grew frustrated, the veins on his hands and neck snapping, and then, that's when he saw the dark shadows crawling towards the ground.

The human-like silhouettes clawed toward the ground and mixed in with the light. I looked back at Beckett to see the shadows pouring out of him in a panic. It clouded the winds, and he stepped forward toward his brother.

"With as much force as you can, Edwin," he said, bringing a hand down to his shoulder. Edwin growled, and then, with a slam, the winds knocked the barrier so hard that the dark magic crept away as it diffused into the forest. Edwin let go, and at the same time, Beckett grabbed onto his body to not let his brother fall.

The wind stopped. My ears rang from the winds, and the silence was too loud. Arabella did not move from the tree. She looked at Edwin with pity and then looked at me.

"I'm alright," Edwin muttered, getting a good balance on his legs. Beckett let his brother go, and he looked at the cabin.

Beckett then looked at me, his eyes blazing with something I could not understand. "Well, go on, lead the way." He said, the crook of his lip forming into a sneer.

I pushed myself off the tree and then ushered Arabella over. She followed, her movement slow with anticipation. My hand reached for Edwin's back, and I rubbed it softly. "Will you be alright?"

He smiled. "Of course. Nothing I cannot handle."

Beckett's expression fell unnoticed when I passed him and headed straight toward the cabin - where Devyn Everard lived. The place was quite big, especially since she had grown up in a small family. The trees around it circled the house, and some of the vines connected with it. Its big windows held themselves with pride, and the balcony on the top had the legs attached to the earth's ground.

It was too big for a cabin, strangely spacious in an area. The private dwelling was quiet, and the authentic grassland got smaller as I approached the stairs. The porch, tiny and primitive, creaked when I took a step forward. The three behind me were unusually voiceless.

I turned around. Beckett was the one closest, while Arabella and Edwin stood close behind. "Is this cousin of yours dangerous? I don't think I should walk in with obedience." I pushed the urge to roll my eyes at the tyrant.

"She's a witch, so I would be cautious of what you say, Brooker," I retort and look back at him. "It's not wise to make a witch upset."

I had expected him to insult me on the spot, but he merely nodded.

The group followed me up the creaky steps of the porch. I waited for them to settle into a nice spot before I lifted my hand to the door. I hesitated, a little scared to see my cousin.

My hands met the door, and I knocked three times before I let my hand fall to my side. I clasped my hands on my sides and waited for the witch to answer—one second…then another.

I stepped forward to knock again, but before my hand could reach the door, I felt the gravity leave me, and before I knew it, my feet hung in the air, and I was falling, and so was everyone around me. The wood opened underneath us, swallowing us into the ground until we hit the rocky bottom of a cold basement.

We had fallen into a trap.

CHAPTER THIRTEEN

We fell into a room with walls as thick as castles, the cement providing a firm foundation for the cabin. The windows that held up a place like a kingdom did not appear here, and there was no light. Having set up a force field, Devyn was wise to know that it wouldn't hold and installed another trap instead.

The slushy water ran through the pipes of the wall. A red light hung from the ceiling, alternating from left and right. Music hummed on the other side of the exterior, where the door locked us in. Chains hung on the wall, swinging back and forth, hitting the wall harshly. Beneath my boots was a thin layer of slushy water.

"Crap," Arabella muttered from right beside me. She was the only one besides us to land on her feet - the perks of being a werewolf. She brushed off the dirt from her knees and looked at the empty chamber around us. "Where are we?"

"In a dark room, it looks like," Edwin groaned. I pushed myself up to my feet and saw the silhouette of his figure lingering in the darkness, and then his brother appeared by him. Beckett mumbled something, shaking his head in displeasure. No doubt, he was very annoyed with the whole situation.

The drumming of music got louder as the volume of it rolled up. I did not notice how far we had dropped from the trapdoor on the ceiling; it had looked about ten feet from above. It would undoubtedly have broken a bone or two if it were a mortal. Beckett came closer to me, his presence a little too close for my liking, until it disappeared behind me. "What do we do now?" Arabella asked.

"We have to get back to the top," Edwin said, looking at the trap door that opened to the earth. "I do just need a boost-"

"Or not," Beckett's voice cooed. His presence behind me disappeared, and we all turned to see him by the door. His hands withered over the doorknob as the shadows played with the lock. It clicked then, and they retreated. The door swung open, and the music grew louder as the light illuminated the dark room.

Beckett did not wait for us. Instead, he disappeared through the door. "Beckett!" I shouted after him—that fool. If Devyn sees him alone, then I have no doubt she will kill him on the spot. I rushed after him until I reached him in the other room.

The two others stepped into the room not a moment later. The room we stood in was a mountain of magic. Cabinets circled the wall, and potions and crystals were on the black counters. The herbs were exposed to the air, making the room swirl with the mixture of Rosemary and Chamomile.

A chair stood to the side, smoke radiating off it as if recently burnt. The music box came from the small corner, another entrance, though this one was covered with violet curtains. "Is that blood?" Arabella asked quietly. My eyes traveled to the floor, where a circle of glass floor lay below our feet, and with it was a pond of blood.

The ingredients, from safe to dangerous, were piled on the desks and hazardously thrown at each other.

Beckett walked towards the curtain, but my hand grabbed him, yanking him back. He scowled at my strength. "Are you daft? I know Devyn the best. It's best if I go first," I tell him and then walk towards the curtains. I brush them aside with my hand and step inside.

A small room - a brown Persian carpet lay in the middle of the floor. Curtains hung from the side pulled back so that it circled a circle. My eyes grew wide when I saw the witch that sat there. She floated mid-air, her eyes closed with concentration while her fingers opened gracefully by her side. Candles gathered around her body, floating with her.

The music erupted into classical music, the beat getting faster and louder. Her mouth moved in a move of a chant.

Devyn Everard had changed. Her once fragile face was not of an innocent child anymore. Her jaw had sharpened, the eyelashes had grown longer, and she no longer had the usual glow she wore. Her skin had grown quite pale as if the sun had no contact with her. The slightest blush rested on her cheeks, and her red lips were pulled apart, saying the incantation faster.

She had cut her hair. It was now down to her shoulder, the slightest curls still in them. She wore a long black skirt with a gray long-sleeved shirt.

I walked to the stereo. My finger moved over the electronic device, and I shut it off. The music stopped abruptly, and with a shake, Devyn's eyes slammed open. She could only look at all of us until her body grew limp, and she started to fall. The candles fell; the fire extinguished before she hit the ground. Her legs landed just in time for her not to fall.

Her blue eyes roamed over us, taking in every detail. A hiss came from the corner when a black and white python slithered from a corner. It hid under the chair, but its body moved fast as it came around Devyn's body. Its tongue stuck out, wagging at us. "Shhh, Sammy," she quieted the snake and then stood up straight.

Her eyes roamed to me, and the tiny smile lifted at the corner of her mouth. "You finally arrived. I've been waiting." I frowned. "I did, of course, expect you to be alone, but..." She looked at the others beside me. "I guess I was wrong." She strode towards Beckett, her finger grazing his dirty shirt. "Their names?"

"Beckett," he replied before I could say anything.

"He's Edwin, and that's Arabella," I introduced them. "Everyone...this is my cousin, Devyn." Devyn hummed softly as she left Beckett's side and went towards Edwin, going behind him and taking a lock of his hair.

He hissed and glared at the witch. She then stopped at Arabella's side. The wolf remained calm and crossed her arms.

Devyn twirled Edwin's hair in her hand and let go, letting it fall. She then turned to me. "You have not changed much," she said, looking me up and down. "Why have you come here?"

"For safety," I say. "My village, it-"

"I know what happened to it," she interrupted. "So then, how did you end up with these fools? Have they hurt you?" Her expression grew hard at that.

"Not yet," I say, glancing at Beckett. "But I did bring them here so we would not be alone. They were driven out of their homes, just as I was with mine."

"Very well." She turned towards them and then held her head high. She was precisely the brother's age, and though she was shorter, she had just as much authority and control of the situation. "But hear me now if you cause any trouble - anything I don't approve of, and you will leave this house without arguing."

The snake slithered around her neck. Devyn leaned her hand down and let the snake climb down her arm towards her hand. It circled around her while Devyn took its head into the palm of her hands. "I do not like being disrespected." She then confirmed. "And Sammy doesn't like it either." The snake hissed in delight as Devyn petted its scaly head.

"Why Sammy?" Edwin spoke out. Devyn turned to Edwin. "You could have named your snake anything."

"I did not choose it," she responded. "He did." Sammy stared at the elf, and its head retracted, daring Edwin to speak again of its name. He clamped his mouth shut. "Well, I guess I should give you a house tour?" Devyn softly grabbed the snake by the neck and put him on her shoulder.

She did not give anyone time to speak as she walked past us. When we knew she could no longer hear, Edwin said: "Well, isn't she lovely."

"I think she's entertaining," Arabella said, the curve of her mouth tilting upward.

I adjusted my corset, frowning at their behavior. "She is not a wild animal. She is a person just like the rest of us."

"A person sent from hell, as the mortals say," Beckett commented and then put his hands inside his pockets.

"I think you are mistaken. Plus, that's not even true." I seethed and then pushed past him. Beckett followed me, his presence close behind. Edwin and Arabella stay back.

"Your cousin barely acknowledged you," he posed further, cocking his head to the side. I did not look at him but only nodded. "Is she usually like that? Or does she just not like you?"

"It's hardly your business," I said. However, the thought of Devyn hating me had me on edge. We walked across the room, seeing the lights flicker back and forth. The witch in front of us had climbed the stairs already, and the door at the top swung open. "And do not mess with her, Beckett. She is a powerful witch. I might be able to control myself, but I cannot say the same about her."

We stop at the staircase. "I did not say I was going to mess with her."

I bite back an eye roll. "But you will."

He sneered, extending his hand out to let me go first. "Ladies first." I brushed past him, my hair whipping at his chest before I walked forward. The top step was close, and the realization came over me - that I would be back to the home that belonged to my family.

I stepped inside the cold house, playing nervously with the ends of my hair. I haven't seen my aunt and uncle for a while - would they even remember me? Beckett nudges me forward, annoyed by how slow I'm walking. The living room had changed - the number of couches was old from the looks of it. A fireplace burned from the charcoal lit the place enough to see that the kitchen was attached to it.

The kitchen was clean. Any trace of dust had been cleaned, and it had looked brand new - as if she hadn't used it in a long time. Devyn stood in the middle of the room, smiling down at the snake wrapped around her shoulder.

My father had a step-brother who was descended from a witch family, making him a complete witch. It was why Devyn was not an elf like me, because my uncle, Cassius, married my aunt, Blair Caddel, who was also a witch. Devyn was their firstborn child, and at some point, they had lived with the mortals but soon vanished into the forest when the mortals started to turn against them.

Witches were hung, burned, and impaled on a stake. The roaring crowds gathered excitedly. That's when the humans officially started to dislike the supernatural.

"Where are Cassius and Blair?" I ask. Devyn freezes at the mention of her family. She looks at me, and her face remains neutral, but her eyes hold a wave of unbearable anger toward me.

"Dead," She responds and then walks forward. I stopped in my steps, even when Beckett nearly stumbled. How long ago had they been dead? Why didn't she tell anyone?

Now, the house was all Devyn's. How lonely and quiet it has become. Devyn moves to the hallway, and we all follow. "One bedroom is down this way, which is mine." She leads us towards them and then stops by the wall as it opens into another room - a library.

Books lined the wall, and I smiled whenever I remembered

that I would hide from Devyn in here. I was always so bad at hiding, but whenever I hid in here, Devyn could never find me. Two couches faced each other in the middle of the room, and a coffee table was in front of them. A lamp stood on it. A staircase leads up to the second level of the library.

"If I'm not in my meditation room or bedroom, I'll most likely be in here," Devyn explained, crossing her hands. "Sammy likes it here, so don't be surprised if you see him crawling around."

I hear Edwin scoff behind me. "Bloody snake," he mutters, crossing his hand stubbornly.

We have about two seconds to look around before she pushes past us again, and we must hurry to keep up with her. She led us back towards the basement, but instead, another staircase led upwards, right next to the basement stairs.

The second floor is just as large as the first floor. You can see the outside from the windows, the way the rain hits the glass in a rush, almost like it was waiting to break it. It dropped the way the blood on my hands did when I had sent those dybbuks to the underworld. I take a deep breath, the taste of blood in my mouth.

"There are three rooms upstairs, which means one of you will have to sleep with another, but I'm sure it won't be hard to decide." She whirls around, the snack hissing at all of us. "I'll be mediating if any of you need me." She walks past us, her hand skimming a loose strand of Arabella's hair that lingers on it before pushing it past her shoulder.

Arabella's breath faltered, and I could hear her heart from here - accelerating and pulsating harshly against her chest. Once the witch disappeared, she put a hand over her chest, calming down her heart.

I looked at the rooms, searching for the one that was Devyn's old room. It was the last room in the hallway. "We should go to sleep." I turn my back towards the three. "It is getting late, and I'm tired from earlier." I look behind. Arabella looks downward.

"Goodnight, all of you," I say, nodding toward the three. Despite only knowing them for a few days now, I could not bring myself to be horrible to them entirely - no matter how awful they might have been to me. Arabella, the one who was the kindest to me, lifted her head to wave goodbye to me.

She did not dare say bye to the brothers. Instead, she walked past them to the room next to me.

I shut the door behind me, feeling the stare of the brothers burn into my back.

CHAPTER FOURTEEN

The rain screamed. The thunder had no mercy as it struck outside, hitting a tree, letting its roots give in, the impact of the tree falling on the ground with urgency. I awoke with a startle, feeling like I had fallen into a big hole. My head battered against my skull. This sinking feeling was familiar, but it hurt worse today than any other.

My heart felt heavy, as if it had stopped beating. My breath stilled inside my throat like I no longer had lungs. My body felt like an empty vessel, and I couldn't describe this feeling. Pain? Sadness?

It didn't matter. I couldn't feel anything.

My abandoned body lay momentarily on the bed, looking at the plain ceiling above me. My head would not stop tingling, and it felt like my knife had stabbed me right through my forehead.

I looked to my side now and looked at the slightly open door. My eyebrows scrunched together, but I paid no mind as I forced myself into the sitting position. Although, if I remember correctly, I swore I shut my door last night. My hand flew to my head immediately. It was worse when sitting.

The bed itself was very comfortable. I threw the silky sage green blanket off my body, feeling the sweat stain the back of my nightgown. It felt too tight on me. I walked over to the closet and opened it.

I stripped off my white nightgown that I had stolen and wore a white sweater with loose pants tied around my waist. The sleeves were oversized, and I scrunched them up to make them fit my hands. I made sure to fasten my dagger in my holster. I then pulled my hair into a low ponytail to secure it away from my face.

Knock. Knock.

My head whirled towards the door. Two simple knocks and my head pounded at the sound. The already open door creaked louder as it sprang open wider. Beckett followed through; his footsteps were heavy when walking in. His eyes met mine initially, and I tried my best not to look as horrible as possible.

"I didn't say you could come in." I snapped.

"Breakfast is ready." He walked closer to me, looking around my room in the meantime. His eyes traveled toward the bed, which was messy from the night before. Then he looked at the window. His eyes then left the window and stared straight at me.

"Are you ill?" He suddenly asked, gazing at my sweaty forehead and my red-tinted cheeks. "You do not look well."

"I'm fine," I tell him, looking away to hide my bright face. I wanted to pound my forehead against the wall - at least then, he might leave me alone, think of me as crazy, and never talk to me again. I did not know where we stood among each other. "I'm not hungry."

"Did you know breakfast is the most important meal of the day?" He questioned, then walked around me, his finger lifting a few strands of my hair. "Maybe then you won't look like the undead." My eyebrows raised at that, and I could see the smirk on his face before he extended his hand to me. "Won't you come, my little elf?"

His eyes dilated, and my heart accelerated when I saw the outstretched hand. He was an exceptionally remarkable man - enchanting and devilish. I hated what feeling came over me.

My cheeks, already red, grew brighter.

Cautiously I let him take my hand and lead me out the door. He closed the door behind us when we reached the hallway. His hand left mine, and I felt the way my hand was overwhelmed with coldness. It was as if he wanted to leave a mark on me, and he did so, successfully.

Damn him.

I whipped around, shuffling forward, trying to get away from him. Unfortunately, no matter how fast I walked, he was always right behind me. He had his hands in his pockets and his head held high as he watched me walk down the stairs and into the kitchen.

Edwin had a brown apron on and some sugar on his nose, and he smiled when he saw my face. On the couch, Arabella sat on the edge, holding a book. She had her hair done in a braid and wore a white summer dress. She crossed her legs and glanced up from the book to nod at me.

"Morning," Edwin said, leaning over the counter as he took me in. "You look gorgeous, darling," he complimented. "Don't you think, Beckett?" I saw him hurry behind me and then sit at the table. A plate across from him sat.

"Sit down, Everard," Beckett commanded. It occurred to me he did not answer.

I sat across from him when I noticed Devyn come into the room. "Morning, Devyn," I said. Her eyes roamed on the people in the room before they landed on me. She gave me a small smile, and Sammy crawled underneath her hair. Edwin scrunched his nose in disgust.

"I'll be outside if any of you need me," she said before she opened the door and walked out. The door slammed behind her.

"Here," Beckett slid a mug to me. Inside contained a yellow liquid. It was half full.

"What is it?"

"Freshly squeezed orange juice. Devyn had it in her fridge," he answered and then grabbed another mug containing the same liquid. He brought the cup to his lips and let the juice slide down his throat. It bobbed up and down. "It's good for headaches."

I looked down at the mug and then went to take a sip myself, only to stop right as the hardened clay touched my lips. "How did you know I had a headache?" As soon as I let the orange juice slide down my throat, I felt the headache that pounded slowly fade away. I frowned and looked at the empty mug. "Did you…"

"It's laced with a healing potion," Beckett explained. Then he leaned forward, whispering, "I stole it from Devyn."

"Why?" I asked, setting down the empty mug. My headache was fading, and though I was thankful for it, it did not make sense why he was doing it. "Why are you trying to help me?"

"Isn't it a common decency to help others?" He asked.

"You don't have common decency," I responded, leaning my back into my chair. I looked at the plate of food in front of me. My appetite was gone entirely, but I was starving, so I took the piece of bread and shoved it inside my mouth despite feeling like I wanted to spit it out afterward.

Beckett sneered, and I felt his foot stepping onto mine under the table, lightly. "When you are done eating, meet me in the library." He pushed himself out of the chair, brushed off any dust on his sweater, and walked away.

The library was quiet. The stacks of books were aligned next to each other. A staircase led up to the same round table where Beckett sat. It was colder up here than down on the ground floor. Then again, the books up here were full of magic. Some were blocked, meaning I couldn't look inside them.

The wood had been scratched, claw marks visible, like a wild animal had a go at it. I let my fingers roam on it, feeling the anger behind it all. Whatever Devyn released up here once did not turn out well.

I dragged my finger on the shelf, letting the dust collect on my finger. I flung it away, coughing at the dust flying around my face. That drew the elf's attention, his eyes roaming to me. "It is rude to interrupt someone when they are reading," he snapped, coddling the book in his lap.

"You are the one that invited me here, Brooker," I clarified and raised an eyebrow at him. "If anything, it is rude that you pretend I am not even here."

His eyes flashed with annoyance, and then he ushered me over. With slow steps, I took the seat across from him. He closed the book, putting it by the other pile of books. His curls fell over his head, and my eyes looked into his dark ones. "What do you need?"

It felt wrong to see him smile, but he did, and his eyes sparkled with mischief while he did. "I want you, my little elf."

I pushed the urge to roll my eyes. "How long do you plan on calling me that? It is getting tiresome. Plus, I am not yours." I kicked my feet toward him, but he made no reaction when my foot met his leg.

"Not yet," he says.

"Just tell me what you want," I demand, my patience growing

thin. It seems with him, I'm always irritated.

"Well, now that we are together, I think I ought to tell you my plans now since you have provided a safe shelter," He says, and I freeze. The blood rushes to my hands and arms, and I go limp. Anticipation rolls through me, and I roll my hands into rocks. "Have I got your attention now?"

"Go on," I say, maintaining my only confidence because now my desperation must look amusing.

He grabs a book from the pile, flipping it open to a random page. There, labeled at the top, is the family tree of the Percival Family. "Tell me, little elf, do you know the history of the Percival Family?"

I scowled. "I know Rufus was killed by a hybrid."

He slammed his hand on the table, and I glared up at him, odious by his immature behavior. "That is not what happened. A hybrid didn't kill Rufus, nor did an elf or werewolf." I frowned, unable to know where he was getting at. "Rufus may have been a good king, but that doesn't mean he was a good person. Rufus was being targeted by someone who knew him too much. Someone of his kind."

"Oh really?" The lucid amusement in my voice was visible. "And how would you know, Brooker?"

He disregarded my question as he pointed to a picture of the vampire. Castor Percival, the king of vampires. He was worse than Rufus he was, indeed, a powerful man who desperately wanted to kill anyone who got in his way.

"Connect the pieces, Everard. Castor wanted power, and his father had all of it." He cocked his head, smiling at me. "Let's see if you're smart enough to figure it out." I knew exactly what he was getting at it; the only problem was, why didn't Castor tell anyone?

"If Castor killed his father, he would gloat about it," I stated.

"Would he?" He leaned back in his chair, veering his head to the right. A smirk spread across his lips. "The only reason why Rufus was king in the first place was because he had murdered the king with the Warlord's Dagger. It was the only way you could become king. Castor had not."

"And how do you think he killed them?" I questioned.

"Well, perhaps he was going to kill them with the Warlord's dagger in the first place but was never able to find it. Only some people can be trusted to know where a powerful dagger like that can be hidden. He killed his mother and father in the middle of the night and tore them to pieces to make it seem like a hybrid did it. The crown easily went to him, and he gained ultimate respect. All loved Rufus, so if anyone knew he had murdered them, he might have lost that power. What's a king without his soldiers?"

"You don't even know if that's true," I retorted. "This might just be some conspiracy."

"It might be, but it's a pretty damn good one, and I don't condone whatever Castor has been doing. Do you?"

I almost laughed and opened my mouth to reply, but nothing came out. I looked away at the dusty books. I could not look at him. "Don't throw this back at me, Brooker. My village was burnt down because of them. My father might be dead because of it. I hate them."

"Then let's do something about it," he enticed. I looked at him, eyebrows scrunching. He stood up, his chair moving a few inches back as he rounded the table. I remained in my chair as he walked around me. "I want to kill the king. I want him gone from the chair, but I can only do that if I have the Warlord's Dagger. It's also the only way they'll...respect me."

I laugh. "Oh, I see. You want to get the Warlord's Dagger and kill the king. Then what? Become king? What do you plan on doing then? The war won't stop if you become king." I stand up and whirl around at the elf. "You're thinking only about yourself."

"It is better than having that tyrant in charge. Our world has been corrupted, and I need to act," he argued.

"And let another tyrant take charge?" I demanded. His face hardened at that, but he did not fight back. Not only that, he knew it was true. "And even if you succeed, why would you tell me all this? I am nothing to you, and yet I could expose your plan."

"Because, little elf, you also play a nice part in my plan." He comes. "You see, you might be an amateur at your powers, but you are no weak elf. You would make a valuable asset to my team."

"I am just an asset to you then?" I scoff, crossing my hands. "I'm just a machine you can use whenever you piss off the vampires too much?"

"Precisely." He answers. The pile of books fell, the dust flew in the air, and the books collapsed on the floor. "You have extraordinary power. Once learned, you could be powerful. You would be unstoppable." He then walked closer, and with a flash, he reached for my dagger and pointed it straight at my stomach, the tip of it so close to cutting me. "Plus, if you do this for me…I will help you find your father."

Despite being an impulsive and horrible plan, I can only help but wonder what it would be like without Castor in charge. What if Beckett took his place? Is it all that different? A tyrant who wants nothing but power would be switched with another tyrant with unknown intentions.

I will help you find your father.

"You are just like him." I trail off, licking my dry lips. "You want power just like him."

"Yes, I am a bit power-hungry," He admitted, taking the dagger away and putting it back into my holster. Though his expression is hard, I could tell their was an uncertainty in his actions – that there was another reason. I fell onto the chair and saw the way his hand extended, the way it would if he wanted a handshake. "If you shake my hand now, you will be on my side. You will fight with me, and if you betray me…" He tilted his head, letting me get the idea in my head.

"So if I help you, you will help me find my father. Locate him and tell me where he is?" I questioned.

"Yes I will," he promises and then extends his hand forward. "Do we have a deal?"

He shuffled towards me and bit the inside of his cheeks. He looked outraged, but I knew I had gotten to him. He needed me… not just a little, but a lot because he knew he could not do this by himself. He needed a team, no matter how powerful he was.

I let my hand enter his, and his fingers cupped my knuckles. I then smiled, cupping his cheek, which was too soft for someone like him. "We have a deal." I let my hand fall, and his eyes enlarged with relief.

Leaving the library, the doors behind me slowly dragged closed. I realized then how much my heart beat against my chest, and I hurried through the hallway and pushed the back door to the backyard, which only contained a garden. Fresh strawberries and blueberries grew in the soil, and on the other side, a row of cucumbers and mushrooms hung from the tiny plants.

Devyn leaned over them as she let the water from her watering can hit them lightly. Sammy, whose eyes were opened, noticed me first, and it hissed, letting Devyn know of my presence. She stopped her movements as I got closer. She didn't dare to look at me.

"Did you need something?"

"You don't seem that happy to see me, cousin. After so many years, I thought you would at least try to interact with me." I could see Sammy hiss something in her ear from the corner of my eye.

"Well, can you blame me?" She demanded. "Why should I be kind to you when you've done nothing but ignore me?"

I cocked my head, raising an eyebrow. "What are you talking about?"

She finally turned around, glaring at me. "Don't act daft, Blanche. I wrote you so many letters, and you couldn't even reply. Not even when my parents died."

"Devyn, I have no idea what you're talking about. I never received a letter from you. Have you been sending them to the right village?" I asked.

"Sammy has been delivering it." She looked at her snake and pet its head. "Sammy knows this forest and never delivers a letter wrong." She suddenly dropped the watering can and then walked towards me, stopping beside me.

"From now on, I suggest staying away from me until your father needs you back," she added, "if he's alive, that is."

My eyes enlarged with anger, and I snapped my head towards her, viciously grabbing her wrist before she could leave. I yanked at her and heard Sammy hiss from her neck, warning me to back off.

"Let me go, Blanche." She warned.

I looked at her snake and watched as he hissed at me. I'm sure it would attack me on Devyn's command, but my eyes met his. Black eyes stared back at me, but I didn't cower. Instead, I stared back at me, nothing but venom coating my veins. "Watch what you say, Devyn." I looked at Devyn. "Your tongue will get the best of you."

I then let her go and watched her walk into the house. It occurred to me then that I had not known Devyn at all. She never once sent me a note, not even when my mother left my father and I.

And until this day, I didn't think she even wanted to talk to me anymore.

CHAPTER FIFTEEN

Pain hit my head, and I could feel the empty feeling in my head, depriving the hole of desolation. My eyes were wide open, staring at the ceiling before me. My shock was inevitable. I should be happy that my dream realities haven't haunted me these past few nights, but I couldn't shake off this deranged feeling. I could feel that something was wrong.

My hand came over my head and used the pain to knock it into the pillow. Tears welled at the corners of my eyes when the pain hit my skull. The knife stabbing at my skin grew harder, and I felt it dragging against the edges of my brain. I twisted to the side and finally let myself sob into the pillow.

I might have grabbed my knife and stuck it in my head if it weren't for the lightheadedness. I have always had lucid dreams, from the time I was ten years old to now. Yet, I have not had a single one these past few days. They all vanished - like they never existed.

I could not understand it. Why? Why had they suddenly gone away?

At some point, I stopped crying. I looked out the window and saw the moonlight still there. I threw the covers off me, the sweat gliding down my legs. It felt like acid sizzling through my skin, and I could not shake the feeling away. I wanted it to be gone.

The last time I felt this, Beckett had gotten me that orange juice that made it go away. We had not spoken since the morning in the library, and it was getting hard to avoid him since Beckett was everywhere I went and saw. However, I never liked being ignored; I'm sure he didn't like it either.

It started with only glances at each other until one of us would kick the other's feet under the table, or we would throw glares at each other from across the room. It didn't help that we planned to work together soon.

I finally managed to get out of my bed. It was still late, in the middle of the night, and not an ounce of sleep could be found in my system. Dizziness made me trip, my hands landing on the table by me.

I breathed. Then another.

What was wrong with me?

I could not stand this any longer. Let Beckett insult me for all I care. I needed that bloody healing potion. I raced out of my room, ignoring the way the room seemed to spin. I jogged across the hallway toward his room. I didn't care if I woke up the entire house. I needed this painful feeling to go away.

I banged my fists on the wooden door. "Beckett!" I shouted and let my fists meet the door at a rapid pace. "Open the door!" I struck the door with my hands until my palms hurt and my wrists ached.

I then tried to open it, only to find it locked.

The door whipped open, and I saw Beckett standing there. He looked at me momentarily, then looked back at his sleeping brother. "Fucking hell, Everard."

I grabbed onto his hand and pulled. "Come with me."

I pushed past him, watching as he closed the door behind me. His bedroom was the same size as mine, except his bed was more extensive - a king-size with white drapes and black covers. Edwin slept there. Large windows faced his bed, the curtains covering them at the moment. Two chairs, both small sofas with white pillows, sat in the middle of the room—a desk was underneath the curtains.

Despite a blazing fireplace, the room was still very cold. My head ached from the intense light, so I turned around to see Beckett against the wall near the door. Putting his hands over his chest, he leaned his shoulder against it. "Everard, what is the point of bothering me at this hour?"

I swallowed down my pride, ashamed that I would be coming to him so late in the night to make me feel better. "My headaches are getting worse. I need you to give me that healing serum," I admitted and then bit down on my lip. "Please."

"I don't have any," he answered.

"Don't lie to me, Brooker," I snapped. "I can practically smell the magic here, and I know it's not coming from you." I watched his lips tilt into a smirk before pushing off the wall. He brushed past me until he reached his desk. He pulled open a drawer and pulled out a vial of yellow liquid. It was in one of Devyn's potion bottles, and he held it in the air for me to see.

"This healing serum?" He asked, moving the bottle back and forth. I stormed up to him, reaching for it, only for him to pull it further up. He clicked his tongue, cocking his head, looking down at me. "Everything comes with a price, little elf. What do you plan on giving me in return?"

Christ.

I crossed my arms and exhaled. Beckett's amusement sends my shoulder swaying. How about I kick you in the balls, and we call it a night?" I suggest with a smile.

He ushers me over, ignoring my threat as he dangles the healing juice over my head. "Come on, Everard. What do you have to offer?" He asks. Like the devil making a bargain, he twirls the bottle circularly.

"What do you want?" I ask.

"Perhaps…" He circles around me. The juice swished back and forth - right to left. "A taste of your magic?" He cocked his head and then used one of his fingers to drag my chin toward him. "I want to see what you're capable of."

"I already told you I don't have any."

"That's not true," he said. His finger grazed the bottom of my chin and then played with the front strands of my hair. "I saw you use them while fighting the dybbuks."

"That wasn't my power. That was just a ritual," I retorted.

"Don't be a fool, Everard." He let go of my chin, but it felt like he had grabbed my heart and stolen it from my body. Something about his touch was warming, and I didn't particularly appreciate how it felt on my skin - it was burning me.

"No elf can do what you did. Elves cannot do rituals like that unless they have dark power to fuel it." His face got closer to mine. "So, it's only safe to assume you have some form of dark powers."

The shadows from his figure appeared around him, on his shoulder, by his arm, over his head. They circled him, clinging onto him as if he was their power and savior - then again, he controlled them wholly. "You will need to learn. You are going to help me kill the king, and what use are you if you can't even use your power?"

"I thought the whole point of this journey was to get power," I remind him and then step back away from his figure.

"It is, but you need power to go against it. Castor is a powerful individual, and to defeat it, you'll need to match it." He opened the bottle of healing juice and put it towards his lips. The aroma itself made me hazy. The sickly scent of lemons and daisies hit my nostrils, making my brain dizzy.

His shadows lifted the bottle, letting it dangle just above his shoulders.

"Then what do you suppose I do?" I demand. "I've never been able to perform magic."

"Let me teach you," he said. "Let me try to make your power stronger."

"You don't know anything about my magic. Why should I put my trust in you?" I queried, crossing my hands over my chest.

"Because I have enough power," he stated. "You are just weak."

I scowled, my fists gathering into rocks. I skimmed over the desk and saw the knife laid out there. As if noticing my eyes, Beckett looked back and saw the object I was looking at. "Or maybe you aren't as weak as I think you are. Maybe you can prove me wrong." His eyes twinkled with mischief as the knife suddenly started to float up with the help of another shadow.

He was baiting me.

Then, with an abrupt motion, with the blade facing me, it shot at me. My eyes widened as my hand shot up and grabbed the knife's handle in the air. It was right in front of my face, and if I had not stopped it, I would have no doubt it would have pierced right through my head.

"I don't need to prove myself to you," I snapped, looking at the amused elf. "I might not be the best with my powers, but I can fight."

From the corner, I could hear Edwin mumble something in his sleep, much too quiet to hear.

"You can fight?" He asked, then went to the desk, pulled open a drawer, and pulled out his own dagger. On the handle, he had engravings of a name: Elodie. It was carved, black, and trimmed on the brown handle. If it weren't for my pristine eyes, I might not have been able to spot it. "Then fight me, little elf." He slammed the drawer closed. "If you are as strong as you say, you will fight me right here."

"In this room?" I asked.

"Yes," he said. "I'll be kind enough to let you make the first move."

"Your brother is sleeping."

"And?"

He stands beside the bed, waiting for my move, but I never make it. Nothing would make me than happier to fight him, but I couldn't - not even if he wanted me to do it. I'm only giving in to what he wants.

"I'm not going to fight you," I say, shaking my head as I turn around. His hand shoots out, and pain shoots through my entire being when I feel the knife slice through my pale skin. I gasped, seeing the dark crimson blood ooze out of the cut, trailing down my arm. "You.." I shut my mouth and felt power course through me at the sight of the blood. It stung me just as it vibrated harshly against my cold skin.

"Oh, come on, Everard." He circled me again, his demanding voice telling me to feel the vexation - to kill him on the spot. "Don't you want to hurt me?" His voice left a trail of anger, and I could see the blood that leaked from my arm and how suddenly, blood was the only thing I could see around me. "Don't you want to hurt me for hurting you like this?"

The dirty blonde hair fell over his forehead, and he waited. Except I could not say anything. The trail of blood ran down my arm as the tiny droplet fell onto the floor. Almost as if a rock hit the water, I felt the adrenaline; the power to prove myself only drove me forward. I gritted my teeth together, focusing on the trail of blood. "Oh, bloody hell, Everard, just do something already," Beckett's voice rang through, and I turned on him as quickly as possible. The knife swung at his cheek.

He did not react fast enough; it cut into his sharp jawline, and blood leaked from it. He cupped his cheek; his mouth parted as he took in my movement. He lifted his hand from his hand, inspecting the blood. For a moment, there was silence, but then his eyes found mine, and he started walking towards me. My feet moved back with each step until I hit the desk behind me.

"Don't cower," he snapped and then grabbed me by my arm.

My entire body fell towards him as he hauled me towards the bed. I fell onto it with a pounce, and he walked forward, coming over me swiftly. His hair dangled as I looked up at his dark eyes. "Push me back, Everard. Show me how strong you are."

"Get off me," I said, pushing at his chest. He doesn't budge, but he lowers his dagger to my throat until the blade makes an incision at my throat. I feel the pain slice at me, and I close my eyes. "Stop it," I thunder, not caring if I wake Edwin. I hit his chest until his hands came over mine and then pushed them back onto the mattress. "Beckett-"

"Brooker," he corrects. "You call me Brooker unless I say not to."

"I said get off!" I shout, wiggling under his touch. This position made me uncomfortable. I was too close to him, and my heart was beating out of control. My heart was going to explode.

"Please, I'm not strong like you," I confess, making all my movements stop, and I watch as he raises an eyebrow. "I'm not as powerful as you are," His smile comes in late, but it's replaced with disappointment as he finally lets go of my hands. He goes to get off me, but then I grab onto his hands again, and this time, I use all my strength to shove him back towards the bed beside me.

I was always good at lying.

His eyes go wide as he takes in my unique trick. His head hits the mattress, and I climb over his body, knocking the dagger away from his hand. I then force the blade right at his throat - just as he has done for me only a moment ago. "I'm more powerful than you will ever be," I confess and smile. "You want power, to control whatever you cannot, but me.." I did not know what drove me, but I knew I wasn't cruel like him. "I'm not something you can control."

Then I felt...something.

It was peculiar like lightning erupted beside me, but I felt it inside my body. It was driving me; voices whispered something into my head to the point where I could not see straight. It was a... euphoric feeling. I was gifted with imaginable pleasure by just feeling him underneath me.

Without thinking, I lifted the dagger right underneath his body. I felt the pain and watched as I drew on my skin with the blade on each arm until blood coated my entire arms. My vision was blurry as I started to write something of my own on his chest.

I realized what I drew as soon as I finished. It was a circle with a star inside, just as I had done with the dybbuks. However, this time, I wasn't sending Beckett to the underworld. I wanted him to feel suffering.

It felt like someone was lifting me, and I loved it - drowned in this indescribable feeling. He lifted his head to look, and his eyes widened. "No, stop it." He suddenly fought back, pushing at me hard, and I used my hands to confine him in place.

"You are a monster, Beckett," I admitted. "I think it's only fair that you be punished like one." I then lifted my hand and guided my bloody hands in front of my head, crossing them as if I were to pray. His voice screamed at me to stop, and that's when I started to remember the Latin verses I had learned about.

My father, who had once cared for me, had also woken me up daily to study the damn books on magic. I could not think of a better punishment than raining hell upon him, but I could not remember the verse very well. So I went with the other option, I would make him relive some of his worst memories.

I muttered the words in foreign Latin, the curse like a song on my lips. The elf under me hissed and pushed as much as he could, but he did not realize just how powerful the knowledge I carried was. I did not know I had this magic, and I only frowned upon how I could finally use it. When the Latin was finally done, with closed eyes, I brought the tips of my fingers to his temples and then opened my eyes.

His face was a blur of anger and worry as I finally managed to suck myself inside his brain, and I watched a memory come together. I explored his brain and used the blood to freeze him entirely until his breath was trapped in his throat. It was one of his worst memories, and I watched it come alive right before me.

A swirl of shadows and light. I watched the shards of glass come together like a memory locked away into orbit. I let myself walk into the glass memory and get sucked into the darkness until it's all I felt. The memory gave away in front of me. The green trees around me became rooted to the ground, and the summer air blew my hair back.

I looked around the area to see I was back at the boy's cottage. It seemed newer than it did now. "Beckett!" A boy rushed past me, and I twirled around to see a young boy. Edwin. He raced past me and straight into the woods.

I ran after him, following him through the trees, jumping over logs to catch up to him. Light cascaded after he ran, the little boy worriedly, calling after his only twin brother. I ran through the dark forest until I eventually caught up to the boy's figure. "Beckett!" He screeched.

I looked up at the tree before him and saw a rope wrapped around his brother's ankles as he dangled up in the air. Beckett's hair was long for a young boy. His features were soft, but his red eyes indicated he had been crying. "Edwin," he whined, his hands extended for his little brother. "Get me out of this," he pleaded.

The blood rushed to his head, making his face go purple. The rope held him only by his ankles. Edwin rushed over to the tree where the rope hung him, and then he dragged a small pocket knife from his pocket. He cut it, causing Beckett to fall instantly. He groaned as his back hit the soil.

Edwin ran over to Beckett, hands clawing at him. Beckett groaned, and when he faced Edwin, I saw how his lips were swollen and how cuts had been punctured on his cheeks and nose. "Come on. We have to go back to the house," Edwin encouraged, trying to help his brother up.

"No!" Beckett hissed and crouched by his brother. "No, don't take me back there. Not right now. He'll put me back here." Edwin used his hand to comfort Beckett, waiting until his body healed. He coughed up a bit of blood as he knelt and threw up all over the ground.

"Bloody hell, Beckett. What did he do to you?" Edwin asked as he cradled his brother in his chest. He was scrambling to look at his brother, and it only occurred to me how Beckett didn't wear any clothes but an oversized t-shirt, and when it rode up, I saw the number of scars he wore on his legs and stomach.

Then Beckett sobbed, and his brother covered his head in his chest. "Why does he always hurt us?" He kept on repeating it when, suddenly, the memory in front of me started to shatter.

Beckett's shadows, I realized, destroyed it all until it was not a memory to be remembered anymore.

And that's when I finally let go of his mind.

CHAPTER SIXTEEN

My eyes fluttered open to the dimly lit room. This place was not familiar, which meant this was not Beckett's or my room. "You're awake?" Beside me was a stool, and on it sat Devyn with a lantern. She held it above my head for a moment before she set it aside on the table beside her.

"Blanche?" Muffled steps came closer, and Arabella appeared on the other side of my bed. Her hair is pulled up into a bun with strands that are loose everywhere. She makes it look nice.

I scrunch my eyebrows. I realize this is Devyn's room. I could feel the amount of magic that swirled around in this room. I sat up, feeling as though my back had lost all its ability to move. I look down at my clothes.

My blood-soaked nightdress is gone, and my replacement is a long shirt instead. There are new bandages on my arms, and through it, a tiny bit of blood stains the cloth. "What happened?"

"You tell me," Devyn says, crossing her legs. "Edwin came shouting to me when he woke up to you on top of Beckett. Your arms were cut, and on him was a bloody pentacle." I felt Arabella sit on the edge of the bed, her hands resting on my back, smoothing up and down.

"You can tell us, Blanche," Arabella says and looks at me from the corner. "I think it was a nice sight, seeing Beckett all bloody."

I shake my head, my mind foggy. My head is blistering from pain. A sudden feeling of nausea makes me curse. I look everywhere, looking for something, and then notice the open window. I jump off the bed, which stuns the two, but I disregard them as I place my hands on the ledge and hurl.

When the remains of my stomach are out of my stomach, I turn back around, wiping my mouth with the back of my hand. Arabella walks up to me, takes out a handkerchief, and then hands it to me. I wipe my hands in it and then my mouth. "Come sit," Devyn said, crossing her hands in her chair. I narrow my gaze at her. "I'm serious. Sitting helps with vomiting."

Arabella leads me to the edge of the bed, where she has me sit down. "Now, tell us what happened," Devyn said. Her elbows meet her eyes as she leans closer to me.

"It's a blur," I finally said, closing my eyes and clenching my teeth when I felt the nauseous sensation again. I push it back down...inhale...exhale. "I remember getting mad, and he was fighting me, and then I started fighting him."

"So, you two got into a physical fight?" Arabella asked.

"That might explain the cuts on your arms, but that doesn't describe the pentacle."

"I cut my arms," I blurt out without even meaning to. Both of them went silent, and I could feel Devyn thinking. She's trying to find solutions but has yet to come up with any. "I drew the pentacle, and I...I was doing the ritual."

"Like you did on the dybbuk's?" Arabella asked.

"No, no...I didn't send him to the underworld or anything. I think I just made him relive his worst memory, but in doing so, I also saw it," I explained, scrunching the handkerchief with my hand. "I don't know how or why I did it. It was just like something I had to do-"

"Hold on, dybbuks and a ritual? What on earth are you two talking about?" Devyn demanded, raising her voice.

Arabella went into detail about what happened. I let her since I could barely keep up with anything anyone was saying. "Blanche, where did you learn that ritual?" Devyn demanded. She looked gravely at me as if she finally knew what was wrong with me.

"I read it in a book," I answered.

"That's a very dangerous ritual, Blanche," Devyn said and then scoffed. "I'm surprised you even survived it." She stood up, pacing back and forth, pondering the new information. "I can't even do that..."

She faced me then. "Blanche, surely you know what happens

if you fail that ritual. You could–"

"I could have sent myself to the underworld…I know," I retorted. I had known it all along. "I knew the risk, but if I didn't do it, then we all would have ended up dead or wounded."

"That's dark magic. Not even a skilled dark witch could do it. It takes a lot of practice and time to actually be able to do it. I'd never do it myself since it's considered satanic, so just how the hell could you have done it so perfectly?"

"I don't know," I retorted. I sat up and immediately regretted it as I felt the vomit slowly come up my throat. I held it down. "I just want to go to bed. I feel awful right now."

"And what about Beckett?" She demanded. "He can't wake up."

"What?" I demanded.

"We've tried waking him up, Blanche," Arabella says and crosses her hands. "We've already tried. He just won't wake. He's alive still but just sleeping. It's like he's in a trance–"

"A curse," Devyn corrects and then looks at me. "You put him under a curse."

"I did no such thing," I argued. "I haven't been able to even levitate a thing since I was born. How could you possibly think I could have cursed him?"

"An elf's power reacts in different ways. While some develop young like most, some also develop it later on, like you. Maybe your powers have been hiding inside of you for so long it's decided to react. Maybe they finally exploded," Devyn explained.

Arabella sat up; she angrily looked at us. "But this isn't about her powers right now. Beckett is currently under a spell, and he can't wake up. He's probably reliving his worst memory as we speak, so put this whole argument aside for right now and figure out how we wake him up."

"She can undo it," Devyn says, looking at me.

"No, I can't," I argue.

"The person who cast the curse can also undo it, which means it has to be you to let him go."

Suddenly, I feel the vomit harshly pound in my stomach. Arabella acts quickly as she grabs a bucket from the corner of the room and hands it to me. I hurl into it, my cheeks red from shame. This position is pathetic. I just want to go to sleep.

I lift my head slightly, looking at Devyn. "Even if I did cast the curse on him, I wouldn't even know how to lift it."

"Well, I'm sure there's a solution to that. We need to read some books." Devyn grabs the chair and yanks it so that its back is against the wall. "That's enough for right now. I think we're all tired," then she looks at me, scrunching her head. "And sick."

I scrunch my nose, glaring at her. I drop the bucket, and I watch as it lands on her floor. "Goodnight," I say before I brush past her. I don't wait for Arabella as I storm out of the room. I walk towards the kitchen and then up the stairs.

I had felt the adrenaline rush when Beckett had hurt me. It was something I had not felt before, and I didn't know how to react to it. Did I want to hurt Beckett? Perhaps I did, but I never put him under a curse. No, I couldn't have.

As I jog up the stairs, I notice the door to Beckett's room is open.

I peek through, and I see Edwin there, sitting on the couch right in front of the fireplace. I push the door open lightly. It creaks, signaling that I've walked in. Yet, Edwin doesn't turn, nor does he acknowledge that I'm here. I walk closer until I'm only a few feet away from him.

I finally look at Beckett. He's in different clothes, and the blood has been washed out, although there is a little stain on the mattress because of it. His eyes are closed, and he's sleeping in the oddest position. He is in a starfish position, except his legs are closed, and instead of looking peaceful, his eyebrows are scrunched together, like he's in pain.

"Edwin?" I say, waiting for him to turn around, but he doesn't. I walk around the couch and see him staring at the fireplace. In his lap, he's playing with Beckett's dagger. "Do you plan on killing me with that?" I ask, trying to get him to look at me. He doesn't, and I sigh, walking right next to him and sitting down. "Edwin, are you angry with me?"

"No," he suddenly answers, and his hands stop, and with the dagger shoots out and stabs the wooden coffee table in front of him. The dagger cuts into the wood, and the handle is left sticking up. "I wish I could be mad at you, but I'm not."

"Why not?" I ask.

"Because I know my brother," he answers. "Which means I also know he had something to do with it." When all I could provide was silence, he asked: "What happened?"

My hands rub against my thighs nervously. "It's all a blur. I can't even remember a lot. All I know.." I look over at Beckett's sleeping figure. "Is that we both were angry," I wanted to shout at Edwin that it was Beckett's fault. I wouldn't have hurt someone like this. I didn't even do this.

Devyn says it's a curse, but I would have known. Curses are evil according to the eleven histories. Most elves that could curse others weren't just regular elves; they were different. Those elves were anthropophagus – even with their own kind. It's been a long time since I read about them, and maybe tomorrow, I will go to the library and try to read some more.

"You are going to get him out of it, right?" Edwin asked, clenching his fists. It was weird looking at him like this. I swore I could see everything in his mind. He might not have been upset, but I could tell he was angry – with me and his brother.

Funny how you can see an emotion so clearly on a person's face the way they're looking at you. From the way their head moves, their arms, legs, nose, and mouth – everything has a meaning behind it.

"I'm going to try."

CHAPTER SEVENTEEN

Edwin seemed more than calm when he sat beside me on the couch, a cup of tea in his hand as he offered me the mug. I took a sip, lifting my legs to my chest as my head fell on the cushions. I had kept his brother asleep for three weeks, and though he had taken the news very well about his brother, he did seem to start to miss him.

"Tell me, elf," he started, bringing the cup of tea away from his face. "When do you plan on waking up, my brother?"

I click my tongue, focusing on the dagger that Beckett would always carry. My fingers touched the name... Elodie. Elodie. El-odie. A unique but uncommon name, and I found it strange, a random woman's name carved on his dagger. "When I know he's learned his lesson."

"Three weeks is not enough?" He asked, just as the werewolf came down the stairs. Her footsteps are soft but loud enough for us to notice them. Unlike the elf, Arabella didn't bother me one bit about it. Instead, she seemed thrilled about it more than I did. Without the horrible tyrant prancing around, the days seemed brighter - nicer to enjoy.

Doing the ritual on him was the best thing I could have done, or as Devyn likes to say, cursing him.

Devyn, on the other hand, disagreed with my actions and continued to call me childish for my actions. She hasn't talked to me since that night.

I'm happier without Devyn nagging me.

Just then, Devyn walked into the room, wearing a flowy black dress. She glared at me before walking past us and through the front door. Most of the time, Devyn wasn't even around. She stayed outside or in the basement. It's where she resonated, and the only time you can hear something is the classical music in her meditation room.

Arabella shoved at Edwin's hair before sitting next to him. The elf glared at the werewolf, fixing his hair before hurrying away. He fixed the collar on his shirt, avoiding the werewolf's eyes. "You smell." he hissed at her, scrunching his nose in disgust.

"It's called lavender, Brooker," Arabella retorted, cocking her head to the side.

I sat up on the cushion, suppressing a yawn. Just then, Devyn came back inside. Sammy twirled around her neck, resting on her right shoulder. Its eyes closed, and she petted his head. Edwin looked at it and scowled before moving to the opposite couch, away from the door.

Arabella used this opportunity to scoot towards me slowly. Once Devyn was out of the room, we turned to Edwin. "What does Devyn think she's doing, carrying around a snake like that? She does know that it could eat her whenever it wants to?" Edwin exclaimed.

"It'll only attack you if it hasn't been fed," Arabella explained.

Edwin huffed and walked out, his footsteps heavy as they descended the stairs.

My eyes were glued to Arabella for most of the time. As if sensing, she turned to me, raising an eyebrow. "You look like you have something on your mind.." I looked away, my shoulders slumping. "You can tell me. I'm not Devyn or Beckett."

"I wanted to ask you about that actually," I breathe, playing with the dagger. I swiped it when Edwin wasn't looking, but I didn't plan on stealing it. I would return it eventually.

"Well then please say it instead of leaving me in suspense," Arabella chuckled, turning her body towards me.

"Well…I was just wondering why exactly you're here? I didn't ask you to leave your home for me, but you did. I practically forced my way into your home and you still don't have a grudge against me. Why?" I asked, turning my head towards me.

Arabella cocks her head, eyebrows scrunching as if she is thinking, but she only shrugs before giving me a small smile. "Would you believe me if I said that I was bored?" As if noticing my dumbfounded expression, she leans her back into the cushion. "It was so boring in my cave, and it was the same routine over and over again. Wake up, hunt, and go to bed until it is winter time."

My mouth dropped open slightly, shaking my head. "So you only came so you could be entertained?"

She nodded, "Exactly, and hell has it been entertaining. I've had more fun in the past few weeks than I have since the war started."

I scoff, the curve of my mouth widening. "You're insane."

She shrugs, a small laugh escaping her. "Maybe.."

Just on cue, Devyn comes strolling back into her room. This time, she's got a big brown book in her hands. Her eyes travel over the words in the book before she looks up at me. "I found a way to undo the curse."

"Ritual," I correct.

She narrows her eyes at me and then takes several steps forward, facing the book in my direction. "It takes some practice to do, and it might be the only-"

"It won't work," I interrupt. Devyn's mouth clamps up, and Arabella raises an eyebrow. "That's a counter spell. That won't work for a ritual."

"It will work on a curse," Devyn retorted.

"I didn't curse him," I say, clenching my hands against my leg. "I couldn't have cursed him because I don't know how."

"You can keep on living in denial for the rest of your life, but I'm not going to ignore the simple signs in front of me. Call it a ritual, I don't care, but you're going to learn this, and you're going to get Beckett out of his deep sleep."

"I prefer when he isn't around, actually," I kick my feet up on the coffee table, shrugging my shoulders. "I prefer it when both of you are not around."

I'm about to smile in triumph when suddenly Devyn's hand shoots out, and the entire coach goes flying, with Arabella and I sitting on it. It crashes against the window, which shatters the glass. We both fall face-first onto the ground, and I wait for the coach to hit us, but it never does.

Looking up from the floor, I see the coach flying. Then my eyes travel to Devyn, who holds her arm out, and from the looks of it, she's trying to decide if she wants to crush us both. Her eyes narrow in on me, her eyebrows raising. "So, are you going to learn it or not?"

I laugh, chewing on the inside of my gums. I look towards Arabella and see her pushing herself off the ground, glaring at the witch. "Well?" Devyn demands, and I look back at her.

"Well, since you asked so nicely…" I answered her. She smiled then and brought the coach back to where it originally was supposed to be, and then, with a swipe of her fingers and a little Latin, all the broken shards formed back into the glass window. "We start tonight," she says, and then walks away.

Arabella helped me up to my feet and then patted down my clothes to get rid of any dirt or dust that might have gone on me. "You're bleeding," she states, licking her thumb before swiping her finger across my lower lip. "Does it hurt?"

"No," I say, breathless, licking my lower lip.

Most of Devyn's hatred was angled towards my ignorance to her letters, but I can tell there's something deeper than what it seems. Like there's something she isn't telling me, and it only made me want to know more.

CHAPTER EIGHTEEN

A book falls onto the table with a noisy thump that echoes throughout the library. "I've been researching." The witch's voice cooed as she rounded the table. In a circle, she pulled her hands behind her back. The book Malice, No Mercy. The binding was screwed shut by no other than the witch's magic. "Ever since I saw how you cursed Beckett, I've been trying to read about your magic more - see exactly what you are capable of."

I suppressed an eye roll and leaned back in the chair, crossing my hands. "Was that when you were ignoring me?" I asked, raising an eyebrow. I don't miss Devyn's glare as she waves her hand. The book opens quickly, dust flying everywhere in my face from the table. I wave my hand in the air, letting the particles fly away from my space.

"This is serious," she snapped.

"As am I," I glared back at her and then sat up. "Honestly, I'm not in the mood." I start to walk away, but when my body hits the railing, I feel something heavy come over me, and suddenly, I'm thrown back a few inches. I stumble, remaining on my footing, and then looking back at the witch. "Let me out."

"Sit down." She shoots the chair right towards me until I collapse onto it, and then it spins around so her body faces me. It moves right towards the table, in the exact position I had been sitting in only a few seconds ago. Devyn's hand shoots out, grabbing onto the chair so that her hand is right next to my head. "I will tell you something, and you will listen."

I huff, pushing at her chest until she let go of my chair. She scoffed at my behavior before she took the book on the table and flipped to a specific page, her finger trailing over the words.

"Do you not want to know about your powers?" She questioned, raising an eyebrow. "You are quite agitating when you're angry. No wonder that elf, Beckett, hates you so much."

I cross my hands, biting back a nasty remark. "Are you friends with him now?"

"Beckett is not my friend," Devyn assured as she flipped a page in the book. Her eyes were unmoving; she bit down on her lip in concentration. "Now, will you stop being stubborn and let me finish?"

I shrugged. "I might as well, considering you forced me down in this chair."

Now, she smiled; it was the first genuine smile I had seen her wear since I had gotten here a month ago. She then drops the book back onto the table. "Elves are tough creatures to understand. With vampires and werewolves, they have their powers and weaknesses, but it isn't straightforward with elves. There isn't just a certain type of elf, but millions of different ones. It's hard to battle one, considering you don't know what the elf possesses." She brushed Sammy's head, which intertwined its body with her neck.

"For example…" She flipped one of the book's pages when a book by a shadow elf appeared. "Beckett is a shadow elf. He's known for possessing shadows, controlling people's minds through his shadows, and influencing their minds until they go crazy. He is a mighty elf," Devyn said. "Edwin is an earth elf. He can manipulate anything as long as the world has created it. He can use the power of dirt itself. It is why he could break through my barrier when you guys first arrived here. He was the only one strong enough to do it. He was the main source even if he had his brother's help." She exhales. "Those two can be frightening together if they fuel each other."

My hands tighten around the arms of the chair, my face scrunching up. I knew that Beckett wanted to kill the king, and then what? What would he do with that power afterward? Would he ruin the world like the tyrant he is? If so, would his brother join him?

Edwin was always kind to me, but his love for his brother was dominant. I have no doubt they would burn the world for each other.

Devyn went on. "But yours…it was hard to pinpoint," she admitted and then sat down at the opposite side of the table. "Your magic is almost like a witch's, dangerous but confusing. I'd like to know, what exactly causes you to be able to use it? Do you know?" She crossed her hands over her chest.

I shrugged. "I don't know."

"You do know," she says, catching me in the lie. My heart accelerates as her interrogation begins because I had never been able to cast magic, not since a few weeks ago. The sight of blood made my adrenaline rush.

"I think I know," I admit. "It's the blood. It could be my own, but it's stronger when it's someone else's. I don't know how to explain it. It's there, and the power - it just takes over. I can control it sometimes, but I break if I get too angry or emotional. The powers take over my entire body until I'm not even there anymore."

"Of course it is," Devyn replies. "It's because you don't know how to control them fully. If they started to show when you were younger, you'd have a much better chance at not letting these powers affect you, but you're a late bloomer, and these powers you possess are ancient. They come from a dark elf."

I scoff. "Don't you dare say that."

"You're being stubborn again," she said, and grabbed the book, flipping to the page where all the information was for dark elves. "According to this book, dark elves are only known to show their powers when confronted with things of the inner body." Her eyes narrow at me. "Like blood."

"They've been instinct–"

"I know that," She snapped. "But not everything you read in books is true, Blanche." She leans forward. "The only thing that's off about them is their personalities. They tend to kill others and feed off them. As other elves say, they are cannibals."

"Even if I was one," I started, rubbing my thigh nervously. "I could not be a full one. My father is a stone elf. My mother was a light elf. The genetics do not match up."

"You don't need genetics to make an elf," she continued, biting down on her lips. "And it's safe to presume your father must have known."

"No," I assured. "My father made me study every day when I was little just to see what powers I contained. He could not have known."

"And what if he were lying?" She queried. My eyebrows furrowed at her accusation, and I opened my mouth to argue, but she cut in. "Would it be surprising if your father hid the truth from you? You are considered dangerous, after all."

"And what about your mother?" The mention of her caused me to stiffen, and Devyn closed the book, binding it shut, and let it float away until it went to its spot on the shelf. "Your mother left you and your father to fend for yourself. Why would she do something like that unless she was hiding something?"

I stood up. "That's none of your business."

"Perhaps she decided that having a dark elf as a daughter was too much," she continued, despite my argument. "Being a dark elf herself was already a lot, and now, she passed it down to her only daughter. It must have been traumatizing. Plus, a young baby's power is always reckless. Maybe she thought she would have been caught if they knew she had passed it down to you."

"Shut your mouth, Devyn," I demand.

"Don't be daft, Blanche," Devyn says, standing up. "You go years without knowing your true powers, and suddenly they appear? Don't you find it interesting?" She walks up to me until her face is only a couple of inches away from mine, and she tilts my head up with her finger so that my eyes stay directly on her. "It's peculiar, and I want to figure it out."

I shove her away. "Well, stop. I don't need you digging into my past or mind."

"Something is happening, and you can pretend all you like, but I won't stand here and pretend that your revealing powers were just a coincidence." Then she grabs another book from the shelf and turns to a page in the book. She shoves it into my chest. "If it isn't a curse, then you can boast tomorrow. You study this tonight, and we put it to the test tomorrow."

I look down at the book and see the counter spell for the curse. When I look up, I see her walking away.

The thought has me on edge, how my mother, who once kissed me on the head at night, disappeared the night she had promised to stay with me forever. Except for the tragedy, it didn't have much effect on me at that age. I knew the moment she wasn't on the other side of the bed with my father, I knew I would not see her again, and yet, it didn't affect me much.

My father raised me well, and as long as I had him and myself,

I didn't need a mother who couldn't care less about my family. I scrunch my nose at the blurry sight in front of me. I wiped my eyelids furiously, curling my hands into fists as I descended the library stairs.

I didn't wait till the next day to try to bring Beckett back. As I walked up the stairs, I entered Beckett's room. Edwin was nowhere to be seen, so it was just me...and him. I walked up to his sleeping figure. With one hand, I carried the heavy book; with the other, I reached down to take Beckett's hand.

I brought his hand up to my forehead and closed my eyes. His skin was cold against mine, and I frowned. It was as if he was dead, but not entirely. His heartbeat was slow, and I wondered what was happening inside his mind. I saw only a glimpse of his worst memory. Right now, I would like to dive in and learn more. Maybe another time.

I let go of his hand and placed it back on his sheets. I look at his face once more. Without realizing my hand trails up to his cheek, feeling the sharp jawline he always seems to clench when he's frustrated or angry. What would he do if he saw I was touching him like this?

Would he slap my hand away?

So, instead of thinking about it more, I sat on the ground, right in front of the bed, and put the book on the floor. In the book, it says to cut my wrists.

Great.

Instead, I took my dagger and made an indent into my palm. If I lose more blood than I have in the past month, I'll have no blood left by the end of it. The same trail of blood runs down my hand until one drop of blood falls onto the page. I curse, feeling like I did last time - when I cursed Beckett.

Damn it, it's not fair.

Why does it have to be blood?

I can feel the way it has my adrenaline rushing, but I ignore it all as I look at the spell once more.

Rub blood on paper before inducing counter spell.

At the top of the page, I bring my palm down on top of it. My hand stings as I move it. Most of these spells are in Latin, and it's obvious this is all witch's magic. However, Devyn is somehow convinced only I can do it. I read the directions.

Say words out loud over and over until the spell is finished.

It doesn't tell me how many times I say it; other than that, I need to keep on saying it over and over again.

I don't have time to think since my mouth moves, and Latin pours like a song. When it doesn't work the first time, I close my eyes and rub my hand even harder on the book, making me grunt. I repeat it.

Nothing.

Again.

Nothing.

Again.

Nothing.

I've said the counter spell about fifteen times before I ultimately give up. I stand back up and round him. I see his eyes closed, barely breathing, only in a deep sleep. I wonder if there was another way…

I thought back to the millions of books my dad made me read. *"You must read every book!"* He demanded and put twenty books down in front of me. *"You have three weeks to read all of these.."* Now, I realized just why he made me read them all. He was trying to bring my powers to life, but I could never see them because the only thing that triggered them was the sight of blood – the feeling of it on my palms. It made me feel powerful.

I stretched my hand until it met his chest, right where the bloody pentagram I had drawn on him with my blood. With the blood, I let it soak into my hand, linking with his brain. I explored without looking too deep. I tried to find just where Beckett was– what he lived through. I started chanting. Latin rasped from my mouth when I finally saw the brightened memory I desperately tried to find.

I did not want to go into his mind, fearing I might see something I shouldn't see. I let my fingernails dig deep into his head, marking the dents I would soon make. I wanted to explore and see what his mind was capable of, but I resisted as the Latin verses slowly ended.

I opened my eyes, let my fingertips go, and then smeared the blood on his chest with my finger.

A gasp, a breath punctured by the hassle of emotions, screamed through the room when Beckett's eyes snapped open, sitting up abruptly. He coughed, green mush coming out of his mouth. Beckett threw up, his hand hanging low in utter embarrassment. He slowly looked at me, and his eyes were teary momentarily like he had been crying.

"Everard." My last name on his lips was breathless, like he had been running miles for weeks. He opened his mouth to say something but threw it all over him and on the bed.

I moved away from him at the horrible odor. His room was a mess of blood and vomit. His eyes were wide, hair a bundle of waves and curls. I took a step back, his eyes throwing daggers at mine.

Then his fists clenched, eyes dilating, as he said: "I'm going to fucking kill you."

CHAPTER NINETEEN

eckett took a handful of water and splashed it onto his face again. I lay against the door, hands crossed, as he patted his face dry from the vomit. He had changed his clothes into new sweatpants and a long T-shirt. Except now, his sheets were stained with vomit.

Weird. The spell had only worked when I touched him.

He rubbed his head one last time and then took a sip of water I had provided him. It was the only thing I could do since I had made him relive his worst memory. Beckett looked at me with narrowed eyes.

He was upset. I knew that much.

"Did you like it?" He suddenly demanded, turning his head slightly to look at me.

I raised an eyebrow. "Pardon?"

"Did you like seeing me all bloody and defeated?" He spoke angrily. He pushed himself from the sink, steps coming closer until he towered over me. I could not move, not even when I begged my own feet to dodge him. He was right above me, my eyes looking up at him. He was so tall, making me seem more petite than I was. His body was so close, and I could hear his heart beat fast - angry? Frustrated? It did not make sense to me.

The doors of my heart were pounding, threatening to explode through the confinements. His body flushed with mine, so close it could be considered unholy. "It wasn't a terrible sight." My eyes enlarged, and my entire body tensed. At the same time, I wanted to push him away and pull him closer. I exhaled and closed my legs to keep from falling. "But I didn't mean to."

He scoffed, face getting closer to mine. "You drew a pentagram on me." Then he cocked his head, a mocking smile coming across his features. "You knew what you were doing."

I scrunch my nose, lifting myself on my tippy toes until our foreheads touch. "You're lucky I didn't do worse."

Suddenly, his hand comes out and wraps around my throat until he slams my head against the wall. My body aches as it lifts into the air suddenly. My feet dangle, and I'm being held in the air by just the force of his hand on my neck. I choke, air escaping my lungs. "Funny how we end up in this position again," he teases.

Choking out, "Let me go."

Then he drops me fast until I crash onto my feet and wobble. I glare at him and shove him away. "I should have kept you in that nightmare," I tell him before I brush past him and approach my bedroom door.

I've woken him up. I could deal with Devyn's smugness tomorrow, but now I must go to bed.

I make it to my door before I realize he's behind me. I turn towards him with my hand on the door handle. "Go to bed, Beckett."

"In my blood-soaked vomit sheets?" He asks, smiling mischievously. "No, I don't think so."

"Then go sleep on the couch with Edwin. He'll be happy to see you're walking and breathing," I snap. He doesn't say anything to that and instead extends his hand until it rests on the doorknob, on top of my hand. He turns my hand, and the door opens. Without wasting any time, he walks forward.

I frown. "What do you think you are doing?"

He starts to lie down on the bed, grabbing the blanket. "Going to sleep."

"This is my bed," I demand. "You can't sleep here."

"Tonight, it's mine," he says and then lifts his head. "Go ahead and sleep on the couch with Edwin." My own words were thrown back at my face. "Unless you would like to share the bed. There is plenty of room." His head falls onto the pillow I usually use. He turns to his side, the blanket covering his body.

I groan. I grab my pajamas and change while Beckett's eyes are closed, and then I go to the other side. I close my eyes, feeling the way my heart skips. I would not sleep with him tonight. I approach his figure and yank the blanket out of his grip. His eyes open, and he frowns. "I'd rather be doused in gasoline and set on fire than spend a moment with you in bed," I snap.

Then I whip around and carry myself out of the room.

When I wake up I'm in bed, but yet, I'm not.

My body is here, physically laying in bed but my mind isn't. I can see dark figures roaming around me, and I shake my head, dizziness forming in my head. I can see the shadows circling around my body. My eyebrows scrunch, but then just as suddenly, I'm not in bed anymore. I see myself laying in bed, my hypnotized body, sleeping.

Then I see him. His blonde hair walks around my room, the shadows exploding around him like a hurricane. It's frightening to watch, and as he comes closer to me I realize that his eyes are directly on my sleeping body - taking me in - exploring me in a way that I have never seen before.

He sits right next to my body, and his hand reaches towards my forehead, and that's when I see it. The shadows from him explode into me. As if my body can sense it, I resist. My body spasming in a few directions, my head moving from left to right, my mouth murmuring something in my sleep. Christ.

I'm confused. Scared to even know what the hell he's doing. Just as my nightmare ends, I feel it. The excruciating headache.

CHAPTER TWENTY

When I woke up from my slumber, all I could feel was the unpleasant headache that occurred. I remember my dream vividly, feeling the pain in my head, and the way the shadows were all over my body. The next thing I notice is the hand currently lying on my stomach. It takes a second for me to realize it's not my hand.

I look next to me and see Beckett, eyes closed, still sleeping. His head rests near my shoulder, his nose almost touching my skin. I close my eyes and swallow the nausea that suddenly hits me.

After swearing that I would sleep on the couch, I was welcomed with Edwin snoring from the opposite coach and realized I had to come back to my room, which I, unfortunately, had the displeasure of sleeping with the vile elf.

I put my hand over his and then rest his hand on the sheets beside me. I then lift myself from the bed as quietly as I can. I face the open window. The sun has no mercy as it blares through and burns my eyes. It's been a while since the sun shined so brightly.

I walk into the closet and grab a pair of pants and a shirt. I look back at the sleeping elf and see his eyes remain closed. With my back facing him, I pull my shirt off and then exchange it with my shirt.

Still, I think about my dream. It seemed so real - too real, which has me wondering, was it truely a dream? Goosebumps appeared all over my body, as if sensing something is wrong. I've known something is very wrong since the moment I stepped into the cabin, but now looking back, I realize it has been like this the moment I had sent those dybbuk's to the underworld.

I didn't get my nightmares as much anymore, instead I woke with horrible headaches. Although my headaches had stopped as soon as I cursed him. So what did this mean?

Was he behind my headaches? Or was I being paranoid?

"Good morning." His voice has my eyes widening, and I turn back to him. He's sitting on the pillow, and hands crossed across his lap while his legs are splayed out in front of him, tangled in the blanket. His hair is a tousled mess on his head, his eyes drooping in drowsiness.

"How long have you been awake?" I demand.

"Don't worry," he says, curling his lips into a mischievous smirk. "I didn't see anything interesting." That insult should send me forward, threatening to curse him repeatedly, but I hold back, my lips bending. "What were you saying yesterday? About dousing yourself with gasoline?"

"Don't let this get into your head, Brooker. Your brother snores, and I can't sleep with him. So, I came back," I retorted while running my fingers through my messy hair.

"I don't like Edwin's snoring either. Maybe I should move in here and keep you company," he teased me.

"I prefer the bed to myself."

I fix up my shirt, removing any wrinkles that might have formed - anything to get my mind off the vile elf. He stares at me, and for a moment, I feel the need to stare back, but I huff and start to walk off when he says: "I'm going to tell them all today."

I stop and turn back around. Beckett is getting out of bed now. I assume he's talking about his plan - to stop the king. The more he talks about it, the more I doubt his plan. I don't fully know his dreams, only his intentions. "Good luck."

"Over dinner," he says next. "I'm going to tell Edwin today."

I frown. "You haven't told him yet?"

He cocks his head, eyebrows raising. "I was going to tell him a few weeks ago, but…my plans were delayed…" I scrunch my nose and then turn back around. I never thought Beckett would keep something like this from Edwin. I'm the only one who knows what he is planning.

I walk out the door and shut the door behind me.

"I see Beckett is awake," my heart jumps when Arabella speaks. She stands just outside her door next to me, which means she likely just left her room. What a coincidence. "And sleeping in your room too." Her lip curls, and I can't see if it's from suspicion or disgust.

"Yes, it was the least I could do since I cursed him after all," I retorted. Not that I wanted it.

"You guys woke me up, you know," she said, and then, with a flick of her finger, she told me to follow her. We walked away from our rooms until we were by the stairs. She's taking slower steps. Her speed is slow, even though she walks pretty fast. "Can I talk to you about something?" I ask.

I needed to tell her about my nightmares, especially last nights nightmare. It was too real.

She stops for a moment, looks up the steps just as Beckett rounds the stairs and starts to head down. "Weird. I needed to talk to you too."

From the look on her face, I could tell it was serious, and as she looked at mine, she realized I was just as serious. Her hand brushed mine, grabbing onto it, and she pulled me towards the kitchen. Her hand was comforting, and a squeeze to it let her know I needed it. Needed her.

We walked past the kitchen, going towards the front door, just as Beckett descended down the stairs. His presence sent a chill through the room, and as if sensing, Edwin turned in his sleep. He was half asleep, but yet as he looked at his brother, his eyes widened.

"You're awake!" He said, before he jumped up and embraced his brother in a big hug. He patted his back and kissed him on the cheek, smiling excitedly.

"Alright, alright," Beckett said, pushing him off and shaking his head, but I saw the amusement in his face, the way he was holding off smiling. He had missed his brother too.

'Where are the two ladies going?" Edwin asked, looking at us.

"Just to the library," Arabella said, before raising an eyebrow at them. "Would you two ladies like to join us?"

Edwin scrunched his nose. Beckett turned the other way, as he grabbed a piece of bread and started to eat it.

She lead me down the hall, her hair in a ponytail whipping at me any chance it could. When we enter the library, she points towards the stairs. I let her lead me up the stairs, towards the back of the floor, where no one could hear us, not unless someone intentionally was spying on us.

We were here now, and I needed to tell her. Tell her something I could not tell others. Yet as I open my mouth to say what I want to say, my words die in my throat. Could I even trust her? I barely know her.

"I understand," Arabella says as if she's reading my thoughts. "It's okay. Just take your time."

Those words bring me ease, because out of everyone here, Arabella should be the one I trust the most. She's grown to be a friend, or at least, close to one. "I have these nightmares." I start to say, my voice shaky. "Normally they're useless. Some of them feel real while others don't, but...I had a nightmare last night. It was Beckett, and he was doing something to my mind...I've never seen anything like it before."

Arabella straightens her back. "Is it his shadows?"

I frown. "Yes. How did you know that?"

She bites her lip, and I can see the clocks ticking in her head, trying to piece this information together. "I didn't want to say anything, but after what I saw last night, I knew I needed to tell you. I couldn't keep it from you anymore." My eyebrows furrow, feeling my legs go numb from anticipation.

"I've been hearing footsteps for weeks now, going into your room. It would always wake me up at night, especially since my hearing is so pristine, but they stopped when you cursed Beckett. At first I had thought it was just you, but then I started to compare your footsteps to the others, and I realized those footsteps weren't yours. They were heavier, bigger and louder."

My head hurts, and I'm not exactly sure what she will say next, but I hope it's not what I'm thinking.

"It was Beckett. Ever since we got here, I've heard him go to your room. So last night I went into your room, and thankfully the door was open, because whatever nightmare you had, I think it had something to do with Beckett. He was using his shadows and forcing them into your mind."

I breathe heavily, feeling the confusion and worriedness disappear from my shoulders as it's replaced with anger and frustration. All at once it hits me what he's doing. His shadows are meant to torture the mind, so why wouldn't he want to torture me or worse, manipulate me somehow.

Is that why my powers have shown more frequently, because he's been messing with my mind?

My fists clench, feeling the burning feeling in my stomach and throat, threatening to lash out.

"But why...I don't understand. Why would he be messing with my mind?" I asked myself mostly, but Arabella shrugs, biting down on her bottom lip.

If this was all true, it meant Beckett has been lying to me from the beginning. He's been using his shadows too...manipulate me - to hurt me somehow, all while I'm asleep. I don't understand it all...but I will.

My fists close into fists, my head dropping, and all I feel is angry, because I told Beckett he wouldn't be able to control me, and like a fool, I've believed it, not knowing he's been playing me like a puppet all along.

CHAPTER TWENTY ONE

I shut the door closed behind me. My mind is plagued with darkness. I can't even trust my thoughts anymore. Beckett might be making me believe certain things. Perhaps he already succeeded in manipulating parts of my mind.

"Your back," his voice pierced the silence, and my eyes widened. I lock the door behind me, my fists clenching on my sides. I put my head down, staring at the hardwood floor beneath my feet.

"Are you alright?" His tone is laced with the slightest amusement, making me want to cry and hit him simultaneously.

'Tell me, Brooker," I start, feeling the way my breath stutters. "Why do you hate me?"

There's silence for a moment, but I don't lift my head from the floor. My jaw clenches, and I control my breathing. My eyes travel up to him. I feel my face grow hot when I see Beckett staring intently at me. Either he knows I know, or he's trying to act innocent.

"Your face is red, Everard," he says, taking a few steps closer. "Are you ill?"

"Answer the question," I demand, and he raises an eyebrow. All he's done is mock and make fun of me for a month now, and I want to know why. "Why is it that you hate me so much? What have I done to you?"

He takes a step closer. "I never said I hated you."

My entire body moves, and I swing my hand at him, only for him to grab it midair before it hits his face. I'm only inches away from his face, and in this position, I should be embarrassed;

instead, I feel nothing but anger and sadness. "Why wouldn't you hate me?! You treat me like scum and then manipulate me." I use my other hand to try to punch him, but just like the other, he catches it quickly.

"What are you going on about?" He demands, pushing me back until my hand hits the door behind me. My eyes widen, and my heart races out of anger. Then, a tear. It escapes my eyes quickly.

"You're a fucking coward," I say, smirking as I look up at him. "You've been using me since day one, right?"

His grip on my hand gets tighter, and he leans in until his mouth is above my ear. "Blanche, you have no idea how easy you are to use."

You have no idea how easy you are to use.

With my leg, I step on his foot. He slightly loosens his hold on my arm, and I yank one of my hands out until I grab onto his hand instead, spinning us both around and slamming him against the wall. It's the first time I've seen him so surprised because, typically, he's in control, and I'm finally letting myself be in control.

"I know you've been manipulating my mind," I argue and clamp my mouth shut, my face growing hot in embarrassment.

I don't like him or consider him a friend, so why does he always make me feel powerless? I can't even think without knowing he's there. I can't wake up without thinking about him. I can't eat unless his eyes are on me. Christ, he's everything I want and hate. "Why did you do it?" I make sure to look him in the eyes. "Why have you been messing with my mind while I sleep?"

The fireplace burned. The raindrops outside clattered on the window that the curtains covered. Instead, Beckett stared, and it made me grow angry. I stepped forward, pushing at his chest until his back was firmly pressed against the wall. "Well, say something!" I demanded.

The clock ticked, and my eyes traveled up to it.

"Do you know the headaches you've been getting?" He suddenly asked, and I looked at him. At my silence, he continued, "Well, I've been the reason behind it. Unfortunately, I can't manipulate your mind without side effects." My eyebrows furrow, and my mouth opens to talk, but he beats me. "Ever since your powers were revealed in the forest when we were fighting the dybbuk's, I wanted to look into them deeper. So when you agreed to my plan, I realized I wouldn't fully have you on my side without that darkness that lurks inside you. I wanted all of you." His breath cascades all over my face. "I want your darkness. I want your light. Most of all, I want you breathlessly under my command."

"So you've been making me your pet, then?" I demand, scoffing.

"No, not my pet. More like a lover," He admitted, and my eyes widened. "It is unholy for you to stand before me and act like you don't know. I want you to be mine."

On command, I see Beckett's shadows suddenly appear, springing from his body fast and surrounding us in a mess of darkness and coolness. One specific shadow wraps around my arm like a glove. It doesn't stir away, but I cannot let Beckett's manipulation get the better of me.

I groan and push at him until his back is firm against the door and might as well break from the force. "You are so bothersome. So unimportant. Why should I help you now? After messing with my mind when you threatened to kill me for doing the same to you?!"

"I was only making sure you'd stay loyal to me," he explained.

"That's not the point," I snap. "You came into my room, messed with my mind, and then helped me afterward to slowly gain your trust. I am not a robot, Brooker, and I won't be commanded like a dog. How dare you treat me like this?!" I felt the burning sensation in my eyes and how my nose stung. One tear fell down my cheek, hurt written all over my face, and I didn't want to know how pathetic I looked standing before him…crying.

"I saw for myself," I admit. "I saw a memory when I cursed you."

"What are you talking about?" He demanded.

"You were tied to a tree and crying," I explain. "You know how sadness and betrayal feel, so why make me go through it too?" His eyes widen with rage, and he pushes me away until I stumble. I manage to catch myself on the bed, nearly tumbling onto it.

"You shouldn't have done that," he argued.

"Oh, like you have a right to talk," I laugh and then look away, not wanting him to see my tear-stained face. I thought coming to Devyn's would be safe, but I've been in danger since meeting Beckett. "Who else knows about this?"

A beat. "Devyn and Edwin."

Of course, his brother knows. Beckett and Edwin know everything about each other, so it made sense they were tricking me from the beginning. I had hoped his brother was different from him, but perhaps I was wrong. However, Devyn I didn't expect. Was that why she desperately wanted me to wake him? So he could keep on manipulating me? "He's been using the tea to poison you or...to make your powers grow." My mouth parted as I remembered the times he offered me tea.

I face to the side and point to the door. "Get out of my room and stay out." Another tear escapes my eye. God, can I be any more pathetic? He doesn't deserve to be cried over. He doesn't deserve anything.

He deserves to be dead.

"Everard..." I turned to him, my eyes red from sadness, and through the darkness, I could see his guilt, but it wasn't good enough. It would never be good enough. "I never went into your mind. My shadows couldn't break through."

I scoff, almost laughing at the ridiculousness of the situation. It was a relief, but a pathetic excuse for his actions. "You have lost all my loyalty. I will never trust you again."

He stood for a moment, before he turned away and walked out of the room.

By the end of the day, everyone knew of Beckett's plans, and I managed to stay the entire day in my room, sharpening my knife and thinking of brutal ways to murder both the brothers and my traitorous cousin. Everyone knew that I now know the truth. Edwin had come earlier, knocking on the door to speak to me.

I didn't want to speak with anyone.

Instead, he wrote me an apology note and sent it under the door.

I crumpled it in my fist and walked to my window. I let the wind take the paper away. I'd never felt so humiliated - so tricked. I had always considered myself intelligent, but I've just been naive. I've been too trusting, and I've not endured the consequences.

The door opened, and I opened my mouth to shout at the intruder to go away, only to face Arabella's innocent face by the door. "Are you going to tell me to go away too?"

I cross my legs and lean against the bed frame. With my face turned away, I answer, "No."

She chuckles and shuts the door behind her. She strolls in. She stops a few feet away, and while she usually wouldn't care about the space, she seems resistant to coming any closer. Whether it be pure personal space or affectionate. I don't want her anywhere close to me.

"So, what do you plan on doing now?" She asks. "Are you still going on with this plan of Beckett's?"

I snap my head over to her. "You know about that too?"

"He told us all a few hours ago," She said back and shrugged. "Devyn agreed and said it would be a fantastic idea. She's getting potions ready for all of us, and we're taking a train."

I roll my eyes. Of course, my dear cousin agreed.

"We leave in two weeks," Arabella finishes.

"Are you coming?" I ask.

She takes a step closer, and although I want nothing but to keep my distance, I feel my heart race faster. My eyes meet hers, and she extends a hand, grabbing my arm. She shifts closer until her head is against my shoulder, and her hand is wrapped around mine. It's like a hug.

"I didn't want to, but if you go, I will," she retorts.

"I have to go," I say, leaning my head on the top of her head. "I still made that deal with Beckett. I need to find my father."

Arabella leans back a little. A bit of her hair sticks in front of her face, but she swipes it behind her ear. She's marvelous - beautiful. "Good. Then I have no intention of leaving without you. Plus, you're the only one that I trust."

"You're right," I say after a few moments. "But I can't trust him anymore. How do I know he won't betray me again?"

"That's the irritating part, Blanche," Arabella sighs. "You can never know if someone is deceiving you unless you know them well."

I look down at her, raising an eyebrow. "Are you saying that you plan on betraying me?"

She smirks and puts her head against my chest. "I wouldn't dream of it."

CHAPTER TWENTY TWO

Two weeks had passed, just when the potions had finished brewing. Between that time, things have grown quiet with Devyn and Beckett, and I couldn't figure out if I was relieved or angry with that. I didn't want an apology. I wanted to get even.

Edwin and Arabella were the only ones that wanted to talk to me. I trusted Arabella more than anymore.

Edwin had been awfully friendly around me lately. I could tell he was trying to win back the trust he had lost, and there were moments where I did give in and trust him, but even then, there was always that deadly thought at the back of my head, taunting me.

Just last night, I dreamt of my father dying right in front of me. I had woken up with a cry, with Arabella by my side. I had been screaming in my sleep, and she had to come to calm me in the dark hours.

It was early in the morning when Devyn called us down to her mediating room. She gave each of us a magical bag to carry all the stuff we needed. Edwin was more than thankful as he gathered all the clothes in the closet. Beckett thanked the witch before he chased after his brother to go pack.

Arabella took one, even though she had packed a decent amount of clothes earlier. She swiped the bag from Devyn, glaring at her before she leaves. "She's always so angry around me." Devyn put her hands on her hips, shaking her head in confusion.

"Perhaps she's mad at you," I say.

Devyn's eyes widened a little as if she was surprised I talked to her.

I spotted the book that she lent me when I was casting the curse right on a brown wooden table. Ever since Beckett stopped messing with my mind, my powers hadn't shown up as much. All I had was constant nightmares and sleep paralysis.

"Blanche-" Devyn starts to say.

"Don't say anything," I interrupt, and my eyes cut to her, my glare visible and directed at her. "I don't want you to apologize." I take a few steps closer. "We can act like a family and pretend that this friendship from our childhood is still there, but it's gone, and I don't want to pretend anymore."

Devyn bit down on her lip before she nodded her head.

We walked back up the stairs together, and Devyn closed the basement door behind me. "I have all the vials, and once I get a transportation portal going, we can go in and then drink the potion."

"Wonderful."

"Good. Then, get everyone situated. I will need some time before we can all go." She walks off towards the hallway, disappearing when she rounds the corner. I hear the footsteps of the others upstairs. Voices were arguing with each other, which I knew only belonged to Edwin and Arabella.

I hurried up the steps. Arabella's door swung open. Edwin came out, hands clasped around his back. When he caught my eye, his cheeks turned red, and he spun around. I almost burst out laughing when I saw the rope tied around his wrists. "Do you mind?" He asked, glaring at me.

I walked forward and untied the knot around his hands. Just then, Arabella appeared at the door. "I'm almost done packing," she said and then slammed the door right in our faces.

"What did you do?" I ask.

"I didn't do anything!" Edwin defended.

I chuckle and then look over at Edwin and Beckett's closed door. "Is he done packing?"

"He should be," Edwin says and puts some distance between us. My eyes remained on the door, but I could feel his stare from the side. There's a moment of silence, full of unwanted tension, that I hate to feel. "I know you still don't trust me, and if I were you, I wouldn't either, but I am sorry, and I know Beckett is too."

"Really?" I almost laughed. "He hasn't said it yet."

"He won't ever say it," Edwin confesses. "You don't know him like I do, Blanche." he says.

Sometimes, I wonder if I really can trust a word that comes out of Edwin's mouth. He's not naive or stupid, and he knows his brother is capable of horrible things, yet he still follows him like a puppy. I wonder, is that what Beckett thinks of him? Just a pet?

Is that why he made Edwin poison me?

I brush past him. This conversation has gotten exhausting, and I'm tired of hearing his name…. over….and over….and over again.

I was still upset at Edwin, and I would live to be angry with him for my entire life for what he had done.

I secure my dagger in my holster. I feel my eyes burn despite me telling myself there is no reason to cry. Yet that doesn't stop the tear that falls down my cheek.

My hand covers my face, wiping my tears as they fall.

He doesn't deserve it.

My hands then turned into fists, and they angrily wiped the tears away. I won't cry again, not for an elf like him. I don't ever plan on crying for him again.

I let the backpack on my shoulder swing on one of my shoulders. Devyn had opened the door to the forest and worked with her hands as she gathered up a small portal. "Do you know when the nearest train to Romanian is going to be?" Edwin asked.

"I looked at the scheduled trains leaving at noon. We'll have to find the train to go to Moldova," she looks back at us, "There won't be a lot of people on the train, but we just have to get past security and we'll be fine." She grabs something from her backpack, and holds up a tiny vial with red liquid. "We'll have to drink these when we get to the cities."

"But why are we specifically going to Moldova? Where is Castor's kingdom anyway?" Arabella questions.

"Brasov is where Bran's castle resides.I can guarantee that Castor is living there and ruling over Romania. But there is no train leading to Transylvania itself. We can thank Castor for that. We need to go to what is close by. And as of right now, that's Moldova."

"Do you have that portal set?" I asked.

"Just about," Devyn said, and then she backed away from the open door. Appearing behind the door was nothing but black. The sunlight was gone and replaced with a sinister black door. "Be careful. I've walked through tons of portals before, but you guys aren't used to it. It might scramble your mind a bit." She grabbed the backpack from the floor. "Alright, who's first."

When no one spoke, she shrugged. "Fine. I'll go." She walked straight through it, her body disappearing from our view.

"My turn next," Edwin said, a little too giddy about this sort of thing. For a dangerous journey, he sure seemed the happiest to go. I watched as the elf followed the witch's moves and then disappeared inside the black hole.

Arabella followed behind until only Beckett and I were left. He looked down at me. "Are you sure you want to do this? This is quite an impossible journey." He teased, his hand flat on my back, playing with the ends of my hair.

I step away from him. I don't look at him, but from the corner of my eye, I can see him staring at me. I can't tell what he's feeling or thinking, and it irritates me. "Are you ever going to talk to me again?" I expect it to come out as more of a tease, but it's laced with something else - something sincere, something like curiosity.

"Apologize," I say.

His eyebrows scrunched together. "What?"

"Apologize, and we can talk." I take a few steps forward. The door, which seemed so far away now, moved farther away from me as darkness coated my vision. My eyes were open, but I felt like sleeping.

Devyn was kind enough to not make this portal so torturous. My hair flew backward, coating my face as I felt myself fall into nothing. I was flying through the air, and then my eyes met something bright - a light - too much light. It was suddenly too bright, to the point my closed eyes were burning.

Then I felt hands around me as I landed on something soft. My eyes opened, and Edwin stood at me with a mischievous smile. "That would have been a rough landing," he commented. I looked around me and saw the place Devyn had taken us.

In a narrow alleyway, where the puddles reeked of murky trash. The opening led out to the city, where a few humans passed by already. In the air, you can hear the hint of jazz playing in the distance, so close, yet so far.

Lines of string went from one window to the opposite building over, and on it held many clothes, from shirts to pants. And on the line there were clothes that I could not imagine wearing. Sparkly black dresses, almost seductive looking.

I smile. I'll have to shop here sometime.

Just then, Beckett came through the portal, and I reclined my head to send him a glare. Of course, he had landed softly on the ground. His eyes traveled over the group until his eyes landed on mine.

Except then, his eyes scanned over Edwin, his hand around my waist, as he held me. He walked over to us, eyes looking at Edwin. "Have you hurt yourself?" He asked me, his eyes unyielding from Edwin. I saw the way his jaw tightened and how suddenly he looked at his brother like he would kill him.

"I'm fine," I reassured.

"Then why are you holding her?" Beckett demanded. A tick in his jaw set tight at his brother, and his entire body grew tense as if he was about to strangle his brother on the point. For what reason, I didn't know.

"She would have actually broken her nose if I didn't catch her," Edwin said and then winked at me. "You owe me a kiss."

I chuckled at his words, unaware of how my cheeks brightened up from the comment. Beckett looked back and forth between us before he stalked away. "Looks like it hit Arabella out," Devyn said, and I looked at the wolf's body from here. She was lying on the dirty ground, hair spread out in different directions, her eyes closed in drowsiness. "Here are the potions."

I jumped out of Edwin's arms and went to her side. She gave us all the vials of liquid. "Just a warning. It doesn't taste great, but it won't hurt," she says. I pop the lid off and smell the atrocious smell of rotten ingredients coating the bottle. I gag and scrunch my nose.

Edwin raises his glass up. "Cheers?" I bring my glass up with his, and our eyes narrow on Beckett. He pops the lid off, sighs, and then brings it up with us. I smile while saying cheers to Edwin. Beckett is the first to swallow it all, following Edwin and me next. My head only spins a little before I taste the disgusting liquid slide down my throat.

A mix of spoiled eggs and magic – hell in a bottle. I feel my inside turn inside out, feeling the liquid travel through my organs. "This is disgusting," Edwin remarks as he clutches his stomach. The bottle drops from his hands.

When I don't feel the burn of the liquid, I raise my head at Edwin and Beckett. "Do I look weird?" I ask Edwin.

"You look the same but without pointy ears," Beckett points out. "If anything, you look less attractive." My mouth slightly drops before he walks towards Arabella. He pulls her up onto her hands and then lifts her up until she's on his back. Her hands are limp, hanging off of his shoulders. Her sleepy head lays on his back. He holds her up, making sure she is stable and doesn't fall. "We should get going. Where do we go, Devyn?"

"We need a car first to get to the train station." She takes out a pocket watch from her pocket. "We have fifteen minutes."

Edwin leans towards me. "Do you know what a car is?"

I look at him, opting to explain. Humans had more access to technology and transportation than supernatural folks. If I had read about it correctly, a car was something you traveled in to get places – far or close.

"How do we get a car?" Beckett asks.

Devyn smiles. "We need to steal one."

CHAPTER
CHAPTER THREE

A car stands outside a city club. There are lights, flashing red, yellow, and green. What I've learned so far is that when it's red, cars stop, and when it's green, cars go. Although I don't know what the yellow light is for.

But that's not the end of the lights. There are blue and purple lights that flash in front of the building. One of them says Cinema, while others are big. It's different here. While the forest is normally quiet, here, it's busy. There's so many people, some of them bump into us, cursing at us when we don't walk fast enough.

I don't know if I like it here.

However, right now, we stand next to a big sign that says bus stop. Not sure what that means, but it's not my main focus right now. My main focus is the man across the street. He holds up a pipe, and inhales it. A stream of smoke leaves his mouth as he blows it out the open car window he sits in. Cars rush past him in a rush, honking.

I had never been to the cities before - my father forbade it. However, it became apparent that this place was much different than our village.

The buildings themselves were made from red bricks, which was impossible to find in a forest.

There were cars here, transporting from one place to another. The humans were lucky to live in this kind of establishment. There was restaurants you could sit at and enjoy food. There was so much here that I wanted to explore, but I could not.

"So how do we do this?" I ask.

"Can't we just go up to him and drag him out of the car?" Edwin asks and then looks at the man smoking. "And what is that? The thing he is smoking?"

"It's called a cigarette. It's what humans do to feel relaxed," Devyn explains. Surely, this was amusing for the witch. She was basically our guide in the cities, as we had never been here before.

"How come there are no cars in the forest?" Edwin demands.

Devyn looks back, crossing her hands. "Cars aren't meant to drive in a forest. It's meant for a road. Now, stop asking me so many questions and help us decide what to do." Arabella shifted on Beckett's back, and he looked back to make sure she hadn't woken.

"I've already given you an option," Edwin pouts.

"If we do this, we have to do it now," Beckett chimes in and looks back and forth on the road. "Hold her." He puts Arabella on Devyn's back. He grabs my wrist and looks for a clearing. Before I could scowl and pull away, he yanks me with him on the road and heads straight for the black van. I curse just as a car whirls past us in a rapid motion.

"Brooker, are you bloody insane?!" I demand.

He yanks open the car door before I can protest, and the man looks at us all in confusion. A cloud of smoke leaves his mouth, and he rests his head on the cushion of the seat. "Who are you?"

Beckett lifts up my skirt, and my eyes widen before I realize he's got my dagger in his hands, and he's pointing it at the mortal man. This is an older man - with pale brown hair and wrinkles all over his head. His teeth are yellow. Some of them had grown black. His lips are chapped, broken, and bleeding in a few places.

"Don't move," he instructed, and the man stopped his movements. The pipe in his hand burned, but he didn't move a muscle at our weapon. Beckett let go of my wrist before he moved towards the man, pointing it towards his neck. "Now, get out of the car."

The man put his hands up. "Hey man, j-just relax. Do you want money? I can give you some money."

"I don't want any money," Beckett glares, the dagger so close that the skin of his neck should be piercing at any point.

"Actually, we could use some money," Devyn interrupts and then looks up at Beckett sweetly. All the others have joined behind us. "How else are we going to get on the train?"

Beckett's hand clenches around the dagger, his jaw clicking

together roughly. "Fine. Give me the money."

Devyn, in the meantime, goes to the back, where she opens the door and then situates Arabella and herself in it. "Let's make this easier." She calls back and then places her hands on his head before she utters a small Latin phrase. "Now, give me all the money you are carrying." She instructs.

Hypnotized, the man pulls out his wallet. The witch holds out her hand just as he places it on it. "Good boy," she coos and then leans into his ear. "Now, go and take a walk, alright?" Beckett and I move out of the way as the man climbs out of the car and starts walking across the street, unaware of the cars heading for him.

They come to a halt, blaring their horns at the man who dared walk into a busy street like a lunatic.

"I'll drive," Devyn says before she climbs into the front seat. Meanwhile, Edwin gets in the backseat, scooting Arabella aside. "Come on, guys, get in!" Edwin persuades. Cars are headed our way, and Beckett makes a quick jump into the backseat while I run around the car and get into the front. Only then does Devyn start the car.

"Have you ever driven a car before?" I questioned.

"No," Devyn answers. "But I've seen mortals drive it, so how hard can it really be?" She goes to press down on the gas, only for it to not move at all. "Why isn't it moving?" She tried to press the gas again, but it didn't move yet again, restricting us in the small spot by the sidewalk.

"What are these things?" I ask, pointing towards a small gear by my side. It had a bunch of letters by it, with a gear to switch from. I had studied the mortal world, and I knew a few facts about it, but I never got to do a full dive into their entire history. I was completely clueless in the cities.

Devyn stares at it. "Maybe if I put it on R..." She shifts the gear up to the R button, and when she presses down on the gas, the car flies backward, causing us to collide with the car behind us. The impact feels like a slam to the back.

"Watch it!" Edwin shouts.

"I'd like to see you bloody drive this thing!" Devyn yells back before focusing her attention on the gears. I look back at the car behind us. The front of it is smashed due to our car. "What about the D..."

She shifts it into drive, and I fully expect us to collide with another car again, but her foot presses lightly on the gas, and that's when the car finally starts to move forward. I sigh, relief bouncing off my shoulders. My relief is short-lived, though, as Devyn pulls us towards the road, in front of many cars, where they honk and blare at us in anger.

"What the-" I hear Arabella's voice. I look back to see she's woken up from her slumber. She's in the middle of the two boys, which is most likely her worst nightmare. "What is going on?" She looks at her surroundings. "Where am I?"

"Good morning, darling." Edwin offers a hand to her, but Arabella slaps it away. "Ouch. I thought you would be a little more appreciative knowing we didn't leave you behind. Beckett even carried you on his back to keep you safe."

Arabella looks at the other brother. "You did that?" Beckett shrugs it off, eyes rolling to look out the window. "You didnt have to do that."

"So I suppose he should have just left you there to rot and die?" Edwin asks. He scoffs and then shifts over to the other side. "What an ungrateful child."

Arabella goes to argue, but Devyn snaps: "All of you stop talking. I can't focus if you are arguing with each other."

Arabella huffs, crossing her hands together. Her eyebrows knitted in frustration as she looked down at the seat. "What time is it?" She asks.

"I don't know. I'm driving," Devyn answers.

"Check whatever that thing is." Edwin ushers towards the electronic radio in front of us. I've seen Devyn have one before, but it was larger and didn't have as many buttons. I look at the screen and press a random button. The sound of classical music starts to play.

The screen also shows the time. Only five minutes till noon.

"We're running out of time," I warn. "Drive faster, Devyn."

"You don't think I'm trying?" She snaps. Her hands whack the middle of the wheel, and a screeching horn sings out of the car. The cars don't budge, and she curses when nothing works. "Damn it, we are going to miss it!"

"Just focus on driving safety," I say, leaning back in the chair.

"Actually, I have a better idea," Devyn explains before Latin leaves her mouth like a song and waves her hand in front of her.

Nothing happened, not anything that I could see, but when she presses down on the gas, I realize she is driving straight toward the row of cars in front of her, full speed.

"Devyn, what are you doing?!" I cried.

"Holy shit–" Beckett curses.

Arabella hides by Beckett, burying her face in his shoulder, while Edwin screeches so loud that even the loud brakes don't have a chance against him.

I close my eyes, waiting for the impact, but instead, I'm met with nothing. "Calm down," Devyn lectures. I look at the road and see that we are driving right through the line of cars faster to the train station. Realization dawns over me.

"Are we transparent?" I asked.

"We aren't," she then looks at me. "But they are."

As we ride through the cars, we take a right. I see the train tracks in front of me. Devyn doesn't try to park like the other cars in the parking lot. She drives up right to the front and stops the car there before she leaves it on the P lever. "Let's go. We have two minutes," Devyn warns.

We all jump out of the car and race towards the entrance. The train station is a mixture of stone and wood. It's built on wooden ground, but the stone exterior has an old effect. I can hear the trains approaching, and we all speed up at the sound. A horn blares and it becomes silent when we enter the inside.

There is a row of lined doors leading to the outside, leading to the outside. "That way," Beckett instructs. We all follow him until we exit to the outside. We walk down the narrow stairs leading to the multiple rails that the trains have parked.

"How do we know which train to get on?" Arabella asked

"We must follow the signs," Devyn says. She pushes past us all, coming to a halt. Her eyes scan over the area. "There." She points to the farthest train to the left. It's a white and red train which looks modern compared to everything I have seen. The windows are fully glass, with blank tints. You can't see anything on the inside. A sign hangs just outside of it, with a man outside.

Moldova.

As we head towards the open doorway, someone stops us. A man - with a black and red uniform. "Pardon me." His accent is not like the others. His hands skim over my arm and pull me to get my attention. "I need your train ticket."

I stare in shock. Train ticket? What the hell is that?

"Sorry, sir, but I'm going to have to ask you to get your hands off of her." A malicious voice comes from behind me. Beckett's looming figure pulls me away harshly before he steps in front of me.

"What do you want?"

"I'm sorry – I didn't know she was – uh, I need to see your guy's train ticket," the man stuttered.

"We're going on the train to Moldova, sir," Devyn exclaims and then steps in front of me.

He nods. "I'm afraid you'll need a train ticket to enter it, ma'am."

As if she were enchanting me herself, I felt the way her magic vibrated off her body. The man stilled, his body growing tense. "Mister, you will distract everyone around us while we enter that train. You won't ask us any questions. You will lead us to a train and make sure no one is suspicious of us."

I nudge her. "You ought to be careful with magic, Devyn. It would be a great scandal."

She raises her eyebrows as the uniformed man in front of us nods and then starts leading us towards the train. As he walks by, the guards wave at each other, and the man does a good job of looking like everything is okay. He stands by the train entrance and then ushers us all forward. Arabella is the first to go, eager to sit down and take another nap. The rest of us follow behind.

Before he could leave, Devyn puts her hand on the man's shoulder. "Now, forget all about what you have seen, mister." He walks away without a second doubt, the witchcraft already mangling his mind.

When we enter the train, we are greeted by a mortal at the entrance, looking delighted as he looks at us. "Heading to Moldova? How wonderful. Moldova is very beautiful. Come, let me show you your compartment." We follow him to our compartment. It's enough room for all of us, but it will be cramped.

"Could we, by chance, have two compartments?" I ask.

He nods his head, and while Devyn and Edwin sit down in the first one, the man leads us to a second one not too far away from them.

It's a smaller compartment, but it would be fine for Beckett, Arabella and me. "There you go, ma'am. I hope you enjoy the ride." He smiles at me but doesn't dare to look at Beckett as he walks away.

I slide open the compartment and let Beckett slide it close behind him. Arabella sits next to me, her presence giving me ease. I sit down by the big window, and put my hands in my lap. I still don't look at Beckett, and as far as he knows, I'm still angry with him.

When the train starts to move, I dread every moment that I made leading up to this plan.

"Are you planning on ignoring me forever, little elf?" I look at Beckett, and see him stretch himself out on the other cushions. "We'll be on this train for a while. Moldova is a long way from London."

I don't answer him.

CHAPTER TWENTY FOUR

Three hours.

Romania is a beautiful country located at the crossroads of Central and Southeastern Europe. It is home to the legend of Count Dracula, Vlad the Impaler - the undead, centuries-old vampire. He was most known for having many enemies and the cruel punishments he would do to them - impaling numerous people on stakes for hours. The slow deaths ceased to have remained in history.

I used to believe that heroes always reigned among villains. It's how every magical story went. The villain did something horrid, and the hero stopped them before it could all happen. Except no one had stopped the villain this time. King Castor reigned in Transylvania. So, are we supposed to be the heroes in this situation?

I look at Beckett. Or maybe the villains.

The train ride had been mostly silent due to the lack of talking between Beckett and I. Arabella had left to go visit the others. Surprisingly, Beckett hadn't talked either. Perhaps he realized trying to play with me wasn't getting him anywhere. Maybe he realized he desired a reaction, and I finally stopped giving him one.

I looked down at my thigh and saw the dagger tightly fitted in the holster. "Do you have your dagger on you?" It's the first thing I've said to him since the train started to move.

He snaps his head to me as if I've startled him. "Are you finally going to talk to me?"

I expect a smirk, maybe even a genuine smile, but he looks curious instead. "I asked you a question," I urged, "Do you have your dagger on you?"

He lifts his head up. "Yes."

"Take it out," I commanded. Without arguing, he reaches into his jacket, pulling out the dagger that he normally used. I stretched my arms out to grab it, but instinctively, he pulled it away. My eyes met his, and his eyebrows scrunched. "I'm not going to do anything. I just need to see it."

It takes a second for him to give it to me, but when he does, the dagger meets my hands like fire. It's cold, big and silver. The blade is so sharp it could cut my whole head off in one swipe. My fingers meet the handle. There's a unique pattern on the top of the handle. Big black crisscross x's.

Then I saw what really pulled my attention to the dagger. I've seen it more than once, and I've always wondered what it meant. *Elodie.*

A name engraved right at the bottom of the knife. It's almost hidden, and from normal eyes, you could never see it, but I can, and I spotted it the day I saw Beckett's knife. I've wanted to know what it is.

"Do you want me to forgive you?" I ask.

Beckett raises an eyebrow. "Did I say I wanted you to forgive me?"

My jaw snaps, and with a split second, I've gone from holding the knife to pressing the sharp blade right at his throat. His back is against the wall, trying to avoid the sharpness, but it doesn't do him too well. "I thought you weren't going to do anything," Beckett says.

I shift in my seat and smile at him. "I can also lie." I see his eyes darken, and his eyes move up from the dagger until they interlock with mine. "On your dagger…there's a name. Elodie. Who is she?"

He smirks. "Are you jealous?"

I press the blade deeper until it pierces his skin. He flinches and closes his eyes before scrunching his nose and looking back at me. He relaxes in his seat, his shoulders unending and his face a blank canvas. "Someone you don't need to know about."

I tense and dread asking this question because the thought had always been in the back of my head, but I had never expressed it in any way. "Is she your lover?" I demanded, trying to keep my voice cool. My heart sprang to life as he turned his head quickly. His mouth opened to respond, but then, he scoffed, and with it, he laughed. He threw his back towards the cushion of the seat and burst out laughing. I frowned. "What are you laughing at?"

"You," He said, trying to control his laughter. His smile gave away the dimples on his cheek and, with it, my dignity. He looked nice, laughing, though he normally didn't smile. "My lover?" My face grew hot from embarrassment. Would it have been a wrong guess? He's an older man - surely, he's been with women before. When his laughing finally cooled down, he looked at me breathlessly. "You never fail to amuse me."

"It's not a bad guess," I argue. "You're twenty years old. I'm sure you've been with many women before." I looked the other way, out the window, where I saw the train moving on the tracks.

I regretted bringing the whole thing up. Right now, I only wanted the silence that Beckett and I had created. I watched as the train jerked and roared outside and thought just a few more hours. By the end of the night, we should be able to be there. Or, at least, close.

I was so close to distracting myself, but as the train hollered, Beckett's voice rang deeper in my ears. I felt the tip of his finger crawl underneath my chin and lightly twist my chin to his side, where I was met face to face with him. His hand reached up and wrapped around my palm on the dagger. With its blade still pointed at his throat, he leaned closer. "I have been isolated in a cottage with my brother my entire life. I have never been with a woman."

He was lying. He had to be. Twenty years, and he hadn't ever been with a woman? What about a first kiss? I nearly gasped as the thought came into my mind.

"What about you, little elf? Have you let a man touch you?" He grew closer till his lips were practically ghosting mine. "Closer than this?"

Curse my heart for speeding up like this. It felt like jumping into a dark abyss whenever he drew close like this. It was exhilarating, but it terrified me, knowing I never knew what he would do next. Breathlessly, I said: "I have."

Something in the air changed, and I could feel him pull away from me. His hand escaped from under my chin, and I felt like he had grabbed my heart and started squeezing it. He wasn't teasing anymore. Instead, his face became tense and full of frustration. "I see." Venom laced his words, and he sat back properly in his chair. "You kissed him?"

I let go of the dagger and let him take it back. "It's really none of your business."

My father made sure that I studied, learned, and trained as a young girl until I knew every scrap of information about the forest, about dark artifacts, and about all the supernatural beings. I was never allowed outside without permission, so I never kissed anyone without permission either. Never let anyone touch me. It was just a simple lie.

His eyes traveled over to me. "So you did. Did you do more than that?" His fists tightened into fists, and for a moment, he looked agitated and angry. No...is he-

"Why are you so angry all of a sudden?" He looked away instantly, and I can sense the frustration that radiated off of him. I reach my hand to grab him, but his own hand reaches out quickly, grasping my hand harshly. His grip is tight, and it hurts as he pulls me closer.

"How dense are you?" He demanded.

My eyebrows quirk up, and I draw back, allowing the corners of my mouth to curve up into a smirk. "Oh my..." I smiled, letting a chuckle escape. "I didn't think you would be jealous."

He immediately let go. "That's nonsense. I'm not jealous."

"Then you wouldn't be so angry," I argue, smiling like an idiot. I relax in my chair and then watch as his face tightens with confusion and frustration. "It's okay to be jealous. Most women and men have their first kiss before the age of sixteen, but I guess in the forest, it's hard to find someone you truly care for. Especially if you have been hiding in that cottage that you lived in."

"Oh, you mean, the one that got infested with vampires... because of your scent." He glanced at me and then shook his head in annoyance.

"Your scent was in that cottage, too!" I argued.

"It doesn't matter anymore because I never plan on going back there. I'll be king in a matter of weeks."

I rolled my eyes. "Of course. An elf as a vampire king. What could possibly go wrong." I crossed my hands over my chest and felt my stomach rise up and down with deep breaths. He was silent, and I turned back to him. "You know, you never answered my question."

He frowns.

"Who is Elodie?"

For a minute he looks like he wants to slap me but then he says, "She's someone special to me. Someone I don't like to speak about. Lets leave it at that."

He turns his head, but I don't push him further. Because Beckett didn't get emotional, you never saw him with his guard down, but I saw now, with his eyes on me, the hint of sincereness and sadness.

The name Elodie haunted him.

CHAPTER TWENTY FIVE

By the time we reached Moldova, it was one o'clock in the morning. It took us a day and a half to get there. During the time we had to cross the ocean, I saw the sea animals playing around while the train rode underneath the waves of the water. I could not sleep, not even when the other elf fell asleep on the bench across from me. I was too cautious. Too afraid he might try to enter my mind again.

Arabella didn't leave my side, and she fell asleep on my shoulder as I stared out the window.

As soon as I left the train, I was excited to feel the air more than I was to actually see Moldova itself. The train was exhausting, and I was only able to get three hours of sleep during the entire ride while Arabella was awake. To my surprise, Beckett slept through the entire night.

Moldova is only a few hours away from Transylvania, which means we could most likely travel on foot, but I knew Beckett wanted to get there quicker. Yet, no one other than vampires was allowed to enter Transylvania, let alone Romania itself. It was blocked off so humans wouldn't get killed.

After all of us had stepped off the train, I looked around. It was mostly empty. The train rattled and then started up again before leaving.

Devyn adjusted her bag on her shoulder. Everyone was consumed with exhaustion. I could tell by Arabella's droopy eyes, Devyn's messy hair, and Beckett's bags under his eyes.

"We need a ride to Transylvania," Edwin announced.

"Actually, we need a place to stay until the potion wears off. We should spend the night somewhere and then find a way in the morning," Devyn says.

"Where are we going to stay?" Arabella asks while yawning.

"A motel will be fine," Devyn says, "Plus, we still have the money we stole. We can use it to get a few rooms."

I scrunched my eyebrows and looked at everyone around me. Devyn caught the expressions on our faces, and then she dead-panned. "A motel is a place we can stay. It has beds and a bathroom, so we can shower."

I see them talk back and forth with one another, but it slows down, and that's when I realize that my mind is growing dizzy. It felt like something was stretching through me, but I didn't know what was causing it, and it was so sudden that it felt like an emotion was coursing through me.

It made me want to puke, but it was the best feeling I've ever felt. The only thing I wanted was to be covered in it - soaked with it, dripping from my mouth, leaking out of my ears, my hands… legs…body, covered in the heaven I found in it.

Then I felt the pain. The mixture of it mixes with the powers in me that have been hidden for so long. They didn't get along well, and my powers, as well as this feeling, burned in my stomach. It felt like my stomach was splitting in half. It shattered into a tiny million pieces.

It was when I looked down at my hands that I realized there was a trail of blood leaking from my left finger. Blood. It was blood that was making me feel like this.

"Everard?"

I don't know who called me, only that their hands made their way toward my body, circling me with their own hands, and everything went dead silent around me. My vision blurred, and I only saw the view of the train station get smaller as I fell to the floor.

I woke up on a white bed.

I did not recognize the place that held itself up. The faint voices of others echo around me. I turned my head to my side and squinted as I saw the bright light of a lamp sitting beside me. It was burning me. *"Is she awake?"* The mumbling voice was distant. The sound of footsteps got closer to her until a figure appeared above her.

I opened my mouth to speak, but the pain of the blood rushing to my head struck against my head, and I groaned in agony. *"Blanche, can you hear me?"* My fingers moved on their own, my hands clouding my forehead. The figure said something else, but I was too out of it to listen. I felt like a fool, drunk on blood.

I moved my hands away from my head and squinted around the figure of the individual. **"Blanche."** Suddenly, the voice of the stranger felt all too familiar.

Black hair with bright emerald eyes. I didn't realize that until now, she had freckles around her nose, brown spots that were so hidden in her skin that they became intangible.

"Blanche, seriously, are you okay?" She knelt beside my bed, so she was face-to-face with me.

"Yeah, I'm okay," I finally responded. I was not okay. Actually, it felt like I was walking on fiery hot rocks. I was unaware of my surroundings, and that freaked me out the worst. "Where...are we?"

"Devyn says it's called a motel," Arabella answered and stood back up. She grabbed my hand and helped me sit up until I saw the thing that was called a "motel."

Gray long walls stood before me, with a painting that was shattered. Beneath my body were white covers, and behind me lay white pillows. Red curtains covered the windows in the room, sealing it dark. The lamp lit the room up, just barely. On the other side of the room was a door to the bathroom, I guessed. Another bed was beside mine, with the same sheets and pillows. Cracks surveyed the wall and looking closely, I could see the specks of dry blood splattered on them. Then, in the middle of the room, lies a small dresser with a big mirror on top. And just beside it, was a small desk, on old chair pulled up to it.

"Where are the others?" I questioned.

"Devyn's in the shower." Arabella ushered towards the closed door, with a yellow light shining through the crack of it at the bottom. "Edwin and Beckett are in the room next to us. Devyn thought it would be a good idea if we just got a good night's rest for right now. We'll need it soon enough."

I felt the dryness of my throat and looked around for something to drink. "What happened?"

"You should be the one telling us that," Devyn sighed. She walked out of the shower with only a towel wrapped around her body and one around her head. She sat down on the bed, the cushion sinking with her weight. "You were the one that fainted on us."

"I–" I open my mouth to explain, but I'm not even sure what happened. One minute, I was okay, and the next, I was feeling dizzy and faint. Then I remembered my cut and how I had been in contact with blood before it all happened.

"Say I am a dark elf, and I really am dangerous," I look back at the two women, "What would you two do?"

Arabella looks at Devyn first, but then she turns back to me. She smirks. "I guess we would have to kill you then." Arabella's smile contorts playfully, but when I look over at Devyn, her face is deadpan, telling me everything I need to know. That she might actually kill me if it ever came to it.

The door rattled suddenly, and a heavy fist slammed into it. We all snapped our heads to it. We all were on high alert, and I even slipped my hand to my thigh where the holster held my dagger. "Come on, let us in!" We heard the comical voice of Edwin, and my hand fell back against the bed.

"Those morons..." I snapped before I stormed towards the door, yanking it open to the two brothers. "What do you want?"

"The beautiful elf is awake and well. That's wonderful," Edwin says, winking at me. I felt the urge to roll my eyes just as he walked past us with a bag full of stuff. Behind him was Beckett. He carried another bag of stuff. He looked at me for just a moment before he sauntered inside the room.

I locked the door behind me.

"Where did you get all of this stuff?" Arabella asked. They dropped the stuff on the dresser, and Arabella didn't waste a second before she started searching through it.

"Stole it from a local grocery store, or whatever was left in it," Edwin says, shrugging his shoulders. "We had to break into it, but nobody was there."

Arabella grabbed an apple from the bag before she cursed. She took one look at it and then scrunched her nose. She drops the apple on the ground, and her mouth thins. "It's all rotten!"

"What? No, it's not," Edwin argues. "I ate an apple earlier, and it tasted perfectly fine."

"She's right," Devyn chimes in, looking inside the groceries. "You broke into an abandoned store, which means you really didn't need to break in at all."

I watched as the three bickered with one another and then turned my head to Beckett. He stared into the mirror as he ran his fingers through his hair. I took a step towards him until my image was right behind him, and we could both see each other in the mirror. He never turned my way. Before I could think, I reached out towards him, and my hand ran through his hair.

He froze and let me fix his hair for him. His hair was soft. He also was so put together, but whenever Beckett had messy hair, it showed just how imperfect he really was. His flaws shone through the surface, and I saw it all in just one single look.

After fixing his hair, my hands slipped back to my sides. "How are you feeling?" I frowned, surprised he even asked such a question. "You hit your head on the cement pretty hard. I don't want you going foolish on me."

I scoff. "I've been through worse," I narrowed my eyes on him. "My mind has been fooled enough." His lips turned into a thin line before he scrunched his nose and looked away from me.

"Will you ever stop talking about that?" He demanded.

I sigh, my hand reaching up to take his chin. I forced him to look down at me. My hand moves down until it comes to his throat, wrapping around it, and he exhales.

Beckett takes a step forward, which makes me take a step back but my foot trips and I start to fall, Beckett's hands reach around my back, holding me up steadily.

I didn't pay attention to the closeness earlier, but now, with so little space between us, it felt like lava was surrounding us. My chest pressed against his, and my hands reached around his shoulders to not tumble back. He leans in slightly, the curls of his hair brushing over my forehead. His lips ghost over mine. It should be unholy for the way he is making me feel.

It feels wrong for my heart to beat for him. Because he's hurt me, betrayed and manipulated me, and it frustrated me to understand why my body could ever feel anything for him.

Then I pushed myself away, feeling myself become completely vulnerable. Not to him. Never to him. "This is a mistake." I whisper, only loud enough for Beckett and I to hear. I look around and see the other three still arguing with each other.

"I don't think its a mistake," Beckett replies, and I look back at him, my eyes widening. He's leaned down again, his mouth grazing my ear before whispering: "I think you yearn for me."

I have to hold myself back from my cheeks reddening, and my eyes widening even more. My bloody heart won't stop pounding. "You're wrong,"I responded, and turned around. My expression hardens and I remind myself of how horrible the man in front of me really is and why I hate him so much. "I'm not interested."

CHAPTER TWENTY SIX

he Bran Castle.

Myths have said that Dracula's castle resides in Transylvania. It is far from where we were, and we haven't stopped traveling. We slept from one motel to another until, eventually, a motel bed felt normal.

Dracula was notorious for punishing many people. He often ordered people to be skinned, boiled, decapitated, blinded, and roasted, but most of all, he loved to cut off people's noses, ears, limbs, and sexual organs. However, this favorite punishment of all was impalement, hence his nickname, Vlad Count Dracula, the Impaler.

Normally, mortals wouldn't believe such a thing, but if you asked a vampire or any paranormal creature that roamed this earth, they would believe it a hundred percent.

The door to our motel room opens, and Arabella walks in with a small towel on her shoulder. She throws it over the bathroom door. "Blanche, you should try the pool some time. It's so soothing," Arabella only wears a pair of underwear and a long shirt over herself. I cross my legs, writing down on the piece of newspaper I found. "I'm running out of clean clothes, so I cannot."

Devyn sits on the bed with a lamp on, and she reads a book of spells.

With each passing motel, our visits get longer, while the motels get emptier. The entrance to Transylvania is blocked. I had read it when the war first started. King Castor had specifically blocked it off, so the entire entrance was unable to walk through. A big stone barrier, right where we should be going. There was one way to get in - to be a vampire.

"There is specific security at the barriers to let vampires in, which means we can't just walk through. We'll have to disguise ourselves as vampires…somehow," Devyn told us a few days ago,

If you weren't a vampire, it was impossible to get in. There were vampires who had blocked off the sky around Transylvania for planes to fly. It was like an isolated Island that was severed from the entire earth. Yet somehow, that same city was controlling the fear of many.

I turn around in the chair. "Has Beckett thought of how to get in?"

Devyn shrugged. "How would I know? I don't talk to him."

"Really? I thought you two were best friends. Especially after messing with my mind."

Her book slams shut, and she drops it onto the nightstand by her. "And aren't you two lovers? Shouldn't you be talking to him?"

My fists clench on the chair, and my eyes widen. "We are no such thing. I don't even know where you got that idea from."

Arabella chimes in, "Blanche, don't act daft. Even I can see it."

My head snaps to her. "We're not lovers. We never have been." I turn around in my chair and continue reading along the lines of the newspaper. Both of them go quiet behind me, and I expect them to stop arguing with me, but then I see Devyn by my side and lift the newspaper away. "Hey, what are you-"

"What are you doing, huh?" she asks and looks at the notes I've made. "Are you drawing?" I cross my hands over my chest. As if I would ever be good at drawing. "Oh, I see. You're trying to keep tabs on the vampires, right? Well, the newspaper never talks about vampires. The mortals don't like to meddle in their business."

I snatch the newspaper away from her. "Why don't you just go back to your corner and leave me be." She seemed surprised by my remark, but just as she opened her mouth to reply, Arabella chimed in.

"Will you both stop?" She demanded. We both look at her. "This trip has gotten unbearable with you two constantly at each other's throats. We're together because we need eachother. So, act like it." She walks into the shower and slams the door behind her.

My foot knocks against the desk, but even now, when I'm standing in front of Devyn, I can't help but look away. She's gotten unbearable to interact with. Each time, let was another argument over something silly, and I couldn't help but fight back.

"She's right, you know," Devyn says. "We're just being childish by constantly arguing with each other." She walks back towards the bed. "Maybe it's best if we act like we like each other."

"We used to like each other," I mumble, but her head perks up at my response. I turn around to my newspaper. "I actually was excited to see you, but…you hate me. For something I never even did."

"You ignored me," her voice rang, and my head turned to the side, not quite looking at her but not fully turning around. "All these years, I sought you, and you couldn't even be bothered to write back to me."

I sighed. "How many times do I have to say it, Devyn? I never got the letters. Your snake must have lost them." With a pen, I got back to circling events in the newspaper that happened a few days ago.

"My snake did deliver them to your doorstep," Devyn then responded. "Your dad wrote me back once."

My hand stops, and the pen with it. I turn my head first and then my entire body. "What do you mean my dad responded? My dad hasn't written to anyone in the past decade."

"He told me you didn't want to speak to me. That you were too busy," She said, shaking her head.

I couldn't respond to that. I had never once thought my father would go behind my back like this. There must have been a reason for it, but I turned around.

"Devyn, I never said that." I promised, but she didn't look my way, but now I saw the truth for what it really was. Perhaps they have been coming, but maybe my father was hiding them. And if he was, why?

After weeks, we've finally found a solution. With a lack of materials, Devyn needed to improvise, and she would be making a potion. It would transform us into a vampire for twenty-four hours. It would help us get in.

My hand reached for the doorknob, and it clamped shut as I tried to walk in. I groan and then slam my fist on the door. "It's Blanche. Let me in," I yell from the outside.

Heavy footsteps echo, and they come close to the door, and then I hear the door unlock. Edwin is the one who opens the door, and he smiles as he looks at me. His hair is a fresh mess on his head, and when he looks down at me, his chest is fully exposed in front of me.

"Put a shirt on, Edwin," I demand, and then search for the other elf. When he's nowhere to be seen, I turn back towards him. "Where is Beckett?"

"By the pool, from what I know. He left an hour ago, so he might be on his way back if you would like to wait." He shuts the door and smiles at me. "Or maybe I can relay a message?"

I raise my eyebrow at him. "How nice, but I would rather talk to him myself."

I walk past him and out the door. I'm walking away from the room when he calls out: "He's probably by the hot tub!"

I walk down the frozen steps. It's gotten colder these past few weeks, and snow has started to fall in Romania. A snow blizzard had appeared the other day, so instead of leaving for another motel, we stayed, and the motel granted us a few more days to stay before we left the next day.

Tomorrow should also be the day that Devyn finishes the potion.

With only my socks on, my feet scrunch in the snow as I hurry down to the outside pool. Beckett has favored the pool at night.

The gate is open, and I pull it open. I spot him before he sees me. He's sitting by the hot tub, his feet dipping into the hot water. His head hangs low, lost in thought. The one thing I hadn't expected to find Beckett was shirtless. It didn't occur to me that he actually was swimming. I thought he was using it to get away from everyone.

My eyes scanned over his body. How desperate I must have become to catch myself in this position, but as I looked down at his sculpted body, it felt like a painting that was made specifically for me. I had seen him shirtless before, but looking at him now felt unreal. I wanted to look away, but he lured me in without even meaning to.

"Enjoying your swim, Brooker?" I ask, walking closer to him.

His head tilts to the side, and his eyes look up at me. He narrows his eyes at me and then looks back to the hot water. "Is there something that you need?"

My head tilts to the side, and I take a seat across the hot tub and take off my socks. He watches me intently as I pull up my thin pants up to my knees and then dip my feet in the hot tub. The hot water burns my feet at first, but it feels amazing after a few seconds. "It occurred to me that you never told anyone about your plan when we got inside Transylvania. I'd like to know."

He looks up. "Is that what you wanted to talk about? A plan?"

My feet move beneath the hot water and create waves with my motions. "What else would I talk to you about?"

He shrugs. "Anything else?"

"You're avoiding my question," I state and lean closer into the hot tub.

He looks up, and then the sides of his mouth curl up, just like it always does when he's going to do something he shouldn't do. He hops off the edge, and his body drowns in the hot water. He ducks down until his entire head is under the surface, and then he rises.

He flips his hair down and then up, the sprinkle of water exploding everywhere, even on my own bare legs. His skin glistens from the water, and my entire body goes still as I look at him.

It's unholy how angelic he looks. My eyes look over his face and then down to his chest, where I see the starting line of his lean stomach and, with it, his abs. I look away for a second, embarrassment flooding me.

He looks much too delicious, and that is not how I should be feeling when the man in front of me is the man I've hated from the very beginning.

"I don't actually have a plan," he answers.

That snaps me out of my trance, and I frown, looking back at him. "You don't have a plan? How is that possible?"

He shrugs, leaning his hands at the back of the edge, and he smirks up at me. "I just don't. I'll think of it when the time comes, little elf. Have some trust in me."

I scoff. "Oh yes, I trust you, my dear elf," I shake my head and then start to lift myself off the ground when his hand comes around my own, and he takes hold of my shoulder. "You should come in."

I look at the hot water below me and then at him. I could tell him the truth and say I don't want to get in because the thought of me and him being so close makes me want to hurl. "No, thank you, I'm not much of a swimmer."

I see his eyes widen slightly, and his pupils dilate. His hand around my shoulder slowly eases up, and I think he'll let go when he trails down my arm and towards my hand, where he intertwined our fingers. He then comes closer, and my entire body tenses when his breath cascades around my neck. "Please."

He slightly pulls on my hand until my head is above his, and his head is right around my neck. My chest heaves up and down. Our arms become tangled with each other, and I can't seem to let go.

I draw my head back for a moment, our eyes locking. My lips parted, and when I stared at him, he didn't look like a man I hated. He looks so much more than just an ally or enemy. "Brooker, don't look at me like that."

He cocks his head, the smile curving. "Don't look at you like what?"

With one final tug, he pulls me into the water, and my pants and a part of my shirt get soaked in the hot water. I narrow my eyes on him. My mouth parts, feeling my feet hit the ground and the hem of my shirt float to the surface. "You're an asshole." I look down and see that he's still holding my hand, even though he's already got me into the water. What else does he want?

"Let go of my hand," I demand, trying to sound as confident as I can, but the slight edge of my voice gives it away, and my legs nearly give it out when he lowers himself into the water. His hand lets go of mine, only for his hands to grab onto my waist and pull me toward him, onto his lap, where he buries his face into my chest, and my head rests against his forehead.

I'm straddling him without even meaning to, and all I can think about is how hard my heart pounds and how I can't seem to move anything in my body. He's taken complete control, and like a fool, I've allowed it. "You have nightmares." It's a statement, not a question, and I cannot deny it.

I have yet to tell him. "How did you know?"

His head leaves my chest and then looks at me, and at the same time, I look down. "I've known for a while." One of his hands moves around my hip until it's trailing around my ribs, up the side of my chest, and then coming around my back softly, his fingers playfully teasing me. "The same way I know you're a dark elf."

My eyes widened, and my hands around his neck tightened. "I'm not a dark elf."

He smirks. "Lie to yourself all you want…" Then, with a harsh pull on my hip, he lowers me closer to him. ".... But don't you dare lie to me, little elf." He's so close, and my mouth dries. I need to get away from him - he's driving me insane.

"We've known each other for two months, Brooker, and yet, you still have not said my real name. Do you even remember my name?" I challenge, raising my eyebrow. He stays silent even though he's been nothing but talkative right now. "You told me that I should call you by your last name unless you told me to stop. Now, I want you to listen to me." My head rests on his, and his eyes flutter close, his breathing getting heavier. "Say my name, Brooker."

When his eyes open again, he looks into my eyes. "I will do anything you ask me to do, but saying your name will come soon enough," he says, and I rest my head on his shoulder from the comfort he has given me. "I am sorry if I have done things that you do not like in the past, and I'm sorry if I have hurt you." My hand slides across his chest until it wraps around his shoulder, and my lips ghost on his collarbone. "You can hate me for however long you want, and I will hand you the knife if you plan to slaughter me, but right now, all I need is you."

My fingers play along the top of his shoulder and slide towards his neck. I position myself so I'm sitting in his lap, and my eyes close, his body feeling softer than the beds I've camped on for the past few weeks. I don't care if he's hurt me or betrayed me because I've never been granted so much pleasure in this very moment.

This should feel wrong - disgusting, to even be touched by an inhumane monster like himself, yet he's too warm - too soft for me to pull away, and all I could think of wanting to do was stab him while he hugged me - while his breath cascades around my neck. This is disgusting.

This is exhilarating.

This is domination.

His voice echoes, "I'm yours for tonight, little elf."

CHAPTER TWENTY SEVEN

I didn't get to celebrate my birthday like the rest of the other children. I was turning thirteen, and my father couldn't provide much for me. I never went to school - I was homeschooled. I never had the chance to make friends, and the only other person I talked to was Anastasia. She was who I went to when my father let me have a break.

So when it was my thirteenth birthday, I was forced out of my bed. Father said that birthdays were meant to train harder. However, recently, our training sessions had shortened, and it felt like I wasn't training much at all. Perhaps this would make up for it.

"Across me," my father commanded, and with the small knife he lent me, I followed. My feet came together in a tense position, and I raised my head high. The dagger holding the knife by my side felt heavier than usual. In the past three years, I've grown fond of having a weapon by my side, and I never went without one.

A weapon gives you an advantage. It gives you power over someone's fear. It is someone's greatest weakness, and with fear and anger, you can conquer everyone.

"Tell me the first step of the fighting process," my father demanded.

He was in the same position as me.

"Assess your d-danger," I stutter.

"No stuttering," my father demands, and he comes forward, circling me like a predator. "Elves are meant to be prey among the supernatural. What do you think of that, little Blanche? Does that make you angry?"

I turn my head, but he comes around me in front of me. His eyes are blazing at mine. My father could be terrifying when he wanted to be, and being a hunter had always made me have nightmares of what he might do *to me if I disobeyed him. Instinctively, I look down to think of what to say.*

Think before you say something. That's another lesson I learned, unfortunately, the hard way.

"Look at me, Blanche, not the ground," he commanded, and I lifted my head.

"Elves can be powerful," I finally responded. "When they want to be."

"Exactly," he says and then kneels down to my saddened face. "Don't look sad, Blanche. I'm going to make you powerful. I'm going to make you terrifying, and no one will dare cross you." He lifted his hand and then intertwined his pinky with mine. "I love you."

I smile and then, with my hands, put my hands around his neck. My father was terrifying, and I feared him the most out of everyone, but he was still my father. The only thing I couldn't decide was what kind of love this was.

By the next morning, Devyn had finished brewing up the vampire vials. I woke up on my bed that morning, though I had no recollection of ever going to my bed. The last thing I remember was being by Beckett. I felt my cheeks burn at the thought of it, and it only made me look down toward the ground.

One by one, Devyn gave each of us the vials. "This potion will last only twenty-four hours, so we must sneak in, find shelter, and immediately come up with a plan." She looks at Beckett, cocking her head. "I assume you already have one."

He gives her a small smile and then steps forward, grabbing the vial. "Of course, I have a plan," He eyes me as he continues, "I wouldn't unwillingly lead us along."

How easily he lies, and everyone believes him. How ironic.

One by one, each of them takes a vial until it's my turn. My hand goes around the small vial. The liquid swirls, creating a thick and red form, and it looks a little like real blood. My body numbs when I think of it, and I have to clear my mind before I examine it further.

"Alright, are we ready? This transformation will be quick, but it might be a little uncomfortable," Devyn says, holding her own vial.

I look at the others. Arabella unscrews it first and then lifts it up. "Cheers." She dips the vial against her lips. The red liquid goes down her throat until there's none left in the vial. Then Edwin and Beckett follow her. Devyn and I dunk the liquid into our mouths.

The liquid isn't delicious, and it tastes a lot like metal to me. The red stains my tongue as I let it slide down my throat and into my stomach. My stomach grumbles at the uncertain fluid that has set itself in my system. At first, I don't feel anything, but then, when my stomach growled again, I feel the effect of the transformation start to begin.

My hands go on my stomach, and nausea hits me, threatening to cough up the liquid. My eyes start to burn and tear up, and suddenly, I feel as though they are shifting around my face, and I'm not able to see a thing for a second. My nose is next. I reach up, gasping when I feel my nose suddenly get pointier. Then it's my teeth, my two front ones sharpening.

When it ends, it feels normal - like I haven't changed at all. My eyes are traveling everywhere, on high alert. Vampires have always had greater eyes, but their senses are what catches me off guard. I can hear everything from a mile away, and I can't turn off the sound - the sound of an ambulance rushing towards safety or the kid a mile away riding on their bike.

"How does everyone feel?" Devyn asks when we've all transformed.

I look at everyone else, I see the difference in all of them. Arabella's skin is brown as ever, but her black hair seems thicker than it normally is, and her eyes are a shade of black. Beckett and Edwin look almost the same except for the fact that their skin is paler.

"I feel great, actually," Edwin answers. "So, does being a vampire mean we'll have to feed?"

I look at Devyn. I hadn't thought about that. Since we are now vampires - do we have the same perks as them? I hope not, since blood has only led me to disaster each time.

"We don't have to feed, nor do we have the urge to do it, but normal food will not taste good for the time being. We'll have to not eat," Devyn explains.

"How wonderful," Arabella deadpans, crossing her hands. "So shall we go?"

"We shall," she says towards her.

By the time we get close to the Transylvania border, I realize how dangerous this plan is. If we are discovered, this could only result in our death. Most likely, once they find out we are not vampires, they won't waste a second before they grant us with their teeth.

From afar, I could make out the lining of the border; a small round booth stood by it, and two guards stood there. Both of them are vampires. "We are coming up on it," Devyn whispers to us. "Follow the plan."

I lift my head and look straight ahead as we start to come closer. The guards are only a few feet away from us when they suddenly notice us. They turn their heads, and on command, they gather in a small line, where they stand in front of the border.

"Good evening. We have safely come into Transylvania, just for a few nights." Devyn is the one that says it first. She's acting confident, but when I look at her, I see the way her hands are closed in fists. She's nervous.

One of them looks at her strangely. Both of them aren't wearing any sort of armor, but they have holsters around their waists carrying many weapons. Yet, as I pull my attention only on them, I realize they are confused.

One of them leans towards the others. "Ce a spus vampirul ciudat?"

The other shrugs. "Poate vampiri născuți pe pământurile muritorilor?"

My eyes widened, and I looked towards Devyn to see her looking at me. I had read about this before - about how the vampires were born. I feel my mouth get heavy with words I want to say but cannot. I had read a lot about vampires - ones born in Romania, ones born in the mortal world, but it would make sense that vampires who never left Romania could never speak English. Ones who were born here never learned English, and as long as we don't know Romanian, we can't get through the border.

Beckett steps forward, and I go to pull him back and tell him it's no use when suddenly his voice is full of Romanian. "Doar trecem prin domnii. Ne întrebam dacă putem trece?"

My mouth slightly drops at his accent. Edwin nudges my side. "Our father taught us Romanian when we were younger," He winks at me before facing the guard again.

The guard seems to relax when he hears Beckett speak. "Și unde te îndrepți?"

"Avem familie în Serbia. Născut pe pământurile Mortal," Beckett replies back to them.

I don't understand a thing they're saying, but I can only hope that Beckett knows what he is doing. He said he had no plan before, so I can pretend that he does, at least.

"Foarte bine, te lăsăm să treci. Îți doresc călătorii în siguranță dragul nostru prieten" Edwin nudges me again to get my attention, although I cannot stray my eyes away from Beckett.

"Multumesc dominator," Beckett replies and then looks back at us. The border in front starts to unravel into an opening that we can walk right through. "We should be able to walk through now," Beckett is the first to start walking, and then following is his brother and Devyn. Arabella and I stay close behind just as we walk through the border and into Transylvania.

In Transylvania, it is exactly like any other state, although there is an odd aura from the moment I step into it. I look around at the little town in front of us. We walked directly into a town with stone houses, stone towers, and blacksmiths. Yet, even in this town, no one is outside.

"I didn't know you spoke Romanian," I say.

Beckett turns to me. "You never asked," he said, narrowing his eyes at me. "I also speak a bit of Latin, so maybe someday I'll have the pleasure of cursing you."

I roll my eyes. "Only in your dreams."

CHAPTER TWENTY EIGHT

I hold a silver dagger behind my back.

God damn them for leaving me in the open like this. I hide behind the nearest corner and look out for the nearest vampire that I see.

"Alright, the plan is…"

Bloody bastards. They left me for dead. I made sure the dagger was beside me in case of delays. I look over the corner and see the red and white train station pop up in the distance. The closest vampire is in front of the steps, talking to a nearby vampire, passing by.

I'm not a vampire anymore, so I have to be careful. The doors behind him are what I need to get through first. I look at the holsters he carries. Two silver knives hang there, and I see the handle of a gun. My eyes widen at the pistol. Christ, where did they even get that? Do they even know how to use it?

I need to get their attention without them shooting me straight to the ground. I can't make myself look suspicious. I duck around the wall until the shadows of the alley wall trap me. I'm lighter on my feet and calmer with my breaths. I'm scared that if I breathe too loud, I'll get discovered.

As the vampire turned towards the left, I lurked around to the right, where I ducked behind another brick wall. My eyes travel up to the title of the building. Post office. I don't know what it's for, only that it must be something mortals use.

Just then, the door swings open to the right of me. Coming outside, a blonde-haired vampire catches my eye. His eyebrows raise, and he looks me up and down. Then he spots my ears, and

I see his eyes turn a different shade, darker and scarier. His eyes swoop at my body, and then, with a hollar, he yells: "Elf!!"

My eyes widened, and I turned around as I bolted down the road, away from the train station. I curse, looking back and seeing the same vampire chasing after me, except now, he's got three others with him. I'm fast, but I can't outrun them all. I'll need to play it smart - simply outsmart them.

I swerve to the nearest alley, hearing the thundering footsteps only a few inches from me. My dagger is in my hand, and I look down at my blood-soaked bandages. Blood, I need blood, desperately. My breaths were uneven, inhaling and exhaling as I ran.

I exit the alleyway, running into a parking lot with trashed cars and the smell of detritus in the air. "Get back here, elf!" I hear one of them scream.

The other: "You can only run so fast before we catch up!"

My legs are starting to get tired, and my feet can only last for just a little longer. As I round the mountains of cars, I drag the knife against it to make it look like I've scratched myself and then slumped on the ground. I wait for them to come, but the silence is frightening.

"Look who we have here." I look up and see the three vampires' heads smirking down at me. The blonde one grabs my hair, yanking me up, ripping my hair out of my scalp. It burns, causing a panicked yelp to tear from my mouth, and tears spring to my eyes as he throws me over the hood of the car. I yank myself onto my elbows, watching as the three loom over with ominous gazes.

"What's an elf like you doing around here, huh?" The brown-haired one says, cocking his head to one corner. "Don't you know this is our territory?"

"Funny, I don't see you trying to stay out of our territory either," I snap, feeling the burn on my scalp. I see the bits of my hair ripped out of my head.

"You have no territory, elf," The blonde one says. He takes a step forward, to which I try to move back, to only slide down the car closer to them. He chuckles, kneeling before me, inching his fingers around the back of my neck until he makes me look up directly at him. He pushes my hair away from the exposed skin on my neck and runs his fingers on the vein that is exposed.

"Take a look, mates. This one still has so much blood left." The boys hover over their friends, looking at me like I'm a piece of meat.

Go ahead, you undead fools. Take a good look.

"What do you say? Take turns, or shall we have to argue for it?" The blonde one smirked at me, and his eyes, already dark, turned into a sinister red.

He looks down, and his lips quirked up into a smile when he sees the dagger I've got and the bandages that wrap my hands.

"What have you got there?" He puts his hand over the dagger, trying to pry it off of me, but I don't budge. "Be a good girl and drop the dagger elf."

Then, a smirk comes across my face. "Since when have I ever been a good girl?" I ask, and I pull my head back before swinging it forward, bumping my face straight with his.

He curses, flying back from the impact. I jump to my feet and look at the two vampires. If they want a fight, I'll give them a fight, and I'll make sure they're on their knees as soon as I'm done with it.

"Vei plăti pentru târfa aia!" The other one says in Romanian, lunging at me, fangs flaring and eyes red. He goes to grab my neck, but his hand misses as I duck and then use my dagger to slash him in the face.

His friend grabs my back, exposing my neck to him. My eyes widen, and I panic, feeling the fang slightly scraped against my skin. I kick, then swing the dagger back towards him towards his side. He lets me go, just as his friend has recovered from the previous accident, and this time, he looks furious.

The blonde-haired vampire rises just as he seizes a knife as well.

All of them seem to come at me at once. The blonde-haired one rips my bandages off, but I disarm him by kicking his back while the other grabs onto my arms. I can fight until blood covers me entirely, but taking three on will be difficult. They are bigger. I'm smaller.

I need their blood. Now.

I look at the brown-haired vampire and see the blood still dripping from his face. "This is three on one, elf. You have no chance!" He hollers as he comes closer, looking at me like I'm prey.

I curse. I need him to get closer, but the other is already removing my hair from my neck. I duck and use his hands that have secured my hands to come forward, throwing him in the air in front of me and onto the pile of cars.

I exhale, looking at them. "You'll need more than three vampires to get me to submit."

I race for the brown-haired vampire. He's got his knife by the side, and the blonde is barely able to reach my hair before I pounce on him, and with a slash of my knife, his throat is slit right in front of me. The blood splatters like glitter on crafts. It's heavenly, and the taste of it is heaven on my tongue.

This is where my power has been all along. It's been hiding, and its sinister power is illuminating my soul like stars exploding in the sky. All the vampires seem to feel it. I need more. I crave more. The vampire's throat is close to sealing up, and I land my hands right on his throat, feeling his crimson blood on my hands.

That's it. That's all I needed to end their miserable lives. I look down at my hands and see black veins pop up on my arms, spreading like branches up my arms and up to my shoulders. My legs, my neck, and then I feel it on my face. The power - that's what I want to feel. The euphoria of it makes me dizzy.

I get up and watch as the vampire crawls away quickly. He's not looking at me, though. He's looking up above where I stand. My eyes travel over me to see the shadows swirl around above me like a bottomless pit, and they're joining with my power. Beckett. He's here somewhere.

I turn towards the vampire, and with a wave of my hand, I cling onto his sorrow until his whole body spasms uncontrollably, until he is aching on the ground, and I watch as his heart slowly stops from the pain. His body comes alight with black flames suddenly, and I lick my eyes from satisfaction. His ashes fly in the air as his screams of agony seem to get louder and louder. I smile, feeling myself for the first time since I've entered this miserable world.

I feel a tear roll down my cheek. I then turn towards the others. They stand, petrified by the sight in front of them. Are they scared? They should be.

I slowly take a few steps, the wind whirling around me furiously, shadows whispering in my ear. *"Good job, Everard."* It's Beckett, his voice clear beside me. *"Show them who you really are."* My fists clench together furiously, and the one thing I want is for them to pay.

I bring my hand up, aiming specifically for the blonde-haired one. I feel his soul, the way it's whole. "Tell me, vampire, have you ever had a nightmare?" He tenses, feeling the way the air constricts around him, and my hand slowly vibrates his neck. His feet leave the cement that we all stand on.

His hands go around his neck, eyes big, mouth open to beg. Yes, beg. Make it pretty for me.

"Kill him," Beckett's voice rings in my ear.

My firsts clench tight at the sound of his beautiful voice. Damn it, get out of my head. I don't need him right now. "Let me show you your deepest nightmare, vampire," I declare, and I reach inside his soul. I see everything I need to see in there, just like I had with Beckett the night I cursed him. Except, when I look, there's only one thing there. It's the king - Castor.

I make him watch him. Castor kills him right in front of his brothers and sisters. How stupid and weak he was. He was nothing but a coward - an abomination to society. "No-" I hear him beg, and then, with the curl of my fingers, his mouth floods with black snakes, making him gag. All of it is a simple illusion, but it tricks him enough anyway.

His hands constructed, snapping in places they shouldn't. His legs turn completely black until they dissolve into dust, and his eyes turn white. I watch as he suffers slowly, replaying his worst nightmare. Suddenly, his fear changes from the image of the cruel king to a dark elf with sinister powers. Me.

Then it all stops as his body floods away like dust, and then his head plops down, blood soaking it. I turn towards the other. He looks scared, looking between his two friends and then at me. He backs away and tries to make a run for it. I don't waste my power on him. He's much weaker than his two friends.

I grab my dagger and then throw it straight at him. It hits him in the chest, where the heart beats, and then stops. I saunter over to him, just to make sure that he's dead. I pull my dagger away from his chest. I feel my power dissolve inside me just as I turn my head to the bloody dagger. My reflection looks back at me, bloody and vicious. I see the crimson blood glide down my face until it drops to the ground, and I feel the ache in my hands as my black veins slowly fade away.

I turn around and see the dead bodies. The vampires I just murdered are gone, for good. They don't even get a chance in the afterlife. I've banished them from the world. The bodies flood around me in a circle, and I put my hand on my head to steady myself.

A headache forms and that's when I hear the distant yelling. I turn around and see a pack of vampires approach the cars, eyes wide, seeing what I have done. They yell something, but it's all muted as the world spins…spins…spins.

Then I collapse on the ground, eyes heavy. I look down. I've lost too much blood. The vampires surround my body and speak with each other, saying something in Romanian. One of them looks concerned, while the other stares down in hate.

My eyes drift close, and the last thing I see is the blonde-haired elf that crosses my mind, and the way he's with me, somehow, he's keeping me safe. Then his voice…

"Good job, Everard. You did so well."

CHAPTER
TWENTY NINE

My body is on fire when I wake up.

My feet are tied to the bottom of a chair, while my hands are secured in the back, just as I had hoped. I can't see much except for a few things around me. The rest is pitch black, and I make out a small wooden door locked with chains. I feel the water droplets fall from the ceiling, and I jump when one hits my forehead. Nothing makes sense, but oddly, I can't help but feel like this place is familiar.

I frown as my surroundings feel as if I've lived this exact scenario already. Hell, I had been here before. I had seen this exact dungeon in my nightmares. I shook my head, looking down at the stone ground. That can't be. Have I finally gone mad?

I tried to understand the meaning of this familiarity, but I felt like I was losing myself in the darkness slowly. Dark elves had many abilities, while being referred to as monsters for their devilish habits, and sinister tricks and curses, but never once had I ever read about predicting the future.

So what does that mean for me?

I shake in my chair, and I try pulling my hands free. I could feel the ropes dig into my skin, causing my skin to burn red, and it only got worse as I struggled against them more. Where is my dagger? Where is my stuff? What the -

My head screams. Get me out of these bonds.

I look more and see my dagger, the one that I specifically stole from my mother after she left me.

Cells are surrounding me. Most of the cells are open, but there's one that's closed, and I try looking inside. The last time I was here, I saw my mother.

I make out a figure in one of the cells.

They are on the floor, their body is laid flat, their arms above their head in a sleep position, but their legs are spread apart weakly. The body looks brutally beaten and tortured. "Hey!" I call out to them. "Can you hear me?" There is silence. I try to jump up so that my chair takes me to them. Slowly, my chair hops over to them until I'm right by the cell. "Hey, answer me. Are you okay?" Now, there is a grunt.

I kick my leg against the cell. The figure finally lifts its head. I see their ears; they are pointy, just like elves. I smile to myself. When the body turns slightly, I realize this is no woman. It was a man, his muscles hard and tired out. He rolls on his back, letting out a deep breath. His hair was completely shaved off. "Are you okay?" I ask.

"I'm fine, I'm..." he turns towards me, and we both freeze when we see each other's faces. "Blanche?"

My entire body, the chains seem too tight around my legs and arms. My heart, since the day I left my village, floods with joy. My mouth drops slightly as I sigh a breath of relief. He's looking at me with happiness, a tear rolling down his eyes. He's wearing a filthy shirt over his bare chest and torn pants. His eyes are not his normal shade, dulled to a lighter blue. He looks like he hasn't eaten in days, and his legs seem weak enough to not be able to walk.

He uses his hands to crawl over to the cell, gripping onto the cells as the light finally cascades over his face. I stop breathing. "Blanche, honey," he says, his tone so sweet and blissful.

A tear rolls down my cheeks. "Dad?"

"Yes, it's me, honey," he clarifies. I try to yank myself out of these chains, cursing when I can't do anything. Even if I had a way to get to him, the cell separates us. I want to hug him - want him to know how much I missed him. I want to tell him how I never stopped thinking about him. I want to apologize for abandoning him. Christ, I want nothing but to feel him again.

Has he been here the whole time? What exactly happened the day I ran from home?

"Dad, I...I have a plan. I just have to wait for the others."

"Others?" He questions. "You shouldn't bring your friends here."

"No, Dad, this was the plan." I bit down on my lip, unsure of how to explain it. "I was meant to get taken." The way I did it, though, was completely unplanned. "I have a few…allies with me." I had yet to refer to any of them as my friends, though Arabella was certainly making her way down that way. "Devyn is one of them."

"Why? Why would they sacrifice you like this?" He demanded, angry.

"You have to trust me, Dad. We've had this plan…to kill the king and-"

"Kill the king?!" He demands, frowning. "Blanche, what on earth are you talking about?"

"Dad, please. I can't explain it now. It's too much. I need to focus on making sure I'm not discovered."

"He will kill you, Blanche, if he figures this out. He has it. He's been using it, Blanche -"

I am about to lean forward to press a kiss on his forehead, but I hear the door open, and I stumble back in my chair. I am still by the cell, and I stay there, unable to move. I see a woman stalk in. Her eyes are now red, masked with malice. She walks to me. "Now, who said you can talk with a prisoner, you naughty elf?" She twists the chair and pulls it towards the center of the room. My father watches me and grips onto the bars, watching me from afar. A cry leaves his lips. "You know, I thought you weren't going to wake up at first, especially after that stunt you pulled. You devious dark elf."

"You're not Castor," I state.

She smiles. "No. I'm far better than him." She then lifts her left hand up, and on her ring finger lays a black silver ring coated in shiny red rubies. "My name is Ambrosia Bloodrose. I am to be the future queen."

I almost laughed at the situation. "Weird. I never thought Castor would even think about sharing his throne."

"Oh, it was very tough at first. He's a stubborn man, and he's very persistent about having power over himself, but I was able to convince him after one night with me. All men are the same after all - even powerful vampires." She pulls my chin up to examine my features. "I can feel your heart beating…strong. Have you ever been bitten by a vampire?"

I yank my head away from her. "Go ahead, drain me dry if you want to. I can't die." Even if she had control over me now, I couldn't show it. To her, I was just another threat. Another toy for her to play with. I would show her how much of a threat I actually was.

"Yes, you can. The Warlord's Dagger does the job right," she grins, biting down on her lip. "I'm sure you are a bit confused right now. I don't blame you. As you know, you're in the dungeons of the vampire kingdom. It's a bit tragic, I know, but as long as you play along with Castor's games, then you'll do just fine." She clasps her hands over her lap just as I frown. "I must say, it was quite a bore watching over you. I can feel all those emotions in you - truly, it's disgusting."

My hands clenched behind my back, and a growl left my mouth as I tried to break free of the chair. She looked amused at my attempt and grinned. A small giggle falls out of her mouth. "You know I didn't plan for you to come here. I've been watching you for quite a while, even before you pulled that stunt. I knew there was an elf in my territory as soon as you walked through the border."

She snaps her fingers, and a chair is in front of her, being dragged from the other side of the room. She sits on it, her chest meeting the back of the chair, while she rests her head on the top of it. "I love how aggressive you are. Especially with that blonde fellow - he seems like a catcher. You guys were made for each other."

"We're not together," I snap.

"Why not?" She questions, raising her eyebrows.

I glower at her. "How have I not noticed you?"

That is her cue to smirk, and she does it. "My sense of hearing is pristine." She points to her ear to emphasize it. I don't answer her, watching as her eyes slowly turn into a darker red. I'm not sure what that meant. "I think you and I have a lot in common."

"We are nothing alike."

She gives me a narrowed look, which I ignore completely. "Oh, I beg to differ. I see the way you look at that blonde elf or both of them, actually. I can't seem to understand if you like or hate them. Or, is it that witch girl?"

"I have no friends or relatives in that group. My relationship with them is...complicated. Plus, they have abandoned me after all," I look her in the eyes, trying not to sound nervous. A half-lie would secure their fate.

"Are you telling the truth?" She asks, eyebrows raising.

I am nervous. She will compel me, just as she might with others. Despite that, I respond: "Yes."

"Hmmm, well, just to make sure." She cocks her head to one side playfully. "Tell me, do you have any friends or relatives that you have traveled with?" I expect to feel the effects of the compulsion, but when I don't feel anything, my eyes frown.

I swallow. Is this one of the advantages of being a dark elf? My hands shake. If my darkness can manipulate and control the mind, that would mean compulsion is completely useless to me. Or... only one that's powerful enough to enter my mind.

"I have no relatives or friends," I snapped. My eyes narrow on her. "Now, tell me, what is it that you want from me?" She clenched her jaw.

Then she sighs. "I don't want you here. I would have preferred you dead, but Castor wants to keep you. Since that elf over there -" she points to my father, "- doesn't want that and refuses to be a loyal subject. Now, he rots in there forever." She trails my jaw softly. It almost seems genuine.

"You've got nice features. I think you would make a good loyal subject. Will you take up that offer?" She asks. My body screams to shout no, but another part doesn't move, and it opts to keep quiet. She would kill me if I disagreed. She won't have the same mercy as she had on my dad. Castor wants power, and what better way by having an elf to spy for him? Although I hate that it had to be me. I look at my dad and see him pleading with me. All I have to do is pretend. I can make them think that I would ever betray him.

I think about the plan. How Devyn put a tracker enchantment on me before they let me loose. If I can play along, they can find their way here sooner, and I won't end up being killed.

"Maybe I'll consider it, but I want something in return," I told her.

She laughed. "I'm not sure if you've noticed, but you're not in a position to bargain here." She looks at the chains restricting me from moving at all. "Plus, Castor wouldn't make a silly deal with you. He wouldn't stoop that low."

"He will if he wants me to be his loyal subject," I shoot back.

"What could you possibly want from him?" Ambrosia questions. "He's not a very friendly man." I knew that. I wouldn't have had nightmares about him constantly if I didn't know that. I didn't want to be reminded of his crimes. He was the King of Vampires, after all. That title was terrifying enough.

"I don't have to explain myself to a king's toy." I snapped. She scowls at me then, and with great force, her hand meets my cheek. Spit flies out of my mouth, my head turning in the opposite direction.

Ambrosia's voice brought me back to reality: "Don't you ever talk to me like that again. When I say something, you answer. I command, and you obey. Do you understand me?" I say nothing. "I said, do you understand?!"

Just to irritate her, I say: "If I do become a loyal subject, I'm afraid I won't be obeying you. I'll be obeying, Castor. I do not serve you." I wouldn't kneel for any of them, especially after what she just told me. You could beat me and torture me, but it would not be enough for my submission. "You have no authority over me. Even if are his queen."

"When I rule alongside Castor, you will have to rule alongside me and the king. You will be my subject as well," she titters. "You will be under my complete control." I have no words. I could be strong and defy her, but what would happen to me in the end? I must play this smartly. They cannot control me, but they can still hurt me. They can kill me. One wrong move, and I will get punished.

Pretend. Tell her what she wants to hear.

"Well, when you become queen, I shall become your loyal subject as well, as long as our king makes a bargain with me." She smiles at that and pats my head. Let her think everything I say is true.

"Now, that's the obedient little elf I want," she says, blowing me a kiss. She smiles. "He's coming." I knew whom she was referring to, and I was prepared for the worst. Maybe he had horns on his head, with sharp fangs that stuck out of his mouth. I flinch when I feel Ambrosia trail her hand down my hair and on my back. "He'll be so joyful to see you. You have no idea how long he has waited for this. I've been telling him about you."

I hear the heavy footsteps of his feet outside. He unlocks the door, and suddenly I see him up close. A realization dawns on me. I had seen this man before...he was in my dream realm. What happened in that nightmare again?

The man who is most important to you shall die on the day you need him the most.

A shiver runs down my spine. He wears a black dress shirt and some black pants. His hair is ebony, just like Ambrosia, and his eyes are as cold as obsidian. When he smiles, his fangs are very visible.

He walks forward, casting glances at Ambrosia. "Thank you, Ambrosia, for doing my dirty work. I knew you could do it."

"Of course, I could. Now, you owe me," she scowls at him. Castor walks to her and places a kiss on her temple. I almost barfed at the sight of them. When they turn back to me, their eyes pierce through me. I'm now in the spotlight, in their spotlight. They need a loyal subject, and they would get one for now.

"I'm sitting right here," I responded. "I'd love to hear the reason why I'm the cause of your interest now." I roll my eyes, causing Castor to chuckle. He leans towards Ambrosia and gives her a long kiss, which both of them seem to enjoy, causing me to stir in my chair.

I don't say anything. My heart speeds up as the blonde elf comes into my mind. How he had held me in the hot water while he breathed on my neck, and how I couldn't possibly stray away from him. He was like a magnet I could not get rid of. Wherever he was, I hoped he was okay now. As much as I still hated him, I wanted to make sure no minor injuries were inflicted on him unless I was the one to hurt him.

When Castor and Ambrosia pulled apart, Castor smirked at me, and Ambrosia winked. I feel like hurling.

"Now, let's get to business, shall we?" Castor says, sitting in the chair that Ambrosia was in. "Has Ambrosia told you anything of what I want from you?"

"Yes, and I've agreed, only if you give me something in return."

He laughs. "I don't make deals with elves. You crossed territory, elf. It's either you do it, or you lose your life," He hisses at me, his fangs showing more. "I have the Warlord's Dagger.

"Then do it," I snap at him. "If you want your future loyal subject to die, then do it. I dare you." I need to pretend. Being an excellent liar has its perks sometimes.

They are both silent until Ambrosia speaks: "Well, go on, Castor. Kill her."

"Silence, Ambrosia," he says. "Leave me alone with her. I want to deal with her myself."

Ambrosia curses. "Fine." She stomps away, her hands clenched, and I see the frame of the ring still on her finger. Her hair whips behind her, and she slams the door next. Castor doesn't look back as he takes a deep breath. His breaths are uneven, but he seems interested in me. *Only* me.

"I don't like making deals with elves that have no significance, but...if you swear to me that you will forever be my subject...I might consider making a bargain with you," he says.

"You already have my word," I explained.

"Your word is not enough," he hisses. "If you do agree to this, you know what you will do? You will murder and kill whoever I tell you to kill, but you shall be showered in jewels and luxury for the rest of your life. I want you to be my subject, so when I say swear your life to me, I mean it." Then his eyes darkened, and I knew he was going to use compulsion. I'm more ready for it than I thought I would be. I wondered if he could get past the barriers of my mind.

"You will serve and be King Castor's loyal subject. You are bound to him as werewolves who have mates. You are faithful to only the queen and the king, only." I feel his words ring inside my ears. I pretend, making it seem like I am under his control. "And then, after this, you may tell me what you want for your loyalty." When he sits down, he expects me to speak.

I take a deep breath. I point to the cell that my father is in. "Let him go. I want him out of his cell and no harm done to him," I say.

Castor looks at my father. "You want your father to leave after not kneeling for me?"

I look up at him with shock. "How do you know he is my father?"

"I know a lot of things about you, Blanche." he leans in, cocking his head to the side. "If I let your father go, then the deal will be set in motion, and there will be no going back." He stands up, walking behind me, and with a whisper, just by my ear, I feel his hot breath on my neck, sending goosebumps up my body. "I will untie you now, but when I do, you will kneel for me and swear to me your loyalty."

He walks to my chair and undoes the ropes. He uses a dagger to rip them. I consider making a run for it, but it would get me nowhere but in a cell, or Castor would end my unfortunate life. When he starts to rip the ropes around my legs, I ask: "Why me?"

He rips them off and raises an eyebrow. "Because you're an elf, and you'll blend in more. Plus, tricking elves is like tricking a kid into a van. It's so...so easy." He takes my hand and roots me to my feet. I stand before him, my eyes never leaving his. "Kneel before me. Swear to me your loyalty."

I press my mouth shut. My pride begs me to not do it, but my head is saying otherwise.

Pretend.

I kneel on one of my knees and the other foot in front of the other. I put my hands together and bow my hands. I look up at the king's face. How can a man so beautiful be so evil? His face contorted to something familiar - a face I see almost every day. A face that I hate but can't stop thinking about. He reminds me so much of Beckett. I almost collapsed trying to find the right words to say to him.

"I swear my loyalty to you, my king. There is no one but you, that I would rather serve more." I look up to see if that is enough to earn his trust. He smiles down at me and pats my head. A feeling of disgust bubbles inside me.

"My dear Blanche, you are going to be my favorite puppet."

CHAPTER THIRTY

astor catches my father before he falls on the stone ground. My father stumbles on his two feet, after not being able to escape the confinement of his cells, I imagine it's pure bliss to be set free. As soon as he is able to carry himself on his feet, he races for me, wrapping his arms around my hips and smothering me in his warm body. He's colder than I imagined, but I lay my head against his chest and feel the comfort that I've needed for a while.

"Alright, let's go. Both of you follow me," Castor says rather impatiently.

My father sighs, pulls away, and puts his hands around my face. "You shouldn't have done that, Blanche." Then he comes closer next to my ear, quiet enough that not even Castor could decipher what he was saying. "You can only trick him for so long."

I put my hand on his back, laying it flat to straighten his back, and gave him a reassuring look. "Don't worry about me. You know your way around the country. Go back to London, to Devyn's house, and you'll be safe." I lower my voice and whisper in his ear. "I'll be fine. We'll see each other again." I look at Castor and see his eyes cast over us suspiciously.

He ushers us towards the doors of the dungeons. "I'll be right behind you." A hint of mischief in his voice, as if daring us to make a wrong move. He is not wearing a crown on his head, but he does have an attitude of a king - self-absorbed and cocky.

I open the door to the large stone staircase. I look and see the mountain of stairs swirling in a circular motion. "Hurry up!" Castor snaps. I look back and glower at his attitude. I whip my head around and ascend the steps with my father and Castor on my trail behind me the entire time. At some point, Castor pushes my father to hurry, making him stumble into me.

I steady my feet, unable to let myself fall in front of the king. As soon as we climb up the stairs, I opened another door. I cover my face when I see the bright light. My father puts his hands on my shoulders, guiding me through. When I uncover my eyes, I realize we are in a big hallway, and I observe every feature.

The hallway looks elegant. There are portraits of many vampires, ones that reigned before King Castor - some as old as Mother Nature itself and some just as young as me. The hallway floor is made of black marble, the walls are ashen, and the ceiling has a chandelier hanging from it. If this was only the hallway, I wondered what everything else looked like. It was the castle that fantasies lived in.

Of course, Castor lives in such luxury, and while he does, others are hunting for food and dying to save their villages. Castor rounds us, checking something in his pocket before he looks back at us. "Take a good look, Everard. I hope you like your new home."

For now.

A few guards walked by us, casting King Castor a gracious bow. All of them who passed looked at him with respect but with a hint of fear.

What would everyone think knowing that a new king might rise soon? An elf among vampires. Beckett would be ridiculed. He wouldn't last a minute before someone assassinated him.

"Dario!" Castor roars.

Only a second later, a guard comes running towards him. He's older than Castor - I could tell by the wrinkles on his forehead and the way he holds himself. His dark skin is tanned from multiple bruises. I spot the scars across his neck, deep and red ones that haven't vanished from his skin. His brown hair is curly and runs down to his neck from the back. "Yes, my King?" He holds his head high, eyes staring only at Castor.

"Take this gentleman to the entrance and set him free. He can find his way home from there." My father holds me tighter around my shoulder, and I look back, giving him a reassuring look. Dario speaks, but it is in a different language this time - Romanian.

My father pulls me in one more quick hug before Dario is by his side, pulling him away from me. "Let's go," Dario says in his

Romanian accent. His hand goes towards my father, and he pulls him away from me.

A tear slips from my eye to see my father pulled away from me again. I only hoped he was strong enough to get out of here alive now. As soon as they are out of sight, I feel Castor close in on me, taking his hands and putting them on my face. "Now, don't cry, little elf. It doesn't suit your face."

I ball my fists and scrunch my nose in anger. *Little elf.* How dare he. Only Beckett was allowed to call me that. I know better than to strike at him. Instead, I push myself away from him, watching him smile wickedly. "Tell me where my bloody room is."

"Oh yes. But first, we need to make a stop at my sister's room," he says, and then grabs my hand, pulling me with him. He walks fast, and I almost stumble, trying to keep up with him. That's when we stopped at a brown door, and on it, engraved was the name Belinda Percival.

Castor knocks on it once, but he walks right in after that, not caring for his sister's privacy. He pulls on my arm and presents himself. His sister sits at her desk, lighting a candle that drips onto her desk. She turns and looks over at her brother. She's much younger than I expected. I assumed Castor was close to twenty years old or even older. Belinda seems younger, around Arabella's age.

"I hope I haven't disturbed you," Castor says, but by the tone of his voice, he doesn't seem to care all that much.

"You always disturb me." Her eyes travel over to me. "Who's the elf?"

"Blanche Everard." His eyes cast towards me. "My new puppet. She'll be running some errands for me for now." Belinda looks at her brother, expressionless. "Now be a doll and show her to her room."

Her shoulders slumped. "I don't know where her room is."

"It doesn't matter. Pick a room that's not occupied," he says. He then turns. His eyes land on me, and he lifts a piece of hair that floats in front of my face. "Behave, elf. My sister can be sensitive."

Without turning, Castor leaves the room, leaving me with the teenager. I see her roll her eyes, annoyed by my presence. "So, do you have a preference?"

My eyebrows furrow. "A preference?"

"For a room," she retorts. "I mean, some rooms are bigger than the others. Then there are the ones that are cold, while the others are too hot. This castle is pretty empty, so whatever you would like."

"Something comfortable. Not too hot or cold." That makes Belinda's mouth quirk in a smile, and then she saunters close to me. My instinct is to back away, but I cut it short.

I need to pretend that I trust her. That's how we kill them.

"You know, vampires have good senses. My brother might be oblivious, but I'm sure as hell not," she explained, and I feel my heartbeat accelerating as soon as she comes closer. "I saw the way you looked at me when you first came in here. You seem too tense to stand before me unafraid. Your fists are clenched, meaning you probably want to hit me right now, which makes me wonder if you're strong. However, if you were strong, you probably wouldn't have gotten kidnapped. So...what is it that you want, elf?"

After realizing how the bundle of nerves in my arms was strengthening, I unclenched my fists and relaxed my body. Truly, vampires did have many good senses, but to think she could read me so easily...

"It's a lot to explain." Truthfully, the way I was kidnapped was not as planned. I didn't plan on killing three vampires or letting my power go out like that. It happened without thinking, and it ended up working, which led me straight here. Just like all of us had planned.

I cringe at the thought of what would have happened instead. Devyn didn't think the plan through. I was bound to die with the original plan. I wish I could talk to them all. For the people I hate so much, I feel so lonely without them.

"Do you want to talk about it?" Belinda asks, and I stare at her, eyes wide. "I'm not my brother. I'm not mean like him."

I smile. "No. I'd rather just go to my room."

"Alright." She shrugs. As much as I'd like to confide, I can't. She's a vampire - an enemy. She'll die with the rest of them.

We closed the door behind us, and Belinda started walking fast, not letting me keep up with her at all. She leads me up a grand staircase. While we go, she points to certain rooms. "That room is where we'll be having dinner," she says, pointing at two dark wood double doors. "The throne room is on the bottom floor, and we'll be using it in a few weeks for Ambrosia's coronation." She turns her head, smirking at me. "She's very excited to be queen."

I jog to her side, my feet almost giving up on me. "Why didn't you become queen?"

"Because that's not how our system works. Castor is the oldest, so he has to inherit the crown. It technically doesn't belong to him. It belongs to the creature that killed my mother and father in the first place. Whoever kills the king and queen is automatically crowned the next king or queen. However, since they disappeared, Castor had to take it. He was delighted, though. It was supposed to go on his head at some point."

"And what if your brother was the one that killed them? Would you want him to be the king then?" I demand, raising an eyebrow. At my comment, she stops, dead footsteps followed by nothing. I stop and look at her. She's looking at me confused, eyebrows furrowed, almost angry.

"Where are you getting your information from?" She demands. "Whoever is telling you these lies needs to come to an end. It wasn't my brother. I was with him the night they got murdered."

She shakes her head, taking a deep breath. "Christ, just stop talking and keep on following me." She wanders off, heading off towards my room. We arrive at a brown wood door, with gold-crests of snakes appearing at the top. "We will have this be your permanent room from now on. Dinner will be in two hours, so relax and get ready. I'll pick you up then."

She leaves me stranded, walking as fast as she can away. An awkward encounter, but I let myself slip inside. The chamber is medium-sized, which is much better than what I've been sleeping in for the past few nights.

The bedroom has a light pattern to it. The walls are grey and decorated with a dark green outline. The bed is big enough for me. I have a similar vanity to the one Belinda had in her bedroom, and after further investigation, the desk appears to be the same.

It reminds me of my room back in Devyn's cabin. I could let this chamber be my bed for the next few weeks. As long as the four came quicker. I touch the back of my neck and feel the enchantment still intact. It's still there. So, what's taking them so long?

A soft knock on the door grabs my attention, and then a woman comes in. She has a white skirt that looks more like a rag wrapped around her hips and a brown long-sleeve shirt. She carries a few ribbons around her hand. "Good afternoon. I've come to get you ready for dinner."

She has short blonde hair that ends at her shoulders, and she has round glasses around her face. She bows before me as if I am some sort of important figure. When she stands, she looks at the ground. "You seem nervous," I say, taking a step towards her. "Are you all right?"

She looks at me. "My apologies. As King Castor's loyal subject, I have to treat you as I would him." Her fingers fidget around the ribbons she has in her hands. "May I fix your hair now?" I nod, and we move to the vanity. I sit in the chair while she grabs a comb from the dresser and starts to brush it. I look at myself. I'm a little confused - *how did she know I was his loyal subject?*

This must be Belinda's doing.

I've never been known for anything important - not that being Castor's loyal subject is that great. I was no one of importance. I was raised by Mallory and Brenner Everard, and I have no brothers or sisters. I have always been alone in the world, even when my father was there for me. I didn't count on anyone. I didn't need another. I was able to train and become strong while still being knowledgeable.

What is better than knowledge?

"How does it look?" The maid asks. I look at myself and see two strands of my hair pulled back to the back of my head. She put some loose strands in front of my face and also put some flowers in my hair. They were a mix of green and silver.

I touched my hair, examining the brown curls. "It's beautiful."

"I'm glad you like it. Now, with your permission, may I put on some makeup." I nodded and let her do my makeup. She painted my lips a dark red, and did my eyebrows and eyelashes, and then painted a black line on my eyelids. When I looked at myself, I praised her. "There are a few gowns in your closet. You can pick whatever you want." She politely brought me to the closet and opened it.

"May I leave, Ms. Everard?" She asks, bowing her head.

"Of course," I say. She saunters out, shutting the door. I skim through the clothes. There are a lot of options. I decided to go in a white long dress. It consists of small straps with an opening in the back. There is lace at the bottom, while the rest of it is flowy. I quickly put it on and then look at myself in the mirror.

I wasn't sure when dinner started, but I kept myself occupied by sitting down at my desk. For the next few hours, I sit back and find something to do. I read books, try to look for weapons, and write letters that I plan on sending one day. I really miss my dagger.

My mind travels to the vile elf. For once, I find myself missing his challenge of authority. I miss his presence and all the wickedness that comes with it. I do hope he brings me a knife - a nice shiny one that looks as sharp as it feels.

I don't know how long I'm sitting and thinking until my door opens. I scramble to my feet, fixing my hair that I had managed to mess up. Belinda walks in and she examines me. "It seems the maid did a good job preparing you. You look stunning," She complimented.

"So do you," I retort.

She is dressed in an all-black dress with a silver lining of diamonds on the collar. "Come on, let's get to that dinner." Belinda ushers me forward, and I follow her reluctantly.

We walk out and walk down the corridors where the dinner will be held. "Mind your emotions at the table. Castor can sense if you are feeling any discomfort or nervousness." I nod, and she twists around suddenly, grabbing my wrist and holding my gaze.

"So, if you're up to something, I don't recommend trying it at dinner."

I yank my hand back. "What makes you think I'm up to something?"

She lets go of my hand abruptly, moving along forward. "I know elves. They may look innocent, but they are far more cunning than any creature I know...especially dark elves." My feet almost fall over each other. She casts a glance just to see my reaction, but I force my face to stay neutral. Christ, has she already figured it out? Can she see what I'm planning?

"I know what you elves think." She twirls around, walking backward. Anyone heading our way moves around her, avoiding the lady with the black dress. "Most of the people in the castle are controlled by him. The vampires in town are the same. Castor loves it. If he didn't drink blood, he would be drunk from vigor. Either you obey him or pay death a long-term visit."

I have thought of Castor as an inhumane monster, and the ones around him who supported him to be monsters as well, but the sudden realization, knowing that not everyone wants it to be like this. They like elves, werewolves, hybrids, and mortals. Some of them might even want the world to be equal to each other.

"But it doesn't matter in the end, does it?" Belinda questions, and I straighten my back, feeling the way the back of my neck dampens, and my hands twist in anxiety. "Because we are the bad guys. We suck the life out of everyone, and unfortunately, we can't just stop. If we did, vampires would be nonexistent. There would be nothing left of us."

"You're his sister. Does he ever control you?" I ask.

"He controls everybody," she replies. She twists around just as we turn and head towards two big doors. With her hands, she pushes them both open. They swing open and then slowly glide shut as I step through the doors and see the room unfold in front of me. The room is big, despite only having a large dining table in the middle of it and surrounding are brown chairs pushed inside. Only a few tables have plates on them, with silverware.

Towards the right, Castor and Ambrosia sit next to each other. He lifts her hand up, landing a kiss on the finger that lays the ring. They certainly deserve each other. Castor then lifts his head and smiles at both of us, which leaves me on edge.

"Both of you, come join us," he says, ushering the chairs towards them. I feel Belinda's hand go through mine as she pulls me forward.

As we walk, I hear her whisper: "Don't show that you're scared."

Listening, I keep my head straight, and then Belinda leads us to two open chairs, on the opposite side of them but still close enough to see them face to face. Her hand goes over to mine, and as if reading mine, she cocks her head, warning me to be safe.

After a short while, I hear the doors open again, but this door was on the completely other side, and that's when I realized they were chefs, all vampires. They all form a straight line with a dish plate in their hands, with a covering on top that hides the food. "I hope you enjoy this food. They aren't used to cooking for an elf, so you must forgive them for not cooking it properly." Castor smiles directly at me.

Ambrosia's hand goes on his shoulder, and my eyes travel to her and see the vexation. She's annoyed not only in my presence but also because Castor is paying attention to me and not her. "I will enjoy anything they serve me." I keep my voice steady, remaining calm.

"Good," he sneers. "You heard the elf. Serve her the food."

A chef opens up the tray to see a grilled chicken with some

mashed potatoes on the side. My mouth waters just by seeing it. I hadn't eaten a proper meal since I had left Devyn's cabin. Edwin used to cook the best meals. They place the plate underneath me and then bow their head before getting the other's plates.

Ambrosia, Castor, and Belinda are being served a steak, uncooked, with some blood or red wine in their cup.

"Care for some red wine, elf?" Castor asks.

I swallow, then nod my head. "Sure."

The chef pours me a glass of red wine and then places it beside me. As soon as everyone is served, they scatter back into the kitchens. The door flaps inward and outward shut for a few moments. "Well, eat up." Castor smiles. He takes his silverware, cuts a large piece for his steak, and places it in his mouth.

Beside him, Belinda and Ambrosia do the same.

I've never had dinner with vampires, and this seems all wrong. Looking down at my plate, I pick up my silverware. Everything seems cooked, and nothing looks out of the ordinary. When I look back up, I realize everyone is staring at me.

"Not hungry?" Ambrosia teases, the curl of her lip lifting upward.

I scowl and then cut a piece of my grilled chicken. I lift the fork until it hovers over my mouth. Castor is practically waiting for me to put it in my mouth, patiently tapping his foot under the table.

My mouth covers the fork, sliding the chicken off of it. Slowly, I bite into it. It tastes like chicken, only slightly chewier and… not seasoned.

"Do you like it?" Castor asks.

Belinda casts a glance at me. She's almost done with her steak, her silverware full of the steak's blood.

"It's um..delicious," I managed to say. I almost barf, trying to swallow it down. I would rather eat my own foot than take another bite out of this. Nonetheless, I take another bite out of the grilled chicken. This time, I can't swallow it, and bile rises through my throat. No, this can't be chicken. Castor has to be lying - it's different - it's disgusting.

As soon as I feel the bile, I turn my head away and then spew all over the floor. The hairs in front of my face catch on the bile, my head throbbing.

As soon as I'm done, I hear Ambrosia say: "I told you she would react like this."

I lift my head, wiping my mouth with the napkin on my plate. "I'm sorry."

"No, I'm sorry," Castor says, sighing. "I should have never served you that." I look down at my grilled chicken. Christ, it's just chicken - how did...

I look at Castor. "What do you mean you shouldn't have served me this?"

Ambrosia chuckles, covering her mouth with the back of her hand, and Belinda puts her hand on my back, eyes widening as if she is shocked. "Well...we don't exactly have normal food on us at the moment, so we had to improvise." His smile turned into a scornful smirk. "We had to make you something we had."

I look down at my food, and I push it away, stumbling away from the table. Oh god, this was never chicken. "What is it?!"

Ambrosia puts her silverware down, chuckling. "Her name was Amber, and she delivered the sweetest blood I have ever tasted. The poor girl was only twelve years old at the time, unfortunately, but she cooperated nicely, and in a matter of minutes, she was dead."

Twelve years old. My hand goes over my mouth, feeling bile rise up my throat. I just ate a twelve-year-old girl. Worse, a mortal - a child. I feel my stomach go up and down as I inhale and exhale.

"Oh god " I steady one of my hands on the table as I head towards the door.

"Now, elf, you can't leave yet." Ambrosia rounds the table, steps echoing in my mind. "Sit down, Everard," she says, yanking on my hair and forcing me to sit back down. "You still haven't been given an order."

I can't even think clearly, and they're giving me something to do? Why? How?

Did Belinda know of this? I look at her and see the shock written on her face, which is just as similar to the one on my face.

Ambrosia sits back down in her chair, and Castor watches me from across the table. Belinda's hand comes around mine under the table. She squeezes it as if to comfort me. I yank my hand away from them, revolted by her - by everyone in this room. "I have my first assignment for you, my dear elf," Ambrosia coos, stabbing the steak with her knife.

I scowl. "I knelt for Castor. Not you."

I see her drawback; look at Castor. He doesn't say anything.

Of course, he doesn't because he doesn't actually care about Ambrosia, and if it were up to him, he would never have married her. This is simply an arrangement, and Ambrosia is delusional to think otherwise.

I feel the anger vibrating off of her. Her eyes narrow. "I'm your future queen. You have to do as I say."

My hands balled into fists. "Exactly. You're my future queen, not my queen currently."

"That's enough, both of you," Castor demands. She faces Castor, eyebrows raised. "Ambrosia, I don't want to hear anything from you…as for you.." He looks at me. "You shall treat my fiancée with respect as you would with me. Although, since she's been acting like quite the brat, we will leave an assignment for you until tomorrow morning."

It won't change anything. He will still be a monster, and Ambrosia will always be his whore.

"Now…" His eyes darken, and I realize he's trying to compel me again. "Go to your room. Get ready for bed, and don't let anyone in your room. You will wake up tomorrow and go to the throne room." My gaze never leaves him, and it's not until his eyes go back to his normal color that I move.

From the corner of my eye, I see Ambrosia look for my reaction. Instead, I lift myself up and leave the dining room without a word. Guards pass me and give me a narrowed look. I can hear Belinda behind me, calling after me to get my attention. I won't risk the idea of Castor discovering me.

He made me eat a human - *a fucking human.*

She stops in front of me. "Slow down, would you?" She says. "Even I can't seem to keep up with you."

"I have to go to bed. Goodnight," I say, trying to walk past her, but she pushes me back, preventing me from going farther.

"I'm not a fool like Castor. I know his compulsion didn't work." She looks me up and down. My breath hitches in my throat, and I know I've been caught. "Don't worry, I don't plan on telling him, I'm just curious to know how you didn't get compelled. Vampires have a very strong hypnosis."

I swallow. For a moment, I think of telling her the truth. She's shown a few times she is different from Castor, and at the dinner table, she looks surprised. She didn't look like she had known.

Nonetheless…I couldn't trust her.

"Walk me to my room?" I ask. I lift my hand, and she accepts my hand gesture, linking our hands together. We travel to my room together, hands linked. For a few minutes, I let my mind roam free. "When I was little, my mother and I were very close. I thought everything was okay, but ever since I left my village, I realized that my life isn't what I thought it was. My mother left me when I was ten years old, and I always thought it was for no reason, but…it's obvious now, that she did do it for a reason."

Belinda frowned. "Why are you telling me this?"

"Because trust can go a long way. I trusted my mother, and look where that got me. I've trusted many people I thought I should trust and I've been betrayed. The same reasoning goes for you Belinda, because you are a vampire, and vampire and elves are enemies."

As if hurt, she withdraws from me. "Your mother…what was her name?"

"Mallory Everard."

Her eyes widened, and she smiled, something in her gaze passing as recognition. "Perhaps, you'll see her again." Then her eyes narrow. "Perhaps, she'll have a lot of explaining to do."

CHAPTER THIRTY ONE

I shivered, the darkness consuming me. No matter how long I lay in my bed, I could not force myself to keep my eyes closed. Fear dwelled in me as nightmares flashed before my eyes. My mother, lying in the dungeon, and I'm reminded of my childhood. I'm reminded how suddenly I truly didn't have anyone except for my father.

I knew as soon as I fell asleep, my sleep paralysis would take over me. I didn't like growing weaker to it, but it truly terrified me. I'd grown accustomed to it, greeting it as a dear friend, but my mind was growing angry, darker than usual, and it affected me harshly.

I was so caught up in my own thoughts that I didn't even notice that my door was slowly opening, and by the time I found out, someone was looming over me. A tall, dark figure, his hair slightly familiar. I opened my mouth in a scream, but their hands clamped down on my mouth to force it quietly.

Without my dagger, I could not defend myself, and that was the worst of all. In a moment of panic, my shoulder snapped out and hit the unknown intruder who dared come into my room. They groaned, feeling liquid on my shoulder.

Blood.

I felt a surge of power inside me, and I kicked my feet out of the sheets before they came across the intruder's face, making them fall over right next to the door. I jumped out of bed, spinning towards my light to see the person's face.

As I turned the lamp on, laughter broke out, and I met five familiar faces that I'd grown to love and despise all at once.

"Damn," I looked down to find Beckett covering his bloody nose, and with the swipe of his hand, he snapped it back in place. Edwin was sitting on the desk, laughter escaping his mouth. Arabella was next to him, sitting on the edge of my desk as she dangled her legs forward.

Devyn stood by the door, smearing something on her lips, making it look redder than normal. Right next to her stood my father, looking as much like a wreck as early, although he looked a lot happier, and I felt the urge of excitement blast through my powers.

Beckett lifts himself off the floor, patting dust off of his shoulder. "That was unnecessary."

"I'm in a whole castle with vampires! I'm lucky to be alive, you asshole! I thought you were going to murder me!" I shouted.

"Be quiet; we don't want to wake anyone," Beckett argued and rolled his eyes, sitting down on the huge bed.

"What took you guys so long?" I asked, crossing my hands, a frustrated groan escaping my mouth.

"Well, we were supposed to get here hours ago…" Edwin looks at Devyn, eyes narrowing towards her.

Devyn sighed, turning around, annoyed by the sudden disruption. "It's not my fault the enchantment stopped."

"It's your enchantment. You're supposed to know when it stops," Edwin argues and then shakes his head, looking at me. "Thankfully, we ran into Brenner, and he told us everything."

Everything? Even my deal with Castor?

"We know you made a bargain with Castor." Arabella read my mind, jumping off the counter. "Honestly, I'm surprised. I thought he would have killed you."

I narrowed my eyes at Beckett. "I should be right now. What happened to the original plan? I thought we were supposed to stay hidden."

Beckett smirks, the corners of his mouth twisted in a sinful desire. "That was the original plan," he released a huff of air. "But it's not a fun plan."

I crossed my hands, feeling like I'd been betrayed.

"King Castor tried to compel me," I say, and everyone focused their attention on me. "It didn't work."

"Well, of course, it didn't work." Devyn stands up, adjusting the dress she wears. "Dark elves are immune to vampire compulsion."

My father gasped as if it was sinful to say. "Don't say such a thing, Devyn."

She turned to him, narrowing her eyes at me. "With all due respect uncle. I've seen Blanche's abilities, and I know she's powerful. I've already studied it."

He looks at me with absolute horror, and I try not to let it affect me. "You can't all stay here. I'm Castor's subject, and he is already aligning a task for me tomorrow. It will look suspicious if you all stay here."

"I'm not a fool," Devyn says, reaching into her bag before pulling out a vial. "I didn't have all the ingredients, so I had to improvise. All five of us will have to camouflage, turn into a vampire, and act a role in the castle. That way, it won't be suspicious while we slowly execute the plan. I suggest we go to the dungeons where no one of importance will be there."

"And what is the plan? Turn yourselves into vampires, and then what?" I demand.

Arabella sits up, walks over to Devyn, and takes the vial. "The plan is simple. We can't risk getting caught. Devyn and I will sneak into the maid chambers and pretend to be maids. As for the rest of you, you'll have to play guards. Then we find a way to strike from there."

"We should go to the dungeons now, then. Almost everyone is asleep as of right now," Edwin suggests. I look back and see the time on the clock.

I walk forward towards my father. His eyes pierce through me, and I wonder if he hates me now that I revealed that I am a dark elf. My father was a hunter, and he hunted many dark elves. "Are you upset?"

He sighed. "We'll talk about it later, alright?" He vanished out of the room. It shouldn't have hurt, but it felt like he had ripped out my heart. I was never angry or upset at my father, though he had shown numerous times he could be with me. It felt disloyal. It felt shameful to disappoint my father that way.

Everyone gathers out of the room, and I feel Beckett skim the back of my shoulder. It stung my skin, making me hot all over. I turned to him for a second, seeing his jaw tight, and then his hands trailed down my back before eventually leaving his spot. Even through my nightgown, I feel the mark he has left on me.

It unsettled me.

The door shuts, and Devyn and I are the only ones left in the room.

I turn around. Her legs are crossed in front of her, and I realize now the last time we were alone, we were arguing. "Did you want to talk about something?" I ask.

"Well, you sound joyful," she teases and then stands up, stretching her hands out in front of her. She's glimmering from her enchantments, and her freckles are darker now. Trauma changes people - especially war. I had never asked what happened to my aunt and uncle, only to spare her feelings, but now, I couldn't care less.

"What happened to Cassius and Blair?" I ask, circling around the bed. Devyn's face, which was normally neutral, grew into one of shock and confusion mixed with a hardness I couldn't read.

"I told you they were dead," she answers.

"How?" I demand. "Tell me. I want to know every detail."

She's not smiling, and I move to sit next to her, putting my hand around her lower back. She looks back as if I've spit on her and scoots away. "It's none of your business," she snaps.

"They're my family. Of course, it's my business." I cross my hands.

"They didn't die during the war, you know," she says and then whirls around, facing away from me. "My mom died before the war even started." When she turns around again, I realize her eyes are red, and she's at the point of tears. Which I know…she absolutely despised.

Though Devyn was strong and, most of the time, stubborn, she hid her emotions. I wish I could hide my emotions like that. Since I arrived at the cabin, I had realized Devyn wasn't the same witch from when we were little. She was more stubborn, cold, hurt, and betrayed. "She went out to get supplies and was caught using magic. My father was with her at the time. He couldn't save her. They pulled her away so quickly because they thought she was bewitching him. Not long after, they burned her."

My eyes widened. "Burned? You mean -"

"They tied her to a pole and burned her," she continued to describe, and a tear fell down her eye. She wiped it away furiously, refusing to look anywhere but at me. "My father soon died after her. He was terrified to ever step foot in the cities again. He had shut me off too because of his grief. He got sick, and he wasn't able to treat himself like the mortals did. He refused to take any medicine the humans made. I was only seventeen at the time, so…I watched my father pass, and then I buried him in my backyard."

She tries her best to hide the sorrow, but she does a horrid job. All these years, she must have felt lonely, hopeless, and lost, and when she tried to write to me, I wasn't there. Fuck, and I never even got the letters.

I go to her and grab her shoulders, but she shoves me away, more tears streaming from her eyes. My feet stumble over each other, but I manage to keep myself from falling. "Did you even read my letters?! I had confided in them, told them everything I was feeling. How could you just ignore them? Ignore me?!"

She bolts towards the door, but I grab her arm, yanking her back. "Let me go, now," she demands, fighting against my grip.

"I'm sorry," I say. "I'm so sorry, Devyn. I just-"

"You just what?" She demanded. I had never seen Devyn cry, not even as a kid. She was the confident one, the one who comforted me. She was the strong one. I was the weaker one. "You forgot?!"

"Devyn...you have to trust me when I say I never got them," I say, feeling her emotions, seeing her sorrow. "You said my father wrote you back?" She stared at me, not saying a word, but I remembered. "I think my father took them."

She wipes at her eyes, frowning. "Why would he do that?"

"I don't know, Devyn," I say, taking a step back. My throat is closing up, and my breaths are ragged. "I trust you when you say that you wrote to me, but you need to trust me too. I would have never ignored you."

Devyn shakes her head. "It just doesn't make sense. None of this does."

It's then that I notice the bags under her eyes, the dullness to them. "Are you alright, Devyn? You seem like...you're not really here."

"I'm fine," She trails off, grabbing her head and looking down at the floor.

"It's alright, you just need to relax," I try to confront. "I love you Devyn. Do you trust me?" I move closer, grabbing onto her shoulders, trying to get her to look at me.

She shrugs, shaking her head. Still she doesn't look at me. "I don't know."

She brushes past me, my hands landing to my sides as she walks away. I watch her leave, the smell of her perfume wafting in the room, and I frown.

I hoped she would trust me again.

I knock on Belinda's door.

My foot taps against the floor. I'm still thinking about the events of before, and the guilt consumes me, but I shove it down just as the door opens up, and Belinda's face comes into view.

Belinda stumbles out, still putting on one of her black heels. Her hair is a mess of black curls on her head, jumping up and down as her body shifts downward and then upwards, looking at me. Her black dress lifts slightly too high, and I kneel down and push it down to her knees. Her eyes widened, embarrassed. "Can I help you?"

"Show me to the throne room?" I ask.

She nods her head and shuts the door behind her. "You know being your escort is a pain in the ass."

"You can thank your brother for that," I retort, smiling at her annoyed expression. She walks past me, throwing me only a playful glower before I follow behind. I keep up with her even though she's walking tremendously fast.

We walk through the corridor. We turned corners and passed other guards, and I even noticed Edwin passing by us. He winks at me, and I give him a small smile that I hide from Belinda. His hair seems a bit more platinum blonde than golden, and his skin has grown paler, his normal shade being tan. He wore a uniform that most of the guards wore around the castle.

I give him a small wink back just as I turn the corner, and he disappears from my view. Finally, we reach our destination. Belinda opens the double doors and then stands by the doorway. With an echo, the doors slam behind me.

All around me, walls of pictures hang like tapestries. They all hold different authority figures, and by the wall, I see our former King, Rufus Percival, standing by his wife, Eden Percival. Gold carvings on the wall are painted with royalty among the banisters. This room radiates the legacy of a true king and queen. At the end of the room, a stage stands with a red chair with gold lining the edges and top.

A red and gold carpet leads up to it, and sitting on the chair, Castor holds a wine cup and swirls the blood in it with his finger.

"Bow to him," Belinda whispers to me. She links our arms together, and we saunter over to him. When we're just a few steps from the stage, she unlinks my hands. At the same time, we bow down on one knee. "Brother. I have escorted Everard to you."

"Good. You may leave now," he instructs, his voice deep and assertive. Belinda shudders before nodding and walking out of the room. The doors slam, and I'm left alone with the king.

I keep my head bowed, afraid that he might see right through me. I hear him shuffle, and then his footsteps get closer…closer… until they're right in front of me.

His fingers come under my chin, and I softly lift my head up to meet his eyes. "My loyal subject. How ravishing you look today." His fingers run through my hair and then lift up one of the little braids that I braided. "Did you do these yourselves?"

"Yes," I say, controlling the tone of my voice.

He smiles and then kneels down so that his face is by me. "I have my first assignment for you." He waits for a reaction, but when I don't provide one, he went on. "I need you to be my spy…" He sighs and then lifts me up so that I'm standing. "…Steal the Warlord's Dagger from Ambrosia."

As if the gods of elves had finally gifted me a prize from the hell I've suffered, happiness sprouts through my entire body. The mention of the powerful artifact spreads goosebumps down my entire body, and my power practically circles furiously at the mention of the darkness that the Warlord dagger contains. I've always wanted to get my hands on it. Never to use it, but to keep it safe. It was truly one of the most dangerous and powerful artifacts in the world.

I frown. "She has the Warlord's Dagger?"

"Unfortunately," he sighs. "Stole it from me in my slumber and hide it somewhere I can't find. I would search for it myself, but I don't have the time nor the patience to do so."

I had to bite the inside of my cheek from smiling because Castor, as brilliant as he may think he is, didn't know how smart I could be. He would never truly get the Warlord's dagger back. I wouldn't allow it – not without him killing me first. For as long as I stood here, alive, I would make sure his greedy hands never touched it again.

"I will find it for you, my king," I promise, spewing lies effortlessly. He smiles, and delight simmers through me.

Keep on smiling. Keep on thinking you have complete control.

"Good, you are dismissed then for the day. I want to see the Warlord's Dagger in my hands in two days. That is all I am giving you." He stares at me before I bow my head to him. I control my breathing, and when I get out, I practically whimper as the tension leaves my body. It amazes me how daft he is.

I duck every time some vampire sneers at me in the hallway, but all I want is to bash their teeth against the wall. Something was wrong with me.

"Hello, ma'am. Can I escort you to your room?" I turn around and spot the maid's uniform. I look up and then see Arabella, her eyes a dark red, illuminating around her dark skin. My eyes widen, and she laughs. "How did that sound? Convincing enough?"

I look around for any vampires, making sure no one can hear. "Holy hell. You look…"

"Weird," Arabella finished my sentence. "This body that I'm in doesn't even feel like mine. Being a werewolf is better. Anything new with Castor?"

"Castor wants me to find the Warlord's dagger. Ambrosia stole it apparently and hid it from him."

She glances behind her and frowned. "Who's Ambrosia?"

"His fiancé," I answer.

She freezes and turns around. She then bursts out laughing, her fangs showing in full view for everyone to stare at, and she only stops laughing when she cannot breathe anymore. She clears her throat. "What woman would ever take him as a husband?"

I whisper: "A mentally insane one. That's what Ambrosia is."

"How long do you have to get it?"

"Two days."

Two vampires appear around the corner, and she shrinks away from me, her head down. When they pass by us, she looks back at me. "I'll tell everyone about the news. I would stay clear of everyone right now. Keep your door unlocked. We'll be coming tonight."

She then bows her head at me, raising an eyebrow in a mocking manner before walking past me.

I walk back to my room, keeping my head high even as everyone gapes at me, their faces showing either disgust or pure anger. As soon as I'm back in my room, I reach for my doorknob.

"Blanche!" I whirl around and watch as Belinda jogs towards me. Her eyes are shimmering with malice, but her smile holds much more emotion that I can't pinpoint.

"I have to show you something," she says, and then pulls my hands. "You'll love it." She walks so fast that I nearly trip over my own feet, trying to keep up. She leads me towards the dungeons, and my heart accelerates.

I shouldn't let her lead me like this, not after knowing she's a Percival. She's just as dangerous, just as vile as the rest of the kingdom.

She wastes no time walking down the stairs, and I try to pull my hand away, anticipation making my stomach hurt. As soon as we reach the doors, she pushes them open and reveals what she has wanted to show me.

A woman is strapped to a chair, just like I had been not too long ago. Her mouth is gagged, and her neck is strapped back towards the chair, making her unable to breathe properly. My mouth drops at how familiar this woman looks - how...she looks so...alike. She seems to be a replica of me.

Belinda walks forward, taking the gag out of her mouth, and then rounds the chair. She places her hands on her shoulders and smiles up at me. "I want you to know you can trust me." The woman growled, her eyes narrowing at me. "This is me proving my loyalty."

"Blanche, meet Mallory Everard," she says, her mouth turning upward. "I believe this is your mother."

CHAPTER THIRTY TWO

It felt like my lungs had been stolen from me. I couldn't breathe, like the sight in front of me was just another nightmare I conjured. It didn't make sense. This woman disappeared such a long time ago, and now she sat in front of me, tied and gagged. My mother was here, alive and well for me to see.

Belinda uses her hands to push her hair to the side, and I see Belinda's fangs reveal into sharp knives, and then, in only a second, she plunges her fangs into my mother's throat. My own eyes widen, and for a moment, I open my mouth to stop her, but my tongue is unable to move.

My mother groaned before she closed her eyes as the sensation of it rolled through her. I can see the exact moment her pleasure was led with pain, her eyes shooting up, and her feet moving, trying to get away, miserably failing through the constraints of Belinda.

When Belinda did release her, she raises her eye, blood coating her mouth hungrily. Her hand swipes across her lips, collecting the leftover blood and licking it from her fingers. "You want to trust me, Blanche? Here." She took careful steps towards me, her violent eyes closing in on mine. "Here is my loyalty to you. I'm gifting you my brother's whore." She looked back at my mother. "Or is it mistress now?"

My eyes snapped to her.

You have got to be kidding.

Her eyes stay on both of us, and the sadness and shock that I felt after burned, and then I feel something different. I felt the dark fury spread through my body. Although my face had no adjustment at all. Before I could go on, though, I turn to Belinda. "It might be better for you to wait outside, Belinda," I said. Although I spoke in a serene manner, there was a warning behind it that was deep enough to be hidden.

Her eyes flickered up to mine for a moment, then she nodded. Before slamming the door behind her, she spared one last look at my mother before walking past me.

Only when the room fell in complete silence did I turn around, looking straight at her. I saw the similarity in my eyes, the same color of blue. I walked forward until I was right in front of her, and I leaned down. "I will take this gag out of your mouth, but understand this now, if you make a move, attempt to call for help, or use any of your magic, there will be severe consequences."

My gaze moved to something silver by her thigh, and I scoffed. I know where I get the habit from now. My fingers met the blade of silver by her thigh, and I pulled it free. It was quite exceptional, perhaps better than the other one I had. It was sharp. *Very sharp.*

She wasn't worthy enough for a dagger like this.

I pushed the tip of the blade toward the center of my mother's neck, threatening to tear her skin until it hung. With my other hand, I reach for the gag, pulling it out of her mouth. She's got freckles around her nose; they're small, but I could still see them.

She opens her mouth to talk, but I push the dagger firmer against her throat to keep her mouth shut. "Don't," I threaten, leaning my head until our noses touch. "You are not allowed to talk until I say you can."

I didn't know where to start. Perhaps I could ask why she had left in the first place or when she had decided to leave, although all of it made me seem just as desperate as my younger self, and right now, all I wanted was my mother desperately underneath me. "So tell me, how has life been treating you?"

Her neutral face showed me she truly didn't care that a dagger was being pointed at her throat, but her lack of screaming showed me how much power I really had over her, and that was exhilarating.

"Interestingly enough," she finally answered.

As I look at her, I can't help but almost think of us as twins. She's so similar, with the same hair, the same eyes, and the same freckles. I walk around her, disgust pulling at my lip.

"So, what have you been up to?" The knife trailed around her shoulder until it reached her upper shoulder. "Have you been busy with other families, by chance?"

She scowled while a sinister smile pulled at my lips. I wasn't going to confront her about this. I was going to make her say it.

"Blanche, please, don't start this now," she commanded.

With a heated look, I ran my fingers through her hair, grabbing one of the strands and rubbing it together before the strands fell back with the rest of her hair. "Don't do what?" I asked innocently.

She turned to me, trying to figure out my plan, but I could tell she didn't have the slightest clue. A cruel smile fell upon my lips. "Tell me, mother. What could you have done that was so horrible, huh?" I kissed the top of her hand, my fingers running through her hair softly.

"Blanche-" In an attempt to explain, she starts to speak but stops short. My hands tighten around her hair, teasing her calmly, but every thought is telling me to rip all of her strands until she has nothing but a wounded scalp. "Blanche, I'm sorry."

My hands suddenly let go of the strands as if I hadn't expected to hear them. Though they tightened just as quick, and I let my anger finally control my body, as I clutched onto her tightly and pulled her head back, with the speed and strength of my grip. She looked up at me through her perfect lashes and her bloody blue eyes.

"You're sorry for what?" I asked, leaning closer so she could see my face better from the chair. I had spent every waking moment wanting this moment to happen. Although I had always thought it would be full of happiness, now I've seen things from a new perspective.

The old Blanche would untie my mother from her constraints and hug her until she couldn't breathe. That old Blanche burned in the village and replaced me. The darkened memory of her.

I had been robbed of this my entire life. There was no goodbye, no warning that she was going, and *finally…. finally*, I was going to say goodbye. Whether it had to be in a bad way or in a good way.

She looks up at me, her eyes wide as if she can see everything in me, but I've locked it away, not letting a single emotion pour out. Not even when I felt the need to run away and hurl.

Then her words cut through me. "I'm sorry I left."

My lips curl up in disgust. I want an explanation, not a fucking apology. I let go of her scalp until I rounded back in front of her. One moment, I'm glaring at her; the next, my hand strikes her face so hard that it bruises my palm. My hand colliding with her cheek sends the whole room echoing the sound against her skin.

"The next time, it will be this knife," I threatened, holding it in my palms tightly. I grab the nearest chair near me and then sit down right in front of her. My hands crossed over my chest, feeling the sharpness of the knife against my chest. "Look at me," I demand. She turns slowly, which almost makes me go mental. "I don't want you to apologize, mother. I want to know why..." A single tear escapes her eye. "Why did you leave?"

"There are many reasons why," she explained, a few extra tears running down her face.

"Well, I've got all day, right?" I ask, looking around for a clock, although it occurred to me that there wouldn't be a clock in a dungeon, so I pointed towards the only window that was in the dungeon, a small window with bars surrounding it so no one could ever escape. "It's still daytime."

She scowled at me now, her gaze narrowing at me deadly. "Well, then, I assume you know what you are, considering you're old enough," she was talking about my new powers. How ironic that this is all happening. "Well then, I'm sure you know by now that I'm a dark elf, too." She shifts in her seat slightly, and I watch as her fingers fidget among themselves. She's trying to figure a way out.

"Keep going," I demand.

She stops her protesting. "I never planned to run away like that, Blanche. I loved your father very much, and I believed he loved me. He was a good man - a wild elf that was a huntsman, and out of everyone, he fell in love with *me*." She stared at me for a moment. "Dark elves were always a hazard. It didn't matter who they were as a person; whether they wanted to use their powers for good or bad, they would always end up dead. So how was I, a true born darkness, ever supposed to tell your father he fell in love with a monster?" She exhaled, tears forming in her eyes, but she blinked them back. "There was one solution, and that was to never tell him."

My eyes widened, but she continued her story. "So, we got married, and no one ever suspected that I was a dark elf, not even Brenner and made sure to avoid my powers. It was so great...I was living my entire life with him, and I was so happy." She looked joyful for a second, but her entire spirit was crushed, her smile turning into a frown. "But then I got pregnant...with you."

Great.

"I was terrified when you were born. I prayed to the moon that you would inhabit most of your father's powers because if you had mine…then all my dreams would be crushed. All of them would turn upside down," she snapped as if this was all somehow my fault.

"When you were only four, you had killed a fox in the forest," she said, biting down on her lip, her gaze softening. "Your father was training you to do it, and you had finally gotten the courage to kill an animal, but when you saw the blood…your eyes darkened, and you smelt it, and…you started to drink it."

I almost stumbled out of my chair and shouted at her for telling me such outrageous lies. Surely that can't be true. I'm not a bloody vampire. Yes, the desire for blood was big with my power, but I had suppressed it for a while now.

"Your father looked at you like a monster, and I'd never seen him so furious at you. He nearly beat you to death, and I had to beg for him to stop; otherwise, he would have broken so many of your bones…" My mother had tears in her eyes as she looked at me. "I had never been more terrified in that moment. I hated him, and I vowed to hate you, too, for spreading us apart like that. If you had never been born, I would have still loved him. My secret would still be safe, and we'd love each other forever."

I scoffed. "So, you hate me because you passed your genes onto me? Perhaps you should take a look at yourself, Mother, before you pass any judgment on me," I hissed.

"That's not all of it," she snapped, and I raised an eyebrow before she continued on. "I knew you were starting to show signs, and as you got older, your powers grew and grew until I couldn't stop them from happening on a daily basis. Your father put his anger out on me mostly, but sometimes I couldn't save you from it."

I shook my head, almost laughing. "None of what you're saying is true. My father would never hit me."

"Nothing that you remember, Blanche," she said, her eyes gleaming. "Do you really think I would let you carry those memories at such a young age?"

I frowned at that statement, and that's when it all hit me. Dark elves can manipulate minds, and my mother was a damn strong one. If what she was saying was true, that meant all the beating, all the insults, all the horrible moments from my childhood…they had been manipulated.

"You messed with my mind?" I demanded.

"I was trying to protect you!" She shouted. "Can't you see?! Your father hated dark elves, and eventually, he started to see it in you, and in me! My secret was out to him, though he never thoroughly admitted to knowing it; I knew he had known, and he despised me for it. He acted horribly towards me, hitting me, ignoring me, and he wouldn't even kiss or lay near me anymore."

Her lips curled up in anger, and for the first time, I'm not sure if she's lying or not. Her emotion shows through her face, and it's hard to tell…hard to pinpoint if this is all made up.

"You're lying," I say, although I'm only trying to deny it. My father was *everything* to me. "I would know if my father went into my mind."

"Dark elves are normally not affected by persuasion, especially by a vampire, although if a vampire, werewolf, elf, or any other creature were to learn how to break past a dark elf's limits, then they would easily be able to perform it. Most persuasion is already powerful, but this kind that you would have to learn would be dark. I believe your father used dark magic persuasion to enter your mind and erase or manipulate any bad memories from your mind."

I wanted to deny it, though as I thought back on my childhood, all I really thought about was how my father always made me study, fight…study and fight…. study and fight. That was my entire life, but I still had shown no signs of my powers. Perhaps they had hidden, but another thought came to mind as fast.

What if my father manipulated my power into hiding? What if he made me study for nothing all this time? In hopes of getting a different power? He wouldn't be that cruel…right?

"You still haven't explained how you left," I said.

"It was simple," she stated. "At first, I was going to take you with me, run and hide away from him, but then a few days before, your father had laid in bed with me, and for the first time in months, he had given me affection, and made love to me. I found out I was pregnant after. I was so happy, but…then that terrifying feeling came back, and I knew I had to leave. I couldn't let this other child suffer because of him like you did."

She sobbed just as she finished. "So, I packed and left. I knew I couldn't save you from him. I'm sure he would have hunted you until the entire world burned, but at least I could save myself and my other child. I left on Christmas, burning all the presents to send a message to never find me. Before I left, I manipulated your memories to make it look like your father was crying and desperately sorrowful at my escape."

A ping of betrayal shot through my heart, and it crashed into a million pieces. How idiotic. She had left *me*. My father was a monster from the looks of it and she had me believe that my father was a good person. That was if all of this was even true. I needed to talk to my father.

Then my mind caught on the way my mother was pregnant. I had a little sister or brother. "Where is my sibling now?" I ask.

Her voice sorrowful, she replied: "Dead. She died while trying to be birthed."

A rush of red shot through me, and my hand shot towards her face again, slapping her harder than I did before. She moaned, looking back at me as if all of this was my fault. She had left me in the clutches of my father, studying and fighting, as if those were my only purpose in the world. I was not allowed to have friends. I was not allowed to socialize with others except for Anastasia, and my heart pinged as I realized the only good memories I had were with her, and now, she was dead.

"And now?" I demand. "What are you doing here?!"

Her gaze hardened on me. "I didn't come here into Romania until years later, but it was because Rufus needed dark elves. He knew there were only a select few rounds, and he had tracked me down, demanded I come and be his subject, and with the loss of my child, I didn't have any other choice. I would be living with the mortals, with nothing. So, I agreed, and when he died, I was passed down to Castor, who gave me to his sister, Belinda."

I crossed my hands, still feeling the knife in my hands. "So, you've been lurking here for years, huh? I'm sure you had access to letters and a bloody quill. You could have written to me."

"I couldn't risk it," she said. "You were a part of my old life that I needed to leave behind."

"I am your daughter!" I shouted, and that shut her mouth. "Do you realize the damage you have done?! The amount of devastation and anger you have caused me to have?! I had loved you, and you abandoned me!" I got up from the chair, kicking it harshly until it smashed towards the wall. At her neutral expression, I sighed. "You don't even care."

"It was my life or yours," she explained. "My life will always be greater than anyone's."

"Oh, I'm sure it is," I mocked. "Or maybe you care about someone else now? King Castor? Really? How could you even bow or get near such a man without rolling in disgust?"

"He has become a good friend of mine," She hesitates to say and then shrugs her shoulders. "He was there for me when I was going through a lot."

"Helping you?" I raise an eyebrow, smiling. "You mean he fucked you, right?"

Her eyes widened. "Blanche, no-"

"I've had enough of this. Figure your way out on your own; I've got other things to deal with." I push myself off the chair, and my mother watches my moves.

"Blanche, untie me," she demands.

"No." I shrug my shoulders. "You left me with my father, and now, I finally get a chance to leave you." I walk towards her and place a small kiss on her cheek. "One day, you won't just be tied to this chair. I will kill you and let your despairing body rot. I won't let you get your goodbyes. Not even to your precious king."

I stormed out of the room, my steps on fire. All I want to do is let the blood inside me run and tear everything that I see apart until it's scattered under me. I want to drown in this anger - I want to let this wrath out of my chest, and at the same time, tears form in my eyes, and I cannot stand to hide them anymore.

Walking up the dungeon's stairs, pathetic sobs escape my mouth. The knife is still firmly in my hands; I draw it up, still feeling the anger slicing into my palm. I cry out in pain at the deep wound, but at the same time, I'm filled with the euphoric feeling of happiness, and it washes over me in a dark hurricane. I'd never felt so happy, angry, and sad, and I wanted to cry, shout, and yell for happiness.

It felt like I was going to collapse. I would kill her for what she did.

I burst through the door, coming into contact with Belinda, who stands outside the castle corridor. "Belinda? You're still here?"

She smiled at me as if she knew what I was doing down there, but then her eyes fell over my bloody palms and the knife in my hand. She raised an eyebrow at me before she stepped closer. "You have to be careful with knives, Everard. They can leave scars." She drew her hand out, but I caught it, ignoring the pain in my palm.

Her eyebrows scrunched in confusion, but before she could let a word out, a guard strolls up to us. His blonde hair seemed all too familiar, and when I looked up into his eyes, I found the same brown eyes that I saw most of the time. I wiped away my tears furiously.

He guided his hand out to both of us. His eyes scan around us, and then he takes a step closer.

He bows his head, looking at me mischievously. "May I escort you to your room, Ms. Everard?"

CHAPTER THIRTY THREE

As the dead of night fell, everyone gathered in my room. My wrists were still sore from my cuts earlier, but the sting of them reminded me of the blinded pleasure I felt underneath. In spite of the fact that the majority of them had vanished, I was delighted to see those that had remained. I sat on the bed, my elbows resting on the mattress as my hands cupped my face.

Arabella sat beside me, her legs criss crossed on the bed while she played with the white drapes of the bed. She was wearing a red nightgown that splayed across her form, and it ended right underneath her knees. She looked marvelous.

Beckett and Edwin were by the door, whispering unknown secrets to one another. It was obvious those two were talking about something serious, but I didn't want to invade their conversation, though my ears perked up, trying to invade. Before my ears could hear their conversation, I turned towards my father, whose eyes were trained toward the ground, deep in thought.

I thought about what my mother said….and about his reaction when he found out I was a dark elf. Everyone had sort of accepted it from me, even when it was the most dangerous elf there was to live. Hell, not even Beckett questioned me about it. Everyone never said anything but my father…he had been disappointed.

I was going to get the truth from him, whether he liked it or not.

Devyn strolled through the room, throwing away the covers and turning on the little lamp by my bed. She put down a huge map that lay on the sheet. "Everyone gather around," Devyn instructed, laying out a big map that unfolded across my bed. Devyn hadn't talked to me since our fight, and we both remained unspoken about it. Right now, the mission was necessary, not a petty argument between us.

Everyone rushed to gather around, and Arabella and I turned our bodies to get a clear view of the map. In the midst of the pain in my hands, Beckett's left knuckles touched mine slightly. I focused on the pain in my hands to combat the horrible aching feeling in my chest.

It wasn't the first time I had felt this way around him. I had an inkling feeling that this nauseating feeling was more than just hatred.

"Word has spread in the town of Ambrosia's coronation, which means that her rising to the throne is soon. We must stop that from happening," Devyn said. She spread her hand out, pointing towards certain areas of the map. There are sections to the castle, four of them to be exact. My room stands in the north wing, where the throne room, dining room, and gallery are located. It's also where the coronation for Ambrosia will be presented.

Each section has a tower, and around it is a big stone gate to protect it. It connects the castle in four parts, and the walkways are held outside on a bridge held up in the air, connecting the towers.

Devyn points to a specific room in the east wing. "Castor's room is located in the tower we're currently in, which also means that Ambrosia sleeps here too." Her hand trails along the towers. "Which also means she could have hidden it here...or in the three towers. And if we were unlucky, she might have hidden it away from the castle."

"Ambrosia likes to tease, which means she's creative. She needed to hide it where Castor couldn't find it."

"Correct," Devyn agrees, avoiding my eyes as she looks at the rest of them. "But nonetheless, it's in these four towers somewhere, and with only six of us...it will take us weeks just to find the bloody thing. There is no way we can find it in two days."

"Well, we have to," Beckett snapped, his hands fisting against the sheets. "If we don't, Blanche is dead." He looks at me, his face tightening. He looks back at Devyn, frowning. "We need her for the plan."

We need her for the plan.

It shouldn't have hurt, but it did. The bait in all of this is what Beckett told me the first time we discussed this plan. I accepted it – played the part, but it only made this sickening feeling inside me grow.

"Even with my magic, I can't do it that quickly," Devyn retorts, crossing her hands over my chest. "So please enlighten me if you have an idea."

"I can use my shadows," Beckett responds, and then, all at once, I feel coldness spread across the room, sending goosebumps along my bare arms and legs. Something whirls around my hands, something black. When I look down, it circles around my arm, a black, small, and ghost-like shadow.

"Christ-" I commented, but the shadow started roaming up my hand until it was by my shoulder and then around my neck. I didn't see any eyes, only movement, but I could hear its whispers, and when I looked around, everyone else had their own little shadow clinging onto them.

Edwin had two of them around him, the shadows whispering to him with familiarity; he smiled down at them.

"My shadows are like ghosts. They see everything around me; they can tell me things I don't see in front of me, but I can't command them to my will. They all have their own mind, and with each sin I've done, another shadow is made until I'm consumed by them. They are sort of like my punishment, but my friends as well."

Arabella clears her throat. "What are you getting at?"

"My shadows are like my personal guide. They warn me when something bad is coming, but they also don't like to listen sometimes." He holds his hand out to me, and suddenly, the shadow around my neck is being pulled towards Beckett, where he then gently guides the shadow around his own neck. "This one here is Shade. He doesn't like to listen and wanders around too much."

A whining noise emanates from the shadow around his neck as if embarrassed, and then the shadow disappears.

"Alright, we get it now. Get your shadows off me," Arabella snaps, and Beckett glances at them, the shadows disappearing. "Alright, so we use your shadows to look all over the castle. Can they do it in two days?"

He sneers. "They can do it in two hours."

"Great," she responds and then looks at the map.

"What happens after?" Brenner speaks up. We all turn to him, and my muscles tense at the sudden tension I have with him. I need to talk to him very soon. "We can't let that monster have the Warlord's dagger."

"You guys are kidding, right?" Arabella looks around the room, raising her eyebrow as if the answer is right in front of us. "We have four elves at our disposal, who happen to be able to craft stuff. We can make a fake one and give it to him without him realizing. We can keep the Warlord's dagger for ourselves and use it against him at the coronation."

"She's right," Devyn agrees. She looks at Beckett, Edwin, Brenner, and me. "Then we keep the Warlord's dagger and save it for the coronation." Her smile turns menacing, "Then we kill the king and queen."

Beckett takes my hand and then looks down at me. "Well, it's a good thing that Everard and I are up for it."

"I never volunteered," I argued, crossing my hands and coming to a stop by a bedroom door. Beckett walked side by side with me. He'd been happy to have me along, but I only felt annoyed as he dragged me into this. I was supposed to be laying low, tricking Castor.

I shouldn't be angry with him. My life was on the line, but it was because of him that I was in this position.

"You whine too much," he retorted before he opened the door and slipped inside. With a huff, I followed, plunging into the darkness and shutting the door behind me.

"Why here?" I asked.

"Shade told me we would find something in here. He didn't say what, that bloody bastard, but he said it was something important," he replied, scanning the room like a predator on a rampage.

I chuckled, and he turned, frowning. "Do you talk to your shadows a lot?" I teased.

"Only when they talk to me." He zeroes in on the curtains and pulls them aside. The moon glows.

This room is so similar to mine, with its gigantic bed, large vanity, open closet, and big bathroom. All of it would look spectacular if it did not look so abandoned. This room had not been touched in ages, and it showed. Dust was lingering on the vanity and desk, the bed was made, and the pillows and sheets looked untouched. Not a soul in sight accompanied this bedroom.

"This was Ambrosia's old room," Beckett says, trailing his

hand over the window ledge, his finger collecting dust. "What could Shade have found in here?" Beckett asks, mostly to himself as he roams the room, his hands spreading across the bed, gathering dust into his hands. He is quiet as he looks up towards the ceiling. I saunter over to the vanity, opening up the white drawers. A moth flies out suddenly, and I stagger back.

I curse, shutting the drawer. My back meets the hard surface of Beckett's chest, and I turn around just as Beckett lets the moth land on his finger. "Moths are beautiful creatures," he explains. "But…they also mean death. Did you know that?"

"Yes, I did," I say. I was familiar with them since I studied most creatures, although I never really cared for them. Moths actually represented a lot of other things. They can mean change, transformation, endings, or even the mystery. Death was one of them, but you can never really see the true meaning of a moth.

"I think somebody died here," Beckett stated; he turned and looked around at his surroundings. I walk past him, opening up all my senses. Beckett's heart increases just as he moves closer to me. "Do you hear anything?"

I look back at him. "Only your bloody heart."

"It beats only when you're around." He chuckles. I would roll my eyes, but the sudden sincereness has my heart speeding up. How suddenly, I feel like I'm falling out of the world into a dark abyss, with him controlling how fast I fall. He then lifts a strand of my hair. "It seems your heart is full of life with me."

I swat his hand away. "Refrain from touching me and my hair."

He shakes his head as he roams around the bed, away from me. His hand skimmed the headboard, listening, as do my senses. I walk towards him, looking down at the bed. As if reading my thoughts, he raises an eyebrow. "I'm not getting on the ground."

Pretentious prick.

I punch him in the shoulder before I lower myself to the ground. I look down under the bed, only seeing the darkness that looms underneath it. I then stick my hand out, feeling for anything. I look up at Beckett, a smile spreading across his cheek. "You look beautiful from this angle."

"I'm sure you love me on my knees," I respond. My fingers move over something, and I freeze. I feel for it again until I feel something wet and mushy, and I pull away, curling my lip in disgust. I groan, sitting up and looking at my hand. A thick black goo is on my fingers, cold but…sticky.

Beckett kneels. "What did you see?"

"Nothing, it was…" I look down at my hands. "Whatever this stuff is. Can you move the bed?"

He smiles, but with only a flick of his hands, Shade, the shadow that had wrapped his body around my neck earlier, comes roaming out, and crawling under the bed. A second later, he comes out and whispers something in Beckett's ear. He looks at me. "Shade says we shouldn't move the bed and that we should drag it out."

I scoff. "Well then, gladly go ahead, cause I'm not sticking my hand down there again."

He put his hand underneath with a roll of his eyes. I can tell when his hand hit the goo. His mouth scrunched up into disgust, and that's when he starts pulling. I see the edge of something black, and then he pulls it out.

The stench burns my nose, and I almost gag as I look at the creature that lies before us - dead. I cover my mouth, inhaling the smell despite my attempts not to. "Holy hell," Beckett says, backing away in disgust. "Christ, what is that?"

I scoot closer despite its horrid smell. "It's a cat; can't you see the ears?" In front of me, a once-alive cat is covered in the darkest black tar. Its ears seem to be the only thing that looks intact. Its eyes are rolled back, and the whites of its eyes are the only thing I see. Its paws have been burned, and its prints darkened. Whatever happened to this creature was a heinous thing.

Shade whispers something again to Beckett, and he turns to him. "He wants us to look inside."

I turned to him. "Look inside what?"

Beckett looks at the dead cat and ushers to it. "Inside the cat."

I look at him, trying to find the amusement behind his eyes. This must be a trick, and he's baiting me yet again. Is that what this is? A test? However, as I looked closer, I realized that he was being serious.

I removed my hand from my mouth, the waft of it making my head hurt. I crawl towards it and, with my hand, flip it over so that it lays on its back and the belly is facing us. I then extend my hand to Beckett. "Give me your dagger."

He grabs it, the same dagger that had once cut me. The name Elodie prints across it, and I feel my blood pump up, my heartbeat growing faster. I held my tongue against the woman's name.

I grabbed for it, but when he lifts it up in the air, I frown. "Be careful. This dagger can feel emotions." He leans forward, his face close to mine. "Just like I can feel you." I glare at him before I grab it and face the cat.

With one of my hands, I position the knife directly at the top of the belly. I take a deep breath, putting my hand on the floor as I start to carve into it. I thought the smell was horrible, but from the inside, it looked even worse. Expired lungs, beating heart rotting, and the blood…Hell, for a dead cat, there was so much blood.

I drop his dagger and then scrunch my nose in disgust. I know what I need to do. My hand slips inside the womb, feeling everything - *everything*. Its blood seeped through my fingers.

"This isn't right. There shouldn't be this much blood," Beckett mutters. He looks up at me. "Do you feel anything?"

I feel my way around its organs, feeling everything. My fingers brush past something big, which could only mean its heart. The surprise hit me as I realized *it was moving*. The heart beat, in such a small pace, that it could have tricked me for a second. This cat was barely alive, clinging to life. The blood sends a rush through me - how suddenly, it's all I want to feel.

Then, my hand hits something hard, and my hand curls around it as I start to pull it out. "Holy- " I start, feeling how heavy it is. It's enough for me to pull out. It falls to the ground as soon as it is out, and I stumbled back from the cat as suddenly, an agonizing screech came out of its mouth.

My eyes widened. The cat suddenly whimpered, shaking uncontrollably. Beckett backs away, and suddenly, I hear nothing. Beckett looks at the dagger and grabs it, but my eyes never leave the cat. My hand is still covered in blood, my eyes watering.

The cat was still alive, and I just killed it.

Beckett grabs for the bloody dagger, wiping some of the blood off of it. I had never seen such a beautiful dagger, and I wanted to hold it. I reached for it, but Beckett drew it away as if I would damage it somehow. From here, I can see the silver handle. Green and gold vines were covering it, stains of vermillion blood. The blade itself was something I could never picture in real life. It was gold. Magical.

On was beautiful gems lining the handle, making it colorful and brighter. It was the most beautiful dagger I ever laid my eyes on.

It was as powerful as the Warlock who created such a thing.

When I look at Beckett, he's smiling right back at me, and it's the first sincere smile I've ever seen him wear. "We found it…" he laughed. "We bloody found it."

CHAPTER THIRTY FOUR

I turned on the sink and washed my bloody hands under it. I could smell the dead stench on me, but I hid my disgust as the sink turned red and the blood plummeted from my hands. I could still see the cat in the back of my mind, but the further I pushed it from my mind, the easier it was to focus on the pain.

"How did you get those bandages, little elf?" I shut the water off and then dry my hands, looking over at Brooker. He leans on the frame of the doorway, his hands crossed.

"I cut myself," I said and then walked straight to him. "Move."

I can see the Warlord's dagger in the holster. He towers over me as he steps closer, and I look up at him. His hands uncross, and one of them reaches into his holster, pulling the Warlord's dagger out. He grabs my hand and then puts the knife in my hand. "I'm keeping it with you for now. I'll need to grab some supplies to make a replica, and I'll come back tomorrow night."

I shrug. "Okay."

I wait for him to leave, and I curl my fingers around the dagger. I can feel the dark magic lingering in the knife, and I'm terrified to even get closer to the blade. When he doesn't leave, I cock an eyebrow at him. "Please, get out of my way."

He chuckles. "Why don't you make me?"

I scoff. "I suggest you leave instead of baiting me right now." His gaze sharpened to me. It didn't matter if I was holding the deadliest weapon in the world right now; his eyes were deadlier.

His hand shot forward slowly as he took a piece of my hair and tucked it behind my ear. "You look like a cruel punishment, dear," he said, his eyes trailing over my face, eyes landing on my lips. His hands came forward, one hand landing on the side of my arm while the other lightly wrapped around my waist, pulling me right into his body.

My body pressed into his sinfulness, and I sighed. His mouth was only a few inches from mine, but his eyes never left mine. I could feel the desire radiating off of him, and something wrapped around me. Shadows, I realized.

Goosebumps spread across my arm.

"Brooker-" I started to speak. It was when his mouth ghosted over mine that my eyes fell close, and I fell prey to the darkness of him. I don't know why he was doing this to me. After everything he has done, must he put me through more suffering?

I bit down on my lip, cracking my eyes open. His lips are so close to mine - I can't do this. I can't let him ruin me and drive me into oblivion. My hands met his chest and pushed him away so that he got the hint.

His eyes opened, and he looked at me, his eyebrows scrunching in confusion.

"I think you should leave," I whispered.

He looked at me for a second, and then he turned around and walked off. I heard the slam of the door, and I clenched my own fists, even the one around the dagger.

There was something strong between Beckett and I. I thought it was hatred, and maybe it still was, but there was no denying that something else was there, and it was exhausting. It was harmful.

Focus on the pain.

When I did, I felt better.

I knew I needed to talk to my father soon, and I didn't want to wait anymore. After the knowledge, my mother presented to me, the aching burning of needing to know what happened blistered. His reaction to my powers had been off, and I wanted him to accept me for what I was, even if he hated it.

It didn't take long to find him. All I had to hear were his familiar footsteps, and I found him in the kitchen. Thankfully, he was alone. When I opened the wooden door to it, I made sure to lock the doors behind me. I didn't need anyone barging in when I confronted him.

He could sense me - I knew he could, but he never turned to me as he gathered scones into a brown basket. I walked up to him, my head held high. Anxiety pooled in my chest. My father was the most important man I had ever had in my life, and I couldn't risk losing him all over again. "Father."

He turned his head to the side, not fully looking at me, but at least he was acknowledging my presence. "Yes, Blanche?"

"You know we need to talk," I state, and he turns around then, his eyes piercing mine. I've seen my father angry before - completely disappointed and fury burning in his eyes until I had no choice but to beg for his forgiveness. "About my powers."

"I'd rather not," He said before turning his back to me again, continuing to pay attention to the basket.

I scoff, my heart pumping loudly to the point where I'm sure my father could hear. "Are you angry with me? You know I didn't ask for this."

"Blanche…" he sighed, turning back to me now. He looked defeated all of a sudden, like he knew this would happen, and he dreaded it. My mother's words rang in the back of my mind, and I wondered if maybe…she was telling the truth. Could it be?

"Being a dark elf is dangerous, so once this plan is over, we have to keep it a secret. You won't be allowed to use your powers. Everyone will try to kill you-"

"That's all you have to say right now?" I demanded, my voice rising in anger. "I have been drowning in this new power since it emerged, and I cannot stop now. Not since it's been so *long*. Do you have any idea how miserable it was to be the only elf in the village that didn't possess power?"

"You have always possessed power," my father argued. "You were just a little later than others."

"Or maybe I wasn't," I shrugged and looked up at him, and I knew the accusation showed in the depths of my eyes. "Maybe you already knew about my power, and you wanted to hide it."

He drew back, raising an eyebrow. "Where is this coming from, Blanche?"

I glanced down at my feet, wanting to tell him everything. "I talked to Mom," I said before I could regret saying it. When I looked back at him, his eyes were wide, and his mouth was quivering as if this news was horrible. It must be, especially since I just learned he hated her. "She told me…a lot."

"You can't trust anything she says," he says.

I frown. "Aren't you surprised, father?"

He shrugged. "I am surprised."

"She told me everything about her leaving…about her dark elf powers. She even told me she manipulated my mind. She said that you have been, too," I tell him everything I know. My hands shake at my sides, waiting for him to deny it, but when he stays silent, I realize that this is no ordinary accusation. It's the truth.

I have memories inside my head that have been manipulated into me believing I had a perfectly normal childhood. I was a good elf who studied and fought, and I had an amazing father. My mouth dropped, and I watched as his features turned into a morph of guilt and anger.

"Is…Is it true?"

He didn't shed a single tear, not even when my tears threatened to spill at the next thing he said. I begged that he would say no and tell me that my mother was insane to suggest such a thing. I begged that he was the perfect father I had thought him to be for my entire life. Then, his head moved, nodding, and I felt my body break into a million shards of darkness and anguish.

A choked sob escaped my mouth, my hand covering my mouth to keep my voice mute. My eyes closed, tears pouring out of me like a waterfall. My lips quivered, and I sobbed even harder. I tried to search his face for any remorse, but it came blank. "How could you?" I sobbed even harder.

I didn't want to cry. I wanted to hurt, but no matter my protesting, the tears wouldn't stop. I tried focusing on the pain in my wrists, but it only made me cry harder. I raised my hands suddenly and lunged at him. My hand whipped in the air, my darkness sending him hurling towards the right.

He fell on the floor, and when he looked up, finally, I saw emotion flicker. It was an emotion I had seen too many times before.

Fear.

"I want them back." I demanded, stalking closer to him until my feet were right by him, and his body was sitting up, looking up at me. "Do you hear me?! I want every agonizing memory back into my brain!" For a second, he stared, and that made me even angrier. "I want all my memories back." My foot hit his stomach and kicked him hard to his side, making him groan, his back falling to the ground.

I continued to kick him hard until I saw blood. His mouth was covered in it, and I raised my foot, making sure to kick him across the face until I heard the crack in his nose. "*Give them back!*" I shouted, and this time, he looked me straight in the face as if I had compelled him myself.

Which I might have.

"It will hurt," he spoke, blood leaking from his mouth. "It will hurt a lot."

"Not as much as you have hurt me," I admitted, and that feeling itself had me feeling weak and desperate. I had promised myself not to feel these two emotions again.

My father sighed before he got back on his feet; despite the blood and pain he felt, two of his fingers met my forehead, and he closed his eyes for a minute, and that's when it all came flooding back in. The excruciating feeling of euphoria for a moment before I screamed, falling back.

My body landed on the floor, only to be sucked into a dark hole where the memories sprouted around me.

I carried a sunflower in my hands. Little vines were attached to it, but I threw them off as I walked over to my father, who sharpened his knife on a nearby wood trunk. He threw me a glance, a smile radiating off of his lips before I appeared in front of him.

"I got you a flower," I said, extending it towards me.

He smiled but shook his head. "No, Blanche, I don't like flowers, but I'm sure mom would love it very much." He took the flower from my hands, got off the trunk, and placed it in the center. "Now, today is the day you kill a fox, dear. I believe you are ready." He took hold of my tiny hand, and I let him guide me through the scary forest.

He stopped when he spotted a fox in the center of the small grassland. He crouched and then handed the knife to me, his eyes gleaming with excitement. "Now, exactly as I have taught you, Blanche." He let go of my hand and then backed away from me. He hid behind the trees while I remembered what my father taught me.

Foxes are sly and mischievous creatures. I had read about them only a few days ago when my father made me sit down and read. I hadn't wanted to, complaining that I wanted to go outside and make friends. He dismissed me with little to no consideration before he made me read two other books about them.

I crept around the tree, trying to find the right position to strike. Until now, I hadn't been able to kill an animal. They always seemed delicate creatures to me that deserved to live, but today was the day I proved my father wrong.

So, as I spotted the fox again, his head perked up, not looking in my direction. I could get it from behind - my attack would be unexpected, but foxes have exceptional senses.

From the side. I would jump at it from the side. Normally, a better weapon would have been a crossbow or bow and arrow, but I had to make it work with a knife.

So, as I turned around the tree, I made sure I was centered with its belly. Quietly, my feet crouched, and when its head looked back down at the ground, I struck. The fox didn't expect it, and its eyes met mine for a brief minute before the dagger had met the center of its stomach. My eyes looked at its stomach, watching as the blood poured from it.

I wanted to hurl as I looked at it. My mouth dropped when I saw the glint of hurt in its eyes, and my eyes teared up. Guilt. I felt guilty. Then the blood met my hands, and suddenly, something about it lured me straight in.

"You did it!" My father's voice yelled in excitement, but I didn't bother to look back, not when the sight in front of me was captivating my entire being, and it was the most powerful thing I have ever felt. I drew my head closer to the blood - needing it - tasting it on my tongue.

"What in the world?!" My father suddenly shouted, and he pushed me so hard that my entire body was thrown to the side. My back hit the nearest tree, and I looked up. "What were you doing?!" He started shout-ing, and he bent down, grabbing me by the shoulders and shaking me. "Why were you drinking its blood?!"

My entire body shook. I was? I didn't know. I didn't mean to. I swear I didn't-

A hand whipped across my face, and my cheek burned from the harsh punishment that my father cast upon me. I looked back at him, tears burning in my eyes. "Don't look at me like that," he snarled, and then *his hand whipped in the air, this time sending me tumbling into the air until my face hit a tree branch, and I fell, my mouth bloody, one of my eyes swollen.*

"W-What's going on?!" Suddenly, I heard my mother's voice yell, and my head lifted from the ground. I saw my father strolling over to her, shouting something at her, but I couldn't hear anything that transpired between them, the only thing I heard was the ringing in my ears. I watched as my father raised his hand to cast the same misfortune on her that he did to me, but she stopped him with a single thought, sending him cascading back.

"You monster!" She shouted before she scooped me up in her hands, and I sobbed, my head buried in her shoulder. "Don't you ever touch her again!"

I felt reality come back into my body, and my eyes opened. I was lying on the kitchen floor. My father was standing over me, his eyes darkening. He didn't look like the father who raised me, and after seeing that, maybe he never was.

"That is just one memory, Blanche," he said, and then he went on, "Do you really want to see the rest?"

Hatred burns, and I feel the utter rage to rip him apart. I hadn't even felt this kind of hatred towards Beckett, who always seemed to rile me up the most. Now, my own father stared back at me, and the only thing that fired inside my body was betrayal, and I needed to hurt him somehow.

His hands then circled around each other, and before I could protest, he shot something my way. I covered my body, but not before the magic hit my head suddenly, and I jolted up. "What did you do to me?"

"You wanted to know your memories, Blanche," he said. "I was protecting you from them, but it seems you don't want that. So now you can drown in them," he said before he walked away.

"Wait!" I shouted, but he did not listen. "You can't just leave! You still have so much to explain!"

He unlocked the door, and before he left, he turned to me. "No, I don't." Then he left, and I felt the tears invading my eyes as they slipped, and sobs escaped my mouth.

This entire time, I had been a shell of a person, believing I was someone I was not when I had been molded into something else entirely.

CHAPTER THIRTY FIVE

I didn't sleep the entire night, and I wish I could curse myself into never falling asleep again. Every time my eyes fell
closed, I could feel another memory stirring behind the
depths of my mind, and I wasn't prepared to face reality just yet.
I cut my legs, distracting myself with the pain, daring myself to
close my eyes again.

It didn't make sense how I had hopelessly fallen into the hands
of the creatures around me. First, it had been Brooker, who I knew
from the very beginning was a monster, but I had been blind -
oblivious to the actions of others around me. Truly, now I have
absolutely no one.

Beckett hadn't come, even though I had expected him.

"Blanche!" A voice called from outside the door, and I spun
around from the desk just as the door opened, and Belinda strolled
in. She looked like she was reborn from the dead of night. Dressed
in a long black shimmering dress that fit her curves in just the right
way, and her red heels stuck out from the rest of her outfit. She
wore a little makeup, which I had no bother doing - considering I
didn't know how to do it.

"What do I owe the pleasure?" I ask in the most monotone voice
I can muster.

"Ambrosia's coronation is coming up, and Castor has said to
pick just the right dress for you," she exhaled and narrowed her
eyes at me. "Have you ever gone shopping, elf?"

My eyes widened at the smile that she conjured. "Yes, I have,
in my village."

"Oh, but have you ever gone to a store in Romania? We have such exclusive styles here. Truly, we must find something of great style for you." She walked forward, her eyes turning a dark red before she smiled at me. "It's not up for choice either, I'm afraid, but I'll make sure to give you the time of your life."

I sighed, narrowing my eyes. "Do you need blood?"

She drew back as if surprised. "No, actually, I don't. My eyes turn red when I express a strong emotion. I can't control it that well, so I've stopped trying, but…if you are offering your blood, I wouldn't mind…" She took another step closer, but I stood up from the chair before she could tower over me.

"Belinda, I trust you more than any vampire in this castle, but I will never let you drink my blood," I snapped, and she narrowed her eyes at that challenge before she stepped back, smirking. "Now, you said we were going shopping?"

We found ourselves roaming the streets of Romania. I never thought I would be outside the walls of the castle, especially after becoming a slave to Castor. Though, as Belinda pulled my hand to a store named *The Popular Chariot*, I couldn't help but feel a little giddy.

I haven't gone shopping like this in many years. In my elf village, there were many shops that the elves went to, but it would never compare to what the mortal world had. We had to use blacksmiths to make our clothes, with as many things as we could bring from the mortal world, but I had never been to an actual store in the mortal world. Even this country was infested with parasitic vampires.

Belinda threw the door open, with a loud cling of a bell falling upon the store. The shop owner stood at the cash register, counting a stack of cash. She glanced at us once, but she flung her head towards us again, and with a whip of air, the cash fell from her hands, and she appeared in front of Belinda suddenly.

Her white hair whipped around wildly, her red eyes widening, and she kneeled on the floor in front of Belinda. "My lady, what do I owe the pleasure?"

"Oh Cordelia, please get up. I just came here to browse around," Belinda answered, and then she tugged me forward with her hand. Cordelia looked up at her, and her eyes narrowed when she looked at me. "And this is Blanche. My brother's loyal subject."

"Yes, I've heard the rumors," she cooed before standing back up on her own two feet. She surveyed me, her eyes glancing down and roaming my entire body until her eyes met mine. "I sense danger coming from you."

I frowned. "Uh…"

Belinda only chuckled and looked back around me. "Don't think too much about it, elf. Cordelia likes to analyze people, and she tends to be a little dramatic about it." Belinda then tugged me so that her hand wrapped around mine, and she cast a smile at Cordelia. "Can you please show us the most beautiful dress you carry?"

Cordelia snapped her head to Belinda, and the eyes that pierced mine became soft. She nodded before she took the lead. I fell into step with Belinda, even though she was going extremely fast. Cordelia led us to the back of the store, where there were separate rooms. It was shaped in a circle, with curtains wrapped around the front.

Cordelia pulled the curtain aside until two chairs stood at the right, and in front was a large mirror. "Sit down. I'll go fetch the dress." She rounded us, casting me a glare, her fangs snapping out before she passed me.

It seems that someone doesn't like me.

"Cordelia is hyper-sensitive when it comes to her senses. She can see things better just by looking at someone. It's no wonder she sensed you were in danger. You're loyal to my brother." Belinda took a seat in one of the chairs, and I followed.

The curtains opened again and closed as Cordelia strolled in. She carried a long red dress. She kneeled once again in front of Belinda and stretched her hands out to offer the dress to Belinda.

Belinda smiled. "Actually, it's for Blanche."

I turned my head in surprise, and at the same time, Cordelia snapped her head to me, her gaze growing angrier, and the wrinkle in her nose said everything that needed to be said. "Uh, no, it's fine. I don't-"

"Nonsense," Belinda said, standing and beckoning Cordelia to stand up with the curve of her finger. Cordelia swallowed and then looked at me. "Castor's loyal subject expects to look the part, Everard. Plus, you would look very delicious in a red dress."

"If I have the most beautiful dress, then won't Ambrosia be upset? It's her coronation, after all," I argued, standing up and crossing my hands.

"Don't you dare back talk, our lady!" Cordelia screamed, pointing a crooked finger in my face. I flinched at her tone, not out of fear but of the business of it. I hadn't really met anyone here yet who was truly extremely loyal, at least not like Cordelia. Everyone followed Castor's orders, but they never got to their knees unless it was out of fear.

Here was Cordelia, who had just kneeled for Belinda multiple times in the span of five minutes without as much as a thought.

"Cordelia," Belinda warned, drawing my attention away from her face. "This is Castor's loyal subject you are talking to. Unless you don't want to get in trouble with the king, I would suggest leaving this instant," she narrowed her eyes at Cordelia, "...And leave the dress."

Cordelia huffed and glared at me as if this was my fault. I rolled my eyes when her back was turned from us, and I shook my head in annoyance. She tossed the dress on top of the chair before she pulled the curtains closed behind her. I didn't need another enemy right now, I'm sure her hatred for me would grow even further, once she finds out what I have planned for the king.

I turned to Belinda, my eyebrows scrunching. *What would you think, Belinda?*

"Well," Belinda said, facing me. "You should try the dress on."

I narrowed my eyes on her, but she just gave me a smile before I walked over to the chair where Cordelia had placed it before she left. I lifted the dress into my vision. It was certainly a beautiful dress. From far away, it looked like a bright red, but looking at it closely, I realized it was a bit darker than it looked.

I looked over my shoulder. "Turn around." Belinda did so as I started to take off my clothes. I dropped my pants to the floor, stepped out of them, and then unbuttoned my shirt, leaving me in only my black underwear. I stepped into the dress, and I was slightly surprised when the dress fit me perfectly.

I whirled around, looking at myself in the mirror. The beauty that the dress held hit me then. It clung to my body like a magnet, and I saw the way it hugged my curves perfectly. It was long, going past my legs, until it hit the floor, with a pool of other fabric around it. The dress itself was made purely of silk, but what caught my attention was the two slits on both sides of the dress. It showed my legs, and in the center, it covered itself with fabric.

On top, long-sleeved lace scratched at my hands, and I took a deep breath as I stretched my neck from one side and then surveyed myself in the mirror. "You can look now," I said, and Belinda turned around.

With one look, her eyes widened with hunger, and then she smiled. "It looks beautiful. You must wear it."

I shook my head. "I shouldn't. What if Ambrosia thinks I'm trying to outshine her? It'll only cause chaos if I wear it." I went to grab at the back of the dress, unzipping it, but Belinda used her speed to whirl around me and stop my hands from doing no such thing. She gazed at me in the mirror, her hands wrapped around mine tightly behind my back.

I could feel her breath right behind me, but it didn't matter if she was a vampire or if she was trying to become my friend; I didn't share any kind of fear, leaving my expression blank. "Don't you want that, Blanche? To outshine others?"

I frowned. "No."

"You should," she said, and then let go of my hands and let them run through my hair before tossing my hair over my shoulder. Her hands wrapped around my shoulders, and she smiled at me. "If you wore this dress, everyone would look at you. Admire you. They might even forget you're an elf."

It was tempting, though I wasn't sure if it was worth it. I looked at myself for a minute and let myself think of what might happen if I did wear this dress to the coronation. I could walk into the room and let everyone's eyes linger on me instead of the king or his future queen. They would whisper. Some might gossip. They would be looking at *me*. Not her.

Then I saw the way Ambrosia's fangs popped out, and she lunged at me before she sucked me dry and found that the dark power that swirled around me wasn't normal and that I was betraying Castor all along.

I sighed. "Even if I did wear this dress, I wouldn't be able to pay for it."

Ambrosia giggled. "I'm Castor's younger sister, and Cordelia is in love with me. I could convince her to just give it to me, although if we are being modest, I can always pay for it."

I frowned. I was trying to kill the king and queen, not impress them. I had no one to impress, but as I said that, Blonde hair and brown eyes flashed in my mind, and I almost cursed when I found him admiring me in this dress, and I felt exhilarated. I felt like myself.

I cursed. "Fine, I'll wear it." I turned around towards Belinda.

"I can pay you back…with due time."

Belinda squealed. "No need, dear elf, I don't need money any-ways," her hand lowered towards my hand, feeling the fabric of lace around it. "Everyone is going to die to get a taste of you, darling elf."

CHAPTER THIRTY SIX

I waited for Beckett as the clock turned midnight. He should have been here hours ago, and I didn't know if I was disappointed or happy he wasn't here. He had not come the night before, and I wondered what was taking him so long. I needed the Warlord's dagger by tomorrow, or Castor would get suspicious.

I felt the Warlord's dagger strapped in the holster that was wrapped around my thigh. It didn't feel safe to hide it in my room. I was terrified someone might steal it from me in the dead of night. I had thought to put it under my pillow, but even a thief would look there, so I stashed it on me. Where I knew no one would touch it.

When the clock strikes five after, I sit up on my elbows, my eyes heavy with drowsiness. I would give Beckett five more minutes.

Except, then, behind the door, I can make out three soft knocks. I swing my legs out of the bed, straightening my dress, hiding the dagger. I hear three knocks again, slightly louder this time. He had made me wait. Surely, he could wait as well.

I pull my hand away from the doorknob, hearing silence behind the door; only a few seconds later, I hear footsteps and then a slight breeze. Shivers run down my back as I see a shadow slip through the bottom crack of the door and come and unlock the door instead. The door opens wide for Beckett.

His shadow retreats back towards his body until it disappears under his skin.

He shuts the door behind him, making sure to lock it so we won't get any unwelcome visitors. He turned towards me, a glare etched on his features. "Why didn't you open the door?"

"You didn't come the night before," I stated and crossed my hands. I stood up. He drew closer, and I immediately felt the way my heart picked up as his footsteps came closer to me. It wasn't fear that was making me feel this way. Perhaps it might have been that way at first, but it's another bothersome nerve.

It's telling me to back away because if I don't, it will make me do something I will regret.

"I was busy."

I look at him and see the bag of supplies hanging on one of his shoulders. "Don't lie to me." I crossed my hands.

"I'm not lying," he retorts. I don't believe him in the slightest. "I can't just wander into your room every night. Someone might get suspicious if they see anything." He moves past me towards my bed, where he sits on the ground, the bag slumping against the ground. He grabs it, pouring the supplies out on the floor in front of him. He looks up. "Will you be staring at me all night or helping?"

I roll my eyes, walking forward, right next to him. "I'm assuming you know how to craft."

He chuckles. "I can do more than craft if you would like me to show you." He then extends his hand to me. "But first, the Warlord's dagger."

My heart beat widely at that thought, and I swallowed before I sat down across from him. I lifted my nightdress up slightly, revealing the Warlord's dagger that was tightened around my thigh. I could feel a weight drop between us as his eyes narrowed on my thigh, and I felt physically sick as he looked back at me.

"Take it."

He took a glance at the dagger, his breaths hot and short as he looked back up at me. "Spread your legs," he demanded, and my entire body grew numb at the thought of giving in to his command, but without thinking, my legs spread open. I used my ears to listen to my heartbeat, but then I heard his….and his was beating like a hurricane.

He leaned forward, his hand brushing my inner thigh. He went to snatch the dagger, but my legs fell close a second before he could snatch it away, and I leaned forward, his hand caught between my thighs, and something sparked in his eyes. I couldn't figure out what it was, but it was there, and It was the only thing I could see right now.

"You think I would give you the dagger that easily?" I asked before reaching down under my dress. I twisted his hand until I pushed him back, and he rolled over onto his back while I straddled his lips.

"You really want to play this game, Everard?"

I smirked. "I do."

Though this was nothing but playful, we both knew it was a challenge. When it came to fighting, we would always challenge each other. I snatched the dagger out of my holster and held it down to his throat. "Now, I think you should apologize for ditching me. That wasn't very nice of you."

He sneered before his hand met my hair, and I flinched when he pulled it back to the point of pain, and he snatched the dagger from my hand effortlessly. He pushed me off of him lightly and I was almost surprised by his gentleness before he tugged me back toward the supplies. "I want nothing but to play with you for the rest of the night, but we've got a Warlord's dagger to make."

I crawled to the space next to him, my back hitting the board hard enough to hurt, but I didn't let it show as I looked down at the supplies. My heartbeat slowed to a steady beat, but I knew if I looked at Beckett again, then it would spike up again, and there would be no hiding it from him.

It took us nearly three hours to get the handle shaped correctly with a slab of silver wood. Beckett used his knife to carve it perfectly and then to shine it down until it matched the Warlord's handle. It took another hour to place the gems correctly, and the vines. The glue was still fresh, the gems nearly falling, but with a push of my fingers, they stayed intact. They just needed to dry. We used a real blade, not wanting to take any risks.

"What if he doesn't take the bait?" I asked, my eyes landing on his. "He will kill me."

He chuckles, going forward. He's standing, unlike me, who sits on the ground. "You can't die, Blanche. Not without the real dagger." He then snatches the dagger away from my hands, and I wince as the knife drags against my skin, making a lower cut on my hand. My hand clenches, my eyes closing in pain.

I curse and sit up. I push past him, my shoulder bumping into his roughly before I enter the bathroom, rinsing off the blood that leaks from my hand.

"You are blessed, Everard. You have such great power in your hands, and yet I'm surprised you haven't used it to kill me yet," Beckett says before strolling inside the bathroom. He's smirking, just like he always did whenever he was up to something.

"Maybe I don't want to kill you," I muttered, hoping I wasn't too loud, but his eyes found mine, and I knew he had heard me. I shut the water off. His hand came around mine suddenly, and I had to force myself to stay still instead of stumbling away from him.

He was like poison, a plague I couldn't heal even if I wanted to. He was always there, right by me. It was exhausting, being played around like a toy, and I longed to make him pay for it. "For example, these cuts…" he looked down at the bandages around my hand. "These should have healed by now, but you've still got them on." He looked at me as if he had me all figured out, and maybe he did this one time. "You keep on cutting yourself."

I narrowed my eyes on him. "So what?" I didn't try denying the fact because it was right. Cutting myself felt exhilarating and after the blood was leaking from my hands, it felt like I could take down everyone that was in my way - good or bad, I wanted to see everyone burn whenever I felt the blood, and I *loved* that feeling.

"I know what it does to you," he said, "It's the same feeling I have whenever I release my shadows, but you can't give into it so much. It will manipulate your way of thinking - it will completely change you."

I scoffed, snatching my hand away from him. "Oh, like how you manipulated my mind? Did it change you when you did that?" I watched his expression drop into a frown. I didn't care if he was trying to be caring or compassionate; I couldn't care less about his feelings.

Nothing could make me forget the betrayal I felt. He deserved to be punished for that, and hopefully, in the future, I would deliver that punishment.

"I never really manipulated your mind," he confessed, drawing away from him. I frowned, opening my mouth to argue, but his hand flew up, and a shadow burst free of his hand. The shadow wrapped around my mouth, keeping me from talking. When I stopped fighting it, I pierced my eyes at him. "Yes, I tried to manipulate it, and maybe I might have succeeded if I dug a little deeper, but your mind was like a cement wall. I couldn't get past certain memories, and your mind was protected by this barrier that nearly drained me of all magic when I tried to get past it. I never manipulated your mind because I could never get past your defenses."

When the shadow retreated, I huffed. "Is that supposed to make me feel better? You still tried, and you can't be forgiven."

"I didn't ask for you to forgive me," He explained, and then his lips curved into another smirk. "Actually, I hope you spend every waking moment trying to come up with ways to punish me." He took a step closer, and I took a step back, hating the closeness of us. This isn't how enemies argued. Enemies weren't supposed to be close or work together. So why did he feel so hot whenever he was close?

"I've been a naughty elf," he said, my eyes widening, my heart pumping loudly. "And I'll be waiting for my punishment." He turned on his heels and then walked out of the bathroom, dropping the Warlord's dagger on the bed and walking out of my chamber.

I ignored how his words sent a shiver down my back, and my hands were consumed with goosebumps. He didn't mean anything to me - he didn't even deserve my attention.

So why is he constantly in my mind?

Dario was the first ever guard I took notice of. I knew he was one of Castor's trusted guards, but I wondered if he grew to resent the king for punishing him in such a way. The first time I ever saw him was when I emerged from the dungeons. He was the one who had escorted my father out. I can still see the bruises fading, just barely on his skin. Armed with a silver sword and knife in his pocket.

I glanced down at my leg, the fake dagger pressing against my leg. I'm right behind Dario, my body tense with anxiety. My fingers played with the hems of my green dress. I look behind me and see three other guards following behind me, all of them... *staring* at me.

"Does Castor hit you often?" I break the silence between us. His figure grows tense, but it doesn't stop him from walking. I ached for him to talk. I didn't like the silence that was growing between us. "You must get angry...I mean, I would."

"*My king*," he responds, blowing out a frustrated sigh. "It is my king to you, and you will not address him as anything else. He's your superior, and you should drill that into your head now before he cuts it off of you."

I frowned, but the curves of my smile lifted up, and I jogged forward until I was standing side by side with him. His lip is cut, making a small red indent on the side of his mouth. There's another bruise on his forehead. I wish I could heal them. "Ah, so you do talk then. That's good to know. It was becoming so quiet, I was starting to think you were mute."

His fangs snap out, a clear indication of a warning, but I only smile brighter.

"The king did not make these marks," Dario says, making my head snap towards him. He roams the place so freely, and he moves to take a right at a corner, all while making sure I'm keeping up with him. "If you must know, it was a werewolf. Vicious little creatures, they are."

My mind wanders to the only wolf I have ever known. Arabella was a force to be reckoned with. I've only ever seen her very angry once. I still remember how the arrow had struck Edwin so harshly and how she had quickly taken down Beckett just as easily. She had almost done the same with me.

I didn't see her use her powers very much, but I knew she had them.

"Werewolves can be very harmless, too," I retort, shrugging my shoulders. "They only attack if they feel threatened, so I have a feeling you probably deserved it." His shoulders sag, and I chuckle. "You weren't being very nice, were you?"

"I'm not allowed to be." Dario looks away. Growing tired of the discussion, he rolls his eyes. "You shouldn't be worrying about me, Everard," he says, and that's when we arrive at the double doors he was instructed to bring me too. "You should worry more about yourself."

"I don't need to worry," I snapped, crossing my hands. His face pulls into a confused frown. "I think one day I'll be even stronger than your king and that one day, you'll all be bowing to *me*."

He smirks, clearly amused by my challenge. "Yes, well, until that day comes, you are just the loyal subject." He bows his head to me, and I smile just before he walks away from me, leaving me to suffer at the hands of the vampire king.

The pit of my stomach screams.

I push through the doors, the breeze making my hair fly back. Fresh goosebumps appear on my skin as I look into the throne room. All the windows are open, blowing in the cold air. The doors smacked behind me, and I looked upon the throne where Castor sat, Ambrosia on his lap.

I take the fake Warlord's Dagger and hold it out for them to see. Castor's eyes gleam, his mouth curling up into a smirk, while Ambrosia's vanishes, her eyes widening. Castor practically pushes her off of her and ushers me forward. "What the-" Ambrosia says, her eyes on me. "Where did you find that?"

"Exactly where you put in Ambrosia," I retorted, walking forward towards Castor. I reach the small steps of the chair and walk onto the platform. Pushing my pride down, I get on one knee, shamefully bowing my head like the good elf I am. "For you, my king."

Ambrosia races for the dagger, but Castor snatches it from me in time for him to push her back. "Ambrosia, you've stolen it from me, so I stole it from you. Isn't that fair enough?"

She scoffs. "You didn't steal it. You let some dirty elf do your work." I ignore her words, even though it takes all my strength to not choke her with my bare hands. I stand back up, my hands interlacing behind my back.

"You might want to try a different hiding spot next time," I suggest, and she turns to me, sending me a scorching glare. "What did that cat ever do to you, huh?"

Ambrosia lunges at me, and I act fast, turning to my side so she misses. Her nails scrap my hand. I don't notice as she lunges at me again, her eyes turning a deep red, a rage so strong, it makes me laugh. She goes to grab for my neck. I dodge again and then trip her, so she falls to the floor.

Her eyes widen at the move, and I almost see her on the ground before Castor comes between us, swooping her up into his arms and dragging her back. "You little-" She says, trying to come at me again.

He looks at her, whispering something into her ear. She looked at him, shame written all over her face before she faced me. Her gaze meets mine, her mouth in a thin line. "A week, Everard," she tells me. "A week before I have full control of you."

She then pushes out of Castor's arms before walking out of the throne room.

I turn to the king. "Ambrosia has always been the dramatic type. No need to worry, Everard. As long as I'm alive, you will always be safe and mine."

I give him a fake smile. "The coronation is in a week. For now, your only job is to look pretty," he says, smiling. "Oh, and please try to look very decent at the coronation. It's a very big deal for everyone, especially myself and Ambrosia." He runs his fingers along the dagger again. "You are dismissed," he says.

I bow my head just before heading out of the throne room. As soon as the doors shut, my back hits the wall next to it, and I let out a breathless sigh that I had been holding. My fingers curl into my palm, and I can't help the sinister smile that appears on my face.

He fell for it.

CHAPTER THIRTY SEVEN

Arabella's coronation went from ear to ear in the vampire palace, and it didn't relent as the day soon came. I heard the whispers of the celebration each time I passed the hallways. With each passing day, the coronation was becoming a bigger deal. When I woke up the morning of the coronation, I had never been as excited as I was today.

Today was important amongst all the other reasons. Today was the reason I had been paraded around as a pet for Castor. It was why I had pretended to be bait. Today, the king died, and I was ready to watch as he cowered.

I look down at the gashes I had created in my skin. With the excitement drumming in my veins, I felt no need to keep on reminding myself of the pain, and slowly, the cuts were starting to heal. The gashes I created were deep, so they would heal within a few hours, hopefully before the coronation started.

I opened up the closet, where the red dress was. My hand smooths over the front, feeling the silk and lace underneath my palm. I grab it from the hanger and push all my clothes off before dressing it on my body. I tightened the back of the dress, making it mold my curves perfectly.

Knock.

One knock sounded on my door, and before I could give them permission to come in, the door opened and revealed Arabella in her dirty maid uniform. She had her hair tied back in a ponytail. "I had to get away," she said before slamming the door behind her. "How is it that every vampire in this place thinks they own everything they touch?" She demanded, mostly talking to herself.

Her eyes met mine, and then she looked at my dress. Her eyes widened slightly, and she exhaled. "Wow, Blanche...you look-" She cut her sentence short before straightening her spine. "It looks beautiful on you."

My cheeks brighten from her compliment. I thought it might have been too much, but Arabella had just changed my mind completely. The lace on my hands feel good, and the silk made me feel like I was still lying in bed. "Thank you." My hand swipes against my mouth, feeling how dry my lips have gotten. I look away, trying to hide away the red in my cheeks.

"Are you dressing up?" I ask.

"I'm still a maid," she said.

"Do you think the plan will really work?" I ask, looking down at her. "I had a nightmare last night."

It had been a whole month since my last nightmare happened. The same thing had happened, the same exact dream from when I was back home.

The man who is most important to you shall die on the day that you need him the most.

The same exact message was written on the wall. It was Castor - he was haunting my dreams. Uneasiness fell over me, and I looked for Arabella for comfort, but her face showed otherwise.

A mask of unknowing. "I don't know, but we have a solid plan." She touches the lace on my hand, and I watch her every move. "I believe we have a chance at killing him."

Believe.

I nod my head, not wanting the discussion to go further. Before I could tell her to leave, the door opened once again, and my eyes grew wide when the familiar vampire came into view. Belinda sways eagerly on her feet, looking between us. "I see the maid has come to help." She takes a few steps closer before looking Arabella up and down. "And what is your name? I've never seen you before."

"Arabella Vandas, ma'am," she replies, bowing her head in a delightful manner.

"Arabella..." Belinda trails off, her tongue running over her fangs. "Well, I can take care of our elf. So, you may leave."

The nervousness in Arabella's eyes is evident as she glances at me and walks away, bowing her head in the process. She rounds Belinda, but before she can escape, the vampire snatches her hand back, claiming her wrist in her mouth. All at once, Arabella's face contorts with disgust and surprise as she gasps.

In a sudden moment, her body relaxes, and her eyes close, a sigh escaping her lips. My eyebrows shot up. I had expected Arabella to at least relent since she had made it clear how she hated the parasites that vampires were. Except now, she didn't look like a woman who claimed to hate them.

Belinda releases her hand, wiping her blood from her mouth. "Thank you," Belinda said before letting her wrist go. Arabella stood, breathless sighs coming from her mouth before her face hardened, red painted on her cheeks. She sauntered away without another word, slamming the door behind her.

When Arabella is no longer in the room, Belinda takes a step towards me. "You look a little too ravishing, Blanche."

"Stop it," I deflect, shaking my head. "Ambrosia will have my head for wearing this."

"Yes, well, no one will do it other than you," Belinda says. I looked down at her black gown, noticing how most of the material was silk, the slit at the bottom of the dress, tiny straps carrying it all. It was simple, but it was marvelous.

I check the clock in the room. The party started only thirty minutes ago, but I hadn't yet done my hair or prepared any makeup. Belinda saunters behind me before she runs her hand through my hair. "Your hair is too simple. You should put in heavier curls. They would look good on you. Come, come." She then grabs my hand before pulling me into the bathroom.

She wets my hair with a brush and then slowly puts in rollers. Once she adjusts them in my hair, she spins me around, looking at my face. "You're a natural beauty. You don't need any makeup."

"I want some," I argue, and then step away from her. "I don't know how to use any of it. Will you do it for me?"

She smiles. "And what do I get for it?"

I cross my hands across my chest. "If you're thinking about my blood, you can forget it. I won't be as obedient as Arabella."

Belinda's eyes widened, and her fangs snapped out, looking at me in a totally different way than what I'd been used to. Belinda can be nice, and she could sometimes look like she could eat me, but right now, she's looking at me in total fascination. "Her blood tastes like heavenly bliss. I don't want to drink your blood Blanche because that maid is now *mine* to drink."

I narrow my eyes at her, growing slightly protective. "I didn't know you could drink another vampire's blood."

"We can drink anything with blood in it," Belinda says, before she forces me to take a seat in front of the mirror. She grabs the makeup that's been provided for me in the drawers of the sink. I have not been able to use it until now. She lays out everything that she needs before grabbing one of the brushes. "Usually vampires are just less tasty, but hers…was different."

She taps one of the brushes against the sink. "I'll only do your makeup, but only if you promise I can get the sweet taste of her blood again."

I frown. "That's not up for me to decide."

Belinda glides one of the brushes on my cheek, and she licks her lips, concentrating on the makeup she puts on my face. "I could feel the way her body was reacting. It was tense and rigid and then soft and fragile. She was disgusted in me, and she made it quite obvious." I don't say anything to that because I could tell as well, but I don't tell her how Arabella reacted afterward.

She then instructed me to close my eyes before she painted something over my eyes and then something wet over my eyelids, following towards the side of my face. When I opened my eyes, she grabbed some red lipstick and coated my lips with it. When she was done, she smacked my cheek lightly with her palm, and I turned my head.

My eyes are very lightly painted, and from afar, you can't see much, but as I looked closer, I saw the brown and the black line following it. My cheeks have been painted a little pink, and my lips are a firm dark red. It's a natural look despite the red lipstick. "It looks good," I say.

"Good, now you owe me," Belinda says before she starts to take the rollers out of my head, letting my curls swoop in different directions.

Her fingers swept through my curled hair, rubbing the ends together. "Shall we?" She then lets the hair fall back into the pile of tresses. She links her hand through mine and led me out of my chambers. Dario passes us, bowing his head at us. His gaze follows us as we walked the other way.

Belinda checks the clock on the wall just as we arrive at the throne room. It's nine o'clock on the dot. The party started only an hour ago. The announcement of Ambrosia's betrothal would happen tonight, as well as the crown being placed upon her head. In only a few short hours, Beckett would be the one to wear it.

"Walk in with confidence," Belinda said, which snapped me out of my train of thought. "They don't exist in your world."

That was the last thing she said before she opened the doors, and we walked in, side by side.

I go unnoticed at first, as most of them despise me, but as soon as they see the red dress, their conversations go quiet. There are soft whispers at first, talking amongst themselves as they look at the divine red dress and how inappropriate it is for an event like this.

"Why is she wearing that?"

"Ambrosia won't be happy."

Belinda puts a hand on my hand, and her words come back to me. *They don't exist in your world.*

It was hard pretending that it was nothing, and I could only make out the shocked and confused faces of the vampires. I was prey among predators, and I walked into the snake's den. Except, I wasn't prey anymore - not after tonight.

I look for the king and his horrible excuse for a wife. My eyes scan the tables of food and the dance floor that only a few vampires have occupied. It's when I spot Castor with Ambrosia, way farther into the room, right up at the throne. Except now there isn't just one throne; there are two, and Ambrosia is sitting in the other one.

By the way, her jaw is set; she's upset. She knows I look better, and if I weren't getting rid of her, I would run - run somewhere she can't find me. My eyes trailed up her black dress and how elegantly it flowed down her body. She would be beautiful...if it weren't for her horrid personality.

"Come, let's go get something to eat." Belinda pulled me towards the deserts on the table. Cookies, brownies, cakes, and fondue aligned together in a neat line on the white tablecloth. All of them are labeled with something, and each of them contains... blood. Belinda looks at me. "I don't know if you would like to try, but brownies with blood are delicious."

"Who did the blood belong to?" I asked, raising an eyebrow.

"Who knows." Belinda shrugged. "The chefs made it, not me. Surprisingly, regular brownies aren't that good, but the hint of blood in them is delicious." My eyebrows scrunch, and she takes a bite of the brownie. She shows me the inside, and I see the liquid blood in there. "Don't look at me like that."

"What do you want me to say, Belinda? That I want a bite?" I ask as I reach over to the large bowl of strawberries and dip it into the chocolate fondue. I take a bite out of a strawberry, the chocolate coating my lips.

"I want you to try it," Belinda said, trying to put it near my lips.

I slap her hand away, my nose scrunching. "Over my dead body."

"Belinda!" An excruciating voice calls her name, and we turn just as Ambrosia strolls toward us slowly. She's smiling at us, and I raise an eyebrow, as does Belinda. "Belinda, if I can have a word in private with our beautiful temptress over here." She looks at me, and her smile fades as she looks down at my dress.

Belinda smiles. "And if I don't want to leave?"

Her head snaps to Belinda. "It wasn't a question."

Belinda rolls her eyes before winking at me and turning around. I stand my ground, eating the rest of the strawberry. Ambrosia's delighted smile comes back as she takes Belinda's place and grabs a glass from the table. "I must say, Everard, your dress is ravishing. Where did you get it?"

I throw the strawberry away. "From a shop in town. Belinda took me herself."

"Of course she did," Ambrosia states, putting the glass under the fondue. "I didn't expect any less from her, considering she'll be dead by midnight." I try to keep my face as straight as possible, but the small frown of my eyebrow and the twist of my lips and Ambrosia sneer. "Oh, you haven't heard? Our sweet Belinda tied up poor Mallory in the dungeon. She came to us distressed and told us of everything that had happened. Of course, she asked if we could kill you first."

I swallow, my fists tightening. My own rage seems to shimmer through my face when I see Ambrosia look at me, amused. "But unfortunately, Castor has refused to kill you, especially since you found the Warlord's dagger, so instead, his decision was his sister."

"You're lying," I say. "He wouldn't hurt his own sister."

"Are you sure about that?" Ambrosia demanded and then leaned in, her sneer emerging across her lips so wickedly. "I guess we'll see at midnight, won't we?"

She then smiles and walks forward. As she does, she takes a sip of the glass before her chest bumps into mine, and the chocolate is flown everywhere, right on my face, neck, hands, and most of all…on my dress.

I gasp as it floods down my dress, the red of the silk, stained now with dark brown. "Oh my…" Ambrosia says, covering her mouth.

I wipe the chocolate off my mouth with the back of my hand. Humiliation spreads through me like a wild storm; I grit my teeth together as I stare at her. Everyone around me gasps and stares at the mess that Ambrosia has made. "You are such a bitch."

"Now, that isn't very polite, is it?" Ambrosia asks, setting the cup of chocolate down. I look at her dress and realize nothing is on her dress. She had planned this perfectly, just for me to get humiliated. "You should be thanking me, honestly. Red isn't really your color."

With a chuckle, she walks away back to her throne, where she rightfully belongs.

I look down at my dress and grab a few napkins. I try to wipe it all off at first, only for it to stain more, gradually making my dress more hideous than before. This is what I deserve, I kept trying to say to myself. I knew Ambrosia would be upset, yet I still went and wore it, just for me to get humiliated in front of…all of them.

"Christ, Blanche." I look behind me and see Arabella coming towards me. She's got napkins in her hands, hands reaching for me. "Let me help you."

I swat her hands away aggressively. She draws back, shocked by my actions. "I don't want your help. I just want to get out of here," I snap.

"But the plan-" She whispers.

"I'll be back before the plan starts. I just need this awful dress off of me." I look at it and feel the tears spring to my eyes, but I don't let them release. Instead, I walk past her, hurrying to get out of this horrible room - this exhausting tension that I always feel whenever I have to come in here.

I'm out of there quickly, jogging to the nearest room I see. I don't bother to care or worry if anyone is there. Mostly everyone is at the coronation already.

The door slams behind me. I look at the room, almost the exact same copy as mine; only a fireplace is there, with a small couch. A coffee table stands right next to it, with papers scattered across it. A trail of ink and a quill sits right on top of one.

Curiously, I walk over and push the quill off the paper. I look over at the paper and see a picture rather than a drawing. It's familiar, two elves standing next to a small, petite woman. Both of them look exactly like…the Brookers.

"Everard."

I jump away from the paper and swirl around as Beckett comes into view. He doesn't look happy, and he takes a step forward, looking down at the drawing I just saw. "Don't you know not to touch things that aren't yours?"

CHAPTER THIRTY EIGHT

I take a glance at the women in the picture once more. The woman has a perfectly cut jawline. There's a smile on her face, but in the picture it doesn't quite reach her eyes. The woman is beautiful - big eyes that seem to plead out in sadness, a mouth that shows nothing but happiness. She's too beautiful - almost as if she'd been crafted to be beautiful, when she should not be.

"Who is that woman?" I demand.

Beckett stares at me, eyes wide with fascination. He doesn't say anything for a few minutes. His head hangs low, looking away.

Except then, I see that he wasn't looking away, only looking down at my dress. He takes it in, stained with chocolate, and scans every fragment of it. He takes in the lace, the silk. He advances towards me, his hand hesitating before his clenched hand comes around my right hand, feeling the texture of it. He looks down at me again, his mouth opened, as if he wants to say something.

"Don't insult me Beckett," I say, and he frowns, before I snatch my hand away from him. "I have been embarrassed enough by Ambrosia, I don't need your criticism too." I try to walk past him, but his body doesn't let me. I'm about to shout at him before his hand shoots up, predicting my next words, and muffling them with his hand over his mouth.

"Do you ever stop talking?" He demands, growing frustrated before he presses me into the desk behind me where my hands bend and the pain of my wrists ached. His eyes look over me again, and my eyes lock with his hungry eyes. "Everard, where did you get this dress?"

"A shop," I say, not letting him take control of me. I bring my hand down on his chest to push him away, but I find it impossible to do as his figure is so rigid. I'm frozen, feeling the need to pull away.

During the past few months, I had grown to despise the vile elf more and more, and my feelings towards him were as clear as day, but when he stands so close…when he touches me so scandalously…there is something else I feel. Something I shouldn't feel. Something forbidden.

"What are you doing?" I whisper in the silence.

My mouth parts when he extends his arm behind me, and pulls out the chair, setting me down in it. He leaves for a minute, walks to the restroom before he comes back with a towel, and in his other hand is a container of water. He kneels down, his head aligned with my knee.

The curls on his head fall over his face, feeling the hotness of his breath on my naked legs. I pull my head up, my eyes piercing into his. "Brooker, what are you doing?"

"I'm trying to clean up your dress.." He says, looking up at me. "Or do you want this to stain your dress?" He waits for an answer but when I don't provide one, he dabs the towel in the water, before he then starts wiping it on the dress.

His touch is soft, and with each swipe, more chocolate is wiped off. He flips the towel over and over again so he doesn't stain my dress more. His touch is warm and even with this dress on, I can feel him.

"The women in the drawing…it's Elodie, isn't it?" I ask. He pauses, glancing up at me before he nods. "I know she's important. I knew she was the minute I saw the name on your dagger…" I shake my head, not able to comprehend the name anymore. "Won't you just tell me?"

His shoulders sag, and he looks at me. "She's…my mother."

A beat. I'm too scared to move, but now everything makes sense.

He looks up at me. His brown eyes are darker now, and he shakes his head looking away, as if the thought of talking about it was horrible. "She died when I was younger."

"How?" I ask, quietly and cautiously, not wanting to overstep.

He frowns, looking up at me now. "My father killed her."

My mouth nearly drops, the shock on my face is evident, and I look away, not wanting him to see my reaction, although I know it's too late. I look around at everything but him because what should I say to him?

When I look back, I muster up a sentence to say but he stops me, a shake of his head. "Please don't say you're sorry for my loss. I don't care for it. I don't want to talk about it." He lifts himself off the ground, and I lift my gaze up, his body towering over me.

Looking down, my once chocolate stained dress is now covered in water, the stain amiss, and I look back at him. "I don't understand, why would you do that for me? I thought you hated me."

"I do," He says, before he starts to walk away.

I stand up abruptly, feeling the Warlord's dagger in my holster start to become heavy. "You never told me why, Brooker," I say, before he could leave. He turns, his eyes narrowing at me.

"I have told you why," he says.

"We both know that's a lie. I want a good reason," I say, walking forward. He turns around completely, looking me up and down. I once looked at Beckett and hated the sight of him, but seeing him now, all I wanted to do is stare at him forever. He was angelic in a way only I could see.

"You want a good reason?" He asked.

My legs tensed, preventing me from falling. "Yes, Brooker. I want a good reason. I don't want excuses anymore." I hold my head high, my eyebrows raising.

His shoulders sagged, and he looked at the ground, almost as if contemplating if he should tell me the truth. I knew Beckett was a tough man - he'd always been, but now I saw something through him that looked not as tough. He looked vulnerable, and I was shocked that I was making him feel this way.

He looks at me. "I hate you because I know what your power can do. It's powerful, and unlike anything I have ever witnessed. You're more powerful than me in every aspect, and I hate it. I hate that you...who doesn't even know how to control them can send me to sleep for weeks. I hate the fact that you are everything that I am not." A beat. I can feel my face contorting to confusion, because I simply am out of words. "And I hate that I can't breathe properly when I'm not around you." His breath is heavy, matching mine entirely. "I hate the fact that every time there is a room full of people, it's you I look at first."

We stare at each other. My confidence wares, but I understand more clearly now. All along I thought I was demented for letting my heart race whenever he was near, but I never realized his heart races too.

I can feel my hands clench, anxiety run through me like a breeze. "I don't know what you want me to say. I've thought this entire time you wanted to hurt me."

"I did want to hurt you." he snaps, looking away and shaking his head. "I thought if I hurt you enough that maybe you would hate me."

My hands clench. "Well you've definitely succeeded in that. You could have made an alliance with me, Beckett. I could have been your friend, used my power for you, not against you. You've disregarded my trust, and manipulated me. You've made all the wrong decisions since I met you."

He nods. "I know, and I still await my punishment."

I scoff, walk to him, and watch as he looks me up and down. "You want a punishment. Fine." My hand comes around his hand, and then I pull him until we're out of the door.

"Where are you taking me?" He demands.

"To the throne room," I say, turning my head and smirking at him. "You will dance with me."

We stop at the doors. "That's your punishment?" He asks, his eyebrows shooting up. "By dancing with you?"

"Yes," I say, before smiling. "If you hate me as much as you claim, I will make this the most miserable dance of your entire life." I lift my head up, facing the doors, and grabbing onto his hand. I knew if I went back into this room, I would only embarrass myself as well. It might be horrible, but if it meant dragging Beckett into this room and making him dance in front of others, perhaps I could handle the moment of humiliation.

I swing the doors open before he can oppose anything. He did ask for punishment, so here it was. I was delivering it. It takes a second for everyone to look at us. Everyone who had looked at me in admiration, now looked at me with disgust, whispering something into their partners ears.

Castor eyes meet mine, and feel his mouth curl up, then his gaze falls down on my hand on Becketts. Ambrosia looks more than merry as she sneers down at me. I ignore both of them as I drag the vile elf to the dance floor. Most of the vampires scoot away from us, as if me being an elf was somehow a disease they could catch.

My eyes scan over the crowd, trying to see any familiar faces. Arabella is by the fondue, but to my surprise, Belinda accompanies her. Belinda smiles, trying to charm the wolf, but Arabella brushes her off before she bows her head and then heads away from the vampire.

I don't see Devyn or Edwin anywhere, but another familiar face is seated at one of the red chairs, and I recognize my fathers distraught face. He's looking straight at me, not like a man who hates me, but of a man who's worried. I look away from him, my eyes focused on the elf in front of me.

"I'm waiting," he says.

"Yes, I'm sure you are," I respond, swaying my hips to the music as I come closer to him. One of my hands reached behind his neck, harshly pulling him closer to me. With my other hand, I grab his hand and pull it around my waist. He tightens it, feeling the way he pulls me even closer, no space left between us. Then with my other hand, I grab his other free hand, lifting it slightly. "Look around, Brooker. Everyone is revolted by my existence, and now they know who you value in your time."

At that he smiles, then he starts to twirl us around in a graceful manner. I didn't expect it from someone like him. "I might hate you dearly Everard, but I have never wanted anyone else but you to value my time."

"Is that so?" I ask, and then shrug.

I open my mouth to talk again, but my gaze lands on the others around me. From the corner of my eye, I could see Arabella looking at me from the corner of the room. When my gaze meets her, she smiles, and then her attention turns back to the vampire who's been chasing her around the entire night. Everyone's eyes are on us, and I'm not sure why. I thought they would all look away after they had their share of disgusted looks.

"Everyone is watching," I ask.

"Let them," he says, before spinning me around in a circle, and then drawing me back, my back hitting his chest, and I felt his breath cascade my neck. "I quite enjoy this punishment."

I snapped my head over to him, before I slammed my heel against his foot, allowing him to hiss before he drew back, turning me around. "I don't want you to enjoy it. I want you to *hate* it."

My guidance of the music slowly grows tiresome, and before

long, I realize, it's Beckett that's swaying us to the music. "Have I told you how beautiful you look tonight?" He then asks, and my eyes widen, my mouth parting, and tongue dry. I wasn't sure how to respond, so I shook my head.

"Good," I frown at his words. "You look sinful, Blanche."

The name itself almost knocks me off balance, which causes me to stumble over my own feet. Thankfully, he catches me before I can embarrass myself yet again. My breathing staggers, and even though I've heard my name said by many, it feels different from his.

He said my name for the first time.

"You said my name," I said, trying hard not to smile. When he doesn't respond, I say, "That's the first time you've ever said my name." I watch his eyes grow, but I can't figure out anything that deepens them. I've gotten used to Beckett's silly nickname for me, but my name on his lips sent a blissful pleasure I didn't know I could feel.

As we swayed around, I looked around and noticed Arabella dancing with a certain vampire. I smile as I catch her eyes. She's gone red in the face, and she is dancing with Belinda. Her hair is loose behind her. Belinda's hands are tangled inside her curls. Belinda turns to me, her eyes mixed with mischief. She winks at me.

I wanted to keep talking to him, but from the corner of my eye, I watched as Devyn walked forward towards us, and instantly, I let go of him. It felt like I had just walked into a dark hole. My body was no longer warm, and it took me until now to realize how cold I actually was.

He looked at me, and he took a step towards me, reaching out his hand to continue our dance. I opened my mouth to tell him, but a small tap made him turn around. Devyn stood there. She wasn't looking at me. Her eyes were on Beckett. "The announcement will be in a few minutes. I suggest we get into place." Then she walks away towards Belinda and Arabella.

Beckett looks at me with a sorrowful expression. He then walks towards me, kneeling in front of me and retreating the dagger without anyone noticing before tucking it in his pocket where it would remain hidden. "We aren't done with your punishment," I say, and his lips curve.

"I don't expect anything less," he says. He stares at me adoringly, the distance between us incredibly hard. Everything is silent around us. I can't hear the chatter. I can't hear anything. I can only hear him, and I can hear how our heartbeats seem to beat in sync with one another.

He doesn't partake in any expression, before his hand comes around my face, pulling my face to his.

His lips are soft against my own, although the feeling is entirely different. I feel the adrenaline I always felt come forth. He was dangerous, and perhaps, I've grown to like that about him. His mouth molds to mine, pulling me up towards his chest so that my feet stood onto his. My back arched, swaying to the heat of his body.

I should want this to stop - try to stop it myself, but I cannot find it in myself to do so. A raw feeling, I realize, this is what I've been feeling. Longing. Desire. He felt good - everything about him was delicious.

I stand on my tip-toes, desperate to feel more of him, and he gives in, our mouths moving in sync as he moves my head to the right, his hand coming behind my head, holding me up slightly.

All the thoughts of betrayal and manipulation flow away - all the sorrowful moments leaving my head. It was as if he had compelled me again, forcing me to forget all the things he had done to me. I should push him away - tell him this isn't what I want.

But it is what I want. From the moment I've met him, he was all I ever wanted.

Times where I thought I hated him was filling me in dread, when I had been nothing but desiring him. A desire that would fill you whole, and empty you completely.

Except the desire that starts, comes to an end when he pulls away, our breaths heavy, staring only at each other. Red flushes on my cheeks, embarrassment flooding. He had just kissed me in front of everyone.

"Remember this Blanche," he says, causing me to frown, "Remember this when you hate me again," he says before he ambles away, leaving me standing on the dance floor.

The chandelier dimmed, as did the throng of vampires that hung in every crevice of the tortuous ball that would wield Ambrosia's betrothal. The vampires looked upon the throne where the king and future queen sat. The throne room was eerie, ghost-like as the king stood up, his hands raised high to give Ambrosia a warm welcome. A second later, the whole crowd erupted with applause at their future queen.

"Let's welcome our new future queen..." He looked back at his fiancée, his future queen, and ushered forward next to him. She follows his moves, lifting herself off the chair. Gracefully, she walks beside him, arms by her side, as she stood next to her husband. Foolish is what they were. How could they stand there and have their celebration knowing everyone else in the world is suffering?

I love how pathetic they look. They'll look even better after our plan plays out.

"Ambrosia Bloodrose," He says, grabbing the crown that sits on the white platform of stone. "Today is the day to remember as we welcome our queen into the kingdom. We have had a rough year, from losing our king and queen to then taking over the land of Romania."

I scoff. "Bullshit," I whisper into the silence. How could they say they had a rough year after claiming war on everyone? I had almost starved to death in my village with the shortage of food. They burned down my village just because they could.

They had no right to complain.

I turned to Arabella, who stood by my side. I could see the twitch of her jaw, how it set. They had stolen everything from her - family and childhood.

I take her hand, and she looks at me. I turned towards the throne, where the king and queen still talked. They caused all of this. Let them rot for what they have done.

"To mother nature," Castor announced, "We would like to ask of you if you would accept our Ambrosia, the queen of our world, to forever dedicate her life to ruling the kingdom beside me." Castor raised the crown above in the sky before he descended it down on her head.

I frowned, looking around. Beckett and Devyn had made it clear that we were supposed to be watching from afar, distracting now and then, but if I was right, Beckett should have stepped in right now.

The crowd was full of the same tall vampires, but none of them were Beckett. I looked at Arabella and watched as her eyes scanned the crowd. Not even Devyn was in view, and Edwin was completely gone. What had happened to them?

Suddenly, something roared in the distance. My whole body vibrated, and I looked down and saw that the floor started to move underneath me like an earthquake.

Castor cackled loudly with it, Ambrosia smiling to herself.

Mother nature had answered.

The rumbling stopped abruptly as soon as Castor's cackling died down, and Ambrosia stopped smiling. Castor faces her then. "Congratulations, Ambrosia. You are my future wife and now, the future queen for the rest of eternity."

At that, applause erupts loudly among the crowd, delighted to see their future queen rise with their king. While they cheer, my face deepens with a frown. Where had Beckett and Devyn been? My jaw tightens, and I look around. "Where the hell are they?!" I whisper.

Arabella shifts uncomfortably. "I don't know, but they better hurry."

I let go of her hand, growing restless and angry as I realized we'd missed our chance. We've missed our bloody chance to do this.

"Thank you so much!" Ambrosia said to the crowd. They died down to hear her words. "I'd like to thank my husband, Castor." She looked at him blissfully before walking to the fron t of the stage. Her hands went around him in a sweet hug, and I frowned. Christ, I would kill Beckett when I saw him next.

Then I felt it. Something shifted in the room - dark and eerie, and I looked around, trying to find the cause of it. "Do you feel that?" I ask, wondering if I had gone insane.

Arabella frowned. "Feel what?"

My mind grew hazy for a second, and I scanned the room. Something was wrong. This place had suddenly gone from welcoming to something strange. The lights flickered for only a second, but it caught my attention, and I lifted my head towards the ceiling, where I noticed the...dark shadow of the ceiling.

It didn't look like a ceiling. It was pitch black, as if a dark hole had been created above us. Arabella noticed my gaze and lifted her eyes to it before her eyes widened. "Beckett's shadows...." Arabella trailed off, her mouth parting in fear.

Everyone else seemed to finally notice, even the king and queen. Castor shoved Ambrosia off of him before striding forward and looking at the ceiling. "What is the meaning of this?"

Ambrosia frowned. "What is that?"

This was definitely not the plan.

"They are my shadows," a voice vibrated, and I recognized it as Beckett's as he appeared behind Ambrosia. She whirled around so quickly that I felt the snap of her neck. Before Ambrosia could get another word out, Beckett retrieved a wooden stake in his hand, and his grin was full of malice as he stuck it straight into her heart.

Ambrosia gasped, and I watched as her face grew pale and her eyes shifted into white oblivion. Then she collapsed on the floor, the crown colliding with wood and bouncing off of her head.

Arabella grabbed onto my shoulder as she made us duck, just as the shadow cast over us.

"What's happening?!" Arabella demands, trying to look for any sign of the others.

I look above the table, inspecting everything going on around me. He was casting the shadows above him that whirled around like a hurricane. It thundered in the room - the whole castle. The vampires ran towards doors, seeking escape only for the doors to shut and lock in front of them. Beckett's eyes flashed with malice, his lips in scornful glare as he stared at the king beside him.

Reaching inside his holster, he pulled out the real Warlord's dagger. They talked among each other, but the wind was unyielding. I couldn't hear a word that articulated between them. I bent down to the floor where Arabella stayed. "Stay here," I demanded, and before she could argue, I tore my heels off before I took off in a sprint.

Havoc winds, screaming vampires, the shadows swept down to the floor, searching for the right host, before going into them, turning the vampires into their own slaves. Their eyes bulged out, hands stretched out for help, but as soon as the shadows were done, they scrambled out of the bodies, and I watched as their souls left them, and they tumbled to the ground, lifeless.

I sprinted towards the stage where Beckett got closer to Castor. "Brooker!" I scream, rage within me. I climbed onto the stage, ready to intervene, when suddenly Shade swooped down from the sky, knocking me off the stage harshly. Beckett turned around just as I landed on the nearest wall near me.

I look up, feeling my head pound. Beckett scowled before ignoring me and turning back to his target. Castor stands up, and I see his eyes glow red before they both start to battle it out. My head burns from the sensation. My hand lands on top of my head, and when I pull it away, blood is pooling on my hands.

"This is outrageous!" Castor curses before lunging at Beckett. He only makes it a few steps closer before a shadow sweeps him up and shoves him to the floor. "You cannot take the crown! It is earned!"

I overhear everything, my ears ringing.

"Earn it?" Beckett replies, tapping the Warlord's dagger against his cheek. "The crown is awarded to the man who killed the king before him, but if not claimed or wanted, the crown is given to the eldest son…" He smiles at Castor. "But…the killer never specified if he didn't want it or not, and my answer is yes."

"What are you talking about?!" Castor demands. "You mean to tell me-"

"Yes, I killed King Rufus, and I've come to claim the crown as mine, brother," he demands.

It seems Castor and I both freeze in our positions. I try to push myself off the ground, but with the new information weighing down on me, I feel a pang of hurt descend upon me. A feeling of betrayal - just as he always seemed to cause me, but this time…he had really gone too far.

His eyes narrowed, drawing back. Just then from behind him, Edwin appeared behind him as the wood from the ground starts to stretch around his hands, and the shadows starts to swarm him madly. Edwin kept him in place, and I saw a hint of bitterness in his features.

He…had been in on this too.

"Our father was a coward," Beckett argued and then stepped towards him, and from afar, I saw a dark vermillion as his eyes lit up in rage. I covered my mouth, a sob itching its way out of my mouth, and my tears finally escaped my eyes.

If all of this was true, then he wasn't Beckett Brooker. His name was Beckett Percival, and his father was King Rufus. Which meant he was related to Castor and Belinda, and that made him…a vampire.

A vampire and an elf.

My eyes burn, hatred seizing through my being. *A crossbreed. A hybrid.*

"Of course, Rufus didn't say a word about us." He ushered to Edwin, and he laughed like a maniac. "Rufus threw us away the first chance he could, all because he grew tired of his wife and needed something new…something innocent. I have been thrown away from the beginning of my life, and now I am here, claiming back what was rightfully mine."

Castor shook his head. "No, that's not true! My father was a good man!"

"He fucked the closest thing he could get his hands on, which, unfortunately, was my mother. At the time, she was just a maid… her name was Elodie. Does it ring a bell?"

Elodie. Elodie. Elodie.

Absolutely mortified by his words, I scattered back towards the ground, where I then sprinted towards Arabella. Bending down to look for her, I saw nothing. Her entire form and position disappeared.

"Arabella?" I said to myself first and then looked up. "Arabella?!"

"Blanche!" A sob, a frightening scream, and then the shadows appeared above me. One of them rushed down towards me, but not before I dove out of the way, catching the side of my arm on one of the knives on the table, and it brushed my skin. I winced, my head hitting the ground hard.

The shadows flew towards me again, and I clenched my fists, raising my hands in the air, and watched as the shadow turned to dust in front of my eyes. I then turned and then ran towards Arabella's terrified voice. She was in the corner, on her knees, as her shaky hands held the masculine face of…my father.

Arabella's eyelids dropped, eyes glistening with tears. "I can't wake him up!" She says, yelling at me. "I-I've tried everything!"

White glowed in his eyes, and my hands made their way towards his neck, checking his pulse. My heart dropped when I felt nothing, my eyes glistening. Hyperventilating, and sobbing, my hand went to his heart, trying to find where his blood system connected. "I need you to push at his chest!"

She cupped her hands over her chest, her hair falling out of her ponytail. She kept on pacing, and I held onto my dad's hand, bringing his mouth to mine, and I blew. I begged that this would work. Tears burned my eyes. This isn't how he dies. He's not allowed to leave yet.

"Blanche!" Arabella screeched, and I reached towards her,

watching her red-stained eyes. "He's dead, Blanche."

I looked at my dad's pale eyes, his eyes closed, and I shook my head, scooting closer to him. "No…No, he's not!" I put my hand over my dad's chest, pressing down so hard I could feel the snap of his bones. I paced for seconds, which turned into a minute, and everything around me became mute.

"He can't be dead…" I trail off, but my hands stopped moving, as I grabbed onto his face, looking at his face. "Dad, wake up!" I screamed, shaking my head. "Wake up, Dad!"

My face contorted into realization, and I lifted my head, frowning. Arabella was screaming something at me, but her voice was muted. I looked around me, feeling everything around me freeze for a second before I came to an awareness of what had just happened.

The man who is most important to you shall die on the day that you need him the most.

I sobbed even harder, my lower lip quivering. I had been predicting it all along. All my choices had led me to this exact moment, and instead of pondering about the message, I had set it aside. It was a vision - gifted to me, and I threw it away as if it was garbage.

I looked down. I could have stopped it.

I could have kept him safe if I had just listened.

"*Blanche!*" Arabella's voice brought me back to the void just as a shadow swept from the ceiling and started coming after us. Arabella hissed before she lifted her hand up, fire spreading out of her palm and exploding the shadow midair. She turned to me. "Blanche, I'm sorry," she said before she took my hand, "But your father is dead."

"It was about time," My back hit the wall as it was thrown back with a harsh pull, and Arabella flew to the side, her head hitting against the locked door with a strong whack, and her body fell beside the other corpses. Blood oozed down the side of her head and down to her neck.

I looked up at the force keeping me there and watched as Devyn strode closer, mouth open, speaking Latin. "What are you doing?! Let me go!"

I saw Castor still tied to the ground, and Edwin held onto his tighter. He was struggling to keep a hold of Castor, and with enough force, I could tell Castor might be able to break out of it, but before he could, Beckett held the Warlord's dagger in the air, speaking something to him before he cut straight into his heart.

I turned back to Devyn. Tears slid down my cheek, and I saw her eyes flash with spite. "You…you knew about this?!" I demanded, and when she didn't provide an answer, I felt the rush of power in my body. "How could you?! My father is dead because of you! Almost everyone in the room is dead."

She leaned forward. "You don't understand Blanche."

"Then make me understand!" I shouted. I look around me and see the destruction Beckett has done to this foreign place. The whole place was tumbling, filled with shadows that were circling on the ceiling. How could I have let him do this?

I led him here - let myself get kidnapped, and now he had planned to kill us all. "No, Blanche, this is what has to happen. We had planned this since day one, and I won't let you mess it up. Brenner was already on our tail about it, and that's why I murdered him. You see, it seems that elves aren't all that immortal."

I let out a vicious scream before I saw the slip of her magic by my hand, and I reached forward, pushing her off of me. She staggers back, causing her to let go of Arabella as well.

She reached for her magic again, Latin on the tip of her tongue, but she didn't get to utter a single word when suddenly, Arabella emerged from behind her. In her wolf form, she jumped onto Devyn, forcing her down on the ground.

Devyn screeched before the wolf calmed her throat with her sharp teeth, and a scream tore from her. It was the last scream I ever heard from her as I watched Arabella chew her in unimaginable ways. Pieces of her skin flew in several directions, and with it, I saw blood splatter everywhere. I watched as Arabella slowly tore her apart with her teeth until there was nothing but skin and blood left.

I gasped for a breath and looked at the stage, only to see Beckett gathering the bloody crown right on top of his head.

I ran past them, heading back towards the stage. He would not go unpaid for his acts - no, he would suffer. He had dragged down so many for his revenge, but not me. I wouldn't let him drag me down.

Blood dripped down my hands, and I let my power feel it all. It felt amazing - having the power of a god - killing everyone that dared to cross me.

It gave me life - gave me oxygen to breathe. It was exhilarating.

I raised my hand towards the ceiling, where the shadows circled around. All of them, sensing my power, came rushing down at me to attack, but I watched in amusement as they all screamed and cried, turning to dust underneath my fingertips. It felt like tearing apart a life - like a vase breaking. It felt breathtaking.

There was no better feeling than this.

As soon as all the shadows vanished, I made my way towards the stage, where the two opposite brothers stood. Beckett was the first to notice, his shadows completely gone - all of them, even his precious Shade. His eyes sparked with recognition as he saw me.

Edwin stood next to him, but at my stance, he seemed to back away. I recognized that emotion. It was fear, and I smiled. "*Walk away.*" With a cock of my head, Edwin grew into my trance, the pain unbearable, and he walked away from us. It was so effortless to get into his mind, and I looked at the vile elf. I wondered if his mind would be just as easy.

"I hope you didn't miss me too much," I coo before I command, "Now be a good boy, and give me the dagger."

Beckett shook his head for a second and then felt the splintering pain that appeared in his head. He didn't dare give me the dagger, though, no matter how much I caused him pain. He was harder to control. "I hope you are proud, Brooker, for everything you've accomplished," I say, walking towards him. "You got your crown, congrats."

He was a beautiful devil with a crown. I looked around the room and watched as the werewolf ran towards us at full speed. "You do not deserve it," I say. I create a barrier controlling his very own shadows before Arabella, causing her to stop in her tracks.

I know she wants to kill Beckett, but she cannot. He was mine to kill.

With a swipe of my hand, I had him crashing toward the wall with just as much momentum as he had given me earlier. I made my way over to him. I usher him to look around. "Look at what you've done! Look around you!" I kneel towards him, my eyes blazing with anger. "My father is dead because of your revenge."

He opened his mouth to argue, but before he could, my hand went over his mouth, and I grabbed the Warlord's Dagger from him swiftly and then used it to make an indent in his wrist, where blood leaked from. I bent down, put the blood right under my mouth, and liked it right off of him, and watched his eyes widen with terror.

I smiled, knowing that not only had I made an indent in his hand, but it was going to leave a scar. Even if it was a small one.

"You got your revenge, but you have obviously underestimated mine," I said before I dropped the Warlord's dagger. With blood running in my system and blood coating my hands, I didn't need a bloody pentagram. I just needed my power.

"You can have your power for now," I felt the burst of energy surge through my body so suddenly it almost knocked me off my feet. I feel the shield clash and see the way the wolf tries to force her way to us. I turn my attention to him, and I put every fiber of my power into my next words - into my next curse. "You are allowed a year of power, to rule and reign and be the king you desire to be because, by this time next year, you will be granted the torture of death."

"Blanche–" Then he started choking, blood came out of his mouth – the illusion of blood that I made him choke on.

My head rolls back, my eyes shutting in pain as I feel all my power leave my body suddenly. I almost scream, but I jerk my eyes open. Darkness of black invades the room until it's all I can see. Then I feel emptiness.

As soon as I back away, I feel my vision go blurry and my eyes droopy from the impact. The barrier around us snapped open, and Arabella ran towards me. She swooped under me, letting me climb onto her.

Hands heavy, eyes weak, I felt myself grow tired, but I watched as she raced towards the door with full impact, slamming them open with unbelievable force and running out of the room in a hurry, her paws sprinting, running faster than ever.

My eyes fell closed as we met the moonlight of the moon.

EPILOGUE

I could not function while waking up from my slumber. This drowning sensation took over my body, pulling me deeper so I couldn't breathe. I had no idea how long I had been unconscious; the only thing I felt was dread, as a reminder of what happened earlier. How the elf had tricked me once again.

A soft voice, a whisper I could only hear from afar. A profanity left my mouth as I let my eyes flutter open, and I pushed myself off the hard surface of the stone. I looked at my closest surroundings and saw walls of stone and carpet underneath my feet, and I looked down at the stone bench I had been lying on.

Around me was carved marble, with names written on top of it. Years dating back from years ago to only a few months ago. I looked to the opposite end of the narrow hallway and saw Arabella, but she was not alone. She was accompanied by the tall man. I frowned, recognizing Dario immediately.

My feet met the dark blue carpet, and that's when I realized I was barefoot. I struggled to balance myself on the carpet as I felt every inch of pain that shot up my legs and down my back. I smelt of blood and sweat, and I'm reminded of everything that just happened when I saw the red dress that I still wearing.

"Blanche," I hear my name, and then Arabella comes towards me, her hands going under mine and holding me up. "Are you feeling alright?"

On the other side, Dario grabs my hand. I hadn't even realized there were new bandages on my hands until now. "Christ." I say, leaning my head on Arabella's shoulder. "I feel awful."

"No doubt," Arabella said, bringing me back to the bench. "You used a lot of power doing that curse. I've never seen someone do a permanent curse," she explained as she made me sit back down on the bench.

A permanent curse. Was that what I did?

If so, I planned on never doing it again.

"Where are we?" I ask.

"A mausoleum," Arabella says. "Oddly, this was the only place that vampires weren't guarding." I looked around, and it finally hit me. These walls held the remains of those who had lost their lives. Mostly mortal, I would think.

"I didn't know where else to go," Arabella admitted, and I watched as she stood up, leaving Dario to hold me up. "I mean, after you cursed the crown and Beckett, everything went wrong, and I knew we needed to get out of there." She bit down on her lip. "I didn't know if we would make it out at first. Everyone was trying to find us, and Dario…" She looked at him. "He helped us get out."

I snatched my hand away from the guard, giving him a suspicious look. "Why would you help us?"

"I never liked King Castor, and after witnessing every horrible thing he had done to me and never suffering the consequences, it felt necessary," he said. "But I can't stay here. They'll know I'm gone, so I need to go back, but…" His voice told me softly, "I will listen to what Beckett says. I'll be your spy for now."

"For now?" I demand.

"Until you come back," he responds.

I draw back, crossing my hands. "I'm never going to go back."

"You might not be able to help it, Blanche," Arabella snapped. She looked at me seriously, and her expression turned hard, eyes sparkled with terror. "They know you cursed Beckett," She kneeled before me. "They think you're the one who killed all those vampires."

"What?" I breathlessly replied, shaking my head. "But that's not true."

"It doesn't matter if it's true," Dario explained. "They aren't blaming the king, and from what I've heard, Beckett has only said one thing." He looked directly at me. "To find you and bring you to him. He's got every guard hunting you at the moment."

"Even you?" I ask, raising an eyebrow.

"I know the truth," Dario explains and then stands up. "I

won't tell a single soul about this." He crosses two fingers across his chest in an 'X' formation. "I swear on it."

"You're wanted, Blanche," Arabella explains. "I am, too."

I scoff, my head hanging low as I take in the evident conversation. Just like that, I had managed to be Castor's loyal subject to a vile woman who cursed the crown - the one who killed their people. Yet, my mind still was hungover from the fact that Beckett let this all happen. He was just a man, so power-hungry that it hurt everyone around him.

Except now I realize, it ran deeper than power. It was revenge.

I snatch my hand away from Dario, stretching my neck out and standing up on my own two feet, even though it hurt. I stormed down the long hallway, taking a right, where I saw the two brown doors. I felt Dario and Arabella behind me as we walked outside into the cold air. I looked upon all the graves that surrounded this place.

I looked back towards them, turning my whole body. "He has one year to rule, and that's all he gets. For now, we stay in hiding until I come up with a proper plan..." My gaze held on the black gate of the cemetery.

A chuckle fell from my lips as I trained my eyes on the graves of the beloved mortals. Beckett had won once again for this, but not without consequences this time. He had stopped the former king, his pathetic brother, but this was no longer about the war of our societies.

This was a personal attack - on me and Arabella.

My mind swirled in darkness as I clenched my fists. Beckett managed to stop one war, but now he had just started another.

He started a war with me.

THE END

ACKNOWLEDGMENTS

Wow. I cannot believe I'm here and writing to you, my beautiful readers. For all my life I've wanted to be an author. I never thought that I would become one. If you are reading this, then I have accomplished my greatest dream, and it is without a doubt the greatest accomplishment of my life.

But…

I wouldn't be able to do this without the most supportive people around me. Firstly, I would like to thank my father for being by my side and supporting me throughout my entire life. I want to thank Dawn for letting me rant endless hours too about my book.

I want to thank my best friend Alyssa for supporting me through several cycles of my book. I appreciate your confidence in me.

I would like to thank my older sister, Denisa, for constantly asking about my book. It meant a lot to me that you are proud of my achievements.

I want to thank my editor, Adrienne, for reading and editing my book, because without you, my book would be a mess of grammar and spelling. I want to thank my graphic designer, Jessica, for making my book come to life right before my eyes. You both helped me so much during this process.

And most of all, I want to thank you, my dear reader, for being able to pick up this book, for giving it a chance.

When I first started writing this, I knew I wanted it to be a romance and a fantasy. It was important to me to create characters who were complex in so many different ways, and I also wanted them to fuse together. That's why when Blanche and Beckett's paths crossed, I wanted there to be manipulation. I wanted there to be desire.

And this story is not only about romance and war. This story is about finding yourself. This is about not letting others bring you down. Even if you don't have a werewolf by your side, or a vampire to capture your mom and tie her to a chair, you have yourself.

And that is enough.

You are enough.

www.ingramcontent.com/pod-product-compliance
Lightning Source LLC
Chambersburg PA
CBHW070450300726

48975CB00007B/2117